The Girls in the Glen

Glasgow-born Lynne McEwan is a former newspaper photographer turned crime author. She's covered stories including the Fall of the Berlin Wall and the first Gulf War in addition to many high profile murder cases. She currently lives in Lincoln and is in the final year of an MA in Crime Fiction at the University of East Anglia.

Also by Lynne McEwan

Detective Shona Oliver

In Dark Water
Dead Man Deep
The Girls in the Glen

The Girls in the Glen

LYNNE McEWAN

CANELOCRIME

First published in the United Kingdom in 2023 by

Canelo
Unit 9, 5th Floor
Cargo Works, 1-2 Hatfields
London SE1 9PG
United Kingdom

A CIP catalogue record for this book is available from the British Library.

Print ISBN 978 1 80436 229 7
Ebook ISBN 978 1 80436 228 0

Look for more great books at www.canelo.co

Printed and bound in Great Britain by Clays Ltd, Elcograf S.p.A.

1

Prologue

On Bield Moss, death is not the end. The boglands fold all in a tight embrace. Time slackens, a sepia tint warms skin and hair. Layers of peat press bone and flesh like flowers in a family Bible. Into the dark ghylls and sykes drain the fear and pain of living, biting through the black soil to run like spent blood beneath heather and pine, until the brine of the Solway washes all clean. The centuries turn and the high moor holds fast. On every surface, life grows upon life.

On Bield Moss, the curlew's warning comes too late. A patch of bog-cotton is a white flag caught among the reeds and starved grass. The pale horseman's shadow swallows the sky. In the hollow, out of the wind, the girl in the glen passes, her last breath faint as a lark's wingbeat. High above, a crow soars with a harsh lament and the circling buzzard creeps closer to inspect the meat.

On Bield Moss, the shadow moves on. An adder unfurls. Sundews reopen, holding out their fragile fingers, but the girl in the glen is off across the heather with the mountain hare. In the rough refuge of the dead, she whispers to the voles and grouse and the nesting plovers. They are coming. They will find me.

On Bield Moss, death is never the end.

Chapter 1

Detective Inspector Shona Oliver examined the photograph of the skeleton she'd just been handed. The skull showed a sharp groove across the crown, the classic mark of a sharp trauma injury, but was it the cause of death? Stop, she told herself as she passed the picture back to the archaeologist. It's a 400-year-old killing and, for once, not your problem. Just enjoy your day out.

Shona waved to her sixteen-year-old daughter Becca, who was kneeling in a trench in the heather, a look of rapture on her face. Next to her, a fair-haired girl, in a hand-knitted green Aran jumper, held up a shard of blackened pottery. Shona and Becca had met Dr Cameron Armstrong at the University of Glasgow open day the year before. He'd been assiduous in answering Becca's emails, and eventually offered her some hands-on experience camping with the current students for a week or so.

Dr Armstrong slid the photo back into a folder. About Shona's age, he was lean and not much taller than her own five feet four inches, with messy dark hair and a long, straight nose. Threads of gold and white showed in his scrappy beard. Muscled forearms and quick movements betrayed a life spent not entirely behind a desk in the Archaeology Department.

'Male, approximately between thirty and forty years old,' he offered. When Shona didn't reply, a grin creased his suntanned face. 'Thought I'd hooked you there. Gonna have to try harder, aren't I?'

Despite the grim subject matter, he was definitely flirting with her, and that was okay. He had a wife, Tanya, and a young son, Lewis, still in primary school. Her own husband, Rob, had cropped up in conversation now and again, too. Shona took it as a sure sign he enjoyed her company. Harmless flirting was all it was.

'Nice try. No cigar.' Shona returned his smile and waved the wad of *Float to Live* leaflets in her hand. 'No work for me. I'm on my jollies.'

The open day at the archaeological dig at Bield Moss, in the eastern uplands of Dumfries and Galloway, was the perfect opportunity for the RNLI to remind visitors about the dangers of wild swimming in the nearby rivers and lochs. Shona, who volunteered on the Kirkness lifeboat fifty miles to the west, was putting in a stint with the station helm, Tommy McCall. He'd grumbled that when he was a lad, they'd just called it *swimming*, but agreed that while the RNLI's remit was saving lives *at sea*, educating the public about the effects of cold water shock, while doing a bit of fundraising, was a good idea. The moorland was also within Shona's policing patch, so if today's exercise saved even a single life, it was win-win as far as she was concerned.

'Anyway,' Shona said, nodding towards Cam's folder. 'Not much mystery how your research subject died. Some big bugger with a sword did for him.'

'I see you're blessed with both brains and beauty, Detective Inspector,' he smiled. 'That would also be my conclusion. It was a common fate for a Border reiver.' He

3

held out a hand, inviting her to walk the short distance towards the edge of the site and a spectacular view down to the Solway Firth. 'You know, that's where the word "bereaved" comes from?' he said. 'It's how you generally ended up if you met one.'

When it came to murder, Shona thought, detectives, or indeed archaeologists, would never be out of business. A couple of Cam's students arrived with a query and drew him back to the trench.

She glanced at the RNLI gazebo. No customers. It was the same for the small pottery, a cheesemaker and a local conservation group. Freya, a cheerful blonde in a dark green apron with the twin stags logo of The Douglas Arms gastro-pub, offered Tommy a shot glass. He sipped it and made a polite grimace. Freya said something, and Tommy's chuckle floated across on the stiff wind.

Shona raised the collar of her fleece and replaced her sunglasses against the bright glare of hard blue sky. The lack of visitors was largely the result of Storm Ailsa, which had powered through the area two days before, leaving blocked roads and flooded holiday cottages; her journey time this morning had been trebled by the aftermath. Hillsides looked as if a petulant chess player had swept their arm across them, upending the pieces and conceding the game. Trees lay at jagged angles, pulled up by the roots, exposing the peaty soil beneath.

From the high moss, the land rolled down to the Solway. Shona traced the border with England, not evident through any barrier or changed geography and marked only by the greater proliferation of wind turbines on the Scottish hilltops.

A faint popping sound came and went on the breeze. It was the Glorious Twelfth, the start of the grouse season, and a shoot was in progress on the Earl of Langdale's estate on the neighbouring section of the moor.

She took out her phone, then remembered that the signal had dropped to zero as she'd abandoned the Audi and walked the rough sheep-track to the site. Her sergeant, Murdo O'Halloran, was in the CID office in Dumfries; he would deal with things until she returned to work tomorrow morning.

Shona fingered the phone and wondered for the hundredth time that morning how her husband Rob's preparations for his trial at the Old Bailey in London were going. A former banker, he'd been charged with 'Concealment and Removal of Criminal Property'. Money laundering to you and me. He'd travelled south last night to stay with friends and meet his barrister to go over the final details.

'Mum!' Becca called. She'd stood up in her trench and was waving. 'Come and see.'

Shona started back along the close-cropped path between the heather. Rob was a victim, caught out by others' wrongdoing, and his former employers, Milton McConnell, had looked for a scapegoat. At lunchtime, she'd renegotiate the hill and catch him then.

'Look what I found in the midden, Mum.' Becca's heart-shaped face, surrounded by the wavy dark hair so like her own, shone up at Shona. They resembled each other in all but height, which Becca had inherited from her father. In normal circumstances, she towered over her mother. In the trench, however, she'd somehow regressed to childhood. Her brown eyes were alive with excitement as she held up a curved piece of broken pottery.

'It's a rim,' Becca said. 'Means there's a good chance of identifying the ceramic type and dating it.'

The blonde girl next to her nodded. They were joined by two younger diggers. Together, they studied the find, taking it in turn to hold the curve of pot with its shiny green glaze and chattering with enthusiasm over what else might be in the midden.

'Oh, Mum, this is Grace Elliot and her wee sisters, Flora and Ashley. They've got the farm just down the glen where we're camping.'

The oldest girl was about Becca's age, with Flora a little younger, while Ashley looked as if she was still in primary school. They all shared straight, almost colourless, fair hair, worn long, and serious grey eyes.

'You enjoying your day?' Shona asked. 'Guess you'll be back at school soon.'

'They're all home-schooled. Like me,' Becca said.

Shona detected smugness in her daughter's reply. In London, there had been an early brush with drugs at her school, followed by persistent issues over bullying and then a general failure to settle when they'd moved north. Her parents had given in to Becca's suggestion of home-schooling as much from fatigue as anything else, but it had allowed their daughter's magpie intellect free rein and the arrangement was generally held to be working.

'We look after the sheep and goats and chickens, too,' Ashley said, proudly.

'I'm not sure I could kill a chicken,' Becca replied.

'It's farming.' Grace Elliot shrugged and climbed out of the trench. 'You give the animal the best life you can, then a clean kill. The deer on the hill don't know a thing.' Her eyes slid to Shona. 'It's not poaching, not on our own land.'

Shona, who enjoyed Rob's venison and red wine casserole, smiled reassuringly. 'It sounds a very sustainable way to live.' She glanced at her eco-aware, vegan daughter and saw that her desire to make friends with the sisters had overcome her natural tendency to lecture others on her views. Shona took it as a welcome sign of maturity, although no doubt the Elliot girls would hear more of the case against meat consumption at some point soon.

'We need to go.' Ashley tugged at Grace's sleeve and Shona got the impression that the youngest girl was in charge. Or at least thought she was.

'See you tomorrow?' Becca said.

Grace smiled. 'Yeah, sure. Can you tell Dr Armstrong we'll be back?'

'Okay. I will.' Becca watched her friends walk off down the hill.

The archaeologists had cut four other trenches at varying angles across the site, but these were largely hidden by the heather. A murmur of student voices, and occasional laughter, floated across. Shona checked how Tommy was doing, and saw he was chatting with two walkers and seemed to have things under control.

'Want me to stay?' Shona said. Becca looked doubtful. 'You can talk me through what you're doing. A midden, right? Why dig up a midden?'

Shona thought she already knew the answer but hoped the question would distract Becca enough to get them to lunch, where a superior digging partner to herself could be recruited from the students.

'Well…' Becca began as she deposited her pottery shard in a green gardening seed tray with other dirt-encrusted objects. She scraped her trowel at an angle across the compacted peaty soil at the bottom of the trench. 'Besides pottery for dating, middens show us what people were eating through things like animal bones. Middens have often been churned up in the past, as materials were recycled, but mostly they go down through history in broad layers, so we can tell when the site underwent periods of occupation.'

'Okay.' To Shona, this sounded like a nugget of information Becca had swallowed whole from Dr Armstrong. At least she was learning things on this windswept moor. Whether archaeology was a fleeting teenage obsession, or would lead to some sort of career, was yet to be seen.

An area of paleness appeared through the peat. Becca tapped it with her trowel, and it made a hollow sound.

'Stone or bone?' Becca grinned as she continued scraping. 'Pot or not?' The sides of a domed object appeared. 'It's what Cam said we should ask ourselves when—' She halted. Fine, wool-like strands, stained orange by the peat, broke against the edge of her trowel.

Shona's breath caught.

'Becca, darling. Time to get out of the trench.'

She reached over to a stack of trays and lifted one, then placed it upside down over the object at the bottom of the trench, concealing it from Becca's gaze.

Becca stood up slowly. 'Is it a…? But it can't be. It's so small.'

Shona took her daughter's unresisting hand. 'Out you come.'

It sounded like the encouragement parents use to get a child out of the bath. Becca looked pale, her eyes fixed on the trench floor. Shona kept hold of her with one hand, while she scoured the moorland for Dr Armstrong. Seeing his slight figure pop up above the heather like a rabbit, she waved her free arm and called to him. He raised his own in acknowledgement and started towards them. As he came closer, he registered Shona's serious expression and his pace increased.

Cam stepped into the trench and hooked a small trowel from the back pocket of his jeans. He quickly confirmed what Becca had uncovered: human remains. A reiver's child, partially preserved in the peat.

'Well done, Becca.' He jumped from the trench and clapped her on the shoulder, grinning with excitement. 'Fantastic discovery. Going by the pottery fragments, I'd say 300–400 years old. Go tell the others. We'll break for lunch now. I'll take it from here.' He sent her to where the students were gathering with flasks and sandwiches.

When she'd gone, he turned to Shona. 'It needs a professional archaeologist to excavate and record this kind of discovery. It can be upsetting for the younger students.'

'I think that's wise,' Shona agreed. 'And you'll inform the fiscal?'

'Of course. We do that for all human remains, even 400-year-old ones.' He rubbed the palms of his hands together with relish. 'It's exactly what I hoped we'd find here in the Debatable Land. It's evidence of family occupation. Not just a skirmish or raiding party.'

'Debatable Land?' Shona raised her eyebrow in a question.

'It's a key part of my research, and a fascinating story.' Energy radiated from him and Shona understood how his students were caught up so readily in his enthusiasm.

'For 400 years,' he continued, 'parts of England and Scotland lay on either side of the official border, but no one was quite sure who owned them and a local Mafia-type system, the Border reivers, emerged.'

'You see Border reivers as Mafia families?'

'Oh, yes. They formed alliances of convenience across the border, played the Scottish and the English parliaments off against one another, and had their own codes of honour. Like the Cosa Nostra, they relied on silence. *Omertà*. It's an invisible power.' He smiled. 'If you're strong enough in numbers, you make your own laws. It's a fascinating area. We've documents, but they were mostly written by those who saw the reivers as a problem and were hoping to wipe them out and, beyond the stone pele towers, we've not much archaeological evidence.'

'Not sure I agree with the personal lawmaking.' Shona shivered. The sun had gone behind a bank of cloud and the wind edged a few points north. It looked a harsh and unforgiving landscape, even on a fine day. 'And this wouldn't be my first choice for a home.'

'It wasn't the reivers' either. When government troops from either England or Scotland came calling, they packed up their women, children and cattle, and vanished into the hills. I'm hoping to prove they retreated here. *Bield* means sanctuary in old Scots. The moss is full of bogs and sinkholes, but if you know your way around, it's a great place to hide. So far, we've no hard evidence they came here.' With a twinkle he added, 'But we both know the absence of evidence isn't evidence of absence, is it?'

Shona rolled her eyes. 'All right, you got me there.'

'The new Earl of Langdale is interested in the area's history and has been very supportive of our dig. People think archaeologists are searching for things. A lost Roman legion's fort, or treasure. What we're really looking for is knowledge.'

Shona glanced over at Becca, who appeared recovered and now the centre of breathless attention among the students, and then checked the time on her phone. 'Right now, I'm looking for lunch.'

She told Tommy she'd swap with him after she'd made a quick call. Cradling an enormous hunk of bread and a Douglas Arms mug with some delicious-looking soup in it, he declared he was fine where he was.

'You'd get a piece at any door, you would,' Shona said with envy. With Becca away camping, and without Rob around to do the cooking, she'd been relying on cereal and biscuits at home for the last few days. He'd left stuff in the freezer for her, but some days, even microwaving a meal felt like too much effort.

'Aye, well, some of us just have a natural charm.' He winked. 'Freya's been looking after me. I'll put in a good word for you.'

Halfway down the hill, a single bar appeared on Shona's phone, but her call to Rob went straight to voicemail. She hung about, hoping he'd reply, until hunger and the chill wind drove her back up the hill.

She'd taken a bite of soup-soaked bread when she heard a vehicle behind her. A police four-wheel drive came to a halt at the top of the sheep-track. A volunteer special constable got out and hurriedly scanned the group. Dr Armstrong started forward. Shona put down her soup and slid her wallet from the pocket of her jeans.

'What is it?' She flashed her warrant card. The officer's eyes flicked between her RNLI fleece and the ID, as if trying to reconcile the two. The look Shona gave him was enough to confirm he'd found the right person.

'On the Langdale estate,' he said, breathlessly. 'A woman. She's been shot.'

Chapter 2

Gravel dinged off the police vehicle's paintwork as they slid to a halt outside a miniature castle with pointed gables fashioned in granite. A group of gamekeepers and beaters, all of similar build and wearing a uniform of wax-cotton and muted tweeds, stared, their eyes guarded and suspicious. The dogs growled but were silenced with a gruff command. A police sergeant came forward.

'Ma'am.' A sly smile flashed across his face. She'd seen it a lot lately, since it had become common knowledge that her husband was up in court. 'Wee Shona' might have been here two years and cleared up a couple of high-profile cases, but she shouldn't get too comfortable in a chair where her sort should never have sat in – that was what the look said.

'Take me to the casualty, Sergeant...?' Shona left a gap for him to rectify his error in not identifying himself to a senior officer.

'Sergeant Graham, ma'am.' He turned towards the lodge's arched doorway and started walking, his long strides inviting her to keep up. 'Ambulance is on its way,' he cast over his shoulder.

A wide octagonal room took up the bulk of the building. The shooting party was scattered in small groups around the edges. A tall young man in tweeds and a ludicrous feathered hat was talking quietly to a fine-featured blonde. The woman, in a wine-coloured gilet, kept shaking her head as if she couldn't believe what had happened. Other guests, white-faced and clutching drinks, tried and failed to ignore the drama at the centre of the room, where a small group was huddled around a figure lying on the floor.

Discarded white towels, stained red with blood, lay beside a woman who was applying straight-armed pressure to the wound on the victim's shoulder. Shona assessed the pallor of the casualty's skin, levels of alertness, and in that second, she also recognised the woman: Nicola Baird, recently elected member of the Scottish Parliament for South Scotland, and the widow of Shona's former boss, DCI Gavin Baird. Shona let this information flow over her as her training kicked in.

'Hello, I'm DI Shona Oliver.' She kneeled as she introduced herself to the group. Nicola Baird grimaced, either in pain or in general distaste that the woman she blamed, unjustly, for her husband's death was here to prevent her own. Shona didn't know which it was, and she didn't care. There was sufficient blood to merit urgent action.

'I'm Eilidh Wilson. I'm a nurse,' said the woman applying the pressure. 'Mrs Baird has a rifle injury in the left shoulder. No exit wound. She can't feel her fingers, so the blood loss and potential damage to the brachial artery are my primary concerns.'

'Thanks, Eilidh.' Shona turned to the casualty. 'Listen, Nicola, the ambulance is coming.'

Shona angled herself away from Nicola's prone body and spoke quietly into Eilidh's ear. 'What else do you need?'

A keeper held a near-empty first-aid box. The nurse looked down at her bloody hands on the rapidly darkening towel.

'This is all we have,' the keeper said, with a glimmer of guilt.

'A shooting estate should have better provision for accidents like this,' Shona mouthed at the keeper, who had the grace to look shamefaced.

'But it wasn't an accident,' the keeper replied.

'What?' Shona stood up. The Special who'd driven her here had said *a woman has been shot* but knew few other details. Shona beckoned Sergeant Graham, who stood a little way off, watching her, hands on hips, and talking in a low voice with some of the beaters. He approached with less haste than the situation merited.

'Have you secured the weapon?' Shona said. A full investigation would be required, and with such a high-profile victim they couldn't make any mistakes. *She* couldn't afford to make any mistakes. With Rob's trial imminent, there were plenty who thought she was a liability to the force and the bosses would be keeping a close eye on her.

'How can we secure the weapon if we don't know where it is?' he replied, as if talking to a child.

Shona's eyes darted to the shotguns chained up in the rack by the door. This was a grouse shoot; there wasn't a single rifle in sight.

'You're sure a rifle caused this?' Shona said to the nurse.

Eilidh nodded. 'Shotgun pellets don't make a hole this size.'

'Where did the shot come from?'

The keeper shrugged. 'Somewhere on the moor.'

'There's a shooter out on the hills and you didn't think to tell me?' she hissed, her lips white with anger. Becca and the archaeologists were up there, not to mention walkers.

'There's a few——' the sergeant began.

Shona held up her hand to silence him, and punched in Cam's number. Her heart soared when he answered. He'd come down the hill in his Land Rover to collect some items from the site hut at the camp.

'Get everyone off the moor,' she said calmly, holding the fear that gripped her throat at bay. 'We're attempting to locate an armed individual. Tommy McCall will help you. Tell any walkers you see, too. Don't approach anyone suspicious. It's for your own safety. Do it now.' She cut the call, then requested authorised firearms officers.

'Seal off the locus,' Shona said to Sergeant Graham. 'Get special officers on the access roads. The strategy is locate, alert, contain and negotiate. Firearms are on their way, so no ill-considered attempts at an early arrest. Understand?'

The sergeant nodded, his expression blank.

'Send a couple of guys up to the Elliot place. The farm track's a potential exit route for the suspect, and there's a campsite full of students. I don't want a hostage situation.' Something sharp and hard turned in Shona's gut when she thought of Becca up there. 'Get the students inside a barn or somewhere else that's secure. Don't let any of them leave.' She fought to drag her mind away from her daughter's safety and back to the job in hand.

'ETA on the paramedics?' Shona said.

'There's an issue with the ambulance coming from Dumfries,' Graham said. 'The fallen trees——'

'Air ambulance?' Shona cut in, glancing at Nicola's pale and sweating face, and calculating the volume of her blood now soaked into the towels. The Royal Infirmary was normally an hour away. It had taken Shona nearly three times that to get here this morning.

'Helicopter's tied up on another job,' the sergeant said.

'Nearest hospital?' Shona said.

The officer stuck out his bottom lip in thought, as if he'd never considered this question before.

'Cumberland Infirmary, at Carlisle,' Eilidh said. 'I work there.' She turned back to her patient. 'Nicola, open your eyes.'

For a moment, Shona thought Nicola Baird was slipping under.

'Call them,' she said to the sergeant.

'It's a different authority. I don't think they'll cross the border.'

Shona stared at him, incredulous. She'd heard of shenanigans like this but never witnessed one. There was, of course, the official way of doing things, and then there was the way things worked in practice, where folk helped each other out. She'd made the effort to establish a good relationship with all the emergency services on the other side of the border, including her lifeboat colleagues at Silloth and Maryport, but perhaps Sergeant Graham had stepped on Cumbrian toes in the past.

They'd run out of options. If they waited for help, Nicola Baird would bleed out on the floor of the lodge. Much as she disliked the woman, Shona would not let that happen.

'Can you get to the Carlisle Road across the estate?' Shona asked the keepers.

'I'm Jim Wilson, Eilidh's husband.' One of the men stepped forward. 'We could do it in a Land Rover, but it'll be rough going.' He looked at his wife. She nodded.

It was clear from Eilidh's expression that she understood Nicola Baird's dire prognosis, too.

'How far to Cumberland Infirmary?' Shona asked.

'Thirty minutes,' Eilidh replied, 'once you reach the road.'

'Do it,' Shona said. 'Anything we can use as a stretcher?' She directed her question to the group of keepers. None of the tabletops, laden with empty glasses, were big enough.

'There's a coffin,' a voice said. 'We could use the lid.'

This was an outfit with an inadequate first-aid box, but equipped with a coffin. It told Shona all she needed to know about their health-and-safety preparedness. The whole place was an accident waiting to happen. The letter she'd be sending the estate owners and the firearms licensing folk was auto-creating in her head, as two men emerged from a side room bearing a teak coffin top.

They rolled Nicola Baird as gently as they could onto her right side and slid the coffin lid beneath her. The back of her pale blouse and her chignon of blonde hair were soaked dark with blood. She let out a series of gasps and sharp cries, and Eilidh murmured reassurances as six shuffling beaters carried the makeshift stretcher out to the Land Rover.

As they manoeuvred Nicola into the back, the MSP reached out and grabbed Shona's fleece.

'Shouldn't you be with me?' Nicola slurred. 'Protection.'

Shona turned to a young special constable who was helping lift the makeshift stretcher.

'This lad's gonna take care of you,' Shona said.

His eyes widened, but his mouth was set in firm determination.

'Get in,' she said, a hand on his arm. 'You see anyone armed on the moor, call it in, but don't stop. Understand? I'm gonna get someone to meet you.'

She made eye contact with Eilidh and her husband, and saw that both understood what was being asked of them and needed no further instruction.

Shona pulled out her phone again. 'Dan?' she said as the number was answered on the first ring.

'It's Charlotte.'

Shona checked the number on her screen. DC Dan Ridley, Cumbria CID.

There was a giggle, and a murmured conversation, then Dan himself came on the line. 'Boss?'

'Sorry to interrupt.' It sounded more arch than Shona intended. 'Need a big favour. Can you get to Cumberland Infirmary, ASAP?' She quickly filled him in.

'Shit. Of course.' Dan was on the move, the jingle of car keys and rustle of clothing clear down the line. 'I'll bell you when they arrive.'

'And Dan,' Shona said. 'Preserve every piece of evidence. Something tells me this won't be straightforward.'

Shona watched the Land Rover turn off the drive and take the steep track that wound up behind the lodge, then dialled her detective sergeant in Dumfries CID to update him, too.

'Any sign of the shooter now?' Murdo asked.

'No,' she said. 'A rifle makes a different noise to a shotgun, but it would've been difficult to pick out in the middle of a shoot. They only have a vague idea where the shot came from.'

'I've put an alert out for an armed individual. With so many roads shut, you're better heading to the Lothian and

Borders team in Edinburgh. I've asked them to give us a hand and they're also sending a negotiator.'

'I forgot. You're from this neck of the woods,' Shona said.

'Aye, Langholm. Just up the road. Want me to come?'

'Not just yet. I need your local knowledge to co-ordinate from HQ. But "stable door" and "bolted" come to mind. I've got uniform sealing off the locus as best they can, but the fella in charge isn't up to much – a Sergeant Graham.'

'Aye, Willie Graham. I mind him,' Murdo said, mildly. 'Been there all his career. Probably never faced anything like this.'

Shona felt a small stab of guilt, but then remembered the officer's lack of respect and urgency. It was no excuse for sloppiness.

'Becca's with a load of students at a campsite. I've sent a unit up.' Shona heard the pitch of her voice rise with anxiety.

'I'll call them, check how they're doin'. Don't worry about that,' Murdo said firmly. 'I'll give forensics the heads-up, too.'

The tall man in his twenties that she'd spotted wearing the ludicrous feathered hat was approaching her. He wore tweed shooting breeks and had Sergeant Graham at his heels like a faithful retriever.

'Thanks, Murdo,' Shona said, reassured a fraction by his steadfast tone. 'I better go. Listen, the signal is atrocious, but keep trying me.'

'Will do.' Murdo signed off.

The young man extended his hand. 'My apologies, ma'am, for not introducing myself sooner. I didn't want to interrupt your operations.' His voice was educated, moderate, and his accent clearly American. 'I'm Alexander Douglas. Anything you need, Detective Inspector – anything – you just let me know.'

'I was just telling his lordship that we're sure to sort this out quickly,' Sergeant Graham put in.

So, this was the new Earl of Langdale. His open, earnest expression, as much as his physical appearance, marked him out from the other guests. At over six feet tall, with broad shoulders, and perfect skin and teeth, he'd have looked more at home on a Californian beach than a Scottish grouse moor. His grip was firm and warm.

'I sure appreciate speed,' the earl said. 'But it's more important the investigation is done thoroughly.'

Sergeant Graham's mouth set in a line at the rebuke.

'Oh, I'm not saying quick ain't good, Willie. But Mrs Baird was my guest and that she should come to harm on my estate… Well, I can't let that rest. I need to know, going forward, how such a thing could have happened, so it's never repeated.' He reached inside his jacket and handed Shona a thick cream-coloured business card with the same twin stags logo she'd seen on the barmaid's apron. 'My cell-phone number is on there. You be sure to call me the minute there's news about Mrs Baird.'

'I will, sir,' Shona said. She wanted to reassure the earl and ensure that the lines of communication stayed open with this key local figure. 'I'm confident she's in excellent hands. The tactical plan now is to sweep the moor. Determine if there's further danger to the public, and detain the individual responsible.'

'Absolutely, ma'am. My men are out searching the moor for the culprit.'

'I'd rather you left that to us.' The last thing Shona wanted was the earl's private platoon on the loose. 'A firearms team are on their way.'

'Excuse me a moment,' the earl said as a stocky man in wax cotton came up and drew him aside.

'The keepers know this country,' Sergeant Graham said. 'Every wee hidey-hole.'

'Maybe so, but armed civilians in pursuit of a suspect?' Shona hissed. 'What d'you think this is, the Wild West? Get them back here, Sergeant.'

As an Authorised Firearms Officer, Shona was a rarity among detectives. Her training was a legacy of her time spent with the City of London police, where the threat of terrorism, stretching back to the IRA attacks in the 1980s, meant most officers were routinely armed. With a shooter on the loose, she'd considered going back to Dumfries nick and checking out a sidearm, but quickly dismissed the idea. Even if she could get there, a handgun wouldn't be much use against a rifle. But if anyone was going to draw a weapon against an armed individual, she would prefer it to be her, not one of the gamekeepers.

'We have a drone up,' the earl said, returning to the two officers.

'That's very helpful, your lordship,' Sergeant Graham said. 'I'll get one of the Specials watching the screen with your lad.'

Shona glared at the sergeant, but she could see how this might safely work to their advantage. The grouse moor was a vast area of open ground. It should be possible to see anyone moving across it. She remembered Dr Armstrong's comment about the reivers hiding on Bield Moss. Sergeant Graham was right about one thing: the local keepers knew the land best.

'Fine,' Shona said, 'but pull your men back. If the drone spots a target, just monitor until firearms get here.' Both men nodded and returned to the lodge, just as Shona's phone screen lit up again with Cameron Armstrong's number. She felt her heart rate climb immediately.

'Everyone okay?' Shona said before he could speak.

'Everyone's fine.' He paused, and for a moment Shona thought the line had dropped. Then he said, 'The burial. It's modern.'

'What?' Shona said, her mind still on the gunman. 'Which burial?'

'The reiver's child. The one Becca found,' he replied. 'I had a quick look when I covered up the trench.'

Shona felt a flash of irritation that Dr Armstrong had lingered on the moor against her express orders, but she supposed he wanted to make his research safe from the elements.

'It's a modern burial cut into an earlier site,' Cameron continued.

'What d'you mean? How modern?' She'd seen it for herself. Experience told her that this wasn't a fresh grave, even with the preserving power of the peat.

'Within the last fifty years, I'd say. There's a clothing label, just visible.' Cameron swallowed. 'It's Marks and Spencer. Looks like a dress. Age eight.'

Shona felt the familiar tightening of grief and dread around her heart. A murdered child, and a cold case to boot. A trail soaked by family grief stretching back decades. Coming on top of an active shooter, she knew this would push her team to the limit. She took a deep breath.

'I don't need to tell you to touch nothing, do I?'

'No,' he said, quietly. 'This is for your people now.'

Chapter 3

The next morning, Shona woke before six a.m. At the earl's invitation, she'd slept for a couple of hours at The Douglas Arms, which sat high on the road that skirted the moss. They'd searched the moor until the day drained away and the sun sank, blood red, behind the western hills. There was no way to lock the moor up tight. Its 10,000 acres were vast and untamed by roads or gates. A police drone, a helicopter sent from Edinburgh and a sweep by the firearms team paired with estate staff had failed to find anything. It was as if the moor had swallowed the gunman whole.

Shona had called Becca and satisfied herself that her daughter was safe, but she hadn't relished the prospect of sharing the barn with the students. The new gastro-pub venture, managed by the earl's cousin, Jack, was still in the process of its final renovations before a grand opening, but definitely presented a more attractive option. Shona could see that the chalk-white walls, tweed sofas and hunting trophies was the sort of deceptively expensive chic pared-back décor that the pub's target customers would savour.

She'd sent a few pictures to Rob, who'd given them the thumbs-up. It wouldn't work for their B&B, but he promised they'd pay a return visit together, if only to properly test the four-poster bed.

Shona appreciated his efforts at reconciliation. His gambling had put them in financial dire straits, and secrets on both sides had placed an enormous strain on their marriage. She loved Rob, and the stark truth was that she depended on him to run much of the domestic aspects of their lives – cooking, running their B&B, ferrying Becca around – all of which allowed her to concentrate on her career. But would a few days at a boutique hotel be enough to reconcile them? Perhaps after the trial they could have a fresh start?

But even as she thought this, she knew there was no such thing as a fresh start – and a tiny, guilty part of her was glad the shooting would distract her from greetin ower spilt milk.

Shona checked her messages and then called the Tactical Firearms Commander who'd remained at the hunting lodge. It was his decision whether the unit was withdrawn. Was there an ongoing threat to life that required continued action from armed officers? Was the subject still at large? What actions were required to locate them? They agreed there was an ongoing threat to life and to reassess in six hours.

Over in Cumbria, Dan Ridley had been as good as his word, dispatching a bike paramedic, an ambulance and a squad car escort to meet the estate's Land Rover bearing the injured woman.

Nicola Baird went into surgery forty minutes after leaving the hunting lodge. Shona's DC, Ravi Sarwar, kept a check on the MSP's condition with the hospital. The surgery had gone well, and the recovered rifle bullet had been biked up to forensics at Gartcosh. Last night, Nicola was still groggy from the anaesthetic and remembered little, but he'd get a statement as soon as she was fit to talk.

Shona went downstairs, pleased to find that, although it was early, Freya had provided a breakfast of coffee and croissants at a table by the window. Thanking her, Shona sat down, and Freya asked after Tommy, who'd returned to Kirkness with his van late last night, after ensuring everyone was safely back at the archaeologists' camp.

There was a rattle of hooves and horse harnesses in the car park. Freya leaned on the deep windowsill and peered out. 'His nibs is back and I'm still in a clatter. Forgive me if I leave you to it.'

Shona had met the earl's cousin, Jack Douglas, briefly last night; with his unconventional clothes and overly familiar manner, he'd struck her as an eccentric individual, to say the least. This morning, as she watched him swing his leg over the head of a great shaggy horse and slide nimbly from the saddle, she sensed she was in for the full experience.

Jack Douglas was tall and slim, dressed in artfully torn jeans, a leather waistcoat and several bead necklaces. His receding and greying-blonde hair was cropped short, except for an area around the crown, which was gathered into a high, thin ponytail. You rarely saw comb-overs these days. Was this, she wondered, the comb-over of the future, and what did it look like when he'd just stepped out of the shower?

He tied his mount and a second, finer pony to a metal post. She heard his boots in the hallway, and then he strode to her table, holding out a be-ringed hand. She hastily wiped croissant crumbs from her own fingers.

'Shona,' Jack bowed formally and squeezed her hand. For one horrible moment she thought he was going to kiss it. If the Earl of Langdale had a boyish charm, his older, Scottish cousin possessed the fully leaded version. 'The moor has a bare beauty this morning,' he said with a smile that made the comment sound both spiritual and erotic. 'I've just been exercising Lady Douglas's mare.'

His decision to take on The Douglas Arms suddenly made more sense. Family connections aside, she could see him working his way through the gastro-pub's female guests of a certain age, eager to sample the romantic Eskdale equivalent of an *Outlander* experience. He was out of luck if he thought she was interested in that particular house speciality.

'I'd rather you didn't go up there until we're sure there's no danger.' Shona frowned.

He batted her comment away. 'I'm used to riding alone. In France, I took the cheese miles over rough country to the weekly markets.'

'Well, I'm sure the French police would give you the same advice,' Shona said firmly.

'It's not like Scotland, though,' he continued. 'The Pyrenees aren't empty. The villages survive, but then, they never had the Highland Clearances.'

Shona wasn't sure how they'd got onto the whole-sale eviction of crofters in the eighteenth and nineteenth centuries, but perhaps the locals' nickname for the new landlord, 'Hippy Jack', was a reference to substances he may have once imbibed, and the resultant idiosyncratic comments.

'Of course, the Lowlands suffered, too,' he said. 'That's how they solved the reivers problem. They shipped them off to Northern Ireland. Well, the ones they could catch. Just what they needed, more disgruntled Protestants.' He winked.

The penny dropped. He was trying out his patter on her. A bit of history and local colour delivered by the attentive host. He leaned in to take her empty plate and cup with a practised speed and dexterity.

'Anyway,' he smiled. 'I've put the small dining room at your disposal. Freya or myself will get you anything you need. More coffee?'

'Thank you,' Shona said. 'But I mean what I said. Stay away from the moor, sir.'

He gave her a small acquiescent nod, perhaps disappointed that his charm hadn't yielded a better result than a repeated police warning.

In a neat dining parlour, she pulled a couple of tables together and borrowed an extension cable. At least the place had good wi-fi. Her open notebook sat next to her laptop. Stags' heads eyed her from the wall, but otherwise the décor was plain and distraction-free.

She scanned through her messages until DC Kate Irving's car pulled into the front of the pub. Shona saw that her other detective constable had dressed the part: Hunter wellingtons, slim-fit pale cords and a wax-cotton jacket. Her fine blonde hair was tied neatly back. As she passed the horses, Kate stopped to give them an appreciative pat.

'Murdo said to tell you he's on his way,' Kate said, once Shona had brought her up to speed with events on the ground, as they were heading to the hunting lodge in the Audi. 'You'd think there was nowhere to hide on such an open landscape. Must have been a nightmare search.'

'Aye, it was,' Shona replied. 'The infra-red on the helicopter kept picking up hotspots, which turned out to be deer curled up asleep in the heather. Have you been here before?' Murdo was a local lad. It would be a piece of luck for Shona if she had two officers familiar with the locus.

'Nope,' Kate replied. 'But I know the lie of the land, so to speak. *Management for Conservation and Water Resources in Blanket Bog Systems* was my dissertation for my geography degree.'

It was a connection of sorts, but Shona wasn't sure how applicable such experience could be.

'How are you going to manage the cold case?' Kate asked.

'It'll probably go to the Historic team in Glasgow. The archaeologist sent me a photo of the clothes label. I'd say it's Seventies or Eighties?'

Despite the urgent matter of a gunman on the loose, and her worries over Becca's safety, Shona had turned over the details in the pictures repeatedly in her head during the night. The preservation of bodies in peat made dating really difficult, Cam had said, and he'd been fooled himself by about four hundred years. Despite Shona's first reaction, she couldn't rule out that it was a recent burial. A child wearing a vintage dress that was a family heir-loom, or bought on eBay. Her own daughter had a few items going back to the Seventies, including an orange crocheted boho top that Shona thought was hideous, but Becca loved.

Somewhere, a mother was missing a child. If the woman still lived, was she watching the clock in the evening, as Shona herself sometimes did, wondering where her daughter was and when she'd return? Age eight, the dress label said. Becca had lived twice as long and was almost a grown woman. Shona felt a sharp, stinging gratitude that her girl had not suffered the same fate, but it did not make her worry any less. Her career in the police exposed her to the worst and she tried not to not always jump to the worst conclusion when Becca was an hour late and not answering her phone. As a police officer, it was hard. As a mother, it was impossible.

Shona was aware of Kate watching her, waiting for an answer. 'Forensics are due up there when they've finished with us. Let's see what they have to say.'

Chapter 4

They pulled up in front of the hunting lodge a little before seven a.m. To Shona's surprise, the Earl of Langdale himself came out to greet them. She made the introductions, and noted how the earl's gaze lingered on Kate. She was an attractive young woman, but a certain cool aloofness – or perhaps it was the job – had so far kept her single.

The earl's attention stayed on Shona's DC as he introduced the stocky man who stood at his shoulder as head gamekeeper Charles Bell. The warm smell of cooked food wafted from tables set against the lodge walls.

'I know you're eager to get up on the moor, ma'am,' the earl began. 'But I've had a light breakfast laid out for you and my shoot staff, who are at your disposal.'

Shona didn't relish the prospect of a day in the hills on little more than coffee and a croissant. There'd been no sightings of the shooter. Forensics wouldn't be here for another hour. Fifteen minutes to take the local temperature and listen to any theories the keeper might have would be useful. She accepted the earl's invitation gratefully.

'Perhaps I could talk you through the next steps, sir?'

'Of course,' the earl replied. 'And I'd like to reassure you, ma'am, that we're reviewing our shoot safety in general and medical readiness in particular.'

Shona nodded. 'That's good to hear, sir.' Her dressing-down of the assistant gamekeeper yesterday appeared to have spurred them into action and might save her some paperwork.

Two young men in white shirts, black trousers and waistcoats, in the estate's signature colour of muted purple, stood by the large silver chafer dishes, but around twenty beaters and shoot staff helped themselves to bacon, sausages and eggs. She texted her daughter, and Becca confirmed they were all fine and breakfast was underway in the barn, too.

Outside, she moved among the men, forking mouthfuls of kedgeree from a plate she'd been handed. She spotted Sergeant Graham, but after a curt nod, he kept his distance. The Tactical Firearms Commander had already sent his team out to do another sweep of Bield Moss.

Given the roughness of the terrain, the keepers thought it unlikely a vehicle had been used, so there was little chance of tyre prints being found. There was one access track of loose gravel; a single B-road with passing places, which crossed the northern edge of the moor. Police vehicles had been stationed at both ends but neither side reported any traffic beyond a couple of locals who obligingly allowed their cars to be searched, fruitlessly, for the rifle.

Shona spied the earl and Kate by the large, framed map that had been brought outside and leaned up against the lodge wall. Kate was jotting down notes, her other hand sweeping across the terrain as she asked questions. It looked like her geography degree had come in handy after all.

Shona joined them. 'We need to remain vigilant,' she said to Alexander Douglas as she sipped a mug of coffee. 'But progressing the investigation and recovering any forensic material from the crime scene are now my priorities.'

'I can take you up there,' he said. 'You know, I was standing right by her when it happened.'

'Good. You can show me.' Shona put her mug on the table and invited him to lead the way, beckoning Kate to follow and ignoring Sergeant Graham's disgruntled look.

The earl insisted on driving. Shona was in the passenger seat. The estate's head gamekeeper, Charles Bell, hunched forward in the rear seat, his face grim. Kate sat beside him. Shona could have sworn the earl angled his rear-view mirror a little more in Kate's direction than was necessary.

'So what's your thinking, DI Oliver?' Alexander Douglas said as they climbed the track that had taken Nicola Baird across the estate. 'It's no accident,' he emphasised. 'So it must be… what? An attempted political assassination?'

Don't get ahead of yourself, Shona wanted to say. This isn't the grassy knoll and Nicola Baird isn't JFK. But the truth was, she'd been considering just this question and had asked Murdo to brief the civilian staff at Dumfries CID. They'd need to trawl the MSP's social media and contact Nicola's constituency staff about any possible threats.

'Gotta be a professional hit,' the earl said. 'With a rifle shot like that.'

'Not necessarily.' The gruff voice came from the rear seat and Shona turned to see Charles Bell's pained expression. She could tell it went against the grain for him to contradict his noble employer, but given the reflection of the day's events on his own reputation, he'd chosen to speak up. 'Plenty of deer in the area. You'd want a rifle for one of those. Every farm, and half the town, has one.'

'So it's possible it *was* an accident,' the earl cut in. 'But not the responsibility of the estate?'

Bell shrugged. Shona knew what he must be thinking. It would be hard to mistake Nicola Baird for a deer in the middle of a grouse shoot.

They reached the crest of the hill. The earl pulled the four-by-four expertly onto a flattened area of heather by the track where one of the armed response vehicles was already parked. They acknowledged Shona's nod.

'We'll need to walk from here.' He gave her an apologetic smile, which Shona thought he must roll out for guests who rarely walked anywhere.

Bield Moss stretched bare in every direction. It was difficult to see how any human hand had ever touched it, never mind tamed it. No roads or farms or even drystone walls were visible. A few miles off, a moving speck caught her eye. She squinted into the distance and finally deciphered it as someone on a quad bike herding some sheep. The figure was so tiny and far away, but she'd seen it just the same. It must be hard to do anything unobserved, despite the remoteness, but somehow the gunman was managing it.

In front of them was a grouse butt: a chest-height horseshoe of drystone walling topped with turf. A small slate tag with the number '1' painted on it hung from a hook. A string of nine more butts progressed along the moor, facing south-west into the prevailing breeze.

The earl strode to a point just behind the butt, then orientated himself, as if replaying the events of the shooting in his mind.

Shona motioned the tall and willowy Kate to stand in for the MSP beside him. Forensics would be here shortly and Shona wanted to narrow down their search parameters.

'Mrs Baird was on my left,' the earl said. 'I was a little in front of her.' He gave Kate a warm smile as he showed her where to stand.

'Talk me through what happened next,' Shona said.

'It was nearly noon,' Bell supplied. 'We were just beginning the last drive of the morning, working in a beat line from the right.' He pointed beyond the earl, and back towards the Land Rover.

'I'd just said how lucky we were with the weather to Mrs Baird and then I heard...' The earl stopped.

'What did you hear?' Shona prompted.

'It was like something passed in the air between us. Then, Mrs Baird was on the ground, and I saw the blood. I tell you, I was shook.'

'Which way was she facing when she was hit?'

'Oh, pretty much how Ms Irving is standing now.'

Kate put her right hand to her left shoulder, showing the wound site.

Shona turned and scanned the moor. There were no points of elevation. The shot must have been fired from ground level. Darker strips of low vegetation lay among the tall sea of purple heather.

'What are those marks?' Shona asked.

'We've been using muirburn and top cutting to stimulate fresh shoots of heather for the grouse,' Bell said. 'It's an experiment to see which best increases our bird numbers.'

An experienced gunman would avoid those areas. Less cover. Shona studied the landscape again and checked

34

Kate's position. She held out her arms to section off a quadrant as the likely position of the shooter.

'This is our initial search area. Would you agree, Mr Bell?' Shona looked at the gamekeeper and he nodded in grim confirmation.

'Aye, right in front of the guns. Must have had a cool head, but then we know that.'

'What d'you mean?' Shona said.

'The moss is a dangerous place. It's always looking for ways to kill ye. The bogs, the sudden weather, the cliffs and sykes. You treat it with respect. Like a beast that might turn on you.'

'Like I said, must have been a professional hitman,' the earl reiterated, nodding his agreement.

Shona could only estimate the distance. Too close and the beaters would have spotted them. Too far and they couldn't be sure to hit the target.

'What was the wind doing?' Shona asked Bell.

He pulled out his iPhone. 'We record all the details for each drive, so I can tell you exactly.' He swiped the screen. 'The wind was west-south-west. Twenty-two miles per hour. A strong breeze to lift the birds and bring them over the guns at a good height.'

The breeze was not an issue for the shotguns, but a significant calculation for anyone firing a rifle. She indicated a widening triangle of moor that stretched out from the butt.

'We'll work inwards from a 250-metre perimeter to avoid contaminating the scene.'

It was likely the shot came from the furthest point of that range. Closer, and the power would have taken the bullet right through Nicola Baird's shoulder, and blood loss and shock from the larger exit wound would have killed her.

'There was only one shot?' Shona asked.

'As far as I know,' replied the earl.

Shona's experience and training told her that a professional would have fired a group of closely targeted shots, two to the head and one to the chest, to be sure of killing their target. A single bullet meant only one shell case to find. It was the proverbial needle in the heather haystack, three or four feet deep in places, and with small pools within the boggy sections.

Behind where they stood, there was a clump of twisted rowans and young Scots pines. It was just possible any other shots fired had gone in there.

'We'll need to search this section, too,' Shona said to Kate, who'd extracted a roll of police cordon tape from her jacket pocket. As she unfurled it, the earl took hold of the free end and tied it to a tree.

Shona turned back to the moor. 'What are those flags on canes?'

'They mark the ninety-degree safe firing area for each butt. Supposed to stop the guests swinging their guns too far and shooting their neighbour's grouse. Or their neighbour,' Charles Bell said dryly.

'Can we borrow them?' Shona asked.

'Aye, fine.'

'Kate,' Shona called. 'You can use those flags to mark the forward search.'

'Okay, boss.'

The earl followed Kate out onto the moor. Shona turned back to the gamekeeper.

'Mr Bell, how are the shooting positions allocated?'

'Pegs are booked in advance. Some guests have a favourite number. They'd be on the estate's computer system.'

'So anyone with access would know Mrs Baird's position?'

'Aye,' he said. 'But number one is always the earl's personal guests, so it might have been a lucky guess.'

Someone planning a political assassination in this remote country in front of a line of blazing shotguns would leave nothing to chance, Shona thought.

Impatiently, she rang forensics. Still half an hour away. Given the size of the search area, and the added complication of Dr Armstrong's find at the dig, they'd said they were happy for the shoot staff to start the search immediately. 'I'd like to get out of there before dark,' Senior Crime Scene Examiner Peter Harrison had told her, as if wolves circled as soon as the sun went down.

As arranged by the earl, the gamekeepers and beaters arrived in a convoy of Land Rovers. Sergeant Graham jumped out to open the door for the blonde woman in the claret gilet who Shona had seen yesterday. Today, the woman wore a fitted tweed jacket, cream jodhpurs and a pink trilby sporting a narrow hatband of small game feathers. The beaters and shoot staff parted with deferential nods. She moved between the men like a gazelle among lumbering beasts, as the earl hurried over to greet her.

As they talked, Shona briefed the shoot staff. 'Look for bullets and spent cartridge cases first, and any discarded clothing, but touch nothing,' she instructed them. Sergeant Graham attempted to organise them into groups but Charles Bell, with the stern look of a sergeant major, quickly took charge.

The earl introduced the blonde woman as Lady Douglas. She gave Shona an appraising look, her hands remaining firmly in the pockets of her jacket.

'Are you the most senior officer available?' she asked coolly. In contrast to her son, her accent was clearly English, and upper-class enough not to betray her origins, although Shona thought London or Home Counties.

The earl looked uncomfortable. Shona wondered if it was Lady Douglas who held the whip hand on the estate.

'I'm in charge of CID Dumfries, so yes, I am,' Shona replied, returning the woman's gaze.

'The rest of your team are, of course, welcome to use The Douglas Arms,' the earl said into the silence that followed Shona's reply. 'But perhaps Ms Irving would like to stay at the house? It's been very unsettling for my mother, and I know she'd prefer an officer nearby for a day or two.'

Several things struck Shona. Firstly, the woman seemed hardly old enough to be his mother. Secondly, her icy stare would be enough to stop any intruder in their tracks and, finally, she clearly looked far from happy at the prospect of having Kate in the house. Shona was tempted to agree purely to burst Lady Douglas's balloon. It wasn't operationally necessary, but Shona immediately realised that Kate's presence in the household would give the investigation an inside track on the dynamics of the earl's estate, as well as how Nicola Baird had come to be a guest and who she might have upset along the way.

Shona glanced at an alert on her phone. A text from Cameron Armstrong. For a split second she wondered if he'd change his mind again about the burial Becca had uncovered and was contacting her to say that it was historic after all. But then Shona remembered the photographs of the dress label and the anguish in his voice, matching her own dread, and knew there would be no easy resolution to this discovery. His message was simple. *Waiting at site for forensics.*

'Okay, sir,' Shona said, dragging her attention back to her surroundings. 'If Kate is happy to take on a liaison role for a day or two, that would be very helpful.'

One look at Kate's face told her she was happy. Sergeant Graham, his place at the earl's side usurped, looked less so. He had promised the earl that the case would be resolved quickly, but it looked like the local officer would have to put up with Shona and her team for longer than he'd like.

Chapter 5

DS Murdo O'Halloran arrived in the passenger seat of the Land Rover with the forensic team. He shook hands with Charles Bell and a couple of the shoot staff, and then, jacket flapping in the wind, tramped through the heather towards Shona, his stocky ex-rugby player's frame high-stepping, his eyes on the ground.

'Nearly trod on an adder up here once,' he said by way of explanation. 'But I guess all this commotion has sent them running. Poor wee things.'

'Got here okay?' Shona said.

'Aye, fine. Bit of a roundabout journey. The blocked roads are a double wipeout for the locals and tourist trade. Mind you, summer in Scotland can be a flighty quine. Late to arrive, and sure to take offence and depart earlier than anyone wished.' He buttoned his jacket, pumping his shoulders up and down against the chill. 'Anyways, where d'you want me to start?'

'Talk to the local cops. You'll get more out of Sergeant Graham than me. We'll need to look at firearms licences. The head keeper said there's more guns than the Alamo floating around this area.' Shona scanned the moor for the officer, but he was nowhere to be seen. 'Who else might have useful intel locally?'

'Well, anyone from outside would have needed to recce the area,' Murdo replied, 'so we're looking for suspicious activity. I'd say speak to campsites, B&B owners. Once we're finished here, I'll get Kate to go over the statements of the shoot staff and see if we've missed anything.' He shaded his eyes. 'Is that the new earl talking to her now?'

Shona told him about the earl's offer to have Kate stay at the house, and the potential advantages to the investigation that might offer. Both of them understood it would also help Kate to regain some confidence after previous cases where she'd struggled to show empathy to victims and potential witnesses whose social status was vastly below hers. She was an excellent officer, but a landscape of addiction, endemic poverty and multi-generational despair was not her natural environment. While not blue-blooded, Kate was obviously more at home in the world of grouse moors and ancient Scottish titles. Success here would spur her on to achieve all the things that Shona knew Kate was capable of. And Lady Douglas, with her disdain and entitlement, would just have to lump it.

'The Douglas Arms is run by a distant cousin,' Shona said. 'That's as close as I'll get to the nobs.' She gave Murdo a wry smile.

'What's the place like?'

'Good,' Shona conceded. 'Jack Douglas is a bit of a character, in the charming old hippy vein. No guests yet and he's offered us space for an incident room.'

'Kate will do a good job, I'm sure,' Murdo said.

In Shona's eyes, his encouragement of younger officers was one of the many things that made him a good sergeant.

'One more thing,' Shona said. 'Get statements from Cameron Armstrong and Becca about the archaeology burial.'

'What are they doing up there?'

'Investigating the Border reivers.'

'Aye, they were a lively bunch.'

'Dr Armstrong told me it's the origin of the word *bereaved*.'

'They invented the term "blackmail", too,' Murdo said. '"Whitemail" was silver paid by farmers to the legal landowners in rent. "Blackmail" was what you paid the reivers not to burn yer hoose down.'

'Dr Armstrong compared the reivers to the Mafia.'

'He's got a point, but they could have taught the Mafia a thing or two.' He cleared his throat. 'I've had a wee think about thon burial.'

'Go on.' Shona closed her notebook.

'There was a series of murders in the 1980s. Five women and girls. They got the fella, right enough. John Maxwell. He was a bad yin. Had a string of previous. Went away for life. The papers dubbed it "the Girls in the Glen". Do you mind them?'

'Of course.' Shona had been a child herself at the time, but the serial killings were big news. 'Wasn't that further east?'

Murdo shook his head. 'Some of the bodies were recovered from hereabouts. Thing is, two victims were never located.'

'You think they found one of them?'

'Gotta be a consideration.'

'Well, let's keep that between ourselves until we've established there's a connection. Dr Armstrong's the only other person who knows it's not a reiver's child. I've warned him not to say anything.'

Shona remembered Becca's shock at the discovery. How much worse would her daughter feel if she'd uncovered not a historical burial, but a murder victim? Uncovering a body in such circumstances would shake an experienced police officer, never mind a sixteen-year-old girl.

Her first instinct was to get Becca away and back to High Pines, but with Rob in London preparing for the trial, and her own presence required on the moor, it wasn't a viable option.

Shona checked the time on her phone. She'd go up to the campsite as soon as she could, as much to reassure herself that Becca was coping with recent events as to see if others had made the possible connection with the historic case.

'Okay, I'll get started and let you know.' Murdo raised a hand to Charles Bell, who pointed to the Land Rover. Murdo gave him a thumbs-up and set off back across the moor, still high-stepping and clearly looking out for snakes.

There was one other person she needed to call. Detective Superintendent Davies. He'd recently replaced the man who'd appointed her and who had been her champion on difficult cases, Malcolm 'Mars Bars' Munroe. This sweet-loving, teetotal super had now retired but not before he'd offered Shona a step up to detective chief inspector. By turning that promotion down, she'd probably lost her best chance of rising quickly through the ranks. But that had never been her aim. For Shona, it was the hands-on aspect of the job that appealed most, and there were also Becca and the B&B to consider. The move north from London to Rob's home village of Kirkness had been all about focusing on family, and she wouldn't be deviated from that course, now more than ever. The DCI's role had gone to another officer, Jim

'Robocop' Robinson, currently on holiday. This forced Shona to deal directly with Davies. So far their exchanges had been stilted, the new super lacking his predecessor's affable authority. She'd call Davies later, when she had an update from Ravi on Nicola Baird's condition.

The painstaking search stretched through the morning and most of the afternoon. Lady Douglas had departed after twenty minutes, but the earl was still out on the moor. Shona sipped from her water bottle and was wondering if the coffee flasks in the Land Rovers were empty, and the flapjacks all gone, when a shout went up from one of the shoot staff.

Senior Crime Scene Examiner Peter Harrison hurried across the moor. The white overalls on his wiry frame swished as he covered the hundred yards to the spot. Shona reached the keeper a moment later. Harrison kneeled down and carefully parted the stiff brushes of heather.

'Anybody here handled it?' he said. The spent cartridge was on the ground.

The young keeper shook his head, dark eyes serious beneath his tweed cap.

'You did well to spot it,' Peter said.

Shona agreed with that assessment. The brass rifle casing tucked in the deep shadow of the heather roots was only the length of Shona's little finger, and a close colour-match to the dried peat.

The earl clapped the startled boy on the shoulder, promising him a bottle of malt whisky from his own supply. Charles Bell added his own gruff approval, then turned to Shona and Peter Harrison.

'Stand the men down?'

Shona looked at Peter, who nodded. 'My team can take it from here.'

'Thank you, Mr Bell. You've been an enormous help,' Shona said.

Peter took out a pair of long tweezers and transferred the bullet casing into an evidence bag. 'I'd say we've got a .243 Winchester rifle cartridge. Good match for the 6.2mm bullet dug out of your MSP.'

'What are the chances you'll get something useful?' Shona said.

'We'll look at fingerprints, but we might also get DNA using direct ammunition recovery technique. We don't swab with a cotton bud, but break open cells *in situ*. It's got a 54 per cent recovery rate, as opposed to 4–5 per cent with traditional methods, and it can throw up multiple profiles – basically, everyone who's ever handled the cartridge, but one of them will be your shooter.'

'Good. Anything else I should consider?'

Peter ran his hand across the close crop of his dark hair. 'It's an open environment, but keep in mind that gunshot residue can transfer from clothes onto car interior fabrics or handles.'

Shona thought of the keepers, beaters and city boys who'd flown in for the shoot. 'I'd bet my house every single person on the moor yesterday would test positive.'

'Exactly,' Peter said. 'The defence may jump on the cross-contamination. So, if you have a suspect, it may take more than forensics to prove they fired the shot.'

As Shona pondered this, Ravi called to say that the statement from Mrs Baird shed little light on who'd attacked her. The MSP was recovering well. Her children were being looked after by her parents.

Shona took a deep breath. She couldn't put it off any longer.

Superintendent Davies picked up after the first ring. Shona outlined the progress she'd made over the Nicola Baird shooting: the recovery of the bullet from Nicola's shoulder, the discovery of a potential shell casing on the moor and the witness statements. As she moved on to the removal of the child's body, and the possible link to the historic Girls in the Glen enquiry, Shona felt she was squarely on the horns of a dilemma. The bulk of allocated resources would go to the apprehension of the gunman, and rightly so. Here was a threat to life, a clear and present danger to the public. But everything Shona had learned, as a police officer and a mother, told her that the resolution of the girl's case – discovering her identity, finding her family – was just as urgent. True justice didn't just lie with a conviction of the guilty; there must be resolution for those whose lives were torn apart by the crime. Only then could the healing begin. The girl could have lain on the moor for decades. Her parents, siblings, cousins would be old now. For them the clock was ticking, and Shona heard it loud in her heart.

'I'd like to assign an officer and a support team to explore potential links with the Girls in the Glen case straight away, sir. Of course, I understand how both cases have implications, politically and in the media,' she said, finally.

There was a pause, a beat, as if the signal had dropped. Then she heard him clear his throat.

'Just stick with the shooting.' He didn't wait for her reply, and instead he said, 'Everything going okay with your husband's trial preparations?'

Shona bristled. Why was he bringing it up now? Was he more worried about the fallout from a DI whose husband was on trial for money laundering than he was

46

about the assassination attempt on a politician, or revisiting a high-profile historic case? There was only so far he could distance himself from her, as her superior officer.

'Everything is fine, sir,' Shona said lightly, fighting to keep the anger from her voice.

'Boss?' Kate approached from the line of grouse butts, her hand in the air.

'I'm sorry, sir. DC Irving is calling me. I have to go,' Shona said, and ended the call.

She crossed to where Kate stood among the sparse green regrowth of heather in one of the muirburn strips.

'Sorry, boss,' Kate said, then stopped at the sight of Shona's expression. 'Everything okay?'

'It's fine,' Shona said tersely. 'What's the problem?'

'No problem,' Kate replied. 'Just checking if you still need me? If not, I'll get over to Langdale Hall.'

Shona made a conscious effort to slow her breathing and focus on the case in hand. 'Kate.' She took a step closer to her DC and lowered her voice. 'This isn't a standard FLO role. The earl and his mother aren't related to the victim. I want a timeline of Nicola Baird's movements on the day of the grouse shoot. Who did she speak to? Was this her first visit? Any upsets? You know the drill.'

'Yes, boss.'

Alexander Douglas was standing a little way off, listening to his head keeper, Charles Bell, but his eyes kept straying to Shona and Kate.

'And Kate,' Shona said, inclining her head towards the earl, 'any trouble from lover-boy over there, call me.'

Kate looked at her blankly for a moment, then coloured as the implication dawned on her. 'I can't see that being a problem,' she said stiffly.

Shona was aware that Kate's nickname around the office was 'the ice queen', due to her fair complexion, her sometimes haughty manner and her almost complete lack of a sense of humour. This, combined with her ambitious professionalism, should be enough to cool any ill-advised advances from the earl.

'You'd better take your car up to the house, in case I need you tonight,' Shona said. 'Otherwise, come to The Douglas Arms tomorrow morning. I'll get Murdo to join us. Okay, off you go.'

Alexander Douglas bent attentively to listen to whatever Kate was saying as they walked to his vehicle. Shona wondered if, despite his gauche charm and obvious fascination with Kate, this arrangement was, for the Earl of Langdale, largely about damage limitation. She suspected the real reason Lady Douglas had agreed to have a police officer in the house was to get the inside track on the investigation and make sure nothing tarnished the estate's good name.

For the next hour, the forensic team searched the area around where the bullet casing was found, and then a strip of moorland between the shooter's position and the number one grouse butt. Shona sat in a Land Rover and attempted to make some calls, most of which dropped at unhelpful moments. Finally, in frustration, she cadged a lift with the gamekeepers back down to the hunting lodge. Murdo was there, his expression as grim as the grey granite walls that formed the backdrop to his conference with two of the local cops.

'Anything?' Shona said when the officers had left, and they were alone.

'Got a list of local firearms that'll take the calibre we're after. No reports of an armed individual but they're widening the search area, checking all the farms around the moss. We've done the statements from Dr Armstrong and Becca.'

'She okay?' Shona asked, casually, though she felt a curl of anxiety that her daughter had been required to relive her experience of finding the girl's body.

'Aye, she's fine.' Murdo wasn't fooled. 'But she'll be better after a hug from her mother, mind. You both will.'

Shona smiled, caught out.

'Do you want to stay here?' she said. 'There's room at The Douglas Arms.' It might be useful to chew over the case with Murdo, but on the other hand there was a chance they'd stay up late talking and she could feel a weight of tiredness sitting on her shoulders. She felt a little relieved when he shook his head.

'I'll get back home, if it's all the same, boss.'

'Okay, Murdo, thanks. See you tomorrow.'

Chapter 6

Murdo drove down the track from the shooting lodge. At the junction, he indicated left. The road was empty, but he still hesitated. The key to his mother's house clinked like a siren call against the steering column. He lifted his knee to still the noise, then flicked the indicators right and made a sweeping turn towards his home town.

Langholm had retained its traditional butcher and baker, and gained a stylish candlestick maker, along with a vintage tearoom. The town was built on muscular proportions, having boomed as a centre for weaving in the nineteenth century. But now its apparel of austere Victorian buildings hung several sizes too big for its population. Broad streets of fine granite houses and robust public buildings were so silent under leaden skies, you could almost hear the hoof-beats and cart rattle of past prosperity. The 'Muckle Toon' was not so muckle any more. But to Murdo it was still home and, given the decline in the face of change he'd witnessed in other parts of Dumfries and Galloway, he felt it was holding its own.

Murdo closed the front door of his mother's house behind him and listened. A pile of mail lay on the floor, brushed aside by his arrival. He bent to pick it up, and stacked the gaudy envelopes and fliers in a neat pile.

He had the fleeting sense that his brother might step in the hall to greet him and his mother call from the kitchen or that he'd glimpse his father in the backyard, busy splitting sticks for the coal fire, but the air remained heavy and unstirred.

Murdo walked along the hall to the kitchen and put the keys in the bowl on the countertop, as he always did. The small table in the centre of the room was bare. His mother's apron hung like a dead bird on the hook, its plumage faded. Her wedding-china cups and plates were grey with dust on the shelf. By the back door, a few boxes remained where they'd sat for a year: items from the nursing home where she'd spent her last months, confused and often unable to recognise him. He crossed to the window above the sink and opened it, as if allowing any lingering trace of her spirit to depart.

Murdo checked the ground floor for any signs of damp or damage. There was little of his father, Patrick O'Halloran, here, beyond a few books in the front room and a framed photograph of Murdo's grandfather, who'd come from Ireland to work on the railway for the munitions plant during World War I and then married a local girl. But in the hall cupboard, the toolboxes were still there, every item in its proper place, clean and ready.

The stairs creaked like old piano keys, sounding their familiar tune. On the landing, four doors faced him. His parents' room and the bathroom looked out to the rear of the house. Murdo's bedroom had become his mother's sewing room long ago, when he'd left to marry Joan. He turned the handle on the fourth door and went in.

The faded orange curtains bathed his brother's bedroom with a golden glow. The single bed with its candlewick bedspread was neatly made; on the walls, posters of aircraft and the solar system.

Earlier that afternoon, Murdo had listened politely to the archaeologist, but it was his brother who'd had the genuine interest in history. Andrew's most treasured possession had been an autograph from Neil Armstrong, the first man on the moon and the descendent of a family of notorious Border reivers. Armstrong had visited in 1972 to receive the freedom of the town. The mayor had caused much amusement by reading him a 400-year-old law that declared any Armstrong found in the town should be hanged. Murdo smiled at the memory of his brother recounting the moment, over and over again throughout his adult life, of how the most famous man in the world had signed his space encyclopaedia, the joy just as fresh as when he'd experienced it at ten years of age. Their mother had been Aileen Armstrong, before she married, so that made the moon-man family.

Drew had suffered what Murdo later learned was called birth asphyxia: a lack of oxygen that left him with brain damage, lack of muscle tone, weakness on one side and seizures. Born sixteen years later, when his mother was forty-three years old, Murdo was a 'change baby', a longed-for and welcome late-life child, who had paid back his parents' joy and gratitude in spades, perhaps because Murdo needed to achieve for both himself and his brother. He'd grown up fast, an ash sapling quickly surpassing his brother's oak. First he'd been a beloved little playmate, then a contemporary, but soon his brother's protector, as their roles quickly reversed.

And now Joan thought it was time. To do the place up and let it to a family – they had no children of their own, but perhaps their nephew might move in. He knew she was stepping carefully around the issue, not pushing him.

Murdo opened the old linen kist at the foot of the bed. Andrew's collection of space memorabilia was neatly tucked between layers of newspaper. He took out the faded photograph of Drew with Neil Armstrong and envied him not only the meeting but that his brother remained that child forever, frozen in the wonder of the world.

There were plenty in the town who thought his death was no loss. People didn't say it out loud, and certainly not to the family's face, but it was what they thought. He'd have ended up in an institution at the taxpayers' expense. Murdo would never have let that happen. He and Joan had talked about it and agreed. He'd come to them when he got too much for Aileen. In the end, it hadn't been relevant. Ten years ago, a petty local villain named Alan Kerr, drunk and high at the wheel of his van, had mounted the pavement and mowed fifty-year-old Drew O'Halloran down as he carefully carried a small cake home, a present for their mother. Murdo knew Kerr, he'd even hauled him in a few times over drug possession, but it seemed like he'd always got off with fines or a sheriff's warning and a rehab order.

And who, now, felt Drew's absence beyond Murdo? Their mother didn't remember either of her boys at the end. Drew had no wife, no children, no professional colleagues. Just his brother.

Murdo went back downstairs, checked the windows and back door, then stood in the hallway again, listening. He'd dealt with death and bereavement all his working life, first as a beat officer and then in CID. He'd seen all the colours of shock, grief and anger, but it seemed to him, when it came to his own, nothing he'd learned made any difference.

He didn't talk about his brother to colleagues or friends. He kept it to himself, as if that act alone could preserve Drew as Murdo had known him: his kind, funny and loving only brother. Murdo stepped onto the front step and, after a last look at the home that had given him so much pleasure and pain, pulled the door firmly shut, turned the key in the lock and walked away.

Chapter 7

Shona came out of The Douglas Arms, breakfast coffee in hand. A joiner and a carpet fitter were at work somewhere inside, their vans the only vehicles in the car park. Last night, the Tactical Firearms Commander, in consultation with Shona and after a final helicopter sweep, had decided to withdraw his unit. There had been no sighting of the gunman for more that twenty-four hours, and all the houses and farms surrounding Bield Moss had been visited and checked. The advice to the public was to be alert and report suspicious behaviour but it seemed clear that the shooter had slipped through their fingers.

Shona's visit to Becca had convinced her that her daughter was in good spirits after giving Murdo her state- ment and her maternal anxiety had returned to its regular levels. She and the other students were treating the whole experience in the barn as an exciting sleepover. None had made a connection between the child's body and the Girls in the Glen.

The pub's granite, two-storey building commanded fabulous views of Eskdale. It reminded Shona of Jamaica Inn on Bodmin Moor, in Cornwall, which she'd visited on holiday with Rob. That pub had been the haunt of smugglers and she wondered if outlaws in the shape of the Border reivers had favoured this one. On impulse, she tried his phone.

She thought it was about to go to voicemail when he picked up.

'Sorry, just out for a run,' he said, breathlessly. 'I'm on the South Bank.' He must have been on the Thames, not far from their friend's flat in Borough Market: a stone's throw from her old RNLI station at Tower Bridge.

'I wish I was with you,' she said, conscious that perhaps it was her desire to be back in the city that had been her home for twenty years, rather than the company of her husband, that made her feel that way. 'How are you?'

'Fine,' Rob said. 'I'm meeting Tessa and Josie for breakfast.'

'And the trial prep?' Shona said, faintly irritated by his laid-back attitude.

'Aye, couldn't be better. The prosecution have nothing.'

They must have something, Shona thought, or we wouldn't be in this mess and the CPS wouldn't be bothering with the expense of a court case. She could hear from his breathing that he was jogging on the spot, anxious to be off again. She pictured him arriving at the cafe, his silver-fox hair still damp, healthy and glowing from his run, wearing jeans and the blue willow-pattern shirt he liked. A kiss on both cheeks for Tessa and Josie, and not a thought for his wife.

'When are you coming back?' she said, tersely. From the sound of it, there was nothing in the trial prep to keep him there.

'Might stay over this weekend,' he said. 'Just a few more papers to get through.'

'And the B&B?'

'I can't tell you, Shona, darlin', how nice it is to have a wee break. It's been flat out since we opened. Why don't you come down and join me for a few days?'

'Are you not following the news? I'm in the middle of a shooting, Rob.' She couldn't believe what she was hearing, but then she could. This was Rob all over.

'You're not the only cop in Dumfries.' He sounded peeved.

'You better go or you'll be late for your avocado on toast,' Shona said and ended the call. She spotted Murdo's blue Astra moving like a pixel along the main road far below, drained her cup and stomped back inside, and took a few deep breaths to calm down.

Shona needed Murdo's local knowledge for another day or two. Back at Dumfries CID office, DC Ravi Sarwar could flex his leadership skills in Murdo's absence. God help the team. Shona took a second cup from the side table, poured her sergeant a coffee from the vacuum flask and topped up her own.

'What's it like to be back home?' she said as they sipped their drinks, having talked through some strategic issues – staffing, vehicles, budgets – and waited for Kate to arrive.

'Aye, it's fine,' he said, eyes on a map of the moor spread out on the table.

Shona frowned, but didn't press him. He'd previously talked warmly of the place, and his days playing rugby for the Muckle Toon. But a case that came close to home was often difficult. He must have been grilled about it by his wife and friends.

Kate arrived with a spring in her step, wearing slim-fit cords and a pale yellow blouse. As she placed a light tweed jacket around the back of her chair, Shona saw the flash of the estate's twin stags logo on the inside label.

They gathered round the laptop and Shona brought Ravi up on the screen.

'How's things going?' Shona said. 'The team behaving themselves?'

'I've done away with the biscuit tin and introduced a samosa-only snack policy. And since I'm the only out-and-proud queen of the south, they've all to address me as *your majesty*.'

If anyone else had made a comment like that, she'd have given them a written warning. But Ravi enjoyed shaking up the status quo and challenging casual prejudices; his light-hearted banter made people consider the power of language to include or exclude.

'I literally never know if you're joking, pal,' Shona smiled.

'Who says I am?' He shot her his megawatt grin. 'Seriously, everything's fine. I've sent you an in-progress doc and Mrs Baird's statement. We're working through the online threats. Her parliamentary agent, and her assistant, gave us a bumper list.'

'Can you whittle it down?'

'Well, so far, we've got a Jim Cameron who wanted Mrs Baird to arrange the cancellation of his speeding ticket. Things quickly escalated to online abuse about her politics and her appearance, and a threat to torch her house. The Edinburgh boys are picking him up.'

'Who else?'

'We're building a profile on Darren Porter, the thirty-eight-year-old ex-soldier with a housing dispute who turned up at Baird's constituency office. When he was told she wasn't there, he pulled a can of mace on the staff. He's previously been sectioned, but has a history of absconding, and his current whereabouts are unknown. I've promoted him to *most wanted* internally. D'you want to go public with him?'

Shona nodded. 'He's made no direct threats to kill, but his military background suggests the capacity to carry out an attack of this kind. Get his name and picture out to the media, but make it clear he's not to be approached.'

'Yes, boss.'

'Anyone else?'

'How long have you got?' Ravi sighed. 'No specific intelligence about a potential political assassination but given she's a Conservative MSP, there's your regular class warriors to consider. Also, she wrote in *The Scotsman* on her anti-independence views – that provoked a few trolls on top of the steady stream of low-level threats she's received since she won the by-election last year.'

'Anyone with a local address in Dumfries?' Shona said.

'Still checking. Her stance on the environment might be something. She tweeted in support of grouse shooting as a key part of the rural economy, and defended muir-burn as lawful and beneficial to the ecosystem. That drew criticism from Friends of the Earth and other groups, and then it was a social media pile-on.'

'Have the constituency staff been in touch with us before about the threats?'

'Her assistant said she'd forwarded emails, but I can't find any record of them.'

Shona turned to Kate. 'How did Nicola Baird come to be a guest of the earl?'

'I've taken statements from Xander and his mother,' Kate replied.

Shona noted the first-name terms – not *his lordship*, but a pet form of Alexander. Perhaps the earl, with his American notions of informality, had pressed Kate into addressing him that way. But it sounded out of place in the context of the meeting and perhaps just a little too friendly.

'I also talked to the house staff,' Kate continued. 'Mrs Baird didn't stay, but travelled down on the day from Edinburgh. The estate is in her constituency and Xander made a donation to her campaign. She's visited a few times before, but it was business rather than a personal connection.'

'Ravi, what was Nicola Baird's state of mind when you talked to her?' Shona turned back to the screen.

'Scared but trying not to show it,' Ravi replied. 'Her team's pushing a line to the media about her fears for her children after the death of their hero father, a serving police officer. They're skirting around any controversial remarks made in the past, but she's demanded armed protection for the family in Edinburgh.'

Shona turned to Murdo. 'What are Lothian and Borders saying?'

'She's got good home security, but they've inspected her office to check and will make recommendations.'

Shona had already received a flurry of emails via Division. The Scottish government were considering a de-escalation and self-defence training course for MSPs, but that wouldn't be much use against a sniper.

'So it's still not clear if the motive for the shooting is political or personal,' Shona said, summarising. The others nodded, and she continued. 'I think the most important factor in the shooting is the terrain. Whoever did this got clean away.'

'So Darren Porter, as an ex-soldier, is the best fit?' Kate said, echoing the earl's line of a professional assassin.

'He was with the Royal Highland Fusiliers,' Shona replied. 'It's an infantry battalion and his last posting was Iraq, so he's capable. My problem is, we've only got one shot fired. It's a small-calibre rifle. Why not use something more lethal? Also, would he have missed? It was windy, but that's a poor excuse.'

'Perhaps the approaching beat line disturbed him?' Kate said.

'That's possible,' Shona agreed. 'We also need to consider if there's an organised-crime connection.'

'I'm not seeing anything so far to indicate that, boss,' Ravi said.

'Dig deeper.'

Ravi rolled his shoulders, a gesture she recognised as him squaring up to argue the point. Shona glared at him.

'Look, boss, there's nothing in Nicola Baird's past or present circle to suggest she's made any enemies among the criminal fraternity. Like you said, it's political or personal.'

Maybe he was right, but Shona felt in her bones that if they turned over enough stones in Nicola Baird's vicinity, something nasty was bound to crawl out.

'We need to be sure,' Shona said stubbornly, but Ravi pursed his lips and shook his head.

'She's not on my Christmas card list either, boss. Her LGBTQ+ stance is medieval, and she'd strangle a kitten on live TV if she thought it was a vote winner, but I just don't believe the criminal angle is there, and pursuing it will take resources from the social media leads.'

Their shared Glaswegian roots gave them something of a free pass in their working relationship to speak bluntly to each other, as natives of the city tended to. But Ravi was edging up to the line of insubordination and pure cheek.

She was giving him a direct order. It wasn't his place to argue.

'Humour me, DC Sarwar,' she said firmly. 'When questions are asked about this case, all the way up to the Scottish Parliament, I want to say my team followed every, and I mean every, possibility.'

'Aye, okay,' Ravi conceded. He'd boxed and won many fights in the ring but recognised, with an opponent this determined, that this was a battle he couldn't win.

Shona wound up the meeting and Murdo left to talk to the local Specials.

'Nice jacket,' Shona said, as Kate opened her laptop and got to work reviewing the statements. 'I saw Lady Douglas with one just like it.'

Kate coloured. 'Yes, it's a sample. The estate's planning a fashion line. I only have the Barbour and a fleece with me. This is smarter, and Xander wanted my opinion.'

'It's probably best if you don't wear it while we're on official business,' Shona said. 'It's a detail the locals won't miss. Accusations of partiality might follow and that could be disastrous for the investigation.' She paused, letting Kate work out for herself the potential impact on her career that would follow such an outcome. 'And it's Lord Langdale or his full title in future.'

'Yes, ma'am,' Kate said, and tossed back her fine blonde hair. 'But there's really no need to be concerned.' She set her jaw in a rigid line and jabbed at the keyboard, not looking at Shona.

'Fine,' Shona said, satisfied that Kate, in contrast to Ravi, could at least take a telling. 'So, any insight from your night at the castle?'

'I doubt the shooting is connected to the Langdale estate or the *earl*,' Kate emphasised the title. 'The housekeeper told me Lady Douglas has been keen to establish the family influence since they returned from the United States and casts a wide social net. Anyone she considers posh enough, or useful to the estate's plans for world domination, gets an invitation.'

It chimed with Shona's impression of the woman. Haughty, socially ambitious and the worst kind of snob. She suspected neither herself nor Kate would make the A-list.

'You recognised her, right?' Kate cast a sideways glance at her boss and saw the blank look. 'Lucy Miller, as was? The model? She was on the cover of *Vogue*, everything, back in the Noughties. Bit of a wild child. Did some TV presenting?'

What had Shona been doing then? Battling up the ranks in the City of London police, while fighting post-natal depression and trying to keep up with the social demands of her husband's merchant banking career. She loved fashion and had probably flicked right past Lucy Miller in the hairdresser's, but her face hadn't stuck.

'Nope. Don't remember her,' Shona said.

'Thing is,' Kate said, and relish crept into her tone, 'Lady Lucy is no lady.'

'How's that?' Shona replied.

'Correctly, she's Mrs Lucy Fernandez. The house-keeper also told me she's not entitled to use *Lady Douglas*, as that belongs to the earl's wife, but his lordship humours her.' Kate grinned. 'Lucy had a brief marriage to the earl's father, the Honourable Alexander Douglas, but he was the third son. A title, but no money, no prospects. She ditched him for Alonso Fernandez, who later traded her in for a younger model, but she got a substantial settlement. His principal fortune came from the importation of white goods and later branched into smart home devices like Alexa, and lawn mowers and vacuum cleaners.'

The housekeeper sounded like a useful source and obviously had no love for Lady Lucy.

'So why did her son inherit the estate?' Shona said.

'Xander's father, the Honourable Alex, died years ago in a car crash in Chile, but neither of his older brothers, who were in line to inherit, outlived the 13th Earl, or had children. The old earl, who was an alcoholic and a very difficult character, only died last year but the estate had been rudderless for a while.'

'Until Lady Douglas and her son took over?'

'That's right. The housekeeper reckons her ladyship is husband-hunting among the wealthy shoot guests, but that the midges and seven months of winter up here will drive her off.'

I wouldn't bet on it, Shona thought. 'What did she say about the young earl?' she asked.

'Unlike his mother, he's very popular. Been living here since January. Went to an elite boarding school in upstate New York, then graduated from what they call a *mountain school*. It's like Outward Bound. He did business at Yale. Then worked briefly for the Fernandez Corporation. His stepfather, Alonso Fernandez, paid for his education, as part of the terms of the divorce.'

'Why was that?'

Kate sat back and folded her arms. 'I think Lady Lucy wanted to keep him in the US. He was her toehold on the Douglas family, the poor state of the estate's finances might also have been a factor.' Kate's attention drifted to the window and the glen beyond. 'I can see why he loves this place,' she said softly. 'He missed out on his family and heritage growing up, and wants to make a go of it now.'

'What do the locals think?' Shona said. 'Is the new earl up to the job?'

'Oh yes,' Kate said with enthusiasm. 'He's the perfect fit.'

Shona had sent her detective constable to the castle to investigate any undercurrents of the estate which might shed light on the investigation. Instead, Kate seemed to have fallen under the earl's spell, just as everyone else had. One thing Shona knew for sure was that everyone had secrets; no one was perfect.

Chapter 8

That afternoon, Kate went back to Langdale Hall to talk to the remaining staff. The Douglas Arms was hosting a boozy prelaunch event for local businesses, and Shona saw it as the perfect opportunity to head across the border to Cumberland Infirmary and check in with Nicola Baird. After crawling behind log lorries, Shona stopped off at an M&S Food on the outskirts of Carlisle for chocolate and flowers. Was it lingering guilt over her boss, Gavin Baird's death a year ago? His actions had cost him his life, but ultimately he'd also saved Shona and Becca, and that was a debt that she felt bound her to his widow and children. But they would never be friends. Their mutual enmity stemmed from something deeper. Nicola had grown up in wealth and comfort, but she was of that deeply Calvinistic mindset that blamed those less fortunate than herself for their own poverty, lack of education or acquaintance with crime – either as victim or perpetrator.

Shona, whose own childhood had been marked by the absence of opportunities, knew only too well the narrow choices and high stakes of such a life. Nicola Baird's instinct was to use her privileged position to lecture folk to do better. In contrast, Shona was driven by a sense of injustice, hoping to correct the balance for those trapped in a cycle of poverty and violence she knew only too well.

Dan was waiting in the hospital car park. His slim-fit, dark grey suit was at the fashionable end of the standard copper attire, and his blonde hair and light beard looked more groomed than usual. She returned his broad smile.

'I hope you gave Charlotte my apologies for ruining your day off,' Shona said casually as they made their way to Nicola Baird's room on the top floor.

'She was fine about it.'

'Been seeing her long?' she pressed. *It's Charlotte*, the woman had said when Shona had called Dan's phone after the shooting, but it was hardly the moment for introductions or small talk.

'Not long.' His eyes were fixed on the corridor ahead. 'She's Charlotte Rutter,' he added with shy pride, as if Shona should instantly recognise the name.

She didn't, but it was familiar. Singer? Social media influencer? At thirty-one, Dan was nine years her junior. They were normally so in tune, she rarely noticed the age gap, but at this moment it seemed like a yawning cavern of cultural references.

'You know, Charlotte Rutter Jewellery?' Dan prompted. 'I gave Becca one of her bracelets for her sixteenth birthday?'

'Of course,' Shona smiled, remembering the birthday gift of handcrafted silver seashells on an upcycled braided band: it looked classy while also satisfying Becca's exacting environmental standards. She was glad Dan had found someone. He deserved happiness.

At the end of the corridor leading to Nicola Baird's room, two armed officers checked their ID. The nurse on the desk studied them over her glasses and said she'd see if Mrs Baird was awake.

'She's had a good night,' she added as she got up.

'Everyone at the office okay?' Dan said when they were alone. 'Ravi didn't give me any details but said you'd got your hands full.'

Shona updated him on the shooting and then, trusting him to be discreet, the child's body uncovered at the archaeological dig, and the complications that might result. He pressed his lips together and nodded slowly.

'Let me know if I can help.'

'Thanks.' Shona smiled. 'Murdo will have a handle on this, Langholm being his home town. Although, I think he's feeling uncomfortable being back.'

Before they could discuss the perils of policing your own patch, the nurse returned.

'Mrs Baird will see you now,' she said, with the air of announcing a royal audience.

Nicola Baird lay propped up, her left arm in a sling, and a surprisingly small shoulder dressing just visible beneath the hospital gown. Her customary prickliness had returned, and she ran a disdainful eye over the bouquet and chocolates. The desperate woman clutching Shona's hand for protection the day before had vanished.

'Flowers. So kind,' Nicola Baird said, although she clearly thought otherwise. Ignoring Shona, she turned to Dan. 'I understand I have you, and the Wilsons, to thank for my life.' She formally bowed her head to him in a show of gratitude. 'Thank you.'

Dan looked a little embarrassed.

'Mrs Baird, who do you think did this?' Shona said, bypassing small talk.

'It was obviously a political hit by a pro-independence group,' Nicola replied indignantly. 'What are you doing to ensure my safety?'

'Armed officers will stay with you until you go home. We're liaising with other forces and checking the list your office gave us. Has anyone approached you? Threatened you in person before?' Ravi had asked this yesterday, but a night's reflection might have brought someone specific to mind.

'You know female politicians are judged more harshly than their male counterparts. We receive more online abuse. My children are bullied at school. You should see the rage-filled messages my office gets from trolls. Any of those unhinged people could have shot me.'

That's just the problem, Shona thought. She wasn't buying the line that this was a pro-independence hit. No one had claimed responsibility, although there was newspaper speculation. She'd encountered extremist groups before, including the Sons of Scotia, who'd pointed out they no longer needed violence when they could successfully press their message through the media and at the polls. Nicola Baird's constituency was solidly Conservative and pro-Union, and the assassination of their MSP wouldn't change that.

'Okay, I won't take up your time,' Shona said. 'If you remember anyone in particular, call me.' She placed her card next to the water jug by the bed. Mrs Baird ignored it.

'Thank you for coming,' Nicola said to Dan. She gave Shona a curt nod.

In the corridor, Dan rolled his eyes. 'Phew. That's the best audition for Lady Macbeth I've ever seen.'

'Don't,' Shona said, suppressing a laugh as the nurse at the desk, who'd obviously fallen deep under Nicola's spell, eyed them with disapproval.

'Fancy a coffee?' Dan said. 'The canteen downstairs isn't bad.'

They took their paper cups of machine coffee to a seat by the window.

'Was the hunting lodge the first time you'd seen Nicola Baird since your DCI's funeral?' Dan asked.

Shona would have told any other officer to mind their own business. But Dan had been involved in the cross-border drug case that had led to Gavin Baird's death at the hands of a dealer, and his smart thinking had also meant that Shona owed Dan her life.

'I'd seen her once since then,' Shona said. 'Let's just say it didn't go well. It suits her to blame me for what happened, but nothing I could have done would have changed the outcome.'

'I think that's a very healthy way to look at it,' Dan said. 'Any idea who shot her? Is it personal or political, d'you think?'

They pushed the different elements of the shooting around, but failed to make the jigsaw fit.

'There is another possibility,' Shona said, as the idea formed in her mind. 'What if Nicola Baird wasn't the target? I mean, Alexander Douglas, the Earl of Langdale, made a point of telling me how close he was to Nicola when the shot was fired.'

'Why would anyone want to kill him?' Dan said. 'Who'd benefit from his death?'

'Good question.'

The new earl seemed popular, as were his plans for jobs and to reinvigorate the local economy. He was handsome and affable, and keen to fit in. A much less likely target than an outspoken MSP.

Shona picked up her phone and called Kate.

'Who'd inherit the estate on the earl's death? What about the cousin who runs the pub, Jack Douglas?'

Shona could hear Kate flipping through the pages of her notebook.

'Next in line is a Ewan Douglas, who lives in Australia and has two sons.'

'So, not Jack?'

'No, he's only distantly related, but Lady Douglas knew him in London years ago, apparently. She told me he's devoted to his younger cousin and re-establishing the family fortunes.'

Jack wouldn't inherit, but he'd struck Shona as someone who pursued his own interests. Given the time and care he lavished on Lady Lucy's pony and the estate's gastro-pub enterprise, perhaps he was looking to extend his power over the earl and his mother by playing on her vanity and acting the benevolent, protective older cousin to the young earl.

'You think Lord Langdale was the target?' Kate's voice took on a worried edge. 'Should I warn him?'

'No, I'm just exploring other possibilities. But check Ewan Douglas's alibi all the same.'

'Okay,' Kate said. 'Given the earl's age, he's likely to marry and produce heirs. I doubt Ewan Douglas has any expectation of inheriting.'

'Good enough reason to target him now,' Shona replied.

–

As Shona returned to The Douglas Arms, she squeezed through cars parked along both verges of the narrow road. The prelaunch event looked well attended. She was almost at the car park entrance when a police vehicle approached from the opposite direction, blues and twos sounding, and swung across her path.

'What the...' Shona jammed on the brakes, then followed them in. A second squad car was already there.

A crowd of men were gathered on the far side of the pub entrance. Dressed in jeans and wax-cotton jackets or gilets, they looked indistinguishable from the shoot staff. All Shona saw were their backs, but it only took a second for her to realise there was a fight in progress. Shouts of encouragement and insults flew through the air. The ring of men blocked the constables who attempted to get at the two individuals scrabbling on the ground. Sergeant Graham stood to one side, his thumbs looped through the armholes of his utility vest. Only when he saw Shona approaching did he start forward and make an attempt to get at the combatants.

'What is going on here?' Shona roared. There wasn't a single other woman in the car park and the sound of a female voice took the men by surprise. The wall of bodies lost its rigidity, and she pushed her way through. The two men on the ground were running out of steam. Both in their twenties, they were coated in dust from the gravel apron of the pub. Both had blood on their knuckles and faces. The red-haired lad looked to have come off worst, but it was a close call.

Nearby, there was a car with its side window smashed and a mobile phone lay on the ground. Broken glass littered the gravel.

'Get them up,' Shona said to the constables. 'Charge them with affray and criminal damage.'

Mumblings ran through the group. Shona would be within her rights to arrest them all for inciting others to commit a crime, but a quick calculation showed four officers and twenty hyped-up men, and it might be difficult to make the charges stick. She needed to de-escalate the situation fast.

'I'm DI Shona Oliver.' She held up her warrant card. 'Whatever this was about, you're doing your friends no favours by letting them fight. You heard of one-punch killings? Have you?'

A few nodded.

'What would you say to the family, knowing you'd stood by, or egged them on? What would they think of you?' Shona looked around the group, making eye contact.

The mood cooled, expressions sobering.

'Go home, gentlemen.'

The brawlers wouldn't get off so lightly. But when Shona turned, she saw Sergeant Graham standing by as the two men got into the back of separate cars and left.

Shona pointed after the departing vehicles. 'Precisely what are you doing, Sergeant?'

'There's always incidents,' the officer replied. 'Low-level vandalism, car thefts, et cetera. The Armstrongs, the Nixons, there's a history between them – you'll no' stop it.'

'I disagree,' Shona said. 'In my experience, when tolerance levels grow, feuds escalate until someone ends up dead.'

'Och, it'll no' come to that.' Sergeant Graham shook his head. 'It all balances out. We police here with the consent of the people. No one wants a waste of resources. They'll not give statements anyway, and the other side generally pays for any damage.'

Professor Armstrong had told Shona that, in the past, reivers would exchange set numbers of cows or goods in a form of criminal accounting. The paradox being that although they were deadly enemies, this system of payback allowed both sides to continue and neither to starve. It seemed the system was alive and well, although cows had been replaced – if the evidence in the pub car park was anything to go by – with repairs to mobile phones and car bodywork. She could pull rank, insist the men be sent before the Sheriff Court and given a fine, or an official warning. But, if Graham was right, it would be a fruitless endeavour and risk alienating potential witnesses in her other cases.

'Get everyone out of here, Sergeant,' she said. 'I will talk to Mr Douglas about damages.'

'Jack Douglas is fine,' Sergeant Graham replied. He took a step closer to Shona, looming over her. 'He understands how things work around here.'

'Does he?' said Shona, staring up at him and refusing to concede ground. 'And does your Super in Dumfries understand, too? Perhaps *he'd* like to explain to me why you're not charging your pals with offences?'

The threat was enough to make Sergeant Graham step back.

Shona went into the pub, her eyes slow to adjust to the darkness.

'Coffee? Something stronger?' a voice came out of the gloom. 'Have you tried our birch-sap liqueur?'

Jack Douglas stood behind the bar in a white linen shirt, his hair in its customary thin ponytail. It seemed Sergeant Graham was right. Jack Douglas smiled at her, utterly unperturbed by events.

'It's a bit early for me,' Shona said. 'Coffee is fine.'

'Ah. Still on duty.' Without waiting for a reply, he set off on a tour of the gourmet delights his gastro-pub offered, stopping only to pour an expert latte and set it on the bar.

'It's still chanterelle season, so we'll run foraging courses,' he continued. 'And you can do so much with heather, from jewellery to skin products. Lucy, Lady Douglas, has some wonderful ideas.'

'The trouble outside...' Shona began.

'They haven't done any real damage.' Jack gave her an indulgent smile. 'A few broken glasses.'

Perhaps this indulgence sprang from his cousin's deep pockets, or not wanting to upset the local customers, but the farm workers and labourers who made up most of that group didn't look like the kind of clientele who could afford gastro-pub prices. They'd probably come to The Douglas Arms this once to satisfy curiosity and mop up any free samples.

'Are you sure?' Shona said. 'You'd just need to give a statement. You don't want a reputation for tolerating this kind of behaviour.'

'I can bar them if necessary, but I have a feeling it won't come to that.' Jack Douglas shook his head. 'Up here on the moss, there's no point in making enemies.'

Shona understood what he meant. It wasn't just that a remote pub might be a target for reprisals. Despite the openness of the country, there was a claustrophobia about the place. Shona had spent most of her life in cities, in Glasgow and London, where it was possible to live anonymously. Here, in this Debatable Land, nothing you did or said went unobserved, and there could be consequences for both.

Chapter 9

Maybe it was the disconnection from all that Shona knew – Rob, High Pines, her lifeboat family, even the daily rhythms of the CID office in Dumfries – but the moor had wormed its way into her consciousness. Even in the village or at the hospital, she had the sense that it waited for her return. It was so different from the coast, just twenty miles away. Here, the weather raged up the firth to squeeze between the gaps in the hills, concentrated and malevolent. Back turned on the Solway Riviera, it embraced a land of wind-scoured hilltops, raging ghylls and sykes.

Since first arriving at The Douglas Arms, she'd had nightmares of burning houses and corpses pulled from the earth, who all had Becca's face. In daylight, the victims of every rape, murder or domestic abuse case she'd ever worked with were suddenly there again like ghosts, their eyes turned to her.

Shona had always tried hard to maintain a mental firebreak between her work life and home, but the thought that Becca could be touched, however remotely, by the evil that had sent that child to her grave made Shona sick to her stomach.

After the fight at the pub, as she walked across the moor to the archaeologists' camp – and despite the bright sunshine and light winds – she couldn't shake the sense that Border reivers lurked in the corner of her vision, on horseback or on foot, weapons raised to end another life, unless she stopped them. Until the individual who shot Nicola Baird was caught, the full weight of public safety rested squarely on Shona's shoulders.

As she approached the Elliot farm and the campsite, a group of men she didn't know stood behind the gate, watching her approach. Had they been at the pub earlier?

Her steps slowed while she assessed the level of threat the group might pose, but then the familiar figure of Murdo appeared among them. He raised a hand in welcome.

'I heard about the fight at The Douglas Arms,' Murdo said quietly, his face full of concern. 'Everything okay?'

Shona's eyes slid to the other, as yet unidentified, men. Murdo saw the look.

'These lads have been here all afternoon telling me about the community land buyout bid,' Murdo said in a tone that Shona recognised as serious.

Most of the men were around Murdo's height and build – stocky and fair-haired – and wore work trousers and green fleece gilets, or blue overalls and boots. Shaking the offered hands felt like a brief encounter with a herd of thick-skinned, muscular animals. Ben Elliot, the farmer who'd allowed the archaeology team to camp in one of his fields, was among them. His hair was darker than his daughters', but they'd inherited his watchful grey eyes.

Mindful that this was Becca's host, Shona smiled and said, 'I hope the campers are behaving themselves. I met your girls the other day, up at the dig. My daughter's very taken with their animals.'

'They're no' pets,' he said.

'Yes, they made that clear,' Shona replied. 'Lovely girls, very polite.'

This seemed to please him.

'So tell me about the buyout?' Shona said.

'The community is raising money to buy Bield Moss,' said an older man with a trim white beard and startling blue eyes. 'We've a grant from the Scottish Land Fund tae match what we've raised.'

'Aye, but his lordship is blocking it,' a voice from somewhere at the back said.

'How?' Shona asked.

'Keeps upping the price,' the white-bearded man said bluntly. 'Originally, he wanted 2 million pounds, but now he wants 4 million because when he reinstated the shoot, he found he could get environmental money by claiming to protect the blanket bog by managing it for grouse.'

'Is that good for the environment?' Shona asked.

There was a round of disbelieving snorts and shaken heads.

'Returning to a grouse-shoot model is a step backwards.' The new speaker's face was deeply lined, his tweed cap perched on grey hair curled like wire wool. 'The earl talks about jobs, but apart fae the two full-time game-keepers, they're short-term contracts, low paid and yer face has to fit. Feudal, I'd call it.'

'We wannae see proper habitat restoration.' White-beard was obviously the group's spokesman, and the others quietened when he talked. 'It's a chance to protect the area's environmental status and monetise that by bringing in eco-tourists, like bird-watchers, walkers, mountain bikers. It'll help the area do its bit against global warming by the reinstatement of the carbon-sink boglands.'

'Nicola Baird's supposed to be oor representative at the Scottish Parliament.' Ben Elliot's face was sullen. His heavy brow seemed to lower even further. 'Whit was she doing up there, anyway? Traitor.'

'In the earl's pocket,' someone else muttered.

'The community buyout is no' a purchase, it's a ransom,' Elliot said. 'Ye ken, who does this land belong to if it's no' the people whose families hae lived here for generations? We didnae elect the aristocracy. The land wis taken by the first Earl of Langdale, fae ordinary people, by force. It wis a war crime. It's him you should be arresting.'

Shona glanced at Murdo. His face was grim, and he was obviously thinking the same thing as she was. They were angry, but were they angry enough to take the law into their own hands and shoot an MSP? There was no shortage of candidates. Every farmer and half the town had a gun licence.

'Let's no' rake o'er old coals,' White-beard said, to murmurs of agreement. 'We're a long way fae all that now. The money's there, backed by the Scottish Land Fund. We'll win this fight. Bield Moss will be returned to her old glory, and when future generations see what we did, we'll be on the right side of history.'

But history, as Shona had begun to realise, rarely stayed in the past. Here, in the Debatable Land, it cast a long shadow over the living. Were reiver notions of redress and retribution soaked into these hills and moors? Had generations of spent blood, a harvest of fire and sword, shaped not just the land but the people who remained? On this sunny afternoon, the rewilding group appeared to Shona reasonable folk, keen on improving the environment. But among themselves, perhaps reiver blood ran true and a different notion of justice prevailed. Taking back your land by violence, the same way it was stolen from your ancestors, would be a satisfying settling of old scores.

Whatever the answer was, it didn't pay to underestimate the weight of history on men who believed they faced such a stark, and potentially fatal, choice.

Chapter 10

Shona thanked the men for their time. She told Murdo she was popping next door to see Becca and he could give her a lift back to The Douglas Arms afterwards.

The students were camped in the neighbouring field, surrounded by a drystone wall, which was equipped with Portaloos and a single mobile shower unit. Shona saw Becca chatting with the Elliot girls.

'Are you eating properly?' Shona said, aware she rarely asked at home, thanks to Rob's household management. She could boil and egg, if pushed, but it rarely came to that.

'We've got a rota going for the cooking,' Becca replied. 'Veggie chilli, lots of noodles. And we have shops, Mum.'

'Becca's a great cook,' Flora Elliot said.

'My dad taught me,' Becca replied. 'He runs this top B&B, known for its food. Uses mainly local products. I keep telling him he should have his own Insta channel. Get into TikTok.'

Becoming an influencer was the least of Rob's worries, but Shona was heartened to see that Becca wasn't dwelling on her father's forthcoming trial and its potentially life-changing outcome.

The Elliot girls looked blank until the eldest, Grace, said, 'Yeah, we don't do social media. Don't have mobiles.

Not much point, no signal. There's a phone at the house, though, and internet, for studying.'

'Great,' Becca hurried on, colouring a little at the idea she'd embarrassed her new friends. 'Who needs social media when you've got all those amazing animals. Mum, you should see their baby goats. Pure dead gorgeous,' she said, in her curious mix of north London accent and local phrases picked up in the couple of years since they moved to Scotland.

Dr Armstrong came over.

'Any problems?' Shona asked, once Becca had gone off with the girls.

'The students are asking questions,' Cam replied. 'I've told them the dating is uncertain, and the fiscal wants to check. We've spent the day finds processing. Any chance we can get back up there?'

'If forensics are happy, then so am I.' She paused, sensing he was a little more muted than usual. 'I'm sorry about your research,' she added. The confirmation by forensics of a modern burial obviously had given a knock to Dr Armstrong's theories about family encampments in the Debatable Land.

'Yeah, about that...' Cam began.

Shona hoped he wasn't about to ask her to give a lecture to his students about the case. He took her arm and drew her aside.

'I'm glad you've come,' he said, his face suddenly intense. He seemed excited, wrestling with choosing the right words.

'Probably best I just come out and say it.'

It was worse than she thought. He was going to ask her out on a date. She liked Cam, and his charm, enthusiasm and energy made him attractive company, but that was as far as it went. She hoped she wasn't going to have to remind him they were both married.

She gave him a stern look. 'What is it you need to say?'

'The burial.' He eyed her from under his shaggy fringe. 'I wasn't completely shocked that it's modern. In fact, I'm pleased.'

'Meaning?' Shona frowned.

'I am investigating the reivers, officially. But d'you remember the Girls in the Glen murders?'

Shona put up her hand to stop him. 'We're not linking your burial to those cases until the evidence compels us to do so.' They were friends, but she wasn't going to speculate with anyone outside the police force. There was a procedure and she'd stick to it. Identifying the deceased and informing family came first. If Murdo was right, and there was a connection to the Girls in the Glen, the media would also need careful management. It wouldn't be long before the questions started over the police response – namely, why had it taken so long to find her?

'But I think the evidence will show a link,' he replied.

She stared at him as he nervously took a pen from the notebook he was holding, and rolled it between his finger and thumb.

'How can you possibly know that?' she said, watching him carefully.

He took a deep breath. 'You'll be aware two of the victims were never recovered: Olivia Thomson and Lilly Scott?'

Shona had gleaned what she could from Google last night. Although the murders were pre-internet, there were plenty of lurid headlines. *Horror of the Girls in the Glen. Evil Stalks the Moor. Murder Riddle of Lost Girls.* And later: *Monster Takes Grisly Secret to His Grave.* A

83

grainy headshot of John Maxwell showed an unremarkable, thin face with deep-set eyes but, as was usually the case, nothing to betray the evil that lurked behind them.

'Yes, I know their names,' she said.

'Olivia Thomson's mother approached me. She's dying and wants me to find her daughter before it's too late,' he said, quickly, like a schoolboy confessing a minor misdemeanour to his teacher. 'She'd read a newspaper story about the recovery of victims of Bosnian war crimes that I'd been part of back in 2013. It mentioned I was now working at Glasgow Uni researching reiver sites in the Borders. She got in touch, asked if I could help her.'

Shona stared at him. They'd been talking off and on for nearly a year. He'd emailed information on heritage open days, and they'd even had the odd coffee when she'd been in Glasgow for meetings and had dropped by the university to pick up books and journals he'd loaned Becca; yet, he'd never mentioned this to her.

'I've narrowed down several potential deposition sites,' he continued, 'where the geophysics show the ground has been disturbed. To gain any further insight, I need to understand what the police have about the other burials and why the killer chose those places.'

'There's no way you can see those files,' Shona said flatly.

'But you could read them and tell me what I need to know.'

She was shocked at his nerve, asking a serving police officer to pass confidential information to him without batting an eyelid. Then a thought struck her. She looked at the students. The Elliot girls aside, Becca was the only school-age digger on the site.

'Do you offer all potential students two weeks' free camping and practical experience? Or just those with mothers who are DIs with access to a series of high-profile murders?'

He attempted a hurt expression, but she could see that his determination to win her over elbowed it aside. If this was academic ambition, she'd arrested less ruthless drug dealers.

'Look,' he said, spreading his hands palm upwards in a gesture of appeal. 'The police are busy. Mrs Thomson has only a few months to live. If it *was* Olivia that Becca uncovered...'

'Wait.' Shona held up her hand to stop him. 'Did you put my daughter in that trench knowing she might find a child's body?'

Her eyes were wide with anger and indignation. A few of the nearest students turned, alerted as much by her body language as the raised voices. They seemed amused that their professor was being ticked off.

'No, of course not,' he replied sternly. 'Think about it, Shona. The police won't put resources into this. Don't you want the Girls in the Glen found with no impact on your budget? And yes, do it for Becca. How much better will it be for her if this is resolved?'

Blackmail. Professor Armstrong wasn't above using the methods of his reiver ancestors. Cam had played on Becca's enthusiasm in order to get access to Shona's position as the local DI, and for that, his card was marked.

'Does your university know what you're up to?' she asked.

'No,' he admitted. 'It's a personal research project.' He shot her a wary glance. 'I just want to help her find her daughter. Surely, you realise I couldn't refuse?'

There was a moment of awkward silence during which Shona attempted to untangle why she was so angry with Cam Armstrong. Partly, it was professional, but it was also personal. She'd enjoyed their email exchanges and chats over coffee. Clearly, though, he hadn't sought her out purely for the pleasure of her company. Perhaps she'd been foolish to assume he had. She cleared her throat, determined to place their relationship squarely on a professional footing.

Shona let out a long breath. Becca was looking their way, a small line between her eyebrows. She'd read the signs that her mother was unhappy with Dr Cameron. Soon, the other students, or Becca herself, might get on Google and guess the reason. It was a gamble. All she could do was calm the situation until they confirmed the ID and she found the best way to break the news to Becca.

'I can't show you the files,' Shona said, 'but as long as you follow the rules and keep the fiscal happy, I can't stop you either.'

It was a truce of sorts.

'So you won't help me?'

'Just be grateful I'm not reporting this conversation to the fiscal's office and advising them to send you all home while they have a good, long think.'

'Okay, point taken,' Cam said. 'Thank you.'

–

Having hugged Becca goodbye, Shona turned and walked back across the moor. Armstrong had made himself scarce. Shona was relieved. Had he stayed, she might have said something she'd later regret.

Murdo stood by his car, waiting for her.

As they wound down the single-track road, Shona tried to push the exchange with Armstrong to the back of her mind. 'The fight at The Douglas Arms?' she said. 'You know Sergeant Graham let the men go?' Her irritation with Dr Armstrong had reignited her anger over the earlier incident.

'Willie Graham needs to have a quiet word with their fathers, or even their wives if they have them, and tell them to simmer down. It'll be more effective than a fine.'

'You think Sergeant Graham was right?'

'Thon archaeologist has a point. The Debatable Land was ruled for 300 years by families where the only law was that which folk took into their own hands. It's no justification, and you're right, he needs to watch things don't escalate. But Willie's been here his whole life.'

'He had the cheek to lecture me on policing with the consent of the people,' Shona said. 'He's forgotten it's not his job to make friends.'

'Aye, mibbae,' Murdo conceded. 'Willie was part of the Girls in the Glen investigation as a young officer. Could say it was his finest hour, him having had his eye on John Maxwell from the start. Seems he'd arrested him previously.'

Murdo had a point. Local knowledge sometimes paid dividends. It was on the tip of her tongue to tell him about Cam's confession, but without an ID on the historic victim, it was pointless exploring any lines of enquiry.

They swung into The Douglas Arms's now-empty car park. The broken glass had been removed, and the granite building sat mute and contented in the golden evening light.

'Okay, thanks Murdo. We can't do any more tonight. You get off home. Apologies to Joan for keeping you late.'

'No bother, boss.'

'I'd like to have another chat with the earl. Kate's staying at Langdale Hall, so maybe you can call in at the office in the morning? Make sure everything's on track and no one needs trauma counselling after a day with Ravi in charge.'

Murdo, who'd turned the Astra around, tooted a goodbye.

Shona stood at the edge of the car park, looked down at the bronze-tipped trees and let the sinking sun bathe her in the last of its warmth. Then, with a sigh, she took out her phone.

Superintendent Davies's office number rang out, and she was about to end the call when he finally picked up.

'Yes?' he said, breathless and irritated.

She pictured him by his desk in the Kilmarnock HQ, coat over one arm, on his way home, and quickly updated him on progress and her next actions. A few reports had come in about a possible Darren Porter sighting, and were being chased up by local cops in Edinburgh and further afield. She took a deep breath.

'Sir, I'd like access to the Girls in the Glen case files.'

He was silent for a moment and then said, 'What d'you hope to gain from this? John Maxwell was convicted and died in jail. He refused to co-operate in locating the remaining bodies.'

She hadn't shared Cam Armstrong's personal mission and she sensed it wouldn't play well with the super.

'Forensic techniques have moved on, sir. I'm aware there's no DNA record from Maxwell and, despite his denials, no questions about the verdict, but I'd just like to acquaint myself with the full facts.'

'You know what the press are like. If it gets out that we're even sniffing around the case, it'll go up like a smoke signal that all wasn't right in the first place. Fake news, Shona. A genie that won't go back in its bottle. It'll cast doubt on our handling of the investigation, which we'll never be rid of. Concentrate on the shooting. We'll wait for the post-mortem on the remains. As far as the historic case is concerned, don't go there.'

He ended the call.

It was what Shona had expected. There was no way she'd share the file with Dr Armstrong, but she didn't like to be blindsided on her own patch. And if he was right about the identity of the child uncovered at the dig, the media would put the case under the microscope all over again. The standards of the present applied to events of the past had a way of amplifying both human and institutional failings. For a moment, she considered getting in her car and seeking out Sergeant Graham for a quiet chat over a drink. Willie Graham was intimately connected with the case and, if Murdo was correct, would welcome the opportunity to revisit past glories. But she dismissed the idea. She hadn't reached the point where she needed favours from a cop like Sergeant Willie Graham.

Chapter 11

Langdale Hall was on the far side of the moor and protected on its other flank by the River Esk. With minor roads still blocked by fallen trees, Shona needed to make a detour towards Carlisle, cross the border into England and then double back at Hall Bridge. She dropped from Bield Moss into the forestry plantations where many of the trees, having barely survived Storm Ailsa, leaned on each other for support.

Murdo had been in touch to say the Specials had swept the local caravan parks, hotels and B&Bs without any luck. It was impossible to run a check on every vehicle that had gone through the town in the past few weeks. Scotland's tolerance of wild camping complicated matters, and it was possible the shooter had made multiple visits to scope out the remote moor without using any official sites, encountering any locals or registering on the few traffic cameras in the area.

Shona dropped a gear to overtake a log lorry just as its empty twin, bearing the green paintwork of Armstrong Sawmills, rounded the corner ahead of her in the opposite lane, forcing her to abandon the manoeuvre. Armstrong, Graham, Nixon, Elliot. The old reiver names now adorned plumbers' and electricians' vans or hung above the doors of shops and estate agents' offices.

Were the ancient divisions or alliances still there, as Sergeant Graham had suggested? A Mafia-network that governed who you'd call to fix a leaky tap, or where you bought your sausages? To Shona, it seemed as unlikely as it was impractical, and she had to admit there was no evidence of the rewilding group's involvement beyond her own vague feeling of unease that local passions on the issue were running high.

The most troubling aspect of Nicola Baird's shooting was the lack of a clear motive. Who had a strong enough grievance against the MSP to come all the way out here to shoot her? Why not just target her at her home or constituency office? It seemed whoever had done this wanted to link it to the moor and the grouse shoot. So why had no one claimed responsibility? The more Shona turned the events over in her mind, the more doubtful she became that Nicola was the intended victim.

She now faced a dilemma. Did she split her team across two lines of enquiry: one with the MSP as the target, the other pursuing the Earl of Langdale? Given that a deep background check on Alexander Douglas would be needed, including his life in America, the whole shooting investigation was taking on the aspect of a rapidly multiplying organism that would soon be out of control. The evidence also raised the prospect that the gunman was local. In such situations, people closed ranks. Nothing she'd seen here had convinced her that this place would be any different.

Shona had left the open farmland around the border and once more the plantations of Sitka spruce loomed dark and uniform, pressing the blue sky into a thin line above her.

The investigation was two days in and opportunities to resolve the case were fast slipping away. The lurid divorce of a high-profile footballer and his wife had replaced the shooting on the front pages of most Scottish media outlets. Soon, that small detail that could turn the case around would slip from people's memories. The decisions she made today would be crucial in either resolving the case or it becoming the kind of nagging, running sore that required reviews, re-investigations and resources stretching on for years. One thing was for sure: Nicola Baird wouldn't let it go; she had every reason to exploit Shona's lack of progress and she would take the greatest pleasure in bringing her down if she could.

Slowly, the forest took on a less rigid and industrial appearance, as Shona neared her destination.

She pulled up in front of the tall gates, which were firmly closed. She stepped out of the car, pressed the intercom and submitted herself for inspection over the camera link. The whole process reassured her that the estate took their security seriously.

At the end of a wide driveway lined with specimen firs stood a pink sandstone building punctuated by tall windows. At its heart, beyond the slate roofs of the later additions, Shona saw the crow-stepped gables of a reiver's pele tower. It was as if in the Border peace of the last 300 years, the stronghold at the heart of Langdale Hall had gained genteel friends who huddled close to that warlike presence, just in case.

The earl himself came out to meet her. He displayed his perfect teeth and shook her hand. Dressed in slim beige trousers and a cobalt-blue shirt that enhanced his eyes, he looked less like old, landed gentry and more like a young royal.

'Thank you for seeing me, sir,' she said. 'I wondered—'

'You gotta have the tour,' he interrupted. 'Everyone has the tour.'

He swept through the entrance hall and rattled off dates. They examined a clock given as a wedding gift to a previous earl by Queen Victoria. Then he hurried ahead like a child keen to show off another toy. They entered the pele tower through a pair of high oak doors and the earl stopped to point out the thickness of the walls, modern whitewash now covering the massive, rough-hewn stones.

'Impressive, isn't it?' the earl said. 'Presidents Richard Nixon, Lyndon B. Johnson, Andrew Jackson and Woodrow Wilson all descended from reiver ancestors. That says something, doesn't it?'

Some might say it showed a tendency to less-than-scrupulous ambition, Shona thought, but kept it to herself.

On the ground floor of the tower, a large dining table sat beneath a high vaulted ceiling. There were swords over the fireplace, and an array of pikes and other weapons in fan shapes around the walls. In one corner, a spiral staircase led to the upper floors.

The pele tower was self-contained: four rooms stacked on top of each other. The dining hall, two sitting rooms, a bedroom. At the top, the earl led Shona out and onto a roof terrace. From here, it was more obvious that the wild-ness of the surrounding forest was artfully constructed. The trees were tall and straight, arranged in conversation groups of oak, copper beach, Douglas fir and sycamore, the tapestry of their colours bright and intricate.

'My ancestor could put 4000 horsemen in the field,' the earl said. 'Autumn to spring was the time for raiding. Traditionally, it was after the last hay was cut, when the nights grew long. They believed all property was held in common, so they had a right to make use of anything they laid their hands on.'

'I've met a few people like that,' Shona said.

'Well, it worked both ways,' the earl said ruefully. 'See that platform there?' He indicated a stone ledge scarred a deeper red. 'A fire was lit at the top of this tower to warn raiders were on their way. Four fires meant a great many horsemen were coming, but none of them ever got inside this tower.' He paused. 'Forgive me rattling on. This house is older than the country I come from. I guess I'm still impressed by that.'

Shona smiled. 'It's an impressive place.'

As she looked out over the parkland to the river, she thought of her own house, High Pines. Its construction was also tower-like, but with a distinctly less martial air. It sat at the top of a steep hill above the shoreline, and she never failed to be awed by the view over Kirkness estuary out to the Solway. The B&B was a success, and despite their problems, she was proud of what she and Rob had achieved.

'It's lovely here,' she said.

'Thank you,' he said earnestly, his tone suddenly serious. 'I feel the burden, too.'

Shona turned towards him. 'What burden?'

'I want to bring a new greener prosperity back to the estate. You know, Bield Moss once held the national record for the biggest bag ever, with 177 brace of red grouse in a single day.'

'Can grouse moors be green?' she asked, remembering what the men at Elliot's farm had told her about their proposed community buyout.

'The moor is a local and national asset, and an internationally important area for some birds of prey,' the earl began. 'It's Scotland's national signature landscape. My business plan makes it financially viable and delivers public goods through increasing biodiversity and mitigating climate change. We've addressed the heather loss through overgrazing with controlled muirburn.'

'That's not popular, I believe,' Shona said. She'd googled it last night after her conversation with the rewilding group. 'It releases carbon into the atmosphere and can contaminate water.'

Alexander raised his eyebrows, conceding she'd made a valid point. 'Controlled burning has a long history,' he countered. 'We follow the code of practice to the letter. Thirty metre-square patches in a quick, cool burn that removes the dead heather without touching the underlying peat. It regenerates the heather and acts as a firebreak, and we only burn from mid-October to mid-April to avoid nesting birds and the driest peat times.

'The shoot business provides jobs, and I want to give it a fair shake,' he continued. 'It extends the regular tourist season into autumn and winter. We've already raised hen harrier numbers with distraction feeding to stop them predating on the red grouse chicks. Other bird and insect species are on the increase, too. The truth is, by maintaining the moor for a healthy grouse population, we're saving it from other kinds of development like forestry or overgrazing by sheep, which would destroy the blanket bog completely.'

His argument and passion were just as clear as the rewilding group's. It was important to the investigation that Shona remained impartial. But her shouts with the RNLI had shown her how a disregard for the natural world had consequences – yachts disabled and their crews in danger, their propellers fouled by discarded fishing, or 'ghost', gear. Or scallop boats on fire after hauling up munitions, dumped in the sea as a cheap alternative to decommissioning. If pressed, her sympathies lay more with the rewilding group than with an individual whose primary aim seemed to be to make money out of posh folk shooting birds.

Of course, she knew it wasn't as simple as that. But in her experience, when an unstoppable force, like the earl, met an immovable object, in the shape of the rewilders, it rarely made for good community relations. She shivered. The sun had gone behind a cloud and a brisk breeze lifted the earl's stags' head pennants on the pele tower's flag poles.

'Let's go down and have some tea,' the earl said. 'My mother would love to see you, and to hear how the investigation is going. Mrs Baird is a dear friend of the estate and we're just so shocked by what's happened.'

Kate stood up when Shona arrived in the pale-carpeted sitting room, which looked out over the formal gardens at the side of the house. Lady Douglas remained seated and held out her cup for Kate to refill. When Shona mentioned the trouble at the pub the previous day, the earl brushed it aside, as his cousin had done.

'Jack handles all that,' Lady Douglas added. 'He's a tower of strength. We're lucky to have him here.'

Shona was surprised at the apparent warmth of Lady Douglas's praise, since she treated everyone else, including her son, with an impatient disdain. She had to wonder at the exact nature of the relationship between these old friends. Had her ladyship fallen under Cousin Jack's libertine spell? Perhaps they had been lovers during their time together in London, either before or after Lucy's marriage to the current earl's father – the wealthier and better connected of the two cousins? However, Kate's encyclopaedic source – the housekeeper – hadn't mentioned it.

Shona briefly outlined the investigation's progress and mentioned that Nicola Baird was recovering well. 'Is there anything you'd like to add to the statements you gave DC Irving?'

The earl shook his head.

'What about those practical jokes?' Lady Douglas said. 'Perhaps the inspector could do something about those?'

Shona looked at Kate, but she just gave a slight shrug.

'Just high-jinks,' the earl said. 'Nothing for DI Oliver to bother about.'

'Well, I didn't find them amusing,' Lady Douglas cut in. 'It doesn't show the proper respect for the family. Xander's too soft,' she said to Shona. 'He wants people to like him.'

The earl shot his mother an embarrassed look but said nothing.

'What kind of jokes?' Shona asked.

'I left my car unlocked and a live grouse was put inside. It sure made a mess,' he replied. 'Then someone spray painted a dozen estate sheep. They sent a picture to the local paper with the story I'd been hoodwinked into buying multicoloured ewes in order to make a new tartan.'

Shona fought to keep her face straight. It was exactly the kind of practical joke locals might play on a naïve American incomer. Kate looked aggrieved. The earl obviously hadn't shared this story, but since he was keen to impress her, Shona understood why.

'Any idea who it was?' Shona asked. The earl shrugged and she continued. 'What about your staff? Is there anyone you've had trouble with recently?'

'Not that I recall.'

'That man you had to sack?' Lady Douglas prompted. 'The gamekeeper turned poacher?'

'What was his name?' Shona said.

'Elliot, I believe.'

'Ben Elliot?' Shona said. Despite the discussion about the moor, Alexander Douglas hadn't mentioned the proposed community land buyout, and here was one of its members with a potential grudge against his former employer.

'That's the fellow,' the earl said. 'I sure hated to let him go, but he had a sideline in shooting deer and selling off the meat. His wife is dead, and I know he has a family to raise, but it's no excuse for poaching.'

'You should have evicted him,' Lady Douglas said. 'He's not the sort of farm tenant the estate needs.'

'He runs his farm well, pays his rent,' the earl said mildly.

'Mr Elliot is part of the habitat restoration group, isn't he?' Shona probed.

Alexander Douglas shook his head in a way that might be seen as patronising to those on the opposite side of a negotiating table. 'It isn't an economically sustainable idea, and anyone who knows me should realise I'd never let it happen.'

'Why is that?'

'I may be a newcomer here, but I love this country. Nothing on God's green earth would make me part with the land my family has held for ten generations. Nothing.'

The earl retained his affability, but Shona saw the hardness in his eyes, and believed him. Whatever the dilution of his reiver blood, by nature or nurture, the earl was an ambitious young man who valued land, money and status just as much as his ancestors.

He crossed to a side table. When he turned, inner sunlight again lit his features. He held up one of the wild swimming leaflets that Shona and Tommy had handed out at the dig.

'I heard you volunteer with the lifeboat in your village. That's impressive. I'm taking part in a swift water exercise with Langdale Mountain Rescue. I'm keen for local people to see I'm part of the community.' He gave her the bashful look that Shona now recognised was a strategic weapon in the arsenal of his charm. 'I wonder...' he said. 'Would you join us?'

The RNLI had a specialist swift water team that did, occasionally, take part in joint exercises with other groups such as the police, fire service or mountain rescue. Tommy had already mentioned a few dates were in the offing with the Langdale group. Perhaps the earl wanted to claim it as his idea. The volunteers would know the truth, but if his lordship was willing to donate time, effort and perhaps, most importantly, money to the cause, he could claim he'd invented the rivers and mountains themselves – and the team would be happy to let him. Besides, it'd give Shona an opportunity to learn more about this new and potentially influential individual on her patch.

'I'll certainly try to be there, sir. Time and the case permitting.' She smiled, and he seemed satisfied. 'We'll leave you to get on now,' she continued and looked pointedly at Kate.

'Of course, ma'am.' Kate put down her cup and went to collect her things. The earl's eyes followed her from the room.

Shona said goodbye to Lady Douglas. While she waited in the entrance hall for Kate, Shona studied a large, glazed map that showed the surnames of the Borders and their home territories.

'Ah. I knew you were one of us.' The earl had come up noiselessly behind her. Shona jumped. He laid one apologetic hand briefly on her shoulder. With the other hand, he pointed out an area in the historic Scottish West March, roughly equivalent to her own policing patch. In the hills above Eskdalemuir, *DOUGLAS* was highlighted in large bold type. Beneath was a smaller surname. Shona read it, and the note. *Oliver, tenants and vassals of the Douglas.*

'Oliver is my husband's name,' Shona said, and then stiffened. Had Willie Graham relayed details of Rob's trial to the earl? The sergeant would hardly resist that opportunity to stick the knife in where Shona was concerned. She cast Alexander Douglas a sideways glance, but he seemed intent on the map.

'So, technically, I can count on you as a vassal in this time of strife?' he said with a mischievous grin.

'You can count on me, sir, to get to the bottom of what happened,' Shona said seriously. 'But I'm from Glasgow.'

'So what does that mean in terms of allegiance?' The earl searched the map, but it didn't stretch that far north and the sight of Kate coming down the main stair with her bag distracted him.

'It means,' Shona said, 'that I'm my own woman.'

Chapter 12

Kate followed her as they drove back to The Douglas Arms. Shona was relieved they weren't travelling together. It gave her time to think and, even without glancing in the rear-view mirror, she felt her constable's malevolent stare boring into the back of her head. Alexander Douglas had treated his guest well. After two nights of the high life, it was time to bring Kate back to earth. She hadn't detected any progression of the familiarity between the earl and her DC, and was satisfied that Kate had heeded her warning about allowing herself to get too close to a witness.

'Melbourne Police visited the earl's cousin, Ewan Douglas,' Kate said, when they reached the temporary incident room. 'His alibi checks out.'

'Okay, well that's good to know. Let's have a chat with Murdo,' Shona replied as she dropped her jacket over the back of the chair. 'He knows Ben Elliot, so maybe he has some background on this sacking.'

She tapped her sergeant's number and put her phone on speaker as she brought him up to speed on the morning's interviews. Ben Elliot had struck Shona as dour and uncooperative, but as a single parent with a hill farm and three home-schooled daughters, his life was unlikely to be a barrel of laughs.

'He's ten years older than me,' Murdo said, 'but he captained the rugby club when I first played. Hang on a minute, I'm just gonnae borrow your chair, boss.'

The background buzz of the CID room diminished as he moved into Shona's office and closed the door.

'Ben told me he'd been sacked. He said he was within his rights to shoot deer on his land, but his face didn't fit at the estate. They've trimmed a few seasonal staff off the payroll. Ben didn't always see eye to eye with Charles Bell, the head keeper, apparently.'

'Kate?' Shona enquired.

'Yeah, that fits,' she said. 'There's been the odd change in the house staff, too, as a few wanted to retire. They offered the younger ones retraining apprenticeships. I called those on the list, mostly to ask about Nicola Baird or previous trouble, and I didn't sense any general resentment.'

'The estate owns the Elliot farm,' Shona said. 'Lady Douglas thought the earl should evict him after the poaching incident.'

'The estate owns all the farms,' Murdo said. 'Ben works hard. The farm's in good nick. It would be a messy business for Langdale to revoke the lease.'

'Publicly messy?' Shona said.

'Aye, I'd say so,' Murdo replied.

'What's the situation at home?' Shona knew the girls' mother wasn't around but was hazy on the details.

'Ben married late, but Carrie died. Cancer. She was a good few years younger than him, so it was a big shock. He went off the rails a bit. Nothing major. Why would he shoot his landlord when he's got those girls to look after?'

'Good point, Murdo,' Shona said. 'Is he on the list of rifle owners?'

There was a pause and the rustle of papers.

'Yep, along with forty-three others in the area.'

'Shit, that many?' Shona said. Charles Bell had been right in his assessment that practically every farmer and half the town owned a hunting rifle. It would be time-consuming and financially prohibitive to check them all in the ballistics lab.

'Okay,' Shona continued. 'Since no threats had been made to the earl, it's more appropriate we focus all resources on Darren Porter. The shooting could be an escalation of his previous mace attack on Nicola Baird's constituency staff.' She ran her finger down the open document on her laptop. 'Where are we with Mrs Baird's social media trolls?'

'A couple are proving tricky to trace, but I've got Chloe and Vinny Visuals working on them, so expect a result soon.'

Shona's youngest civilian staff members – data analyst Chloe Burke, and visual investigations officer Vincent Grieg – were chiefly tasked with CCTV and surveillance tracking but had a solid record of winkling out information from other electronic and digital sources. To Shona, the fresh-faced twentysomethings had a dash of the dark arts about them.

'Good. Is there—' Shona began to ask, but Murdo interrupted to say she should hold on, as Ravi needed to talk to him. When he came back on the line, his voice was more sober.

'Boss,' he said, 'the DNA is back on the child from the archaeology dig. Forensics confirmed the ID as Lilly Scott. PM report from Slasher Sue in your inbox.'

Sue Kitchen was professor of forensic pathology at the University of Glasgow, which held the contract from the

Crown Office to provide post-mortem examinations for the Procurator Fiscal. A former national fencing champion, Professor Kitchen coached the student team, and was a notoriously fast worker at the autopsy table, hence 'Slasher Sue'.

For a moment, Shona struggled to process what Murdo had said. Vicky Thomson had approached Cameron Armstrong to find her daughter Olivia.

'Lilly was Olivia Thomson's friend who went missing with her,' Murdo supplied, as she hesitated.

'The other Girl in the Glen?' Shona said, wincing at the tabloid label she'd adopted to clarify what she was hearing. 'We need to inform the family.'

She was playing catch-up. If the super had let her go through the files, she'd know the background and be better prepared.

'I don't think there is family,' Murdo said. 'I heard that the mother, Gail Scott, died in a road traffic accident in Australia about five years back. The father had a heart attack not long after the trial. Mrs Scott emigrated. Wanted to start fresh. Can't really blame her. But she did a DNA swab before she went, in case we needed it.'

'Let's double-check both parents are dead before we make an announcement, and let's find a next-of-kin if we can,' Shona said, then took a deep breath and updated Murdo and Kate on how Armstrong had been approached by Mrs Thomson, and his unofficial quest to find Olivia's body.

There was a moment's silence as both officers processed the significance of Shona's words.

'Does that mean thon archaeologist will keep looking?' Murdo said, eventually.

'I can't see any reason he'd stop,' Shona said. The university excavation had two weeks left to run. After that, Cam could begin to look at other sites. Lilly and Olivia, had they lived, would be the same age as Shona. Though she wouldn't admit it to Cam, she understood his desire to fulfil Mrs Thomson's dying wish to find her daughter so they could be buried together and be reunited, if not in life, at least in death.

'How did the university come to be digging there in the first place?' Murdo asked.

'Didn't the muirburn reveal something?' Shona began, then looked at Kate.

'There were some stone features that might be *rees* or *rands* – enclosures in the open for penning cattle or sheep – that possibly date from the reiver period,' Kate replied. 'For the university excavation, Dr Armstrong would have started with previous dig reports covering Bield Moss and the Anglo-Scottish border in general, and compiled map regressions looking at changes in the landscape over time. He told me he'd surveyed his target areas using LIDAR and geophysics, and noted anomalies. It has parallels with what we do in the police. Gather evidence, form a hypothesis. Finally, in his case, he'd test it by excavation.'

'So it's possible he could have pursued his side project of recovering Olivia Thomson under the guise of his Border reivers research for the university?' Shona said.

'Absolutely,' Kate agreed.

To Shona, it showed a cunning disregard for his employer's time and resources, and she wondered what else he was up to that wasn't entirely above board. But then she'd already experienced that first-hand in his manipulation of their friendship.

'It's just,' Murdo began, 'when I talked to him about the case, he knew an awful lot.'

'Perhaps he did his research thoroughly,' Shona replied. If what he'd told her was true about Olivia Thomson's mother contacting him, he'd had a few years to prepare for this Bield Moss excavation.

'How did he know that John Maxwell's wife was dead, and that we moved the family to protect them?'

'Did he hear it locally?' Shona said.

'He might have, but we kept it very quiet. Reprisals. Many people didn't believe the wife knew nothing. Back then, things were different. She didn't get the support she needed. I can't see how he learned it through contact with Olivia Thomson's mother.'

'Things leak out, don't they?' Shona said.

'True,' Murdo conceded. 'Did I tell you Nicola Baird is being discharged this afternoon?'

'No,' Shona said. A single, clean bullet wound could heal fast in normal circumstances, with the right medical attention. The surgeon had told Shona that the shattered collarbone and potential nerve damage were likely to give her the most trouble, and she'd need ongoing support for many months to recover the full use of her arm. 'Do we need to arrange close protection officers?' she asked.

'All done,' Murdo replied. 'Mrs Baird is going back to Edinburgh, and Lothian and Borders are looking after things. She's still insisting it was an attempted assassination by nationalists, so expect more media attention.'

Shona nodded. 'I think we'll wrap things up here.' There was nothing to be gained by staying in the area if the press came calling, and they'd got all they could forensically from the crime scene and the local area.

'You'll be wanting your chair back,' Murdo said.

'Looks like it,' Shona replied.

'And Ravi's been missing you, Kate. He'll have the kettle on,' Murdo added.

Shona smiled. The sparring between her two detective constables was, at times, deadly serious, and the office in Dumfries must have been dull without Kate rising to Ravi's bait several times a day. Both were ambitious, and the competition helped to keep them on their toes, each eager to surpass the other. Inevitably, one, or both, would be drawn back to the bright lights of their respective cities – Glasgow and Edinburgh – when promotion beckoned.

'Well, I haven't missed him,' Kate said, deadpan. 'It's been nice to have some intelligent company for a change.'

'I'll tell him,' Murdo teased.

'You do that.' Kate folded her arms and slumped back in her chair.

'Don't expect us in the office until tomorrow. Kate will draft a press statement before we go,' Shona said, raising her eyebrows questioningly at Kate, who nodded. There were no other pressing matters, and it seemed fair to give her the rest of the afternoon to adjust to a less exalted way of life. The journey home should be easier, but diversions were a possibility with the tree cutting.

'Message us with any queries,' Shona said. 'I'll go up and see Dr Armstrong before I head off.'

'Will you tell him about the DNA result?' Murdo said.

'No reason to keep it from him,' Shona replied. She'd considered it, out of spite, but she wanted to see his reaction first-hand. It might tell her nothing, but there was the old adage: *keep your friends close and your enemies closer.* If Dr Armstrong was meddling in things he shouldn't be, she wanted to keep their communication channels open. 'I'll also give Vicky Thomson a ring so she doesn't hear the news from anywhere else. Poor woman, she must be on tenterhooks. I also want a sense from them both about what they'll do next.'

While Kate worked on the press release, Shona went into the empty bar next door and dialled Mrs Thomson's number. It rang out so long she thought it would go to a messaging service.

'Hello?' a frail voice answered cautiously.

'Mrs Thomson, I'm DI Shona Oliver.' She paused, unsure how to phrase the reason for her call. 'Dr Armstrong told me why you'd contacted him.'

'If you're phoning to tell me I shouldn't have then I'm sorry, I've no patience left in me, Inspector. I haven't got long and I'm tired.' The tone was wearily defensive, but determined.

'I understand that, Mrs Thomson.' The idea that, as a police officer, Shona was calling to criticise, struck her as profoundly sad. A mother had lost her child in the worst way imaginable. No one could condemn her for her search.

'I'm calling with some news.' Shona didn't want to raise the woman's hopes for even a second, so she hurried on. 'But it's not about Olivia. I'm sorry.'

'Tell me.'

'There's a confirmed ID on the remains from the dig.'

Shona wouldn't say it had been her own daughter who had scraped back the soil to reveal the small skull and its strands of peat-stained hair. She was acutely aware of how that would rub salt into the wound. Your girl is gone. I still have mine.

'It's Lilly Scott, I'm afraid.'

'Oh, thank God,' Mrs Thomson cried. 'Thank God. Her poor parents didnae live to find her, but at least my

Olivia's wee friend is home.' She sobbed. 'Thank you, Shona.'

Shona swallowed. She'd expected a different reaction. Anger. Grief. Hopelessness.

'There's no need to thank me,' Shona said. 'I wanted you to be the first to know. There'll be an announcement tomorrow and I'm on my way to see Dr Armstrong.'

'Tell him thank you, too. He's given me hope.'

—

Shona took the Audi as far up the track to the dig as she could. She got out; her straightened bob whipped into her eyes and made them water. She'd changed into jeans and a fleece. As she laced up her walking boots, a mountain hare darted from its hiding place beneath a mound of dried heather, its long legs scrabbling for purchase as it vanished into the vegetation. It wouldn't have gone far and as Shona climbed the last half mile to the site, she had the sense that out on Bield Moss, the hare, and a thousand other unseen eyes, were watching her.

Chapter 13

On the high moor, the wind tugged at the small blue gazebo, the only shelter in the sea of heather. Inside, a few students were gathered around a table, washing up bowls and toothbrushes to hand, cleaning pottery sherds. Becca wasn't among them. Dr Armstrong stood by the nearest trench, intent on a clipboard of paperwork that flapped in the breeze. As Shona approached, Cam looked up and gave her a tentative smile of welcome.

'Quick word,' Shona said, and stepped away to a flattened area of heather out of earshot of the students.

'There's news?' Cameron said, his features pinched and anxious.

Shona updated him on the DNA result. A series of emotions ran across his face like clouds: a moment's elation, followed by a frown and then a calculated look which finally settled into a neutral expression of gratitude at her visit. Shona couldn't catch hold of his true feelings. Was he worried about the impact on his research or reputation? Or a potential book deal he glimpsed disappearing into the undergrowth like the hare? He'd found the Girl in the Glen, but not the one he'd set out to uncover. A recalibration was necessary.

Shona explained that she'd need to see some of his research to understand how he came to be digging there.

'You're not suspected of any wrongdoing,' she said. Cameron would have been a very small child himself when the girl disappeared. 'This was a high-profile case at the time, and we need a comprehensive witness statement from you. DS O'Halloran will be in touch again.'

'That's fine,' he said.

'Have you had any contact with the victims' families, beyond Mrs Thomson?' Shona said.

'Vicky approached me,' he reminded her. 'There was no need.'

It wasn't what Shona had asked.

'I've talked to Mrs Thomson,' she said. 'I'd ask you not to discuss the confirmed ID with anyone else, especially the media, until we locate Lilly Scott's next-of-kin.'

He nodded. 'Of course.'

'What will you do now?'

'Keep looking,' he said simply.

'And the university are happy with that?'

Cam looked awkward. 'It's not strictly part of the funding remit. I'll pursue it in my own time.'

To Shona, it didn't seem right that the police were leaving the resolution of this case to the part-time activities of a university professor, but reality was governed by resources. Until Cam provided at least the outline of that last piece of the jigsaw or her Super reconsidered, Shona would have to tread carefully if she wanted to continue to pursue this particular case. She had no doubt those more senior than her would be happy to see Lilly Scott's recovery, and any remaining search, swept quietly under the carpet on the grounds of resources and the nagging spectre of a reappraisal, in the media at least, of the original investigation. But Shona knew that justice would only be fully served when the last victim was found. The clock, ticking down Mrs Thomson's life, suddenly sounded loud in Shona's ears.

Her previously easy exchanges with Cam had acquired a stiffness. Shona had no doubt whose fault that was.

'Becca is sieving over by trench two,' he said eventually.

Shona thanked him and stepped through the heather towards the far side of the site. Her daughter was absorbed in shaking a large rectangular tray with a mesh base, suspended from the repurposed frame of a child's swing. Fine soil dropped into a wheelbarrow below. Becca leaned forward and picked through the contents of the sieve.

'What are you looking for?' Shona said, putting her arm around her daughter's shoulders and giving her a squeeze.

'Small objects,' Becca said. 'A coin would be amazing.'

'Listen, darlin'…' Shona began. 'The DNA on the body you uncovered has come back.' She explained in broad strokes about the murders that had taken place in the 1980s and that there'd been two unrecovered victims. 'It's one of the wee girls.'

'What's her name?' Becca asked.

'She was called Lilly,' Shona replied. She saw a tremor run through her daughter and stepped forward to hug her.

After a moment, Becca stepped back. Her face was composed, but it was obvious to Shona that her daughter was making a huge effort not to cry.

'What about the other one?' Becca said.

'Her name was Olivia Thomson,' Shona said.

'And she's still out here somewhere?'

'Maybe,' Shona replied. 'The police at the time made a search in what they thought was the right area, but she might be miles from here.'

Becca was silent, but Shona understood she was having difficulty processing how a child could vanish so completely.

'I was talking to Grace Elliot about uncovering the remains.' She shot her mother a quick glance to check for disapproval, but found none. 'She was really upset. I suppose if you look after your two wee sisters, it's hard to think of a girl left out on the moor.'

Becca, an only child, had no inkling of sibling responsibility. That she had hit upon the reason for Grace's upset showed a maturity that made Shona proud.

'That's an astute observation,' she said to her daughter with a smile.

'And the Elliots were reivers once,' Becca continued. 'Maybe Grace thought the wee girl might even be related to them, distantly. What will she think when she finds out it's Lilly Scott?'

'Right now,' Shona said firmly, 'you must keep Lilly's name to yourself, because we need to tell her family.' Becca nodded, and Shona continued. 'Look, I'm going back to High Pines. Why don't you come with me?'

Shona could see her daughter's emotional state, even as she tried to hide it. The secret of the recovered girl's identity was a heavy burden for someone her age to carry. Dr Armstrong might be used to keeping information to himself, but it would be hard for Becca, among the students. Also, if she confided in the Elliot girls, it would be round the whole town soon after and there was every chance it would hit the local papers before the family were located.

'No, I'll stay,' Becca said firmly.

'Just for a couple of nights? I'll bring you back,' Shona coaxed. 'Don't you miss your bed and all your teddies?'

Becca smiled at her mother's teasing. 'Yes, a bit. But I'm learning so much here. I'm fine, Mum, honestly. And I won't say anything.'

'Are you sure?' Shona replied. The truth was, she also wanted Becca's company to fill the empty echoes of the family home.

'Have you heard from Dad?' Becca asked quietly.

'Just that the case preparation's going okay. There's a lot of information from forensic accountants to get through.'

'How much longer?'

'His QC reckons they might be finished this week,' Shona replied. 'I'm sure Dad will be home straight after.' She wasn't sure, but that wasn't something she wanted Becca to hear.

'I'll come home then, too,' Becca said firmly. Shona realised her wish to be absent was about more than a potential career choice. Rob was integral to High Pines in a way Shona wasn't. She earned the income that kept them afloat, but it was Rob, with his meals, schooling, picking up of friends and near-constant presence, who made the wheels turn every day. There was nothing to do but accept it.

–

When Shona got back to Kirkness, she microwaved a bowl of Rob's pasta from the freezer and ate it standing in front of the sitting-room windows. The sun sat low over the wooded hills on the far side of the estuary. Golden waves edged with fire lapped against the moored yachts that rode the last swell of the incoming tide.

She left the empty bowl in the sink, showered, and then pulled on clean jeans and a fleece. Outside, the twilight blue of the sky lay on the smoothed surface of slack water. In an hour, the sea would turn again and race with the river out to the Solway Firth.

Shona walked down through High Pines' steep, terraced garden and let herself out through the gate at the bottom. She turned left along the quiet shorefront road. A few drinkers lingered at the tables outside the Royal Oak hotel, bathed in the warm light from the windows. For a moment, she thought of popping in for a drink – Callum, the village postman and her RNLI crewmate, had a girlfriend who worked behind the bar. But the shooting of an MSP was big news and locals knew she was working the case. She really couldn't face being grilled.

A little further along shone the lights of the lifeboat station. Tommy's van was parked in front of his boatyard next door. He often stopped off in the evenings, doing odd jobs or catching up with paperwork.

The tall doors to the station's boat hall were closed so Shona went along the alley to the side of the two-storey stone building that had once been a pair of fishermen's cottages. Inside, immersion suits hung upside down by their yellow boots in the crew changing room like colourful bats. The D-class lifeboat *Margaret Wilson* sat quietly in her cradle. Shona called out as she climbed the stairs to the mezzanine level, with its small training room, kitchen lounge and views over Kirkness estuary.

Lifeboat helm Tommy pushed a still-warm mug of tea across the table towards her.

'Saw you were back home,' he said.

'Am I that predictable?' Shona said as she drew out a chair and sat down.

'Reliable is a better word,' he smiled. 'Thought I might get an apology from you for running off like that on the moor. D'you know how hard it is to get a gazebo into a bag in that wind? If it hadnae been for the students, I'd still be up there wrestling wi' the bugger.'

Shona smiled. 'Sorry.'

She knew none of this was true. Tommy had played a key part in getting everyone safely down to the campsite when news of the shooting reached them.

'Any shouts?' Shona's previous experience at Tower station in London, the busiest in the UK, made her Tommy's first choice when the alarm sounded and the crew members arrived, but she didn't carry her pager outside the village. The Kirkness station was well supported with around twenty other volunteers.

'All quiet,' Tommy said. 'Becca okay?'

Shona took a gulp of tea and nodded. 'The body she uncovered turned out to be more modern than Dr Armstrong thought. We're looking into it.'

Tommy pursed his lips and let out a sigh. 'And Rob?'

'No real news,' Shona said and hurried on. 'But you and I have had an invitation from the Earl of Langdale himself, no less.'

'Oh, aye?' Tommy looked sceptical.

'The swift water exercise with Langdale Mountain Rescue. He asked if we'd like to be involved.'

'That'll be the exercise we do every few years with them, will it?' Tommy said.

'The very same.' Shona slapped the table lightly with her hand and smiled. 'Humour him. He wants everyone to know he's a good guy and has offered The Douglas Arms as a base for the exercise.'

'Fine by me,' Tommy said, to Shona's surprise. She'd expected a tussle over the aristocracy throwing their weight around, before he agreed.

Remembering the other stalls at the open day, Shona smiled. 'It's that barmaid from the pub,' she teased. 'Got to you with offers of birch wine.'

He coloured a little but didn't deny it. 'Freya's a nice woman. Her people were boatbuilders, too. Fae Orkney.'

'She is nice. I guess that gives you things in common,' Shona said, taken aback by the sincerity of his expression.

'I'll need to retire from the helm in a couple of years, when I'm fifty-five. Might be time to think of a life beyond the boatyard.'

Shona felt a hard lump come into her throat and realised she'd just assumed Tommy would be in Kirkness forever. 'But you can stay on as Launch Authority, run shouts from the shore?'

'Oh aye, it's possible,' he agreed. 'You see, I've a nephew who's just finished a traditional shipwright's course down at Lyme Regis. He might be looking to buy the yard. It's been in the family o'er a hundred years. I wouldn't let it go to just anyone.'

Tommy was a good man. He'd never married, but she'd heard rumours of a long-term girlfriend who'd moved on just before Shona arrived in Kirkness. She couldn't picture how things would be without him. The phrase Lady Douglas had used about Cousin Jack – *a tower of strength* – came to mind. That's exactly what Tommy was to her. They'd appoint a new helm from the station crew. She got on well with all the candidates, but it wouldn't be the same.

It seemed like the ground was moving under her feet. Becca would soon be gone to university in Glasgow. Perhaps Ravi and Kate would leave, too. She'd lost a champion in Chief Superintendent Monroe when he'd retired. Even Dan in Carlisle had someone important in his life now and the idea that he'd transfer to Dumfries, as soon as a vacancy arose, was mentioned less and less often. Change was part of life, but it was all happening so fast. The house already seemed empty. Then there was the question mark she was trying so hard not to think about: Rob's trial. Shona loved this place, but would it still be the same without the people she loved in it? She didn't know the answer.

Tommy must have seen her stricken expression. He covered her hand with his own.

'Don't look so worried. Nothing's decided yet. A wee trip out with the crew will take your mind off your other troubles.' He winked. 'Who knows, you might even develop a taste for thon birch wine yourself.'

Chapter 14

The streetlights outside Cornwall Mount police HQ came on. Murdo had stayed later than he'd intended. He wanted everything sorted before his boss – Wee Shona, as the staff dubbed her – returned in the morning.

A list of updates sat on her desk. Ravi had done a good job in the sergeant's absence, but he couldn't be expected to cover all bases in the way Murdo had over the last twenty years. Some jobs needed doing before they sailed over the horizon, and he'd developed a sixth sense for what was coming. The general housekeeping of available vehicles, overtime budgets, training courses and staff rotas were all under his eye, and he knew the pinch points. Parents who needed a few hours off before Christmas for their kid's show. Pool cars that were clocking up the mileage and weren't reliable. Who was moving house and who had elderly parents with issues over carers. He did his best to accommodate them all and keep the CID office running.

Most people were grateful and repaid his attention to the detail of their lives tenfold. The force operated with a small crew for such a vast geographical area, which stretched north for fifty miles from the English border and over a hundred miles west to east. Wee Shona had built a strong team. His job was to smooth all paths and keep it working at its best.

Murdo emerged from Shona's office. His own desk was in the far corner, near a pair which accommodated the CID constables, Kate and Ravi. Beyond, in the other section of the L-shaped room, were the civilian staff's workstations. He switched off a couple of computers and made sure no papers were visible on desks, then let the CID door close behind him.

As he passed the small conference room next door, PC Christine Jamieson reached the top of the stairs opposite and paused, breathless. Along with her partner PC Kirsten O'Carroll, they formed the formidable 'Two Kirsties': beat cops whom Murdo termed 'handy lassies' and rated highly.

'Murdo, how are you?' Christine said.

'Aye, I'm doing fine,' Murdo replied. 'How's yourself?'

'No' bad, no' bad,' she replied with a smile. 'Just getting my daily step count in.'

Being a Wednesday night, it was fairly quiet. Many street officers liked to do the round of the building, catching up with colleagues they didn't have a chance to chew the fat with from behind the plexiglass screen of the custody desk next to the cells.

'Listen,' Christine began, 'I don't know if you've heard, but Alan Kerr passed his parole board.' She stopped, letting the significance of her words sink in.

'That right?' Murdo said, his tone casual, hiding a tightening sensation in his chest.

'Served two-thirds of his sentence. He'll be on licence for the next four years. Of course, he'd have been out a few years back if he hadn't got into that bit of bother in jail.'

Murdo always knew the day would come when his brother's killer was released, but still, it had crept up on him. Perhaps it had been there, curled in the darkness at the back of his mind when he'd come down from Bield Moss, made the turn for his home town and stood in his mother's house listening for ghosts.

'So where's he registering?' Murdo said, sliding his hands into his pockets and affecting an air of calm indifference.

'Back to Langholm,' Christine said. 'He'll need to check in weekly at the local nick and there'll be a compulsory resit on his driving test at some point.'

Alan Kerr's fourteen-year sentence for causing death by dangerous driving, with a minimum disqualification period of two years, was a matter of record, but his new residency wouldn't have been easily available in advance of his release. Murdo's time on the beat earned him many friends and allies. Christine Jamieson, who hailed from the tiny neighbouring village of Craigcleuch, must have done a bit of digging on Murdo's behalf. He'd have done the same if their positions had been reversed.

'Aye. Good to know. Thank you.' Murdo held himself upright and gave Christine a slight nod to emphasise his appreciation for her act of consideration for a fellow officer.

'Look after yourself, Murdo,' Christine said, as she turned and jogged back down the stairs. Murdo let her go, kneading the leather fob of his keyring between his fingers until his knuckles showed white. Then he followed her down, but stopped by the window on the half-landing so there was no chance they'd meet.

The sky retained the last rays of sunset, and the slow stream of cars and holiday campervans adding their headlights to the streetlamps gave the scene a carnival air. It was the end of another day his brother hadn't lived to see. Alan

Kerr had taken Drew's life as surely as if he'd pointed a gun at him or slit his throat with a knife. Kerr had shown no remorse. Drew never regained consciousness. There was no chance to say goodbye.

Murdo left Cornwall Mount by the side door and got into his car. He sat for a moment, considering the implications of what Christine had said, playing forward the variety of scenarios that presented themselves. He'd have to tell Joan before someone spotted Kerr swaggering down Langham's main street and took a gossip's glee at being first to the family with the news.

Murdo was a churchgoer with genuine faith. When he wasn't at work, he and Joan helped at local charities. He understood the social pressures that could result in someone committing a crime. But when it came to his brother's killer, he saw no way to reconcile himself with the man's behaviour. Why had this happened? For ten years, he'd searched for an answer and found none. If God knew, he wasn't letting on. Perhaps evil existed to balance out all the good in the world. Evil had concentrated itself into Alan Kerr and snuffed out Drew's life in the process. That was the *what*, but he was no nearer to the *why*.

Telling Joan would open a discussion he didn't want to have. He relied on his wife's strength and support, but it wasn't her brother who'd been murdered. A brief conversation in the morning, just before he left for work, would cut the opportunity for discussion. But tonight, he would carry the news alone.

Chapter 15

On Thursday morning, Shona crawled through the Dumfries traffic, caught in the twin streams of holiday-makers and quietly jubilant parents on the first school run of the new term. Earlier, she'd stood at the door of her daughter's room at High Pines and scolded herself. Becca would be back soon and it would be another year before she could start university in Glasgow. But the spreading of her wings had begun and Shona couldn't help but imagine the empty nest her daughter would leave behind. It might make the issues she and Rob faced in their marriage easier to work through, but it was also possible that Becca's daily presence was the glue that held the family together and, without her, Shona and Rob would find themselves further apart than ever.

It was already warm, and Shona switched on the Audi's air-con. She'd chosen her favourite navy blue Hobbs suit and purple silk blouse. They were three days into the investigation and no arrests. Reviewing the evidence last night, it was clear that another appeal to the public for information was needed if they were to find their prime suspect, Darren Porter. Her Super would require some live meat for the media and it was likely she'd be the one making a statement in front of the cameras. Of course, once the shooter was in custody, the top brass would be happy to resume that role.

As she entered the CID room, Murdo hurried over. His shirt came loose from the waistband of his suit trousers, and he hauled them up. Behind him, she saw the front page of the BBC Scotland news website open on his computer screen.

'What's this about another attempt on Nicola Baird's life?' he demanded.

Shona held up her hand. 'It's all fine, Murdo. Get everyone in the conference room for a briefing.'

Shona placed the laptop bag on her desk and ran her eye down on the action notes Murdo had left there. She messaged Rob. *Update me at lunchtime. Love you XXX.*

A minute later, Murdo tapped on her door.

'Ready, boss.' He held out her Charles Rennie Mackintosh mug filled with black coffee. She took it and followed him through, her low heels clicking on the vinyl tiles of the corridor.

A ring of expectant faces greeted her in the conference room. Chloe Burke and Vincent Grieg had tablets in front of them; the other civilian staff were ranged around the rectangle of pushed-together tables that almost filled the room. The windows that ran down one side had been inched open. Ravi pulled his notebook out and clicked his pen repeatedly in anticipation. Kate stared at him, but he continued, a smirk on his face. Murdo frowned until Ravi placed the pen on the tabletop and folded his hands, the silver bangles on his wrists clinking to silence.

'You'll have seen the news,' Shona began. She drew out a chair and placed her mug on the table, with her phone and Murdo's action list. 'First thing to say is Edinburgh Police are happy this wasn't an attempt on Mrs Baird's life.'

A call from Lothian and Borders cops had woken Shona from a light sleep after midnight. Nicola Baird had reported shots fired in the lane behind her Victorian villa in the city's Belford Park, and a firearms team had been quickly dispatched.

'The main concern,' Shona continued, 'was that we had the same shooter or even a copycat incident, but the local DCI called me to say a forensic team searching the lane early this morning found spent fireworks behind a wheelie bin and concluded it was a prank.'

'Less *Day of the Jackal*, more "*day of the jackass*",' Ravi said, to a couple of sniggers from the junior staff seated around the table.

'That's a little unkind, Ravi.' Shona fought to keep her expression severe, despite the fact she saw the dark humour in his remark. 'The poor woman's been shot.'

'There's nothing poor about her, 'cept her empathy levels,' Ravi muttered. 'She's a politician. Probably paid someone to do it herself, for the publicity.'

It was true Nicola Baird had spoken to the press almost as swiftly as she'd pressed the panic button on her personal security device. The story of a second assassination attempt, once out there, had had more traction than the later update that it had been kids messing about, and Nicola Baird stayed on the front pages.

'Okay,' Shona said loudly, quelling the rising murmur of comments. 'Let's not forget her children were in the house. It must have been very frightening.'

'No officers with them?' Kate said.

'The security assessment on the property showed CCTV and alarms, so they made a budget decision to withdraw protection officers and send a patrol car round every hour.'

'Somebody will be for the high jump,' Murdo said.

'I don't envy the local cops who made that call,' Shona agreed. 'They were right to do so at the time, but it doesn't look that way this morning.' She took a sip of coffee and ran a finger down the action list. 'Which is why there will be renewed focus on what we're doing to catch the individual who shot Mrs Baird. Ravi, where are you with potential organised crime connection?'

'None,' Ravi said flatly. Then, catching Shona frowning at him over her glasses, he reeled off how Nicola Baird's main property business, and her father's position as the *Carpet King of Edinburgh*, put her at charity events with other, less above-board, individuals, but there were no registered business or social links to any organised crime outfits – and a contact in Lothian and Borders had confirmed that her name had never come up in any investigation.

'Okay.' Shona was forced to swallow that for now.

'Oh, and we can exclude the happy speeder, Jim Cameron,' Ravi added. 'He was up before the sheriff for non-payment of his fine on the day Mrs Baird was shot. Pity. He could claim bagging a Tory was doing a public service. We could have had a whip-round for him.'

'That's enough, Ravi,' Shona said, and shot him a final look of warning before turning to her sergeant. 'Murdo?'

'The key individual we need to eliminate is still Darren Porter. Vinny's got a bit of background.'

The visual investigations officer leaned back, crossed one skinny-jeaned ankle over the other knee and scrolled through his tablet.

'Darren Porter dropped out of sight three months ago. Hasn't used a cashpoint. No social media updates,' he said. 'Previously, he always withdrew his total benefits payments as soon as they hit his account. No credit cards.'

'So, he could have done this in preparation for the attack?' Shona said.

Vinny shrugged in a way Shona used to find infuriating, but had learned to tolerate. His take on life was literal. It was his job to winkle out evidence, not draw conclusions.

'Edinburgh have checked out homeless hostels and previous addresses,' Murdo added. 'No registered vehicle. No known family or girlfriend.'

'What about his prior social media posts?' Shona said.

'Couple of red flags there,' Murdo said, and waited for Vinny, still intent on his tablet, to supply the relevant information. When he didn't speak, Chloe, who sat next to him, nudged his arm and repeated the question.

Vinny blinked, then said, 'Porter's Facebook friends list includes individuals from hard-line pro-independence groups.'

'So Nicola Baird's theory about a politically motivated hit could be correct,' Shona said, turning to Murdo. 'Perhaps the mace incident at the constituency office was a dry run to test security?'

'Also,' Vinny cut in without waiting for Murdo's reply, 'his "likes" and reposts on both Facebook and Twitter reflect a pattern of pro-union support.'

Chloe cleared her throat. 'It would appear Darren Porter has affiliations on both sides of the debate. Most of his contacts are ex-servicemen, including some members of the Sons of Scotia.'

'He has skills,' Shona said. 'Is it possible he was being recruited?'

'Yes,' said Chloe, whose ability to extrapolate the data into potentially useful chunks of evidence exceeded Vinny's. 'On balance, I'd say he's more engaged with the pro-unionist material, but that might reflect prior friend-ships. There are specific invitations to join meetings and demos, but no evidence he attended.'

'So, he could be flirting with both sides?' Shona said. 'Or even laying a false trail?'

Chloe nodded. 'Both are possible.'

'No sign of him at any of his associates' addresses?'

'It's a short list, and Edinburgh have already checked them,' Murdo said. 'There are a few pictures of him wild camping, all on the west coast, nowhere near here.'

Shona, exasperated, turned back to Vinny. 'How is it that he's gone under the radar like this?'

Vinny shrugged again, and Shona fought the urge to bark at him to sit up straight and look at her when she was talking to him. Although he'd worked for her for nearly two years, she'd be hard-pressed to say the colour of his eyes.

'Decentralise your data,' Vinny said. 'Don't use your registered home address. A burner phone. Encrypted internet connections, hide your IP, use a VPN.'

'Virtual Personal Network,' Kate said, responding to Shona's blank expression.

'Throwaway email accounts. Use cash or cryptocur-rency. Dress in nondescript clothing. Don't draw atten-tion to yourself. Don't get arrested. Obviously.' Vinny grinned.

'So he's gone completely off-grid?'

Vinny considered this, his attention still on the tablet, then nodded. 'He must be good if I can't find him,' he said, with no hint of irony.

'Could Porter be using any or all of those strategies Vinny just listed?' Shona said.

Murdo nodded. 'He's unstable, but resourceful. Unlikely he's hung around here. He's from Glasgow originally. The local cops there have had no joy, but they're keeping a lookout.'

Take your revenge, then hide in a city with over a million and a half people, only ninety minutes up the road, where you're not a recent face, but can find your way around. It seemed to Shona like a solid plan and one they'd have difficulty picking apart.

'Any other thoughts?' Shona threw it open to the team.

'There's a lot of drone footage from the estate we haven't looked at,' Kate said. 'Before and after the shooting. If we can pick up anyone on the moor who isn't accounted for, we may find a new witness, or even the shooter themselves.'

Kate's understanding of the landscape would be useful in such an exercise, but it was the sort of boring task most DCs would rather avoid. It surprised Shona she'd volunteered. Perhaps Kate was thinking of resurrecting her geography degree or, more likely, hoping for a glimpse of his lordship striding across the heather. An unidentified person on Bield Moss would be a reason to call Xander. But it was a good idea and might throw up a fresh lead.

Shona gave the idea the green light, tasks were allocated and the meeting broke up. As everyone trooped out, Shona said, 'Ravi? A word.'

Her DC's normal line of patter, guaranteed to raise smiles around the table, had edged into something darker during the briefing. The undercurrent of compassion, present even in his most ferocious teasing of Kate, had vanished where the MSP for South Scotland was concerned.

She waited until they were alone before she spoke. 'Nicola Baird – she's really got to you, hasn't she?'

Ravi shook his head angrily. 'If she'd just got shot ten miles up the road, it would have been entirely a Lothian and Borders problem. I wish it was. She was on the radio this morning. Going on about anarchic individuals of all kinds with no respect for human life, who take the law into their own hands.'

Shona had heard it. 'Does my head look like it buttons up the back? I know her game, but we don't have to play it.'

'Basically,' Ravi said, 'she's having a go at anyone who doesn't think like she does. If you object about local developments, or sign a petition, you're one step away from shooting your MSP. Frankly, I'd say she's putting that idea into people's heads every time she opens her mouth.'

'Right or wrong, it's not our judgement to make. Protect and serve, remember. We don't get to choose.'

Ravi sighed. 'Sorry, boss. It's just… Martin's had a lot of stick lately at work. Seems like folk are getting less tolerant and people like Nicola Baird make it worse.'

Ravi's partner, Martin, worked in addict rehab for a Dumfries-based project. They'd been together for six months. Shona was pleased to see her DC happy and settled. It was another reason for him to stay in his job and not move on.

'Tell me what happened,' Shona said, sitting back against the desk and folding her arms.

'The usual,' Ravi replied. 'Mouthing off about dirty queers. But this time, he got slapped about a bit, too.'

'Did he report it? I won't let stuff like this be swept under the carpet.'

'I fixed it.' Ravi's eyes hardened. 'Don't worry, there won't be any comeback.'

Ravi was slim, groomed and always fashionably dressed, but he was an accomplished boxer and she'd seen him deal with much larger fellas, thanks to the speed and precision of his movements. They'd be on the ground in handcuffs, still wondering what had hit them, and Ravi would be dusting off his favourite yellow cashmere sweater and smoothing his impeccably cut hair back into place.

'I'll pretend I didn't hear that, DC Sarwar,' Shona said, pushing off from the desk. Her face softened, and she put a hand on his arm. 'You don't have to do this alone, pal.'

'I know, boss,' he said, then grinned.

'What?' Shona smiled back.

'I'm just thinking what you'd do if anyone assaulted Rob.'

'No one would ever touch Rob. As Murdo once said, Rob could charm his way out of hell and get the devil to give him a pension.'

It was true that her husband had led a privileged life – expensive boarding school, followed by a good university and then a lucrative job in the city – and he took his good luck as if it was his due.

'Let's hope Murdo's right,' Ravi said, his face suddenly serious again.

She appreciated his concern, and knew he was hinting that her husband's luck might be about to run out, but she wasn't about to discuss the forthcoming trial.

'Murdo's always right,' Shona said and ushered Ravi out the door. 'Back to work.'

–

Shona updated her Super on the hunt for Darren Porter. The public appeal had generated calls from across Scotland, which local officers were following up. Chloe had digitally enhanced two new pictures of Porter, and Detective Superintendent Davies decided that issuing these images with a statement including the line that every available officer was working flat out – and no one was available for questions – would send the right message. Shona was relieved she wouldn't have to face the cameras just yet and justify why a gunman who'd shot an MSP still hadn't been caught.

She'd spoken to Dan Ridley at Cumbria CID, who would also issue the pictures on the local news. A team in Glasgow visited an address on the south side of the city and one of their detectives re-interviewed the staff at the Sons of Scotia office, but neither action resulted in any new leads.

At lunchtime, Rob called, his tone more sober than the previous day.

'I've just run through what it'll be like on the stand,' he said.

'Imogen give you a grilling?' Shona said with relish. She'd met Rob's barrister and was glad the woman was on their side. It was time Rob understood what he was up against.

'She did, but I've lived with you all these years, so I'm used to it,' Rob joked. 'Anyway, they need to show I concealed the movement or ownership of assets, or gained from it.'

'Rob, I need to know you're taking this seriously,' Shona said. 'Listen to Imogen.'

'I am listening. Don't worry, it's all fine. I'm just gonna give Becca a buzz. Love you.'

After he'd hung up, Shona sat staring at the screen as if it would somehow provide the reassurance she sought. In the end she decided there was nothing more to be gained by replaying the call in her mind. She turned the phone face down and went back to her case files.

–

In the afternoon, Shona read through the file on Darren Porter again. His picture showed what Vinny had described. A nondescript individual in plain clothing, with cropped fair hair and an unremarkable face. As long as his behaviour didn't spiral out of control, it was unlikely anyone would pay him the least attention.

Murdo tapped on her door.

'Boss,' he said. 'Forensics are back on the shell case recovered from the moor. Multiple DNA found.'

'And?' Shona said.

'There's a hit on one of the profiles.' Murdo's face was serious, his lips pressed together in a thin line.

'Who?' Shona felt a prickle of excitement run down her arms.

'Ben Elliot. His DNA is on the system from an assault two years back. Bit of a rammy with a holiday-cottage owner over a fence. I heard about it, but I didn't think it had got as far as the courts.'

They had the bullet dug out of Nicola Baird's shoulder, but Shona knew it would be tricky to match it with the shell case recovered from the moor. In court, a lawyer would argue that Elliot had previously handled the casing, and it may have lain among the heather for some time, perhaps from the deer-shooting incident. It would be enough to put doubt in the jury's mind. However, a bullet's distinct striation was caused as it passed down a rifle barrel. The weapon's firing pin also made a unique mark on the casing.

Shona chewed her lip for a moment, then said, 'We need to look at Elliot's rifles.'

'Aye, we do,' agreed Murdo.

If both the bullet from Nicola's wound and the case from the moorland could be matched to this weapon using separate ballistic techniques, they'd have a link that placed Ben Elliot squarely in the frame.

'Ravi talked about Nicola Baird's social media comments on muirburn,' Shona said. She remembered the charged encounter with the rewilding group, Elliot's anger at the delays to their purchase plans for the moor, the general sense that Nicola Baird was in the earl's pocket. 'You know the man. D'you think her opposition to green policies and support for the earl's plans is sufficient motive for shooting her?'

Murdo let out a long breath. 'I'd say violence was out of character, but the incident with the neighbour shows how a small thing can escalate. He'd been sacked by the estate, now here's his MSP shooting grouse on the moor his community group's trying to save. If he wasn't thinking straight, it might have been the last straw.'

Shona leaned her elbows on the desk, steepling her fingertips together and pressing them to her mouth. She trusted Murdo's instincts, especially since he had prior knowledge of the man. She had the DNA match and a motive. The priority now was to secure evidence and interview Elliot under caution.

'I agree, Murdo,' Shona said. 'Draw up an arrest strategy for Ben Elliot. He has weapons at the farm, so book a firearms team. Let's get up there first thing in the morning.'

She hoped she was right in her assessment of the evidence. Going into a family farm armed would send shockwaves through the community. If she was wrong, they'd close ranks against her team: outsiders who'd taken the earl's side against a hard-working farmer who'd already lost his job for standing up to the Douglas family. She'd lose any chance of keeping local people on board. She could picture Sergeant Graham's gloating face and hear her Super's self-satisfied whine: 'Bad call, Shona, perhaps it's time for you to step down.' With Rob's trial looming, he'd jump at the chance to be shot of her. But she had the DNA result, the matching bullet and shell cartridge.

All she could do now was pray she was right.

Chapter 16

The archaeology students normally left the Elliot farm campsite at eight a.m. and rarely came back until after four p.m. Shona wanted them out of the way before her team went in. She'd discussed Ben Elliot's likely routine with Murdo, who made a few discreet calls. Shona remembered the view down the valley from the front of The Douglas Arms. There was little cover anywhere, and they'd need to approach along the main road. A conga-line of police vehicles would be visible miles away and if Elliot spotted them when he was out feeding his sheep, he might be tempted to make a run for it. Murdo reckoned that Ben would be back at the farm just after eight a.m. for his own breakfast. Shona decided they'd make the arrest then, when the chance of a hostage situation developing, or other danger to the public, would be minimised.

They met with the firearms team at a pre-arranged point five miles from Langholm. Shona reviewed the briefing notes with the inspector in charge. The Elliot farm had a long stone barn at right angles to the main two-storey house. Anyone approaching the front door would be at risk of ambush from this farm building, so it would need to be cleared first. It was likely the two sheepdogs would signal the team's arrival, so the entire operation needed to procced at speed. Shona reiterated the possibility that Elliot's home-schooled daughters might be inside; her number-one priority was their safety. A police dog-handler was also on hand to deal with any canine issues.

Shona put on her body armour vest and checked her sidearm. She wouldn't play an active part in apprehending the target and would go in only when the firearms lead had declared it safe to do so.

But Ben Elliot knew these moors like the back of his hand. If he somehow absconded, and they were forced to pursue him, there was every chance he could outfox them. If he resisted arrest and turned a weapon on her team, Shona wasn't taking any chances by going in unarmed.

'We're looking for a .243 Winchester calibre rifle,' Shona said.

The firearms officer nodded. 'Lot of farms round here have them for shooting small deer, like roe or sika.'

She handed Ravi her car keys. 'You drive.'

Shona got into the passenger seat. Ravi swept his long dark fringe back from his face in a gesture Shona recognised as nerves. It was good to be nervous, to check everything twice.

'Okay, pal?' she asked.

'Aye, fine,' he said.

Murdo was in the lead car. When the convoy reached the bottom of the Elliot farm track, he stopped and lowered his window. Sergeant Graham got out of his vehicle and leaned one arm on the roof of Murdo's as they exchanged a few words. Another patrol car sat on the verge. Once Shona's team were on the way up to the farm, the Specials would block the track to prevent anyone else arriving or leaving.

Murdo's voice came over the radio. 'Good to go. Ben Elliot's Land Rover went up to the farm about fifteen minutes ago. No students on site.'

'Sierra–Oscar copied that. Thank you,' Shona said, then fitted her earpiece so she could monitor the firearms comms. The team leader gave the order to proceed.

The farm track ran for half a mile. They left the tree cover that edged the road and within a few seconds were travelling across a landscape of rough pasture. A few Elliot sheep lifted their heads as they passed, one or two skittering away from their feeding spot by the fence. The road became rougher and the Audi bounced over potholes. Halfway up, a side track branched off to the right, which led ultimately to the top of Bield Moss and the dig site. Another local patrol car came to a halt, blocking it. Thirty seconds later, the firearms van, with Shona's Audi behind, pulled into the yard. Murdo's Astra drew up behind Elliot's Land Rover, blocking it in.

The firearms team of six officers exited their vehicle. The front door of the farmhouse stood open, a potential risk, so four men made straight for it, and the remaining two peeled off towards the bolted entrance to the barn, as a wave of frantic barking began inside.

Shona got out and stood by the Audi's passenger door, scanning the fields on both sides of the approach track in case neighbours, remote as they were, had been alerted by the convoy of vehicles and came to investigate.

'Police, show yourself!' the point officer roared as he entered the house.

A flash of red caught the corner of Shona's eye, and she looked over her shoulder. A party of walkers were in the field behind the barn.

'Shit,' Shona hissed. They must have come cross-country and missed both police vehicles further down the track.

Ravi turned to see what had drawn his boss's attention, his hand on the driver's door as he made to get out, but she shook her head.

'Ravi, stay with the team. I'm just gonna head those people off.'

She jogged back down the track, skidding on the loose gravel, then climbed over the metal five-bar gate. At that point, the lead walker lifted his head. Shona waved both arms above her head, then pressed her palms forward in a motion that said, *go back*.

The red-jacketed walker glanced to his left and spotted the police vehicle further down the track at the junction to the path. He gave her a double thumbs-up to show he understood, turned the entire group around and they quickly retraced their steps.

Shona was now level with the rear entrance of the barn. Over the earpiece, she heard the team inside the house move from room to room, calling *clear*. The partially open barn door swung wide and, in a split second, a flash of a green Barbour jacket told her this was not a black-clad firearms officer. Her hand flew to her sidearm. She drew the pistol in one practised motion and levelled it at the figure. The barking had reached fever pitch within.

'Police! Show me your hands.'

The phrase was no sooner out of her mouth than she realised she was looking at two terrified girls. Both dropped the animal feed bags they carried, frozen to the spot.

'Mum!' Becca's face was a white oval of shock. Next to her, the youngest Elliot girl, Ashley, in an oversized wax-cotton jacket, looked about to scream.

Shona holstered her sidearm and moved swiftly towards them. 'Get down.'

She grabbed both by the scruff of the neck, her daughter's fleece bunching in her fist, and Ashley struggling in her grip. Shona pulled them around the gable end of the barn furthest from the house and pressed both into the lichen-covered stonework.

'Where are Grace and Flora?' she said, looking from one to the other.

'At the dig,' Becca stammered. 'We're gonnae join them when we've fed the goats.'

Shona relayed the location of the rest of the family to the firearms team, then put her fingers to her lips to shush her daughter's questions.

A moment later, the team reached the kitchen at the back. *Target located.* Shona heard a shout, a scuffle, then an exchange of low voices. *Alpha-One to Sierra-Oscar, target detained.*

'Sierra-Oscar, received, thank you.' Shona wanted to punch the air, but she kept her face impassive as she turned back to the girls. Ashley let out a sob, but before Shona could do anything, Becca gripped the eleven-year-old girl close.

'What are you doing?' Becca spat at her mother. Her moment of terror had turned to anger. Her cheeks flushed as she rose from her position, backed against the wall, and towered over her mother. 'You're scaring Ashley.'

One look at Ashley's malevolent frown said the girl was more likely to take a chunk out of her than collapse from fear. Shona couldn't allow emotions to build further.

'Becca, I need you to do me a big favour and look after Ashley. Get her safely into the back of my car,' she said calmly.

She took hold of Becca's arm and keeked around the barn wall to make sure they had not brought Ben Elliot out of the house. She didn't want Ashley to see her father in handcuffs.

'Becca, look at Ravi,' Shona said. Her DC stood by the driver's door, alerted to the sounds from the barn. He waved and smiled at Becca.

At the sight of her mother's car and Ravi's familiar face, Becca's anger ebbed a little, but questions lingered. She looked from the police vehicles to her mother's sidearm.

'The man who shot the MSP? Is he hiding at the farm?' Becca asked, breathlessly.

'Where's my dad?' Ashley demanded.

Becca's expression told Shona that she'd put two and two together and made five, thinking that Ben Elliot was the gunman's latest victim.

'Your dad's fine,' Shona said quickly to Ashley. 'Becca, please, just go to the car.'

Ashley made a face that said she didn't quite believe Shona, but Becca, given the task of protecting the younger girl, didn't question her mother further and took her to the rear of the Audi.

Ravi crouched down by the open door. 'Hello darlin', my name's Ravi. Your dad's fine. He's just gonna come with us for a bit.'

Becca shot Shona an incredulous look. 'You don't think...'

'Why?' Ashley began to struggle in Becca's grip 'He's done nothing wrong.'

'Wait,' Shona said to Ashley just as Becca was about to push her into the car. 'Is that your dad's jacket you're wearing?' The girl nodded. 'Can I take it?' Shona continued. 'He might need it.'

'No way,' said Ashley, stubbornly. 'I want my dad.'

'There's a new fleece of Becca's in the back,' Shona said, lightly. 'Would you like to borrow that?'

The girl's eyes fell on the pink top and her angry resolve wavered.

'You can keep it if you like,' Becca said. It had been an expensive, but unwanted, birthday gift from Rob's brother, Uncle Sandy, and his formidable wife, Aunt Caroline.

Shona slipped on blue gloves. 'Quick now,' she said, briskly, as she slipped her fingers under the collar of the Barbour and slid it off, before Ashley could protest further.

She held the garment at her side, careful not to touch it against her own clothes. Becca helped Ashley with the fleece but, once it was on, the girl made a dash for the farmhouse. Ravi caught her, but Ashley lashed out at him with her boot. His childhood with four sisters had obviously taught him something, and he dodged her swipes.

'But I want to see him now!' Ashley wailed as Ravi struggled to keep hold of her.

Shona hung the coat on the car's wing mirror and, crouching, caught hold of the girl.

Ashley struggled but Shona kept the light grip on her arms, allowing her some movement, but not too much. 'Ashley, Ashley,' she said calmly, until the girl began to run out of steam and finally looked at her.

'Your dad will be fine. Becca is going with you to find Grace. You can come back here soon. I promise.'

At that, Ashley calmed a little, and Becca took her hand and led her back to the car.

'We'll need to find next-of-kin or a care team for the girls,' Shona said quietly to Ravi.

'Grace is eighteen,' Becca cut in. 'She can look after her sisters.'

'It's a lot to ask,' Shona said gently, picking up Ben Elliot's coat again.

'She'll do it,' Becca said. 'And they can't leave the animals.'

That was true. From what Shona had seen of the girls, they had a maturity beyond their years – Grace in particular. Ravi looked at Shona, who nodded.

'Let's find Grace,' Becca said, ushering Ashley into the car. 'My mum needs to chat with your dad. It'll be boring stuff.' She smiled and rolled her eyes at the younger girl, who looked suspiciously at Ravi.

Ravi twirled Shona's car keys around his long fingers. 'Hey, Ashley, d'you want to drive?'

A flicker of a smile appeared.

'Thanks, Ravi,' Shona said. 'Listen, keep your wits about you with Ashley, and I don't know how Grace and Flora will react. I'll send up a couple of Specials. The girls need to stay at the dig for a bit. I'll radio you with an update. Murdo might know of somewhere the girls can stay local for the night, in case the search of the house drags on.'

Shona walked through the farmhouse's whitewashed hallway. Through an open door to the right was a short passage that led to a scullery, a stone sink and a tiled floor visible beyond. Kate and two firearms officers, still unidentifiable in their balaclavas and helmets, were going through the contents of a tall metal cabinet. At the sight of Shona, Kate pointed to two rifles leaning against the wall.

'One's a .308 Winchester calibre for shooting large mammals like red deer,' the masked firearms officer said. 'But the smaller one could be the weapon you're after.'

'Perfect,' Shona said. 'Good work. Thank you. Have you retrieved his clothing?'

Kate looked up from the paperwork she was filling in. 'Those two evidence bags have jeans, a dark green jumper and boots. I'll check in what he's wearing now once he's back at Dumfries.'

Shona handed over the jacket and Kate placed it in a third bag.

As Shona came into the kitchen, an officer was righting an upturned chair, but beyond that, there was no sign the suspect had resisted. Ben Elliot sat at the kitchen table, his cuffed hands resting palms down, his gaze fixed on the floor. Murdo stood behind him, a hand loosely on Elliot's shoulder so that he'd feel any tensing of the man's posture that might signal a change in his placid demeanour.

Murdo had formally arrested and cautioned Elliot, the sergeant's face grim at the turn of events that had led them all here. Shona repeated the offence he was being arrested for and advised him again of his right to silence. But he continued to stare at the floor, as if he hadn't heard her.

'You understand this is a very serious offence, Mr Elliot,' Shona pressed. He seemed unmoved by the morning's events and she wondered if he'd been expecting them.

'You understand I'm arresting you for the shooting of Nicola Baird?' She pulled out the kitchen chair opposite him and sat down. The man wouldn't meet her eye; she found it hard to judge if he might, in the next minute, react with violence or break down completely.

After a pause, in a voice barely above a whisper, he said, 'I'm sorry for the woman's pain.'

'Mr Elliot,' Shona leaned forward and put a hand over his. She expected him to recoil, but he merely looked up at her with grave, grey eyes. 'Mrs Baird,' Shona continued, 'wasn't the intended target, was she?'

His eyes hardened, and he pulled his hand away. 'That man has no place in this glen. In my heart, I wanted him gone. So for that, you must arrest me.'

Shona sat back. She had been right. Juries liked strong personal grudges and Ben Elliot's animosity towards the Earl of Langdale, who'd sacked him and perhaps put the family farm in financial danger, was an obvious motive.

She hoped he'd consider the implications of what he'd done while sitting alone in his cell. It might induce him to co-operate with the investigation. A speedy conclusion for Shona would also be an opportunity for Elliot to reduce his sentence.

Shona couldn't shake off the image of Ashley's shocked face. It was a familiar feeling. As always, the elation of arrest had quickly evaporated, and into the gap rushed all the concentrated essence of wrong turns and broken lives that both preceded and would follow it. Whatever Elliot had done, his girls had already lost one parent and should not be punished for their father's sins.

'You understand you're facing a lengthy prison sentence?' Shona said.

Ben Elliot looked at her calmly. 'Some things are worth the sacrifice.'

Shona looked at Murdo, who stood behind his friend. He frowned and shook his head. It was clear the reassessment of his one-time rugby teammate was hitting him hard, but Shona knew she could rely on Murdo to remain the compassionate professional he was.

'C'mon, Ben,' Murdo said. 'Let's get you on the road.'

Chapter 17

After Ben Elliot's arrest, Becca insisted she remain at the campsite to support the Elliot girls. Shona reminded her that she was there to gain experience for her studies.

'I can do both,' Becca replied, and promptly switched off her phone.

Murdo and Sergeant Graham found a local woman with a nearby farm who knew the girls, and who'd keep an eye on them all. Shona had called Social Services. They'd visit and offer support when they could. With his confession and strong forensics, Ben Elliot wouldn't be coming home anytime soon. The burden placed on eighteen-year-old Grace Elliot to look after 200 sheep, over a thousand acres of moor, her younger sisters and assorted other animals would only get heavier as the months rolled by.

Shona sat in the small dining room at The Douglas Arms and pondered what would help the Elliot girls most, when Superintendent Davies's name flashed up on her phone.

'Just checking you're all set for the press conference,' he said.

Despite Shona's assumption that it would be in Edinburgh or Glasgow, which offered easy access for the media, and that the top brass would polish their medals and elbow each other aside to own a success on camera, it had been decided to hold the briefing at The Douglas Arms, and that Shona would do it.

When she'd questioned the location, Davies had made noises about her being on the spot, and 'rural engagement' and 'inclusiveness', but it was clear that the Earl of Langdale had friends in high places. Alexander Douglas would use it to promote his plans for the estate. That The Douglas Arms's official opening was only a week away wasn't lost on Shona. Even Hippy Jack Douglas was getting something out of it.

'The chief constable would like it underlined that this was an individual with a personal grievance against the earl,' Davies said.

'Yes, sir,' Shona replied.

'Shut down any lingering idea that an MSP's assassination campaign had somehow got past us,' Davies continued. 'Or that the shooting is proof of a police intelligence failure to identify deepening divides between campaign groups over Scottish independence. Do you think you can manage that?'

Shona bristled, but checked her tone. 'Yes, sir,' she replied, evenly.

His motive in letting her handle the press was clear. He was handing her a chance to fail. Any critical coverage would be another nail in her career coffin.

'Not expecting any ill-feeling locally, are we?' Davies said.

Shona thought he sounded almost hopeful. A rammy at the press conference would suit him fine. She picked up her keys and suit carrier, the phone wedged against her shoulder. The map of allegiances that hung in Langdale Hall came to mind, but she couldn't recall where the Elliot name was placed. It was ancient history, anyway. Ben's admission of guilt should head off any trouble.

'No, sir. DS O'Halloran and Sergeant Graham are liaising. Local cops will be on hand to keep things low-key.'

Shona had impressed upon Willie Graham that if there were any cock-ups, he'd be for the high jump. It was his patch and public order was squarely uniform's responsibility, although Davies would, no doubt, try to lay it at her door.

'Good,' Davies said. 'Anything else to report? Things okay at home?'

Her new boss's cool manner had never encouraged Shona to confide in him but, with Rob's trial ahead, was this the moment to test the water over exactly how much practical support she could expect? She'd need time off to go to the Old Bailey, and wanted to make sure she was around to support Becca.

'Well, sir—' Shona began, but Davies cut her short.

'Talk to your police federation rep if you're in difficulty.'

It felt like a tribal division had formed between those officers who supported her – her own team – and those, like Detective Superintendent Davies and Sergeant Graham, who believed she was irrevocably tarnished by Rob's forthcoming trial, and her allegations of sexual assault against her former boss in London, DCI Delfont, that were currently under consideration by the CPS. They hated disloyalty more than they hated corruption. Shona knew she couldn't blink, and she wouldn't back down. Her record as an officer would demonstrate her true character. All she wanted to do now was get on with her job.

'Keep me updated,' Davies said stiffly, and ended the call.

At least Shona had her answer. When the chips were down, Davies's support would amount to absolutely zero.

–

That afternoon, it soon transpired that Shona did not need to worry about a local backlash or excessive press attention over police actions. There was only one circus in town, and that was Lady Lucy Douglas.

The Douglas family arrived like movie stars at a film premiere. Lady Lucy wore designer Wellington boots and a floaty dress beneath a fitted estate tweed jacket, as if she'd just exited backstage at Glastonbury. Her blonde hair flowed around her shoulders and her subtle make-up hinted at effortless glamour. With the earl at her shoulder, she looked every inch the star she clearly believed she was.

The media surged towards her, but Sergeant Graham and the local cops maintained order. There were no faces in the crowd that Shona recognised from the rewilding group.

A long table, faced by rows of chairs, was set up in the largest dining room. To a packed audience of ranked photographers and TV cameras, Shona gave her statement and the earl, sat next to her, thanked the police for their speedy conclusion of the case. Lady Lucy, on the earl's other side, was asked how she felt.

'It's been hell. I'm just so relieved my son survived,' she whispered, clutching his arm. Alexander Douglas patted his mother's hand and smiled reassuringly at her, and an eruption of flashes momentarily blinded Shona.

The story had everything. A glamorous former model who'd married into the aristocracy and her clean-cut

American son cheating a bullet – all set against the landscape of the estate, wild and rugged and romantic. Nicola Baird would be watching on TV at home. Shona felt a sneaking satisfaction that she'd been so comprehensively upstaged. The earl must have thought the same.

As an afterthought, he said, 'Of course, we send Mrs Baird our best wishes for a speedy recovery and hope to welcome her back to the Langdale estate as our guest, real soon.'

Shona wondered if the earl's generosity would extend to the Elliot girls. Would the Douglas family treat them as charitably? That was a question for later. For now, she was relieved that Lady Douglas's presence had deflected tough questions from the media about how the gunman escaped the moor in the first place, and why the police had taken five days to find the suspect, who was right under their noses. It wasn't excessive, as cases went, she would argue. But perhaps Shona's competing concerns over the recovery of Lilly Scott, whose family still hadn't been traced, had made it feel longer.

While the earl remained to shake hands with as many in the room as possible, Cousin Jack cleared a path for Lady Douglas. The earl soon followed. Outside, there were calls for more pictures. Lucy Douglas and her son obliged, but Jack hung back, smiling ruefully and shaking his head.

'Not joining them?' Shona said as they stood in the doorway.

'I'm more of a background kind of guy,' he smiled. 'No question who the best Douglas brand promoter is.'

Shona watched the former model run through a variety of poses and subtly manoeuvre her son for the cameras. Couldn't argue with that. Lady Lucy knew all the tricks, and commanded attention wherever she went. At the far side of the car park, the dig students stretched on tiptoe and filmed the scene with their phones. Even they weren't immune to the glamour that Lucy Douglas provided.

Dr Armstrong stood beside his Land Rover. His eyes met Shona's, but he hurried away. The blankness of his expression made the hairs on the back of her neck prickle. What on earth was he up to? A moment later, she saw the Elliot girls and Becca among the students.

Grace Elliot climbed onto the Land Rover. Shona started forward, wanting to stop her. It was unclear what the girl's intention was, but something in the grim set of her face alerted Shona that trouble was coming.

The crush of press still filled the car park. Murdo was nearer the Land Rover. Shona tried to catch his attention, but he had his back to her, talking with two Specials who were trying to clear the exits.

'My father is innocent. My father is innocent!' Grace cried from the Land Rover's roof.

For a single beat, there was silence. The journalists, photographers and camera crews turned like a field of sunflowers towards this fresh opportunity. Lady Douglas frowned at the interruption.

Shona took advantage of the confusion to push through the crowd. It was clear from Alexander Douglas's expression that he did not want a public run-in with the daughters of the man charged with his attempted murder. He took his mother's elbow and steered her back inside The Douglas Arms. When some journalists tried to follow, the door was firmly closed, but all the attention was now on Grace Elliot.

'My father is innocent, and we'll be campaigning for his release.'

She was tall, and well-muscled from her farm work, and stood like a modern-day Joan of Arc, in jeans and T-shirt, fist raised. The students formed a tight ring around the Land Rover, preventing anyone from getting near. Dr Armstrong had vanished.

Murdo reached the front of the crowd first. He held out a hand and said something to Grace that Shona didn't catch. The girl ignored him. Two Specials were close behind, ready to assist. Murdo gave Shona a look of enquiry as to whether he should proceed, but she shook her head. The last thing she wanted was footage of Ben Elliot's distraught daughter being manhandled by the police. Let her get it out of her system. Lady Douglas would still take the top-news spot.

'But today I'm also speaking up for someone else,' Grace continued. 'Someone who can no longer speak for themselves.'

Shona frowned, an icy hand on her spine. 'Today, we're announcing a crowdfunding campaign to find the last Girl in the Glen,' Grace said.

Whatever Shona had been expecting, it wasn't this. Becca had mentioned Grace's reaction to the discovery of the 'reiver child', as they had at first believed her to be: she'd felt connected to the girl by the Elliots' own reiver roots. It seemed Grace had taken things even further by revealing it was Lilly Scott who'd been found. Becca might have let something slip, but only one person could have confirmed it.

Bloody Armstrong.

The journalists looked at each other. Everyone in Scotland knew that phrase and what it meant. Shona almost heard an audible bump as the earl and Lady Douglas slipped down the news agenda.

As a clamour of shouted questions engulfed the car park, the students began passing out leaflets. Shona reached over the shoulder of a photographer in front of her and took a sheet. It showed the picture of Lilly Scott, with her blonde plaits, and Olivia Thomson, dark hair held firmly back by a pink headband, so familiar from the newspapers at the time of their disappearance. Beneath was a link to a website and JustCause, a charity crowd-funding platform.

Questions were pouring in from all sides, but Shona ignored them, as the Specials pushed back the journalists nearest her.

'Grace. Get down. Now,' Shona barked.

When the girl hesitated, Shona grabbed the wing mirror, put her foot onto the front tyre and hauled herself onto the bonnet. Dr Armstrong is behind this, she thought, and he's paying my dry-cleaning bill. She smoothed back her hair and turned to face Grace, still defiant on the roof.

'Grace,' she said, leaning as close to the girl as possible. 'Your dad's in jail. What happens to your sisters and the farm when Social Services see this fracas on telly?'

The girl flinched. It was a low blow, but the fastest way to get her safely down and out of the media's glare.

'I won't arrest you if you come down now,' Shona said, and held out her hand.

Grace dropped into a crouch on the roof, her face level with Shona's, and she thought the girl might spit at her.

Instead, Grace said, 'My father wasn't on the moor when Langdale was shot, and he didn't poach the estate's deer. It had broken its leg. He put it out of its misery and gave the meat to a widow with kids, instead of it just being burned. You're taking the Douglases side.'

'I'm taking no one's side,' Shona said. She felt all eyes in the car park on her, and heard the whirr and click of cameras. 'This is not the way to deal with your father's arrest, or to help the Girls in the Glen and their families. You're only making things worse for them.' John Maxwell's name would be resurrected, once again on people's lips, ambushing the surviving families on screen and in print in a way that could only twist the knife in their hearts.

'We'll see,' said Grace. She turned, and before Shona could stop her, she jumped from the back of the Land Rover and disappeared into the crowd of students, with Flora and Ashley close behind.

Murdo was on the radio, sending Sergeant Graham and the local cops after the girls, but Shona put her hand on his shoulder as she climbed down, and shook her head.

'Let them go. Pointless chasing them over the moor.' She put her mouth close to his ear so they wouldn't be overheard in this bear pit of journalists. 'That conniving, sleekit little shit Armstrong put Grace up to this. He's the one with questions to answer.'

'Want me to pick him up?' Murdo said.

'Aye. I do,' Shona replied. 'Put him in a wagon. Get him down to Dumfries police office. Arrest him if you have to.'

There was little she could charge him with, beyond a minor public order offence that was unlikely to stick, but he'd pissed on her chips, and she wanted to return the favour. She needed to know, and quickly, what else he might have planned.

The earl's Range Rover pulled out of the car park and the remaining media turned her way.

'Becca!' Shona roared in a way that stopped her daughter in her tracks. The girl stood with her arms folded, a familiar, obstinate pose, as her mother marched up to her.

'Did you know about this?' Shona demanded once they'd pushed through the press and Jack Douglas had admitted them to the cool, tiled hallway of the pub. The students appeared to be playing a minor role, and the Elliot girls weren't nearly web-savvy enough to have come up with a crowdfunding campaign on their own. Her daughter had volunteered with environmental groups and counted a few dyed-in-the-wool activists as friends in the past.

Becca bit her lower lip, but she remained defiant. 'I found Lilly, didn't I? I've a responsibility to help find Olivia.'

'Whoever put that idea into your head?' Shona said, although she already knew the answer. Bloody Armstrong.

'Her mum's going to die,' Becca said, tears shining in her eyes. 'What if it was me? You'd want to find me, wouldn't you?'

A lump was working its way up Shona's throat. 'Come here,' she said.

If only Becca knew how often that thought had occurred to Shona, over and over again, since the revelation that it was a modern burial.

Becca stepped forward, and Shona put her arms around her daughter's rigid body.

'It's not your responsibility,' Shona said quietly into her daughter's hair. 'Leave it to me. I'm a police officer and, more importantly, I'm your mum. I'm telling you, it's not your job to fix this. Leave it to me.'

Becca's posture softened, and she leaned against her mother and sobbed, but she soon pulled back and wiped her eyes with the heel of her hand.

'If I hadn't uncovered Lilly, maybe it would be different,' Becca said. 'But, if I don't do what I can to help… when I go to uni… every time I pick up a trowel it'll be like there's this other wee girl following me saying, *I'm waiting for you. Come and find me.*'

Shona swallowed hard, smoothing her hands down her daughter's arms as she fought the urge to curse Dr Armstrong out loud for everything he'd done. Becca didn't need to hear that. Shona and Armstrong would have their own reckoning. But Shona knew what it was to be haunted by past wrongs. The urge that drove you to do everything in your power to lessen others' pain. Asking Becca to come home would be pointless. In that way, she was her mother's daughter.

Instead, she said, 'You understand it may not be possible to find Olivia Thomson?'

'I know, but I have to try. We need to give her a proper funeral.'

Shona pulled her daughter close again. There was a week left on the university dig. Any money raised would go to a professional archaeology team. There was time to look at other courses for Becca. Or perhaps Dr Armstrong would no longer be in post once Shona had finished with him.

'Be careful,' she said. 'I'm not far away. Call me anytime, even if it's just for a wee chat.'

Becca nodded.

Outside, Murdo lingered nearby. The car park had cleared, except for Dr Armstrong's Land Rover and a few students. Becca went to join them and cast a last watery smile back at her mother.

'Cat's out of the bag then,' Murdo said, with typical understatement.

Shona visualised the evening news and tomorrow's newspaper headlines.

'Out of the bag, clawing the furniture and about to shit in the petunias,' Shona replied grimly. At that point, Shona's phone buzzed, and she took it from her suit jacket pocket. Detective Superintendent Davies's name flashed up, right on cue.

As she made to answer it, Shona jutted out her chin towards the moor. 'Murdo.'

Murdo followed her gaze, towards the slight figure of Cameron Armstrong, who was walking down the single-track road that passed the pub. He swung his arms, relaxed and serene, fishing his Land Rover keys from his pocket. When he saw Shona, he stopped.

'You know what to do,' Shona said to Murdo, and turned away to answer the call.

Chapter 18

Shona left Cameron Armstrong to sweat in the cells at Loreburn Street police office. He'd be released after twelve hours, unless Shona had grounds to authorise extending his detention. She was fine with letting him go at four a.m. He could fight the nightclub drunks for a taxi and make his own way back to the campsite. She hoped it cost him a packet.

Shona sat in her office and scrolled through the news websites, trying not to wince at the headlines. Detective Superintendent Davies had delivered the tongue lashing she'd expected when he'd spoken to her but, much to his irritation, even he couldn't lay Grace's announcement at her door. The press office at Kilmarnock HQ issued a brief statement confirming the identification of Lilly Scott's remains and appealing for anyone with information relating to the Girls in the Glen case to come forward.

Thirty years was a long time. Memories faded, witnesses died. With John Maxwell caught and jailed, even though he'd gained national status as a bogeyman, the story had long ago slipped from front-page news to surface occasionally in true-crime documentaries and the odd podcast.

But Olivia Thomson was still out there. Her mother made a powerful appeal on the evening news for anyone with information, who'd perhaps concealed it for personal reasons, to come forward and make amends. Davies reiterated to Shona that until that happened, he wouldn't formally reopen the case, and if he did, it would go to another detective. Shona hoped the publicity might also help to trace Lilly's surviving family and give her, at least, a proper funeral.

She took a sip of her coffee and opened the JustCause crowdfunding page.

Detective Superintendent Davies thought he could bully her, but he was wrong. She'd worked for some right vicious bastards who took pleasure in humiliating their colleagues, particularly female officers, and one DCI in particular whose cruelty and hatred had been less evident on the surface, but whose true nature had been revealed by the bravery of his victims.

The crowdfunding page had a link to Dr Armstrong's profile. It was more detailed than the two-line blurb which appeared on the website of the University of Glasgow's Archaeology Department.

Shona leaned forward across her desk and called through her open office door to where Murdo sat in the far corner of the CID room. He'd commandeered the remaining contents of the Krispy Kreme doughnuts box that Shona had brought as a small thank you for the team's work on the arrest. It was Friday night. Once they'd dealt with Armstrong, she'd take them all to the pub. When Murdo looked up, she angled her laptop towards him.

'You seen this?' she said.

He wiped the sugar from his fingers and narrowed his eyes. Then he got up from his desk and came over to study the web page.

'Did you know Cameron Armstrong was ex-military?' Shona said.

'Nope.' Murdo scrolled to the bottom of the screen.

'He told me he'd worked in Bosnia in 2013, as an archaeologist,' Shona said. 'And Becca mentioned he was with the UN, gathering evidence for war crimes. But I wasn't aware he'd previously been an infantryman with the Royal Highland Fusiliers... shit.'

Shona looked at Murdo and saw he'd made the leap, too.

'Darren Porter,' he said. 'Armstrong's about the right age to have served with him.' Murdo looked at her, his face full of questions. 'You don't fancy Armstrong for the shooting, do you? Were you no' with him?'

'I was.' The irony that she was the archaeologist's alibi wasn't lost on Shona. He'd already played her over the Girls in the Glen. But what if that was just a distraction from a deeper deception? 'I can't swear he didn't leave the dig around the time Nicola Baird was shot. It's too much of a coincidence that his former mucker in the army, whom we can't locate, has been in the frame from the get-go.'

'Where does this leave us with Ben Elliot?' Murdo said. His face returned to a careful neutral, but this spark of hope that they'd been wrong about his old friend, who'd already lost so much in his life, must be an enticing one.

Shona scrubbed her hands through her hair. The forensics were clear, and Elliot had confessed, but if the case was on a shoogly peg, she wanted to know sooner rather than later. She checked the clock. It was just before six p.m.

'Murdo, ask the team if anyone can stay for a bit. I want everything on Cameron Armstrong, from when he cut his first tooth to his preferred pizza toppings.'

There were groans from the office, but Shona promised that, besides drinks, she'd stand them all chips if they'd just give her another hour of their time to make sure their case had no leaks.

At seven p.m., Shona walked to the whiteboard in the CID room and stuck up two headshots. One was from Cameron Armstrong's profile page, the other was the police record shot of Darren Porter.

Kate and Ravi swivelled around in their chairs to face her, and the remaining civilian staff – who Murdo confirmed didn't have pressing family commitments – came forward to perch on desks or stand with their arms folded behind them.

'Armstrong and Porter served in the same regiment, at the same time, from 2001 to 2006,' Murdo began, reading from the notebook he held and tucking his shirt in with his free hand. 'But no hard evidence yet that they knew each other.'

Shona frowned. 'Absence of evidence isn't evidence of absence. Armstrong said that to me at the dig. If he's playing some sort of game with us, he's going to be very sorry.'

'He did his degree with a military bursary after he left,' Murdo continued. 'Worked his way quickly up the pecking order of speakers at conferences. Main undergraduate and master's degree interests were Iron Age and Roman forts, but his doctorate was on the Border reivers period, circa 1400–1700. He's from Glasgow originally.'

Another link to Darren Porter, Shona thought.

'There's only one problem,' Murdo continued. 'Cameron Armstrong doesn't exist.'

Shona stared at him over her reading glasses. The others looked up from behind their screens.

'Enlighten us, Murdo,' she said.

'I've an extract from the register under that name that lists an adoption, at age four. But Social Services and the National Records office say the file is sealed. We'd need a court order.'

'But we've a continuous timeline for him after that?' Shona said. 'No gaps?'

'No, it all checks out,' Murdo admitted.

'I can't see how that'll help,' Shona said and turned to the others. 'Armstrong said the earl was a history enthusiast and funded the dig. There's no indication they fell out over any of this. Any other potential motives come up for Cam Armstrong with either Alexander Douglas or Mrs Baird?'

'His Facebook page shows him at a pro-independence rally in George Square,' Ravi said. 'Along with half the city. But no arrests, and he's never been a person of interest to us.'

'Armstrong was smart enough to absent himself from Grace Elliot's performance today, so if he was involved with an extremist agenda, perhaps that's not surprising,' Shona said.

This brought them back to a political motive. Nicola Baird's crowing would have no end if she was proved to have been right all along. But Shona knew she'd have to follow this thread deeper into the labyrinth if she wanted to find the answer. Whatever lurked in there would have to be faced.

'Wait a minute,' she said. 'Are we overlooking the obvious? What if Cameron Armstrong's been masquerading as Porter? We're lacking a significant digital footprint on Darren, right?'

Vinny Visuals looked non-committal, but Chloe nodded in a way that signalled it was possible.

Shona stared at the two faces in the photographs in front of her. Armstrong was short and slim, with thick dark hair and a distinctive long, straight nose. Porter's face was rounder; he carried more meat. It would be difficult for one to pose as the other, even disguised in jeans and a hoodie.

She tapped the picture on the left with her pen. 'We're sure this is Darren Porter?'

Murdo returned to his desk and checked the screen. He nodded. 'They took the mugshot of Porter after the mace incident. It matches the social media images we have.'

'If we assume that Armstrong and Porter were mates from the army,' Ravi began, 'it's possible Armstrong knows a lot of personal details about his old pal. Maybe he cloned Porter's identity and created a false trail for us to follow.' He looked at Chloe and she nodded again in agreement. 'It's a matter of record that Porter carried out the mace attack at Nicola Baird's office. It doesn't explain why we can't find him now.'

'If Armstrong was involved in the shooting,' Kate said, 'I think it's more likely he facilitated Porter. Perhaps he had a weapon hidden among the dig equipment.'

Shona shook her head. 'The forensics are conclusive. The rifle you recovered from Ben Elliot's farmhouse matches the bullet removed from Nicola Baird's shoulder.'

Elliot's Barbour jacket also had tested positive for gunshot residue, but that might be explained away by the deer poaching incident.

'The archaeologists are camped at the farmhouse,' Kate said. 'Maybe Armstrong removed the rifle, passed it to Porter, and returned it later?'

'They found no DNA other than domestic contacts on the weapon,' Shona said.

'Armstrong is forensically aware,' Kate reminded them.

'What about the drone footage from the estate you were reviewing?' Shona asked.

'Still got a bit to get through,' she sighed. 'We've a couple who appear to be walkers, and two separate individuals we haven't IDed and who've not come forward to be eliminated.'

'Might any of them be Darren Porter?'

'It's possible, but the Southern Upland Way, a coast-to-coast path, runs nearby, and it attracts people from around the world. It's over two hundred miles long and gets even more remote beyond the Langdale estate. They might have just gone home without knowing what happened. Vinny enhanced the grabs. I can chase up the local cops who're showing them round.'

'What about Elliot's confession?' Ravi said.

That was the hump they couldn't get over. Elliot had means, motive and opportunity, but his behaviour still troubled Shona. The doctor who examined him in custody thought he was depressed, and his solicitor would likely arrange a mental health assessment before the case arrived in court.

'Well, let's see what Armstrong has to say about Porter.' Shona nodded to Kate and Ravi. 'You two are doing the interview.' Given the complication over Becca, she didn't want either Armstrong or his solicitor claiming she had a personal reason for pursuing this, even if it was true.

Chapter 19

Shona sat at a desk in Loreburn Street police office and plugged in her headphones. The screen in front of her showed the camera relay from the interview room, where Cameron Armstrong waited with the duty solicitor: a middle-aged man in a creased suit who kept looking at his watch. Opposite them, across the scuffed table, Kate arranged her notes.

Ravi repeated the caution that Armstrong had been given at the time of his arrest. Armstrong gave a slight shake of his head, then sat back and folded his arms.

Kate put it to Armstrong that he'd formed a disorderly crowd, contrary to common law.

'I wasn't present during the incident. I'd walked up the hill to assess the landscape, as part of my ongoing research into the Border reivers. What the students did was ill-advised,' Dr Armstrong said carefully. 'But I refute the idea that they were disorderly.'

Shona studied him. According to Cameron Armstrong's records, the Royal Highland Fusiliers had seen action during Operation Telic in Iraq. It was likely he'd had some interrogation training. After his initial impatience, his demeanour was neither passive nor aggressive. He made eye contact with Kate when required, but no more than that.

When asked if he knew Porter, there wasn't a flicker of recognition. Ravi pushed Darren's mugshot across the table. Armstrong looked at it and shook his head. The solicitor, alerted to the shift in questioning, asked for clarification on the offence he was being interviewed for.

Cameron looked directly up at the surveillance camera, and Shona felt the same unease that had assailed her on the moor, the sense that she was the one being watched.

'I want to talk to DI Oliver,' he said. 'Alone.'

Shona went down to the interview suite. Ravi and Kate stood in the corridor. Armstrong had dismissed his solicitor.

'You sure about this, boss?' Ravi said. Scots law required the corroboration of two police officers for anything said to be admissible as evidence.

'I'm sure,' Shona said.

'Well, Kate and I will be out here if he kicks off.'

'I think I can handle an archaeologist,' Shona said with a tight smile.

'Indiana Jones was an archaeologist, and look at the trouble he caused,' Ravi replied.

She appreciated his attempt to lighten the moment as much as his offer of backup.

Shona composed her expression, turned the handle and entered the room.

Armstrong glanced up, checking that the surveillance cameras were off. Then he said to Shona, 'Give your phone to DC Sarwar. I don't want what I'm going to say recorded. It might put me at risk of reprisals.'

Shona stared at him, but when it became clear he wasn't about to elaborate, she handed it over. Ravi, after giving her a last glance to check she was okay with the direction that events were taking, stepped out and closed the door behind him. There was an alarm button and a station full of cops. Armstrong, ex–military or not, wasn't daft enough to try anything violent.

'So what's your association with Darren Porter?' Shona began.

'None,' he replied flatly, and shrugged. 'There's over five hundred soldiers in a battalion. If you say we served at the same time, I'll take your word for it.'

'Why should I believe you?' Shona said. 'You weren't straight with me about the purpose of your excavations on Bield Moor, Dr Armstrong. And then you pulled that little trick at the press conference.'

'It was the students' idea. Remember, archaeologists are investigators, too. Once your forensics guys came, it didn't take them long. We need funds to find Olivia. The uni won't back a non–academic operation. The students came to me with the crowdfunding plan. I couldn't have stopped it.'

'You had no right to put Grace and Becca through what you did,' Shona said, anger bubbling up inside her.

'I'm sorry about that,' Dr Armstrong replied. 'It was never my intention. But Becca's tougher than you think. If she makes forensic archaeology her career, she's gonna have to deal with a lot worse. I know.'

It was no excuse, and she didn't need a lecture on her daughter's qualities.

'So,' Shona made a show of looking up at the wall clock. 'You claim you don't know Darren Porter? What is it you want to talk to me about?'

Armstrong took a breath and pressed his palms together before him on the table.

When he didn't answer, Shona said, 'My sergeant, DS O'Halloran, told me that when he took your statement, you knew a lot of things about the Girls in the Glen murders that aren't common knowledge.'

Cameron continued to stare at his hands, as if weighing up his reply.

When he still didn't answer, she said, 'And your birth record is sealed.' She watched him carefully.

'I knew you were good.' He smiled and pointed a pistol-like finger at her, then leaned forward on the table and his face became serious. 'I was sure you'd find out eventually.'

Shona studied him keenly. 'I'm listening.'

'I always knew I was adopted,' he began. 'I thought about it in my teens. Who were my parents? Why did they give me up? But I was busy with the army and then studies and my own life, and it didn't seem to matter. Then I married and became a father. It seemed like something was missing. I knew my parents were from southern Scotland. And I thought about my mother. I remembered the violence she suffered, and I thought, now I have something to give her. The chance of a happy family. A grandson.' He smiled ruefully.

'I found an address for her, from the early Nineties, and talked to a guy there who was really cautious. Maybe he thought I was a journalist. He passed on a message to her and she agreed to see me. She was polite, but I didn't feel the connection I'd hoped.'

He sighed. 'Perhaps I'd built it all up in my mind. How I could help her, rescue her from the past? When I asked about my father, if they were still in touch, she just stared at me. Then she told me. My birth name was John Cameron Maxwell.'

Dr Armstrong waited until he saw the recognition dawn in Shona's eyes.

'Your father was John Maxwell,' she said. 'The man convicted for the Girls in the Glen killings?'

'I thought about my dad for years, then I discovered he was a murderer.' He shook his head and smiled sadly. 'My birth mother believed I must've known, but I had no idea.'

'What did you think when you heard this?' Shona said.

Armstrong shrugged. 'She told me I was lucky I'd been adopted. If I'd grown up with him, he'd probably have killed me, too. I thought about all the times I'd lost my temper. The idea that I carry the genes of this man made me hate myself.' He began turning the cup of water before him in small circles on the table. 'It was my wife who helped me see I wasn't him. Your birth, your family name, these things don't define your identity. But perhaps it was the idea I might become him that really scared all the anger out of me.'

'What happened to your mother? Is she still around?'

Cam shook his head. 'I tried to stay in touch with her. She met my wife and son, but she wasn't interested. I noticed she didn't like to look at me. Perhaps I reminded her too much of the man, that monster, who did those unspeakable things, and who ruined so many lives. Then I heard she died. Heart attack. She was cremated, no grave. She had no other kids. Apart from me, and those terrible newspaper headlines, it's like she never existed.'

'So this is why you're here on Bield Moss?'

'I think that's what she really wanted. If she could have wiped out what happened to those women and wee girls, in exchange for her own life, she'd have gladly done it.'

'You should have been honest with me from the start,' Shona said.

'It's not the sort of thing you tell people, is it? My father was one of Scotland's most notorious serial killers.'

'Believe it or not, I'd have understood,' Shona said. She'd grown up without her violent father or addict mother in her life; her gran had brought stability. But she knew what it was like to be constantly looking over your shoulder. To live in a haunted present. He was on a mission, as much as she was, to lay to rest the ghosts of the past.

He acknowledged her words with a small nod.

'Does Olivia Thomson's mother know?' Shona said.

Armstrong shook his head. 'When she got in touch, it seemed like fate was giving me a chance to make amends. For my mother's memory, and to prove I'm not my father's son. When Mrs Thomson called me again recently and told me her cancer diagnosis, I knew time was running out.' He tilted his head to one side in question. 'So, will you help me?'

'My Super said I wouldn't be assigned the case, even if they reopened it,' Shona replied. 'And I can't get you unauthorised access to the files, if that's what you're asking.'

Cam made a theatrical show of denying that's what he'd implied.

'Another thing,' Shona said. 'I can't speak for Grace Elliot – although you should think very carefully about the pressure she'll be under at home – but I don't want Becca involved in this. She's a sixteen-year-old girl. She needs to experience the good in the world before she tackles the evil.'

'D'you not think what I'm doing is good?'

'You have your own reasons. I don't condemn them. But I do condemn your actions.'

They stared at each other until Armstrong gave way, lowering his chin in a gesture of atonement.

'Look,' he said, 'the archaeology is clear. We won't find Olivia Thomson where we're currently digging. There's a couple of geophysics anomalies on the far side of the moor I'd like to look at next, but a commercial company will do the excavation once we have funds. I'll operate as a consultant and lead archaeologist on the project. We'll keep you, or whoever has the case, informed.'

'Thank you,' Shona said.

–

Murdo had hung on at Cornwall Mount. He looked up as Shona came into the office.

'I've released Armstrong and sent him back to the campsite in a patrol car,' she said, dropping her car keys on the desk. 'You were right. He had some inside information.'

When Shona updated Murdo on Armstrong's history, he let out a low whistle.

'In the name of the wee man,' he said, shaking his head. 'Imagine finding that out.'

'Armstrong's been gathering evidence on the Girls in the Glen burials for years, under the guise of his Border reivers research,' Shona continued. 'That'll be why you picked up on stuff he shouldn't have known, when you took his statement at the dig.'

Shona often thought of Murdo as her 'walking Wikipedia' of local knowledge. Without him spotting this anomaly, and querying the sealed adoption file, they might not have uncovered Armstrong's true motives so quickly. And not knowing about them could also have potentially undermined Ben Elliot's arrest for the shooting. If the defence got a whiff there had been an unresolved line of enquiry, they might convince Elliot to withdraw his confession and submit a *not guilty* plea. Despite the strong forensics, sometimes all it took for a case to collapse was the introduction of doubt in a jury's mind.

'Well done, Murdo,' Shona said.

'Nae bother, boss,' Murdo said quietly, his eyes on the notes before him. He cleared his throat. 'What's happening with Rob's trial? It's due to start soon, isn't it?'

'Yes,' Shona replied, but didn't elaborate. She'd been ignoring Rob's calls recently, since they always seemed to end in a row.

'You'll be heading down to the Old Bailey then? Show of support, and all that?'

'It might be better if I'm at home, working hard as a police officer and running the B&B and supervising our child's home education,' Shona said, sifting through the paperwork on her desk, avoiding Murdo's gaze. 'Maybe it'll send a message to the jury that we're just ordinary folks, that we're not flush with cash. Underlines Rob's innocence. If he was guilty, where are the ill-gotten gains?'

Murdo was tactful enough not to mention Rob's gambling as a possible cash black hole. 'He'll want you there, boss.'

But was it what she wanted? Her presence was vital for Rob's credibility. A devoted father and husband, a police-officer wife who kept the public safe. The barrister had already said as much. But the closer the trial came, the harder it had become to supress the bitterness Shona felt towards her husband. He'd gotten himself into this mess by not keeping a close enough watch on what his team at the bank were up to, then choosing to turn a blind eye and take a payoff from directors, keen to hush up a financial scandal. If Rob was convicted, she'd be tarnished by association. If she walked away from him now, it would look like she was trying to save her own skin. Either way, she might lose everything: job, home, family.

When she didn't reply, Murdo said, 'The office won't go to the dogs if you're not here, you know.'

'Even with Ravi in charge?' Shona smiled.

'He'll no' be in charge – I will,' Murdo replied. 'You should go. Be nice when all this is behind you.' His smile was kind and genuine, and Shona appreciated the unshowy support he offered.

'The team's down the pub, waiting, boss,' he said, slipping on his jacket.

'Tell them I'll be five minutes,' Shona said.

When Murdo had gone, she took out her phone. There was no point in updating Detective Superintendent Davies. If he asked about Armstrong's arrest, she'd say the matter had been resolved. She'd agreed to Cam's request to keep his birth information quiet. No one beyond Murdo, Ravi, Kate and herself need know.

Shona's finger hovered over a contact name in her address book. After a final moment's reflection, she dialled, apologised for the late call and chatted for a few minutes.

–

Ravi was by the jukebox when she arrived at the pub. She signalled to the barman, who took her credit card off her and began issuing the promised drinks and baskets of chips, then she crossed to Ravi and joined him in studying the track list. When he asked about her interview with Cameron Armstrong, she repeated what she'd told Murdo and asked Ravi to keep it to himself.

'Aye, course,' Ravi said. 'Jeezo. That's the sort of thing that'd cost you a fortune in therapy.'

Shona pursed her lips in agreement. 'I heard you were off to Glasgow tomorrow,' she said.

Ravi nodded and smoothed a hand across his head. 'I'm desperate for a decent cut.'

To Shona, his hair appeared as impeccable as always.

'Having a spot of lunch anywhere nice?' Shona said.

Ravi looked at her and tried to fathom her interest. The boss was up to something.

'I hate eating alone,' he said, curious. 'Anywhere you'd recommend?'

'I was thinking your old boss might like to see how you've turned out.'

'DCI Paterson?'

'Always good to keep up with old friends.' Shona smiled. DCI Paterson, now head of the Homicide Review Group at the Historical Cases Unit, had agreed to offer some advice about the Girls in the Glen. It was a gamble on Shona's part, sending Ravi. He was a good officer and Paterson might decide to lure him back to the bright lights of Glasgow.

'Is the table booked?'

'At two p.m. at The Ubiquitous Chip. I'm afraid I won't be joining you.' Shona didn't want Detective Superintendent Davies to know she was in touch with Paterson. Police Scotland was a small pond, and someone was bound to spot them lunching together. She also really needed to check in on Becca and there wouldn't be time, with a round trip to Glasgow. 'But lunch is on me.'

'Belter.'

The Girls in the Glen case wasn't strictly Paterson's remit. It was solved, the verdict unanimous. If there had been any doubt, the jury could have gone for a third verdict – a peculiarity of Scottish law, *not proven*, which resulted in acquittal for the accused and a lifetime of not knowing for the victim's family. That always felt like an accusation for a police officer: if you'd done your job better, we'd know for sure. At least the officers working what must have been a tough case were spared that. The killer had gone to jail, giving the families some small measure of peace. But for Olivia Thomson's mother that peace would only come with her daughter's recovery and burial, and Shona planned to do everything she could to make sure that happened.

Chapter 20

On Saturday morning, Shona woke with a headache. She'd only had one drink with the team last night, as she'd needed to drive back to High Pines in Kirkness, half an hour away. She didn't like to admit that – with the B&B closed and her salary servicing their debts – she couldn't really afford, in addition to Ravi's forthcoming lunch expenses, the eighty quid it would have cost her for a taxi home, as well as another back to collect the car in the morning. Even if she'd wanted to take the bus, none ran into Dumfries from the village at the weekend. On top of drinks for the team, and probably a curry, last night's end-of-case celebration costs would soon have mounted up. She self-diagnosed the headache as due to a lack of caffeine, and headed downstairs to the kitchen.

She swallowed a large cup of coffee, a vitamin pill and two painkillers, before heading back upstairs and pulling on her running gear for the first time in a week. The floor-to-ceiling bedroom windows looked out over Kirkness shore. Shona saw it was slack tide, and the sea covered the mudbanks of the estuary, peaceful and impossibly blue. A few yachts from the sailing club were preparing to leave for a day's sailing when the tide turned. She calculated that by the time she'd done the five miles to Knockie Point and back, they'd be well on their way.

She ran hard out, feeling some of the tension of the week slipping away, then jogged back along the seafront. The shooting case file would soon go to the Procurator Fiscal. She'd set the wheels in motion with DCI Paterson. In one more week, Becca would be home. That brought her back to Rob. They hadn't been in touch for a couple of days, beyond a few stilted goodnight messages, and part of her was happy to keep him at a distance.

Outside the lifeboat station, Tommy stood with a couple of other volunteers, talking to tourists who'd come to browse the shop and see the *Margaret Wilson*, named for the Solway Martyr, a young woman drowned for her beliefs.

Tommy waved, then his hands motioned a 'T' symbol, but she shook her head.

'Sorry, Tommy,' she called. 'I'm going up to see Becca.'

The tree-cutting teams had cleared more roads, and the journey was smoother, but delays were still possible, and she wanted to have at least a couple of hours up there before she headed back.

He gave her a thumbs-up. She'd be in tomorrow for their regular Sunday morning training session and she could update him on all that had happened at Bield Moor since he'd been there – although, since he hadn't texted to ask, she had a feeling that Freya, the barmaid from The Douglas Arms, was keeping him up to speed.

Before she left, Shona called Rob. It had to be done. Becca would ask what was happening. Rob told her that his barrister felt everything was going as planned. He was looking forward to her coming to London and suggested booking a restaurant with friends. It irritated her that Rob was his usual upbeat self. Didn't he realise that he might go to prison? Then, as he talked about visiting places in

London where they'd first fallen in love, she wondered if it this was his diversionary tactic to avoid talking about the trial. Either way, she felt drained by their conversation and wrapped it up with the excuse that she needed to get up to see Becca.

Two hours later, she pulled in at the small car park below Bield Moss. A couple of journalists and a film crew were packing up their kit, so she sat in the Audi and avoided their gaze, in case they recognised her. Shortly afterwards, the vehicles left.

The campsite at the Elliot farm was empty, the tents laced up and silent. Shona saw Ben's daughters in the distance, all three carrying heavy buckets of feed up to the sheep. Ashley stopped to rest her arms. Flora looked back and shouted for her to hurry up, but Ashley turned and stomped off.

Shona took the bag of clean clothes and other items she'd brought for Becca out of the car, laced up her boots, and headed up the track.

The day was warm, despite the stiff breeze. The shadows of a few high clouds raced across the moorland. Like the view of the sea Shona had just left, it was a place of farness; rolling horizons with few verticals. Above, she heard a lark, an intense, burbling stream of piercing sound. The heather's bloom, which only lasted a couple of weeks, was at its peak: an intense swathe of purple among the golds and browns, and its faint, musky scent came and went in the air.

Shona felt the stiffness in her Achilles tendons as she climbed the last half mile to the excavation site, and wondered at the wisdom of this morning's burst of exercise *at her advanced age*, as Becca might say. Forty was nothing. Cramp gripped her calf muscle, and she stepped off the track, looking for a place to sit down, but found herself in a fissure of boggy ground between the stiff brushes of uncut heather over a metre tall. Water oozed over her boots and she slipped sideways.

'Dammit.' It was almost impossible to distinguish solid ground. She grasped a brittle heather stalk and hauled herself to her knees. Moss water stained her jeans. She clambered back onto the path, her footprints sucked down by the moss.

Ahead, a couple of familiar figures had emerged from a side track and were walking up the hill. The Earl of Langdale turned to DC Kate Irving. Then he stopped, pulled her close and stroked her blonde hair back from her face. Kate gazed up at him, returning his smile.

Shona was frozen to the spot. They were obviously unaware of her presence.

Slowly, Alexander Douglas leaned in and kissed Kate passionately on the mouth.

So, this was what Kate was doing with her day off. She felt an intense burst of irritation at her DC. The earl was a witness in the case Kate was working. It would be professional misconduct to embark on a personal relationship with him. She was putting her career at the gravest risk.

When Shona reached the dig, the earl was in conversation with Cam, and Kate stood on the far side of the excavation site, gazing out at the moor.

The nearest students greeted Shona. They had all witnessed her attempt to talk Grace Elliot down from the Land Rover yesterday, and heard of Dr Armstrong's detention, but when Becca clambered out of her trench and hugged her mother, they returned to their trowelling and said nothing.

'Everything okay?' Shona said.

'What happened to you?' Becca eyed her mother's wet jeans.

'Fell in the bog,' Shona said.

Becca snorted with laughter. 'Were you taking *a shortcut*?' She motioned an inverted commas sign in the air. 'Even I've learned not to step off the sheep-tracks.'

Shona could hardly reply that she'd wanted to sit down for a wee rest without provoking greater ridicule, so she asked how the digging was going.

'Great. We've getting some pottery and metalwork from horse harnesses,' Becca replied.

'Great,' Shona agreed, unaware precisely where these items sat on the scale ranging from a bit of rock to the Holy Grail. 'What did the journalists want?'

'Just to interview Dr Armstrong about the crowd-funding,' Becca said lightly. 'He said only he should talk to the media now.'

'That's sensible,' Shona said. 'So how far are you from your 10k target?'

'Oh, we made the target in the first couple of hours,' Becca said. 'There's nearly fifty thousand pounds in the fund now.'

'You're joking.' Shona was torn between pride at her daughter's success and frustration at how hard she'd have to lobby for that amount of cash for a similar operation. Pride won over. 'Well done. You can leave the rest to Dr Armstrong.' Shona sensed that an explicit warning to keep away from the archaeologist would have no effect. But now he had the cash, perhaps he wouldn't need the students. 'What will happen to any money left over, assuming the project's successful?'

'Cam's hoping to start a forensic archaeology course at the university,' Becca replied. 'And perhaps work with

Police Scotland on other cold cases. He knows that pathologist friend of yours who wants me to join her fencing team. If I get a uni place. Slasher Sue?'

'Oh,' Shona said, eyebrows raised. She couldn't fault the man's ambition. If successful, it would bring both funds and glory to his department. But then she remembered their conversation last night, in the interview room at Loreburn Street, and what was driving him. No matter how many cold cases he solved, how many lost victims he reunited with their remaining family, he'd never escape the legacy of the DNA he carried. She wouldn't condemn him for trying.

Becca was watching her intensely, ready to judge her mother's reaction.

'That's an interesting proposal,' Shona said,

'I'm glad you think so, Mum.' Becca stepped forward and hugged her again, and Shona was surprised to feel that some broken connection, bound up in the complex geography of her daughter's approval, seemed to have been reforged.

Becca gave her a last squeeze and stepped back. 'I'd better get back to work. I think I'm nearly down to the natural on this context.'

'Is that good?' Shona said, peering at the bottom of the trench.

'It means I've hit the undisturbed ground, and there's no more archaeology to be done,' Becca said.

Where her daughter was concerned, Shona thought this was good news. The sooner she was off this moor and back home at High Pines, the better.

Shona left the bag of clean clothes and snacks in the small marquee where other students were washing finds.

The Earl of Langdale greeted her warmly, pumping her hand up and down in his firm grasp. Dr Armstrong's welcome was a careful neutral, the intimacy of their previous conversation banished as firmly as if it had happened behind the seal of the confessional. As he excused himself, the earl took Shona's arm and led her away from the students.

'DI Oliver,' the earl began, 'while I fully support Dr Armstrong's work, there's a little local unease that the area's back in the spotlight for all the wrong reasons.'

He was right. This sensational case had quickly eclipsed the success in apprehending Nicola Baird's shooter.

'I'm a little concerned myself,' he continued, 'that it will damage our revival as an upmarket tourist destination.' His handsome face was earnest. He likely had little idea about Dr Armstrong's personal mission. Shona wondered if he'd now been primed by his mother, or Cousin Jack, to mount a charm offensive to protect the Douglas brand. She wasn't sure what he expected her to do about it.

'I appreciate your concern, sir,' she said. 'I'm as keen as you are to see this resolved quickly. Dr Armstrong has assured me he also intends to keep his search for Olivia Thomson as low-key as possible, in order to deter unauthorised trespass at potential sites.'

'Thank you, ma'am,' he said. 'I'm sure you'd like to see a prosperous local economy, too, given the beneficial effect it has on crime rates.'

'Yes, that's always a good thing,' Shona agreed.

'I'd love you to come back and stay at The Douglas Arms as our guest. A little personal thank you for your diligence,' he smiled. 'I understand from Jack that you and your husband run a boutique B&B. We have some excellent deals on our estate produce. I'm sure we can be of service to one another.'

His tone was light, his smile convincing. Perhaps it was his accent, combined with his choice of phrase, that made it sound like a line from a gangster movie and a bribe that she had no intention of accepting.

'That's very kind,' Shona said in as polite and evasive a manner as she could muster.

'Good,' the earl seemed satisfied. 'I'd better go check if the students are making off with any of my ancestors' treasure,' he said and excused himself.

Shona crossed to where Kate stood.

Since Shona had arrived, the earl and Kate had orbited the excavation site and hadn't so much as looked in each other's direction. Shona affected surprise that Kate was here on her day off. She explained in fulsome detail how her previous visit to Bield Moss had reawakened her interest in upland landscapes.

They made small talk about the dig's progress, then Shona cleared her throat. 'I walked up from the car park,' she began, 'and I saw you and the earl.'

Kate looked as if she was about to deny everything, but her blush gave her away.

'You think he's too posh for me, is that it?' Kate said, defiantly. 'It didn't stop you marrying Rob, did it?'

Shona stared at her. It was known among the team that Shona had grown up on a Glasgow housing scheme, Garthamlock, notorious for its poverty, social problems and high crime rate. Rob's family owned a well-respected and prosperous firm of auctioneers based in Dumfries, now run by Rob's older brother, Sandy. When Shona and Rob met, he was a rising star at Milton McConnell merchant bank and she was rising equally fast through the

City of London Police. Both had their eyes on where they were going. It didn't matter where they'd come from.

At the sight of Shona's expression, Kate's blush deepened. 'I'm sorry... ma'am,' she stammered.

Shona took a step closer and pointed a finger at Kate. 'Listen to me, lady. I'm giving you fair warning. Conducting a relationship with a witness leaves you open to the disciplinary charge of *an abuse of power in a public office.*'

'Xander isn't a vulnerable individual,' Kate countered.

'If Elliot's solicitor or the fiscal hears about it, it's you that'll be vulnerable,' Shona snapped. 'And don't think I'll turn a blind eye because you're a woman and not some jack-the-lad constable. Sort yourself out, Kate. Decide what's important to you, because if you wreck your career there'll be no second chances.'

Shona turned on her heel and set off back across the dig site to the tent and hugged her daughter goodbye, making her promise to call or at least text her tomorrow, if she could get a signal.

As Shona made her way back to the car, Murdo's name lit up her phone screen. With Ravi and Kate off, it was his turn to provide CID cover. Unless there was a major incident, Shona was rarely called at the weekend, leaving her free to help Rob at the B&B and carry her lifeboat pager when she was in the village.

'Hi Murdo. What's up?'

'Nothing to worry about, boss. Just letting you know that Ben Elliot's asked to see me. I'm going over to the jail on Monday.'

'Did he say what it was about?'

'Nope.'

'I think it's best if I tag along,' Shona said.

'You think he might withdraw his confession?'

'Do you?'

There was a pause, and she heard Murdo sigh. 'Surely his solicitor or the fiscal would be in touch if that was the case?'

Elliot's statement had been brief. He'd walked to the shoot, lain low in the heather, fired at the earl, hit Mrs Baird by accident, and in the resultant confusion slipped away and returned to the farm.

'Aye, you're probably right,' Shona conceded. 'Let's see what he has to say and take it from there.'

She told Murdo about the kiss she'd witnessed on the moor. 'D'you think Kate's likely to get herself into trouble with the earl?' She was talking like an old woman, she thought, with her *into trouble*.

'Kate's a sensible lass,' Murdo replied. 'The earl's a handsome fella. I might be tempted to let him kiss me an' all.'

Shona snorted. 'Stop. That's not an image I want in my head.'

'I think the days when his lordship had rights over the local lassies are long gone, although young Xander could cut a swathe, if he fancied it.'

'I think that's more in Jack Douglas's line,' Shona said.

'Well, he's no' my type, so I'll take your word for it,' Murdo said, then his tone grew more serious. 'I'll have a word if you like, but with the case about to be handed over to the Procurator Fiscal, technically, Kate could argue any resulting relationship doesn't affect her work.'

Murdo was right. Kate's love life wasn't Shona's business beyond operational matters. But she still thought Kate was risking her professional reputation and chance of promotion.

'Murdo, what title does the wife of an earl have?'

'Well, the old earl's wife was Lady Douglas, Countess of Langdale.'

A countess? Kate would love that. But Lady Lucy was sure to have something to say about the matter, and Shona wouldn't wish her as a mother-in-law on anyone.

Chapter 21

Shona sat on the kitchen worktop and swung her legs, which Rob usually told her off for, then put the empty instant porridge bowl in the sink next to last night's supper plate, to be washed later. Dressed in shorts and a T-shirt, she was ready to head out for the regular Sunday morning lifeboat exercise.

The local radio station was running the Girls in the Glen story, and inviting people to phone in with their comments and opinions. She'd listened in the vague hope that someone might call with fresh information, but it soon became a conveyor belt of people wanting to bring back the death penalty or who thought they were entitled to a rebate in council tax since students were now doing the police's job for them. She turned it off.

Shona's phone buzzed. She glanced at the screen as she answered. 'Did you bring me a doggy bag?' she asked.

'Better than that, boss,' Ravi replied. 'I've brought you a wee present from DCI Paterson.'

Shona jumped down from the worktop. 'Where are you? Can you come over?'

The CID office would be empty, but it was probably best avoided if she wanted this clandestine foray into the Girls in the Glen case to remain between Ravi and herself.

'You're in luck. Martin's at his mum's in Carlisle. I'm all yours.'

'Come for lunch,' she said.

'That means bring lunch, doesn't it?'

'Probably best,' Shona admitted. There were fancy crisps in the cupboard, but that was about it. Rob had been gone over a week and his home-made frozen meals were running low. 'I'm out with the lifeboat this morning, but I'll be back by twelve thirty.'

'Okay, see you later.'

Shona jogged down the hill. Tommy had the boat-hall doors open. She went to the crew room and put on her dry suit. When she returned, the *Margaret Wilson* had been backed to the water's edge on the slipway opposite the lifeboat station, and she climbed aboard.

She spent the next two hours helping to train a couple of new members with the station's 35 kg dummy, dubbed 'Dead Fred', to simulate the shared recovery of a person in the water. Then they ran through the equipment on board, and Shona demonstrated how to enter the water and reboard the D-class lifeboat safely at various points around the inflatable rib.

She left them washing down the *Margaret Wilson* under the keen eye of Tommy and the village postman Callum, who'd been a trainee himself when Shona had first arrived in the village a couple of years ago, but was now one of their most useful crewmates.

Ravi's car was parked on the shore road. She let herself in by the garden gate and climbed up the steep steps to find him sat in a deckchair on the sheltered kitchen terrace. He wore tailored grey shorts, a pressed, white linen shirt and flip-flops. His eyes were closed, black Oakley sunglasses perched on his head which was tilted back, and his arms hung loosely by his side.

'All right for some,' she said.

Without opening his eyes, he raised his hands. One contained a carrier bag full of food, the other a memory stick.

'Aye, right enough,' Shona laughed. 'Come on in.'

Shona left him in the kitchen and went for a quick shower. When she returned, the dishes were done, and two plates of cold meats, cheeses, olives, salad, and a basket of bread sat on the table. She felt her stomach rumble as she reached into the fridge and poured them each a single glass of chilled white wine. Just the one, since Ravi was driving and she was on call for the lifeboat.

'Nice haircut, by the way,' Shona said. It was no different, as far as she could tell, but perhaps that was the mark of a good hairdresser.

'Cheers, boss.'

While they ate, Shona scanned the notes Ravi had printed out, marking some with the highlighter she'd borrowed from Rob's office across the hallway.

'Let's take our wine and coffee upstairs to the lounge,' she said when they'd finished eating and Shona had topped up their mugs from the cafetière.

Ravi walked to the deep curve of floor-to-ceiling windows that formed one wall of the room. 'Oh my God, you can see right down to the coast. Do your lifeboat pals just wave a flag when they need you, or do boats contact you direct?'

Shona tapped her RNLI pager, with its small LED screen and yellow button, which she'd placed next to her open laptop on the coffee table.

'There's a phone app, but most of us still like to carry one of these. If I get a shout, I'll have to go, so let's crack on.'

'Want me to walk you through the cases?' Ravi said and took out his notebook.

'Please.' Shona tucked her legs under her on the thick beige carpet by the coffee table, as Ravi sat on the corner sofa. She inserted the memory stick and opened the file, ready to check any points that came up, then turned her attention to Ravi.

'The first victim was eighteen-year-old Harriet Jackson,' Ravi began. 'From Keswick in the Lake District. She'd hitched her way to Gretna Green to work at the Famous Blacksmith's Shop.'

'Is that where she disappeared?'

'No. She became the girlfriend of the haulier, Jimmy Fraser, who'd picked her up when she was hitching. He worked above Langholm on a log lorry. She was last seen leaving his caravan at six p.m. on Saturday 9th October 1985, to walk to a local shop. He was interviewed but had a concrete alibi.'

'Where was her body recovered?'

'Shallow grave, here.' Ravi shuffled through the printed pages until he got to the map and pointed to an area of woodland north of the town. 'Found by a dog walker ten days later.'

Shona turned to a fresh page in her own notebook. 'Who's next?'

'Cindy Jardine, a forty-five-year-old sex worker. She disappeared off a street in Edinburgh on Friday 5th November 1985. Body found ten months later by workmen installing a field drain on the edge of Bield Moss in January '86.'

'And the third victim?'

'A tourist down from Glasgow,' Ravi replied. 'Last seen on the morning of Tuesday 19th December '85. Karen

Anderson, aged thirty. Her car was located on the edge of Bield Moss, where she'd gone for a walk. Her husband had some business in Langholm and when she didn't meet him for lunch, he raised the alarm. It had started to snow, and it was assumed she'd got lost. Her body was found the following spring, in April '86.'

Shona took a sip of coffee. 'And that brings us to the two girls.'

Ravi nodded, his face sombre. 'Olivia and Lilly, both aged seven. Disappeared on the night of Saturday 22nd February 1986. Lilly's father worked on the Langdale estate. It's believed they were taken from their beds during a sleepover at the family's cottage, next door to John Maxwell's, although they could have been lured outside.'

'And the three women whose bodies were recovered were all strangled with a rope ligature and stabbed?'

Ravi drained his mug, then nodded. 'The coppers on the case initially believed it was a Yorkshire Ripper scenario. Someone who travelled around. A lorry driver or salesman.'

'But John Maxwell was local.' Shona flicked back to the page of highlighted notes. 'How did he become the prime suspect?'

'He was questioned over Olivia and Lilly's disappearance, but the case was built on his personal knowledge of the deposition sites on, or close to, Bield Moss. He'd worked as a gamekeeper on the Langdale estate, but had been dismissed and the family were due to be evicted from their tied cottage next door to the Thomsons.' Ravi ticked the points off on his long fingers, the silver bracelets slipping down his arm to rest on his turned-back sleeves. 'The day Karen Anderson disappeared, Maxwell's car was seen parked nearby. When it was searched, they found a knife which forensics confirmed was the murder weapon, and the same type of twine used in tying up the victims. Finally, and crucially, he'd confessed about his little hobby to a third party, Eddie Graham, who's dead unfortunately, but was a keeper still working on the estate. His brother was a local police officer.'

'And John Maxwell obviously had previous for sexual assault and a history of violence?' Shona said.

Ravi nodded. 'It's not clear if his motive was sexual, due to the decomposition of those bodies that were eventually found, but the psychiatrist diagnosed him as having clear psychopathy, with violent revenge fantasies. Even after conviction, Maxwell talked of reprisals and killing those who had put him in jail.'

Shona frowned and tapped her finger against a line of text on the laptop screen. 'The motive for his attack on Lilly and Olivia was an ongoing dispute with the father, Alex Thomson.'

'Thomson called the police and tried to intervene a couple of times when Maxwell was battering the living daylights out of his wife.'

So far, this tallied with the picture Cam Armstrong had painted of his father and his own early memories of life before his adoption.

'What about the deposition sites?' Shona said.

'Marked on the plan,' Ravi said. 'Okay if I make some more coffee?'

'Sure,' Shona said, and handed him her mug.

Shona scrolled through the files on the laptop. She wasn't sure what she was looking for, other than anything that might reveal a previously unnoticed pattern to the burials, or an elaboration on his motives, something John Maxwell had refused to do. There was usually more to it than the label 'psychopathic murderer'. While many killers took pleasure in revisiting and detailing their crimes for anyone who'd listen, just as many revelled in their opacity, and clinical staff's unsuccessful attempts to unravel or categorise them.

She jotted down some notes, in case they prompted the undetected pattern to appear like a postcard image. A mountain view, a distinctive tree. Then all she'd have to do was find it. Pin the image on Google Maps and it would all be over: she'd have the location of the last, unrecovered victim.

She threw down her pen and lifted her near-empty glass of wine, rolling the stem between her fingers. The face of Olivia Thomson stared back at her from the file photograph, a collected and endlessly reproduced family snap memorable from posters, TV appeals for information and newspaper articles, like an image repeated forever in fairground mirrors. The round face with its pale, freckled skin, the dark hair, and pink headband.

'Where are you, Olivia?'

Shona ran through the search reports. Teams had combed Bield Moss and the surrounding glens for days, but found no sign of the girls. John Maxwell had been arrested in May 1986, soon after Karen Anderson's body was recovered. He'd grown up in Langholm, and was listed as a junior gamekeeper and agricultural labourer who'd worked seasonal jobs abroad in France and Germany on the grape harvests and fruit picking. The cursor on the screen hit the bottom of the page and stopped. Shona flicked through the sheets and then ran through the on-screen files again.

'This is all there is?' she said to Ravi as he returned and handed her the refilled mug.

He raised his eyebrows and let them fall back.

Forensics and the quality of the evidence weren't up to the mark required today, but it was important not to judge the past by the standards of the present. Even so, the case was weak, the jury probably swayed by horror and pity for the victims.

'Were there no other suspects?' Shona said. 'What did DCI Paterson have to say when you saw him yesterday?'

A worm of worry was working its way into Shona's mind. She'd expected Ravi's old boss to give him a verbal appraisal of the key points of the cases, which Shona could mine when required, not an illicit copy of the whole file.

'A few journalists have been on to him,' Ravi replied. 'It isnae his remit, as the Historic Cases Unit are all about the unsolved or not proven, but he's a belt-and-braces kinda guy, thought he should check it out. Plus, he's got a bit of time on his hands. Did you know his wife Liz left him? Frank's a lovely guy. I know people say it's hard being married to a cop, but I think she needs her head examined.'

'And?' Shona said, impatient with Ravi's diversion into his ex-DCI's private life.

'You can see for yourself, boss. If we went to the fiscal with a case like this, we'd be told in no uncertain terms our bums were oot the window, and to come back when we had some decent evidence. I mean, don't get me wrong, Maxwell was a nasty piece of work, and deserved to go away. It's as if they lumped three unsolved murder cases together with the girls' disappearance. There are no bloodstains. No fingerprints beyond Maxwell's being on the window of the girl's bedroom, but given he was a neighbour, it's hardly conclusive.'

Shona knew there was little awareness of *confirmation bias* back then. Once a suspect was settled on it was possible for officers to begin disregarding evidence that pointed in another direction. Anyone reviewing it further up the chain of command would see an open and shut case. Once the press dubbed it *the Girls in the Glen*, the story had taken on a life of its own and the pressure to find the killer had been intense. John Maxwell fitted the profile.

'Cindy Jardine disappeared in Edinburgh, not locally, she doesn't fit the pattern,' Shona said, rereading the scant victim profile in the notes. A pair of haunted dark eyes above prominent cheekbones stared out of an ID photo taken for a soliciting charge. Cindy's previous places of work had included Leith's prostitution toleration zone of Salamander Street, and she had a history of drug abuse. 'From her charge sheet, she seems to have had friends in high places.' Shona angled the screen for Ravi to see. Most of her arrests were marked '*NFA*', no further action, but that might also have reflected a lack of resources or the recognition of a hopeless case.

Ravi rapped his knuckles on the printed sheets. 'There's also a missing person list they didn't even eliminate from the enquiry.'

'You think there are other bodies out there?'

'Got to be a consideration. Look at the size of Bield Moss and the glens that run off it. And our pal Cameron Armstrong is out there, making it his business to find bodies.'

Their eyes met.

'Shit,' Shona said under her breath.

'Aye,' Ravi agreed.

The gaps in the original investigation and the renewed media focus on the search for Olivia Thomson meant they might no longer be looking solely at recovering the final victim. The Girls in the Glen was one of the most notorious crimes in recent Scottish history, up there with the unsolved Bible John murders. The difference was, the Girls in the Glen killer had been convicted in 1986, and died in jail. If Shona was right, this could be a miscarriage of justice on a colossal scale and not the ending they all hoped for, but the start of a horrific whole new chapter.

They both jumped as the piercing pips of Shona's pager punctuated the still air of the sitting room. *Launch ILB Kirkness* followed by the date and time tracked across the small screen as Shona silenced it.

'I've gotta go,' she said to Ravi over her shoulder. 'Can you lock up? There's a spare key on a hook in the kitchen.'

'Nae bother,' he called, as she ran down the stairs.

Keys, shoes, fleece.

She was out the door and gone.

Chapter 22

For the rest of Sunday afternoon and evening, she had no time to pursue the implications of the sparse file Ravi had brought her. A ten-metre yacht with a family on board had run aground on the shifting Solway sands on the opposite side of the firth. The D-class *Margaret Wilson* could get closer than the larger B-class, Atlantic lifeboat, the *John Shenton* – operated by their colleagues in Silloth, on the Cumbrian coast – so a joint exercise was launched. Tommy had opted to take a back seat and sent Graham Collins, a prime candidate for his replacement, out with Shona and Callum, to reinforce his experience.

She'd pushed the Girls in the Glen case and the hunt for Olivia Thomson temporarily to the back of her mind, but the sense of unease she'd first felt up on Bield Moor had returned with a new intensity, compounded by the short, slapping waves of the shallow sea, a family in danger and the knowledge they were operating among the treacherous quicksands of the Solway.

The skipper of the *Barebones* was experienced and the yacht well equipped but, with the wind rising and the light falling, lifeboat helm Graham Collins decided to transfer the mother and the three young children, all under ten, into the safety of the *John Shenton*, and back to Silloth station to warm up, until the tide turned, and the family's boat could be re-floated and checked for damage.

For the next three hours, as the tide slowly crept back up the Solway, the *Margaret Wilson* stood off, providing reassurance and support for the *Barebones*' skipper. The returning sea meeting the opposing force of the Solway's rivers – combined with an estuary bed where currents mined deep beneath the sands and popped up in eddies and contrary flows – made for an uncomfortable time.

Shona was torn between doing all she could to help Cam Armstrong find Olivia Thomson and whoever else was out there, and the can of worms that would be opened if he uncovered another body that, once investigated, might blow the original case apart.

Actually, 'can of worms' didn't begin to cover it. 'Giant bucket of venomous snakes' would be a more appropriate way to describe the situation. The image of Murdo at the shoot, picking his way carefully across the heather of Bield Moss to avoid stepping on an adder, came to Shona's mind. For now, she and Ravi had agreed to keep their reservations about Maxwell's conviction to themselves, but Shona was sure that Murdo would have no such doubts. *Tell the truth and shame the devil* was one of his favourite expressions.

When the yacht had righted herself, Shona and Callum went aboard to help check her over. The hull was undamaged, but the rudder and propeller couldn't be relied on, so they fixed a tow rope and, along with a service vessel for Robin Rigg wind farm, made the slow journey into Silloth, where the family were reunited and the yacht could undergo repairs.

After a restless Sunday night, Shona drove straight to Her Majesty's Prison Dumfries and Murdo's pre-arranged meeting with Ben Elliot. Shona rolled her shoulders as she sat at the lights in Dalbeattie Road, ready to make the turn that would take her up to the jail. She was stiff and sore from the buffeting she'd received. It had been after ten p.m. and dark when they'd made it back to their home station. Graham Collins had been nice enough, but she'd missed Tommy McCall, one of the most experienced skippers on the Solway. Shona had fallen into bed, but found herself unable to sleep and gone back to the lounge where the case files still sat. The post-sunset glow in the western sky bathed the room with an eerie vividness. Another sift of the file had revealed little. The light streaming through the windows had woken her at six a.m. on the corner sofa.

When she met Murdo in the prison car park, he seemed more subdued than usual.

'Any idea why Ben Elliot asked to see you?' Shona said. Since he'd called her on Saturday, it was unlikely Murdo had thought of much else and, in the intervening day, something Elliot had said during his arrest or interview might have triggered a possibility in Murdo's mind.

Murdo just shook his head. 'Heard nothing from his solicitor, either.'

That was good news, at least. Shona didn't relish the prospect of Elliot withdrawing his confession, despite the forensics, and provoking a reappraisal of the evidence by the fiscal which would send Shona's team back to square one to comb through everything again.

'Well, only one way to find out,' Shona said, and held out a hand and invited Murdo to lead the way through the electronic doors of HMP Dumfries.

Beyond security, where they deposited their phones and warrant cards in lockboxes and emptied their pockets, the familiar figure of the prison governor, Elizabeth Fraser, was waiting for them. She was a neat blonde woman in a navy blue suit. Her compassionate expression gave her the air of a family GP or an empathetic church minister, rather than the person responsible for keeping the public safe from the fifty or so remand prisoners currently facing trial for everything from violent assault to rape and murder.

Shona took her outstretched hand. 'Hello, Liz. How are you?' she said.

The woman returned Shona's warm smile. 'I'm fine. I'm glad I caught you two. This is a social visit, isn't it? I'm a wee bit concerned about Mr Elliot. You're the only people he's asked for.'

'It's understandable he wouldn't want his daughters to see him here,' Shona said.

The governor turned to Murdo. 'You're an old friend?'

'We played rugby thegither, way back. I've no' seen him much recently,' Murdo replied, cautiously.

Elizabeth Fraser put her hand lightly on Murdo's arm. 'Obviously, I can't discuss his medical details, but try to get him to listen to the doctor.' She turned to make sure Shona was included in the request. 'He'd benefit a great deal by engaging more with our staff.'

'We'll try,' Shona said. It sounded as if Ben Elliot was having trouble, like many others before him, adapting to life inside. For a man used to the freedom of the moors and being his own boss, being locked up must be a struggle.

They were shown into a small visitors' room, normally set aside for legal chats with solicitors, where Ben Elliot sat. As the prison warder stepped back and closed the door, he inclined his head to indicate he was just outside if they needed anything.

Ben Elliot seemed to have shrunk inside his prison uniform of jeans and a pale-blue polo shirt. The hard sparsity of his frame, honed by perpetual physical work in all weathers on the high moors, now gave him an air of worn fragility. His neck was scrawny above his shirt collar, and his badly shaved cheeks were sunken. He seemed unsteady on his feet as he rose to shake Murdo's hand.

'How 'ee daein?' Murdo said, dropping into their shared Langholm dialect.

'Fine. Whit aboot yersel?' Elliot shot a glance at Shona, then gave his old friend a reproachful look.

'Ye ken, if you want to tell me onything aboot what happened,' Murdo said gently, 'DI Oliver needs to be here.'

Elliot slumped in his chair, resting his elbows heavily on the pockmarked yellow vinyl tabletop between them.

Shona sat down next to Murdo and waited. Murdo had been the arresting officer, a situation that often led to enmity, but she was the stranger here, and uninvited to boot. Her best strategy was to become as invisible as possible. She'd deliberately moved her chair back a little, allowing the men to inhabit their own circle of space.

'Ah'll no hae ony mair to say aboot whit happened on the moss,' Elliot said so quietly that Shona had to strain to catch the words.

'Ben,' Murdo said, equally softly. 'I'll do whate'er I can. You just micht say sow like.'

Elliot seemed to wrestle with that task, and Shona thought he was someone whose life was generally so self-reliant that asking for help, or opening up to others, be they prison officials, doctors or even old friends, might be what was taking the greatest toll.

'Ma lassies,' Ben said eventually, turning his serious grey eyes on Murdo. 'You and Joan ha' no bairns of yer ain. I want you to tak' them.'

Murdo looked taken aback. Whatever he was expecting, it wasn't this.

'I'll go up tae the farm as much as I can,' Murdo replied. 'Thon neighbour woman's in everyday and Grace is adamant she'll no' leave the place.'

Elliot made a sound somewhere between a laugh and a sob. 'She'll not get the choice.'

'Whit d'you mean,' Murdo frowned.

'You think Langdale'll let this lie? Even if I'm in the jail, it'll no' be enough for him. He'll hae them oot of the farm, and if he cannae do it legally, his men'll come at night and pit a match to the place. My lassies are alone up there. They'll tak' their revenge ony way they fancy.'

To Shona, it was now clear why the prison governor wanted them to persuade Ben Elliot to listen to the doctor. The Earl of Langdale – this cultured but slightly gauche American business-school graduate, desperate to be accepted in his ancestral homeland and the tolerant butt of practical jokes – was about as far from a Border reiver as it was possible to be. She didn't doubt the Elliot farm was a risk, with Ben as the leaseholder heading for jail, but she thought the intervention of Social Services was as likely to end the girls' stay at the farm as a band of vengeful horsemen arriving in the night. Some misguided thought had led him to the idea that shooting his landlord was a way out of whatever troubled him. Now, he seemed convinced that the threat from the Earl of Langdale had only multiplied.

'Div ye ken onybody who's threatened them?' Murdo said, but Elliot shook his head, as much at the absurdity of even asking as at the question itself.

'You and Joan tak' the girls,' Elliot urged, his eyes wide with hope and encouragement. 'Yer mither's hoose is standing empty.' He leaned across the table and grabbed at Murdo's arm. 'Come away back hame tae Langholm. No harm'll come to ony of my girls with you aroon'.'

'Mr Elliot,' Shona said, leaning forward.

He looked at her as if he'd forgotten she was there.

'Mr Elliot,' she repeated and touched his arm. He moved back in his seat. 'My daughter is on the moor, too, camped at the farm with the archaeologists. If I thought there was any danger, I wouldn't let her stay.'

She watched as he processed this, fitting together blocks of information that Shona couldn't quite see.

'Your lassie found thon Girl in the Glen, didn't she?' Ben said, momentarily distracted from his previous train of thought. 'Wee Lilly Scott.'

'That's right,' Shona said. She quickly calculated Ben's age. He'd have been in his early twenties when the murders took place. 'Do you remember when it happened?'

He thought for a moment, then nodded. 'Wee Lilly's faither, Findlay Scott, worked on the estate with thon other lass's dad, the gamekeeper, Alex Thomson. She wis staying there 'cause of a fire at their tied cottage. It wis thought poachers did it. Then both lasses disappeared.'

'Why did people think poachers did it?' Shona frowned. This hadn't been mentioned anywhere in the case file she'd seen.

'There'd been a few previous incidents wae his live-stock. Some of his sheep were took, an' his wife's pony wis harmed. Retribution for a couple of poachers he'd caught. Instead of turning them o'er to the polis, he skelped one in the face wi' a rifle butt an' broke his neb. It wis only they deserved, but some took it amiss.'

'Can you remember who the poachers were?' Shona asked. Had these men escalated their retribution from livestock to the gamekeeper's daughter and her friend? Perhaps they'd only meant to frighten the father, but the plan had gone wrong, and the girls had died.

Elliot furrowed his brow and looked at Murdo, who shrugged. He'd been a lad of twelve or thirteen. Old enough to remember the cases but not old enough to let it distract him from his new-found prowess at rugby and his deepening interest in Joan Storey, the bonny lass with the red hair in the next street.

'Couple o' the Nixon callants,' Elliot said, eventually. 'Course, it wis well-kent that Findlay Scott was in dispute wi' the estate o'er grazing rights that were part of his lease. They basically bullied him oot o' them.' Elliot's mood turned darker again, and he seemed to fold in on himself. 'But that's aw ancient history. It's ma girls ye need tae be thinking aboot now, Murdo. The Douglases dinnae forgive and they dinnae forget.'

When they got back to the car park, Murdo leaned his back against the Audi and let out a long breath.

'You okay?' Shona said.

Murdo nodded, then rubbed his checks and chin with both hands, as if trying to wipe the last vestiges of shock from his features.

'What d'you make of that?' Shona said. 'D'you think the girls are at risk of reprisals? We'll need to inform Social Services if you do.' She let the implications of that sink in.

Murdo shook his head. 'We'd have heard if something like that was in the offing. Willie Graham, for all you dinnae rate him, he wouldnae let that go. He kens his own patch.'

Shona felt the mild chastisement in Murdo's words.

'There's no chance Ben's protecting someone else? One of his rewilding buddies?'

'What makes you say that?' Murdo frowned.

'Ben's fifty-six. Seeing him today…' she paused. 'It made me question if he's fit enough to have carried out the shooting and escape afterwards? And as an experienced deer stalker, would he have missed?'

'He's got an old rugby injury to his back, but he's strong enough to run a hill farm,' Murdo countered, then sighed. 'I'd rather it wasnae him either, boss, but this is not something you'd hold your hand up for to help a neighbour out. No one else had a motive like Ben's.'

'You're right, Murdo,' Shona said and raised her hand to wave the thought away like a particularly annoying wasp. 'I'm seeing shadows and ghosts everywhere.'

'Aye, it's the Bield Moss,' Murdo said. 'It gets into your head.'

'You've felt it, too?' Shona said, unsure if he was making fun of her, a city girl with romantic notions of wild moorland spirits clutching at the hems of unwary travellers.

'Well known,' Murdo said, a small smile of kindly mischief returning to his otherwise sombre face. 'People have seen troops of reivers on horseback that vanish into thin air. They've heard screams and smelt smoke when there's nothing.'

'You talk about it as if it's true,' Shona smiled.

'Maybe it is,' Murdo grinned. 'Just cause I havenae seen them, doesn't mean they're no' there.'

The absence of evidence is not evidence of absence.

'What do you think to Dr Armstrong's chances of finding Olivia Thomson?' Shona said. Her smile faded as the girl's freckled face and dark hair flitted before her once more, like one of Murdo's ghosts.

'It's a big place,' Murdo replied. 'But if anyone's gonnae find Olivia, it'll be him. He's got the knowledge, and he has a stronger motive than most. But it all depends on one thing.'

'What's that?' Shona said.

'It depends if the moss is ready to give her up.'

Chapter 23

It was only as Shona followed Murdo's Astra through the streets of Dumfries, back to Cornwall Mount, that something Elliot had said came back to her: *Yer mither's house is standing empty*. Was Murdo really considering a return to his home town? He had twenty-five years' police service under his belt, but not once had he mentioned retiring. His mother had died over a year ago.

Was another of Shona's stalwarts leaving her? It seemed like every way she turned, change caught her out. Perhaps it was just a combination of circumstances. More likely, she'd just been so caught up in her own troubles that she'd failed to see life moved on, whether she wanted it to or not.

Shona nabbed Murdo as he got out of the car. 'The house needs a bit of work,' was all he would say, which Shona interpreted as neither a conformation nor a denial.

'Come upstairs,' Shona said. 'There's something I need to talk to you about.'

The morning's interview with Elliot had confirmed that if she was going to unpick any more about the Girls in the Glen case, and locate Olivia Thomson's remains ahead of Dr Armstrong and his media circus, local knowledge would be key. She needed Murdo more than ever and wasn't ready to give him up.

Shona and Ravi ran him through the file that DCI Paterson had surreptitiously passed on to them, the thinness of the information on possible deposition sites and the original case itself. It was a credit to Murdo's natural equanimity that he didn't look the least put out that they'd not initially shared with him that they were looking into such an infamous case in his own home town.

'I wondered why you were asking Ben about the girls at the prison this morning,' Murdo said.

Shona explained the alternative theory of a reprisal by poachers that had escalated into the girls' killing.

Murdo nodded. 'So you're de-linking Lilly and Olivia from the other three murders?'

'What did Slasher Sue say about Lilly Scott's cause of death?' Ravi cut in.

The pathologist's verdict had been unequivocal: sharp force trauma to the chest and a fractured hyoid bone in the neck.

'Same as the other victims: stabbing and strangulation,' Shona said. 'And I'm not de-linking. I'm reconsidering each case separately, based on the evidence.'

'Will you ask the super to reopen the case?' Murdo asked.

'No point now. I've seen the file, and Davies would have a coronary if he thought there might be more bodies.' Shona shook her head. 'It pains me to say this, but I think the person who's looked most deeply into the girls' disappearance isn't a police officer.'

'You think Dr Armstrong's not told us everything he knows?'

'I'd bet my house on it,' Shona replied. 'It's time I had another word with him.'

'Want me to come?' Ravi and Murdo said in unison.

'Thanks for the support, guys,' she smiled. 'But let's not make this official. I'll just be dropping in to see my daughter and check on the welfare of the Elliot girls, and I'll have a wee cup of tea with the good doctor while I'm about it.'

—

As she passed the car park of The Douglas Arms, she saw Cam's Land Rover and parked her Audi next to it. Spots of rain dotted her windscreen. She pulled her waterproof parka from the back seat. A small group of men was gathered by the pub's closed doorway. They had the ruddy faces and pale hair of the shoot staff, but their paunches, barely concealed by tailored suit jackets, marked them out as having more sedentary occupations. They reminded her of Rob's B&B cronies. But Shona soon realised they could move quick enough when their dander was up.

Seconds after she'd got out, they surrounded her, demanding she put an end to the media storm over the Girls in the Glen. It was damaging the area's reputation and affecting the tourist trade. The hunt for Olivia Thomson's remains was ghoulish and should be stopped. The press stories must cease.

Mrs Thomson might disagree with the men's assessment of the effort to recover her daughter as 'ghoulish' – and Shona could argue she was powerless to prevent either the media coverage or the archaeological hunt – but Shona's experience told her that reasoned argument would have little effect when passions ran this high.

'Gentlemen,' Shona said, as her outstretched hand signalled for calm.

The sky seemed to darken as a wall of navy and grey suits pressed in, close enough for her to smell a fetid mixture of sweat, cheap aftershave, stale beer and garlic breath. She felt her stomach contract and wanted to order them to *move back* in her best police voice. But these were businessmen, not a football crowd. They would respond to authority without force.

Instead, she calmly said, 'I understand your concerns. Police Scotland take the impact of these crimes on your community and business very seriously.'

''No' seriously enough.'

She was jostled from behind, a shove in the small of her back. There wasn't room for her to turn around. Her handbag slipped from her shoulder, and she stumbled sideways. She put out her hands automatically, brushing cheap serge and jacket buttons.

'Police assault,' someone said, and there was a round of sniggers.

Since arriving in Dumfries and Galloway, she'd never carried the extendable baton that, along with her sidearm, had been standard issue in the City, but she wished she had it now.

'Enough!' she roared, and jabbed her elbows outwards into the soft bellies of the men nearest her, earning a satisfying 'oof' from their owners. 'How'd you gents like a trip tae the Sherriff Court?'

Faces hardened, the light squeezed out of the circle.

The Douglas Arms was a better bet than trying to get back into her car, Shona reckoned quickly. She picked out a short man with a horseshoe of grey hair above a saggy face, who stood between her and the pub door. She'd put him on the tarmac of the car park if he got in her way. But before she could act, hands were clamped on a pair of shoulders and their owners peeled back like two quarters of an orange.

'Lads,' Jack Douglas's grimace of a smile appeared. 'DI Oliver is the estate's guest, and I'll thank you to keep it civil.'

Cam Armstrong was with him. He took her arm, hoicked her out of the group and pushed her towards the door. Jack Douglas barred the way, putting a hand flat on the chest of the first red-faced man who tried to follow, still shouting about the police and public accountability. Shona looked back and wondered if she needed to call in the local cops as backup.

Douglas growled a 'no' at the red-faced man, who appeared diminished, as the landlord swelled in size and menace. Even posh gastro-pubs, it seemed, had their fair share of troublesome clientele who required a physical intervention. And no one was getting past Jack Douglas today.

He followed them in, and closed and bolted the door. He turned, a smiling picture of serenity. 'You're not hurt?'

Shona straightened her jacket and shook her head.

'Coffee.' He lightly touched her elbow with one hand and showed with the other that she should go through. Cam Armstrong followed her as Jack disappeared behind the bar.

'Sorry,' Cam said. 'They nabbed me, too, and I took refuge.'

'A lynch-mob of hoteliers,' Jack said sardonically as he poured them both a cup. 'What is the world coming to?'

'I can see their point, if not their methods,' Shona said, and shot a reproachful glance at Cam.

'I doubt it'll put visitors off,' Jack said. 'If anything, it'll add spice. Look around you. Murder and mayhem. It's what they come for.'

Shona saw the walls had gained a series of tastefully framed black-and-white line drawings as final touches to what the menu board told her was now dubbed the Reivers Lounge. The scenes showed armed men on horseback, galloping across a landscape ablaze, axes and swords raised.

'Murder and mayhem as a marketing tool is a cynical view, not shared by your cousin,' Shona said. The coffee had revived her, and she'd already stopped reproaching herself for how she'd misjudged the strength of feeling she'd just encountered. 'The earl's also bent my ear about public image.'

'Nothing that can't be taken care of,' Jack said, smoothly, but Shona thought it would need more than a few glossy photoshoots and upcycled furnishings to distract from a story as big as the Girls in the Glen.

'And you'll need to be more careful up on the moor,' Shona said to Cam, aware that someone who'd served in Iraq probably didn't need her advice. Although there were also the students and Becca to think of. The sooner her daughter could be persuaded off the moor, the better.

'Xander's provided a bit of site security,' Jack replied. 'Men from the shoot staff.'

'So there have been other threats?' Shona raised her eyebrows and turned from Jack to Cam, and back again, looking for the genuine answer in their expressions. Both men remained impassive.

'Oh, no,' Jack batted away her concerns.

She thought about the Elliot farm hosting the diggers. Did some locals see them as collaborators in the town's bad press? Could that have been in the back of Ben's mind when he talked about fearing reprisals? In his agitated state, it might be enough.

'While history is a useful brand to tap into, tourists need to feel safe,' Jack continued. 'We don't want the media to get the idea we haven't evolved from all this.' He smiled and indicated again the pictures on the wall.

'Well, I should hope you have,' said Shona, and pointed a finger at both men in turn. 'Because I'll be down like a ton of bricks on either side if there's any tit-for-tat incidents.'

She already had cause for concern about Sergeant Graham's laissez-faire attitude to local rivalry, and she wouldn't let this slip.

'There'll be no trouble,' Jack assured her. 'That group today? What they're really interested in is crumbs from the estate's table. They came up for a nose around. It was bad luck they ran into Dr Armstrong. When we're fully up and running, they'll be too busy counting their money to cause trouble. The estate will make them an offer they can't refuse. It's good business, after all.' He gave her his most seductive smile. 'And I rarely take no for an answer.'

Shona felt the full force of his charm. She almost felt sorry for any women who might head to the rolling Borders hills in search of romance with the sort of hero who appeared in a Walter Scott novel, only to be fodder for Jack Douglas's ego. If he was chocolate, he'd eat himself.

But she was reassured, if only because the combined charm tsunami of Lady Lucy, his lordship and Cousin Jack would sweep aside any local resistance to their plans. That should be enough to keep the peace.

Cam looked out of the window. 'Well, they've gone anyway.' He turned back to Shona and Jack. 'I'll leave you to get on with your business.'

'Actually, it was Becca I came to see,' she lied.

'Oh, well, why don't I give you a lift up in the Land Rover?' Cam smiled.

'Perfect.'

'I'll be back later,' Cam said to Jack and swung his jacket around his shoulders. 'Freya's doing a dinner for the students,' he explained to Shona. 'Gives them a break from camp food. You should come, too.'

'Okay,' said Shona. She had nothing to get back to and nothing in the fridge, and it would give her more time with Becca. 'That would be great.'

And who knows what Cam Armstrong might let slip about his research. He had the skills to find Olivia, but so did she. If only she knew where to look. Bield Moss would need persuasion to give up its secrets and Shona was prepared to do whatever it took to make that happen.

Chapter 24

Shona swayed in the passenger seat as the Land Rover headed up the rutted incline to Bield Moss. Rain threatened, so she'd brought a wool beanie hat and her dark grey parka, and swapped her low heels for her wellie boots. Summer in Scotland. You could never be too prepared.

'So how's it going?' she asked Cam.

'The dig's going fine. We're into the drawing and recording phase. We'll be done by the end of the week, then I've got some leave. I've talked to a commercial company about Olivia. We'll begin as soon as we can, before winter sets in.' He paused, as if choosing what he said next carefully. 'Have you anything that might help me?'

'I'll be honest,' she sighed. 'I've had sight of the file.'

He gave her a sideways look, hope blooming in his expression.

She shook her head. 'It's sparse. We made extensive searches for the girls at the time, but nobody interviewed…' She was about to say *your father* but thought better of it. 'Only a cursory attempt was made with Maxwell to find the outstanding deposition sites.'

Cam's shoulders slumped. 'It's what I expected, but still not what I wanted to hear.' He glanced across and briefly met Shona's eyes. 'Does this mean if I do have questions in the future, you'll help me?'

'Let's just take this a step at a time,' she replied, and returned her gaze to the moor. Ahead, on the brow of the hill, the dig gazebo stood, the blue canvas sides vibrating like a fast heartbeat in the wind. 'You asked me about profiling Maxwell to help locate the deposition sites. What can you remember about that time?'

'Hunger. Fear,' he said, bleakly. 'I kept asking the foster family for a big red bus, apparently, a toy I'd left behind, but I can't even remember it now.'

'Did he ever bring you onto the moor? What about people who came to the house? Friends of your father?'

He shook his head.

'And your mother didn't mention anyone when you reconnected?'

Again, the head shake, this time with a flinch of pain. The memory of his troubled reconnection with his mother had obviously left its mark. But, given how he'd manipulated her, Shona was in no mood to treat Armstrong with kid gloves.

'Any other family who might shed light on what happened?'

'Not that I know of,' he said. 'At one point, I thought about registering my DNA, looking for my mother's relatives. But then I knew everything would come out. Unsurprisingly, I'm not that keen to connect with my father's side.'

'What about Olivia Thomson's mother, Vicky? Was she much use to you?'

He frowned. 'I know you think I'm manipulating the situation for my own benefit, but I just want to find the truth. Vicky Thomson is desperate to lay her daughter to rest before she dies.'

'You have no problem using her grief to finance your excavation, which will enhance your standing and give you a massive career boost.'

He pulled the Land Rover to a halt and, elbow on the top of the steering wheel, turned to look at her, his expression a curious mixture of hurt and anger.

'We've spoken about the Girls in the Glen a few times now,' Shona pressed on, watching him carefully. 'Each time your story about why you're so involved changes. From a police point of view that rings alarm bells. You want my help, but is there anything else you're not telling me?'

He seemed to deflate, sitting back and rubbing both hands across his messy, dark hair.

'Forgive me if I've sounded a little oblique,' he said eventually. 'It's just my habitual reticence. We researchers like to hang on to our secrets. The entire publication process takes so long we're naturally tight-lipped about sharing the information we've found. Shocking, isn't it, but academics aren't beyond pinching research or ideas.'

His face had returned to affable self-depreciation. He smiled but Shona didn't smile back.

'Well, you can trust me with your secrets,' she said. 'I've no plans for an academic career. And it really is in your interest to be straight with me.'

He turned away and started the engine again, jaw set in a hard line. 'What d'you want to know?'

'How many potential depositions sites have you identified?'

'That's what everyone, from the press to the pub land-lord, keeps asking. Jack Douglas is a mine of information about local history, by the way.'

Shona wasn't deflected. 'So, now I'm the one asking.'

'Five,' he replied. 'I have five potential sites.'

'How did you find them? Did anything about Maxwell's earlier burials suggest a pattern?'

'Nope,' he replied. 'It was grunt work. The sites are scattered, but I prioritised those with access tracks or bridle paths. Even after forty years, they're still clear in the landscape. Published papers and journal articles helped me exclude known ancient sites. Then, I spent my weekends with students doing geophysics, and studying satellite and drone footage. The muirburn revealed a few possibilities. I excavated here first purely because it's a salvage operation. The earl plans to put eco-ledges on the site. If he can get permission, any archaeology would have to be recorded as part of the planning process. Given what I knew, I wanted it to be me who excavated the site.'

'Are you prepared to share those potential deposition sites with me?'

'There's still some work to do processing the data,' he replied, not looking at her.

So, no, his vision of co-working didn't involve sharing anything useful just yet.

'Did you get any tip-offs?' Shona said. 'Interview any of the victims' families?'

He shook his head. 'Didn't see any point. What could they tell me? To publish, I need a clear academic trail, not the opinions of psychics.'

It was an obvious dig at the police, who were rumoured to have used mediums in the past. No force would admit to it, but she remembered a Dutch clairvoyant who'd been brought in during the Bible John investigation and had proved useless. Shona ignored the comment.

They'd reached the site. Cam turned off the engine but made no move to get out. On the far side of the site, she saw an estate Land Rover with two figures inside. Langdale's men.

'Anyway, I didn't want to face them,' Cam said, staring out across the heather. 'All that pain my father caused. Would you want to see that, knowing there was nothing you could do to change what happened? Vicky Thomson is different. I can help her.'

'Have you any idea what your father's motive was?'

He looked surprised, as if he'd never confronted that question.

'He was just evil,' he shrugged. 'You must see it in your work. Evil in individuals, people just bad to the bone. But it's also there in systems and societies. Bosnia showed me that. Perhaps that's what drew me to the Border reivers. I'm fascinated by it because I want to recognise it when I see it again, not because I admire it.'

He turned to face her, one hand ready to open the driver's door. 'We're not so different. I think that's the reason it compels you, too. If you understand it, you can protect people. Be a shield for others.'

Shona felt an unexpected jolt at this bullseye. He was right. They felt the same threat and wanted the same outcome. But here, in the Debatable Land, she took nothing for granted.

Shona got out of the Land Rover and was surprised to see that Dan Ridley had come over from Cumbria, and was waving to her from the shelter of the tent.

'Tying up some paperwork at my end over the shooting,' he said. 'I was hoping to see you.'

'Something I can do?' Shona smiled.

'Not really,' he said.

Shona felt a prickle of pleasure at the possibility he had orchestrated this visit just to see her. The truth was probably more prosaic. Dan hated his boss, and the feeling was mutual. The less time he spent in the office, the better.

Becca came over and hugged her mother. Her jeans were damp and muddy at the knees, and she was wearing a thin hand-knitted yellow jumper that Shona didn't recognise. Her long hair blew in a tangle around her face, but she looked happy.

As Shona let go, she felt her daughter shiver. 'Where's your coat?'

'Forgot it,' Becca said.

Shona took off her parka. 'How could you forget it?'

'Because she knew you'd be along with a replacement in a minute,' Dan said.

Shona laughed. 'You make me sound like a clucky mother hen.'

'I'd better talk to Dr Armstrong,' Dan said. As he walked away, he turned to look back at them, then adopted an exaggerated walk and flapped his arms like a chicken.

Shona and Becca laughed.

'It's nice to see you smile for a change, Mum,' Becca said, as Shona zipped up the parka, as if she were a child on her way to school.

'Sorry, I haven't felt much like smiling lately, what with everything that's happened,' Shona said.

'How is it going with Dad's trial preparation?'

'Fine,' Shona replied. It was all Rob said each time he called. *Fine*. Like it was a minor inconvenience. A puncture or a delayed train.

'Then it's okay to be happy,' Becca reassured her. 'And Dad will be all right, he always is.'

'I know,' Shona smiled again, but this time it felt more like an effort. She didn't want to think about Rob. 'How are the Elliot girls?'

'Okay.' Becca pressed her lips together and nodded. 'Grace expects her father home any day. Journalists came to the farm and interviewed her.'

It was a cynical bit of newsgathering. The Elliot girls were click-bait for any media organisation. Pretty girls with appealing baby animals. They might promise to campaign for Ben Elliott's release, but he'd been charged, and they couldn't print anything – because of the sub judice rule – until after the trial. If he stuck to his confession and pleaded guilty, there wouldn't even be a trial, just sentencing. She couldn't see any grounds for an appeal. Ben Elliot wasn't coming home soon.

'Best if she doesn't talk to the media,' Shona said. Becca opened her mouth to argue, but closed it again as Grace, with Flora and Ashley in tow, stalked past with finds trays in their hands, on their way to the dig gazebo. Becca made her excuses to her mother and went back to her trench.

Dan came to join Shona.

'How's things in Cumbria?' she asked.

'Great,' Dan replied, his eyes lighting up. 'Charlotte's been in London this week, visiting buyers. Her jewellery designs are really taking off. She'll be back tonight. I'm cooking.'

Did this mean Dan was considering resurrecting his plan to join the Met? He'd previously mentioned transferring to Dumfries, when a job came up, but she had no idea how long that might take. He'd said he wanted to work for her, and he was exactly the sort of officer she could make something of. Here was another of her close connections that seemed to be fraying under the pressure of circumstance.

They walked to the edge of the dig and looked down across the green-and-gold hills to the border. In the distance sat the outline of the decommissioned nuclear plant at Annan, sticking up like the horned remains of some half-buried beast. Beyond, in the hazy platinum of the Solway Firth, was its successor, the Robin Rigg wind farm, its turbines waving like feathers in the sand. To the south-west lay the dark fells of the Lake District, crowned by a curtain of rain and, to the right of them, stamped faint on the horizon, the triple triangle of the Isle of Man. Bield Moss felt both remote and intimately connected to the world.

'You know... There is something you can do for me,' Shona began. Maxwell's first victim, Harriet Jackson, had come from Keswick, in Cumbria's Lake District. Shona sketched the bare details of her concerns about the Girls in the Glen case, and her desire to trace any family.

'Maxwell's conviction was based on a confession and local knowledge,' Shona said. 'But how well would you have to know the area to deposit the bodies here?'

'How d'you mean, boss?'

Shona remembered her conversation with Cam and her assertion that profilers looked for a work, rest or play connection. 'Say it was someone who'd visited this area?'

'Wouldn't they need some good local knowledge?'

'Kate didn't. She understood this terrain perfectly, yet she'd never been here,' Shona said.

'So, you reckon the killer might have been a homicidal geography graduate?'

'You know what I mean,' Shona said. 'How much knowledge would you actually need? I've asked Ravi to have a look at any other body depositions, with strangulation or stabbing, in southern Scotland for the period, say, five years either side of the Girls in the Glen. Can you also do the same for Cumbria?'

'Sure,' he nodded, his face serious. 'So you want cases after the conviction, too?'

'If it wasn't John Maxwell, the killer wouldn't stop. These people don't stop. Look at Operation Anagram or Op Enigma.' Both were UK-wide investigations launched after the conviction of separate serial killers and explored potential links to dozens of other unsolved murders. 'We need to learn these lessons and incorporate them into our thinking.'

She looked up at the sky and rubbed her arms. 'You parked at The Douglas Arms?'

'I am.'

'Let's get back there for a coffee before the rain starts.'

–

Dan headed off before the students arrived for their dinner at the pub. Becca and the Elliot girls weren't among the first arrivals, having opted to go via the farm and check on the sheep.

Freya smiled as she put a plate of venison stew and mash in front of Shona. She asked after Tommy, but Shona thought it was pure politeness.

Shona indicated the lounge bar. 'Everything's ready for some proper customers, I see.'

Freya shook her head in disapproval. 'Those pictures give me the shivers. Aw that bruck aboot raiding. What

224

are we really talking? Murder, theft, kidnapping your family or cattle for ransom, like some kind of mafia.' She gave Shona a smile and patted her shoulder. 'And they didn't even have the police to call on back then.'

The students, initially frosty, slowly warmed to Shona as she asked them about archaeology, having picked up enough from Becca to sound vaguely knowledgeable.

Kate was right: investigating the past wasn't so different from investigating a crime. Gather evidence, form a hypothesis, then test it.

Soon, the students were bombarding her with questions better suited to her pathologist friend, Slasher Sue. She did her best to answer, finding herself caught up in their enthusiasm for their topic. Cam sat at the bar, deep in conversation with Jack Douglas. It must be a relief to have his charges occupied for the evening, but she had the sense he'd sought the landlord's company as a way of avoiding her.

Outside, it had begun to get dark. Shona checked the time. No sign of Becca and the Elliot girls. The expected rain had arrived. She picked up her plate and went through to the kitchen to make sure a few portions of veggie stew for Becca and venison stew for the girls were kept back.

The rear door into the yard was open. Shona heard voices and stuck her head out, searching for Freya, who was talking to two drenched walkers. Her face turned to Shona, illuminated by the security light, and she immediately knew something had happened.

Shona stepped towards the couple, whose waterproofs were pasted on like a second skin. 'I'm DI Shona Oliver. What's the matter?'

When they told her, she started running.

Halfway up the hill, blurred by the driving rain, she saw Becca lying by the side of the road still wearing her mother's coat. But Becca was also standing over the prone figure. For a fleeting moment, it was if she could see her daughter's spirit bidding her body farewell. Instantly, she was back to that fateful evening just over a year ago, when she'd found her daughter by the roadside, near their village, bleeding and semi-conscious after a hit-and-run.

'I'm fine, I'm fine.' Becca, upright, saw her mother's anguished look and guessed at the resurrection of old horrors. 'It's Flora. A car clipped her and didn't stop.'

For the briefest second, Shona felt nothing but the immense, dark presence of the moor around them, as if it was pushing her face into the wet peat, suffocating her. She took a deep breath to steady herself and kneeled by Flora, reassuring her. In the light from Becca's mobile phone, Shona saw that the girl was conscious, but rain and blood coming from a deep cut above her eye streaked her pale face. Shona began checking her over – pulse and breathing were fast, but regular – and urging her not to move, until the howl of the ambulance siren and sweeping blue lights patterned the wet road.

When the paramedics had loaded Flora into the ambulance, Shona looked up and down the road for any sign that the driver had had a change of heart. It was empty. The rain had turned the tarmac into a slick black snake that slid off into the distance and disappeared into the moor. Eventually, she led a soaked and shivering Becca down to The Douglas Arms, where Freya fussed over them both and Sergeant Graham took Becca's statement. Whoever the driver was, they weren't coming back.

Chapter 25

Shona got to CID before seven o'clock the next morning, but Murdo was already at his desk. He got up and followed her into her office.

'How's Flora?' He looked like he hadn't slept. His normally ironed shirt was creased and had crept from his trouser waistband earlier than usual.

'She was lucky,' Shona said. 'The gash on her head needed gluing. No concussion, but plenty of bruises.' Shona dumped her handbag under her desk and began unzipping her laptop case.

'Does Ben know?' Murdo said.

'I've sent word to the prison and asked the governor to give him an extra phone card, so he might be in touch.'

Murdo nodded thoughtfully. She could practically see the cogs going round in his head. Ben Elliot's words at the prison about the girls' safety were obviously weighing on him.

'No evidence it was deliberate,' she said sternly. 'So don't go blaming yourself for not protecting the girls.'

He raised his eyebrows in a way that said he was reserving judgement. 'Any ID on the vehicle?'

'Dark blue or black. Probably a hatchback. Not a fourbie,' Shona said. 'That narrows it down to about half the vehicles in the area.' She opened her computer and the screen immediately sprang to life. 'I had to chivvy our friend, Sergeant Graham, to collect my coat from the paramedics for forensics. You can tell his finest hour was thirty years ago, nabbing John Maxwell. He's been coasting ever since. You know what he said? Something to the effect of *if drunk lassies walk down dark roads at night, they can expect to be hit by tourists.*'

Murdo frowned and shook his head. He pointed through the glass partition to the kettle.

'Aye, please,' Shona said. The caffeine boost she'd had at High Pines was already ebbing.

'Why'd you want your coat checked by forensics?' he said over his shoulder, as he headed out into the main office.

'Possible some paint residue rubbed off when the vehicle hit Flora.'

Murdo walked back to her open door, the handles of his rugby mug and her Charles Rennie Mackintosh cup looped loosely over his chubby fingers. Shona saw a series of emotions cross his face and knew he was about to question her thinking.

'I know,' Shona said, holding up one hand to stop him speaking, while she tapped her keyboard with the other. 'It's unlikely, a long shot, but I don't want Ben Elliot's solicitor saying we didn't take threats to his family seriously.'

'Why was Flora wearing your coat?'

'Because I lent it to Becca when I went up to the dig. She lent it to Flora. It's what lassies do, the teenage merry-go-round of outfits. Ashley's got Becca's pink fleece. Yesterday, Becca had on a yellow jumper I swear I've never seen before, probably Grace's... what?'

'How d'you know you weren't the target?'

Shona stopped scrolling through her messages and stared at him.

'What d'you mean?' she said, but already it had dawned on her. Flora was about Shona's height. It was dark and raining. The girl had her hood up and was in Becca's company. The Audi was plainly visible in the pub car park down the road. An ember of anger ignited in her.

She told Murdo about the altercation earlier at The Douglas Arms, witnessed by the landlord Jack and Cam Armstrong. He put the cups down with a clatter, marched back to his desk and snatched up his jacket.

'I'm no' having' this,' he said, and his previously pale cheeks reddened with fury. 'There'll be some well-kent faces among that lot. One way or another, I'll get tae the bottom o' it.'

She'd never seen him so angry. Murdo had always had a quiet authority, and could be physically imposing, but he never raised his voice. He didn't need to. When he told you to watch your step, you heeded that warning or paid the price, whether you were a junior officer or a criminal. But is seemed to Shona that something about Flora's hit-and-run had triggered a reaction in Murdo she hadn't predicted.

She put a hand on his arm to stop him, felt the taut muscle beneath his jacket, and thought he was about to throw her off. Instead, he stood still, and his eyes closed for a second as though whatever pain he was feeling might overwhelm him.

'Murdo, the accident was not your fault,' Shona said.

'I shouldae seen something like this coming,' he said, shaking his head.

'D'you not think I've been telling myself the same?' Shona said. 'It could have been Becca, I thought it was...'

She stopped, aware of the emotion pushing through the cracks in her voice. 'Look, it can be tough policing your home town. Maybe it's better if Ravi goes up there.'

'No,' he said firmly. 'Ravi's a good lad, but they'll no pull the wool o'er my eyes. I know these callants, known them aw ma life. Best let me handle it.'

It was more order than request and Shona was tempted to put her foot down, but he was right. There was no one she trusted more to get to the bottom of this than Murdo.

'Okay, but listen, Murdo, this is no' like you to get so het up. Sure you're okay? Nothing wrong at home, is there?'

'Everything's fine, boss.'

She was almost convinced, but whatever was troubling him, beyond the safety of the Elliot girls, he didn't seem keen to share it.

'Okay, but keep in touch.' She watched him go, unsure what it was she was missing about his reaction. The Girls in the Glen murders had cast a slur on Bield Moss, the same way no one could hear the names Saddleworth Moor or Soham without thinking about the atrocities that had occurred there. Perhaps Murdo carried some of the latent collective shame that so terrible an act could have occurred in the place they called home. The identification of Lilly Scott's body brought it all back and a resurrected John Maxwell stalked the moss once more, in print if not in actuality. No wonder Murdo was finding things hard, Shona thought, but it was unlike him to react with such a display of anger.

She turned her attention back to the hit-and-run. Had someone from the business group deliberately targeted her? Perhaps they'd just meant to splash through the puddles lining the rough tarmac, soaking her for a laugh, but misjudged the space? Either way, they'd crossed the line into criminal behaviour. Murdo would rattle cages until the culprit dropped out.

By the time Ravi came in an hour later, Shona had a plan for the remainder of her workload. She called the Edinburgh CID officer who'd dealt with Nicola Baird. When she identified herself, his resultant intake of breath told her it was not a task he wanted to repeat. She mentioned the Girls in the Glen and spun him a line about updating the contacts list for Cindy Jardine, the sex worker who was the second victim, should Dr Armstrong's search throw anything up. Could he supply her with details of any family or co-workers in the city or Leith that were still around? He said he'd have a look and get back to her.

Shona called everyone into the briefing room. Indignation met her explanation for Murdo's absence, along with concerns for her future safety. She reassured them that she was fine, in no danger, and that they could safely trust Sergeant O'Halloran to prevent any further incidents.

She held up her hand, keen to move on with the day's business. 'Let's leave everything to Murdo, and the local lads and lassies for now. Kate, where are they with the Ben Elliot case? Is there much more to get through for the fiscal?'

After the initial paperwork, some minor points of clarification and witness statements were needed. The CCTV from the estate drones hadn't thrown up anything new so far.

'Nearly there, boss,' Kate said.

They discussed some local cases that had come in, before tasks were allocated and the meeting broke up.

Shona returned to her office and called to check how Becca and Flora were doing after the accident, then rang forensics for an update on tracing the car. Nothing useful had been found on Shona's coat, so the best lead was still the witnesses' description of a dark coloured hatchback. She messaged Murdo, then made a start on the monthly crime figures report, but quickly realised her mind wasn't fully on the numbers and went back to recheck her work.

Thirty minutes later, Shona switched off her laptop, pulled her grey suit jacket over her white shirt and picked up her handbag. She gave Ravi the nod.

'We'll be back later,' she said to Kate.

'Where are you going, boss?' Kate eyed Ravi, who stood by the office door and teased her with a small gloating smile. He could be off to unblock a drain, but he'd happily let Kate think she was missing out.

Shona had been careful to say nothing in front of Kate about the Girls in the Glen case. The Earl of Langdale had the ear of folks at Police Scotland HQ and would be happy for the whole thing to fade into ancient history, despite his apparent support of Dr Armstrong. A little pillow talk between Xander and Kate would blow the whole thing sky-high.

'I'm taking Ravi with me to a meeting in Glasgow,' Shona said. She racked her brain for the least appealing topic she could come up with. 'Budgetary reviews.'

Kate looked mildly interested.

'It'll be your turn next month,' she promised, and that seemed enough to mollify Kate, who went back to her screen.

'C'mon you,' Shona said to Ravi, shaking her head at him in exasperation.

–

Shona and Ravi showed their warrant cards to Craig Anderson in the plush offices of Anderson Bell Solicitors. Anderson was a trim man in his early sixties, dressed in a pale linen suit and tie. When she told him she'd like to talk to him about his first wife, Karen, the third Girl in the Glen victim, he looked like he'd seen a ghost from the past.

He had. In the nearly thirty years since his wife's death, and John Maxwell's conviction, Anderson had rebuilt his life. He'd married again and his three children were now grown up. Even though he thought about Karen every day, the rest of the world had moved on and her name must rarely come up.

'It's just a chat,' Shona said. She'd expected resistance, and perhaps some legal questions over the police's interest, but he pointed readily to the pale leather chairs in front of his beechwood desk.

'Obviously, I've seen the stories about the MSP's shooting and the search for Olivia Thomson's remains,' he said with a resigned smile. 'I was half-expecting a visit. But I don't see how I can help. What do you want to know?' He touched the chunky gold signet ring on his left pinkie in an unconscious action that made Shona wonder if it had been a gift from Karen.

'Is there anything that's come back to you that perhaps you didn't mention to the police at the time? Anything that's since struck you as odd about the case or the place they found her?'

Anderson, with his lawyer's comprehension, was as close to an eyewitness as Shona was likely to get.

He sat back and his gaze searched the ceiling, as if looking for answers, then he sighed and shook his head. 'Karen's body was found close to her car. That seemed to fit with her encountering Maxwell, whose own vehicle was seen parked nearby.' He paused. 'What's stayed with me all these years is that somehow it was my fault.'

It was a common reaction in those close to victims.

'I needn't have taken her with me that day,' he continued. 'My business with the Langdale estate was at an end, but Karen was a keen walker, and she wanted to see the moors in the snow.'

'You worked for the estate?' Shona said. It was another detail omitted from the file, although it was hardly relevant, since he was never a suspect in his wife's disappearance.

'A complex land sale. There were nine separate parcels, some without deeds.' He sighed. 'To be honest, I was glad this was the final visit. I don't know if you are aware, but the current earl's grandfather was a drinker and had a furious temper. The estate was deep in debt, but he blamed everyone else. He threw a whisky decanter at a colleague of mine. We didn't do business with them again.'

'Did you or Karen ever meet Maxwell?' Shona said.

'Not that I'm aware,' Anderson replied. 'Karen had never been up that way before. Ironically, I was convinced she was safer with me than at home. There'd been some vandalism. My car was set alight on the drive.' He shrugged. 'Lawyers collect resentful clients, as I'm sure police officers do.'

Shona gave him a sympathetic smile. 'Yes, but we tend to refer to them as *the accused*. Once we've caught up with them, that is.'

Someone in Langdale was about to acquire that label over the hit-and-run on Flora, if Murdo had anything to do with it.

Craig Anderson smiled sadly. 'It was a difficult time. We still trade as Anderson Bell, but my partner Edwin Bell, who did most of the land conveyancing, died in a car accident a few months after Karen was murdered, so I sometimes question my own recollection of that period.'

He stood up and offered his hand to Ravi, then Shona. The interview was at an end.

'It's an odd coincidence that the man you've charged with the MSP's shooting was the one who found Karen's body, but I suppose it's a small community there,' he said as they turned to leave.

'Ben Elliot found your wife's body?' Ravi asked.

Anderson nodded. 'At Blackriggs, on the edge of Bield Moss.'

Ravi's surprise confirmed to Shona that she hadn't missed the statement from Elliot in the file. It was either lost or had never been taken. Elliot himself hadn't mentioned it when they'd talked about the Girls in the Glen in Dumfries jail.

'He came up to me after the trial,' Anderson continued. 'Offered his condolences. I remember it because no one else did. Everyone else was celebrating the guilty verdict. Ben Elliot struck me as a profoundly compassionate man. Who would have thought he'd be facing an attempted murder charge years later?' He smiled sadly. 'But as we both know, DI Oliver, in the justice system, it's never wise to underestimate the human capacity for good or evil.'

'I can't argue with you on that score,' Shona replied.

'Please don't think me rude,' he said, crossing to his office door. 'I hope you find Olivia Thomson. Karen's body was recovered and I'm thankful for that. Her killer died in jail. Just let her rest in peace.'

Murdo arrived back at Cornwall Mount just as she was packing up. She'd already sent everyone else home. He threw his jacket over his chair and sat down heavily, then took a piece of gum from a container in his desk drawer. When Shona went over to him, he was chewing furiously and staring at his screen.

'Any luck?'

'Oh aye, Willie Graham fancies Archie Nixon for it,' he replied. 'Apparently, it's not the first time he's tried to turn someone into a human bookmark. Jack Douglas confirmed Archie was in the car park wi' you.'

'So I was the target?' Guilt at Flora's injuries flooded over her. The Elliot family had every cause to hate her.

'Well, Nixon's been mouthing off about the Elliots an' all. He's no' talking, but traffic are going over his car – a navy blue Honda Jazz – with a microscope. Claimed he was at home. Willie's hunting down CCTV that says otherwise. Oh, and I'm moving into the Elliot farm.'

Shona blinked. She pulled out a desk chair and sat down next to him. 'I'm not sure that's a good idea.'

'How no'?' Murdo challenged.

'Do they need official police protection, DS O'Halloran? Is there enough evidence to get this past Division? Is Joan going?'

'She cannae leave her work at the hospice.'

'What about your work?'

'It'll just be at night. I'll come into the office.' Murdo folded his arms and leaned forward on his desk, his mouth set in a firm line. She, and many a rugby opponent, had seen that look. Murdo was immovable.

'Did you know it was Ben Elliot who found one of the Girls in the Glen victims? Karen Anderson, who was recovered at Blackriggs.'

Murdo looked thoughtful, then shook his head. 'I didnae know that, but it doesnae surprise me.'

'Why?' Shona furrowed her brow.

'Ben's no' the sort to talk about an experience like that,' Murdo said. 'He'd think it was disrespectful to the family. What does his statement say?'

'There's no statement in the file.'

'Probably lost,' Murdo replied. 'We've got the forensic report from the site. D'you want me to ask him about it?' Murdo looked doubtful and Shona conceded it was unlikely to be of any use, particularly in Elliot's current state of mind. It was just another of the shadows she couldn't pin down.

Murdo looked up at the office clock. 'If you don't need me, I'd better be off.' The determined set of his jaw returned. 'Be better if I was at the farm before it gets dark.'

Shona threw back her head in a gesture of frustration and defeat.

'Okay, look, I'll cobble together something about homeworking on compassionate grounds. A family emergency. Division think everyone in this neck of the woods is related to everyone else anyway. But Joan must go with you.'

Murdo looked ready to argue the point, but Shona shook her head. She could be implacable, too.

'Remember Grace Elliot on top of the Land Rover? Speaking as someone with a single teenage daughter, they'll run rings round you. Ashley's a handful on her own.'

Shona could see why Murdo would want to keep an eye on the girls: a mixture of his natural compassion and a desire to protect them, rooted perhaps in guilt over his earlier inaction at Ben Elliot's request. And for Shona, there were advantages to losing her sergeant for a few days. With him embedded in his network of home-town contacts, she'd get an early warning of the local mood, and what was happening at the dig. She didn't trust Dr Armstrong to come to her before making a dramatic announcement in the press.

And there was another, acutely selfish, motive. Any threat to the Elliot girls extended to Becca, too. High Pines had good security, but if she couldn't get her daughter back there, Shona would sleep a little more soundly with Murdo at the farm.

'Well, just caw canny,' Shona said, deploying the all-encompassing Scottish warning to *be careful*. 'I'll be up to check on you tomorrow afternoon,' she warned.

'That's no' necessary,' Murdo bristled.

'You're not my only person of interest, Murdo,' she said. 'Tommy and I are joining a swift water rescue exercise with Alexander Douglas and Langdale Mountain Rescue.'

'Gey public spirited of you,' Murdo replied.

'Aye, isn't it?' she said, getting up and patting Murdo on the shoulder.

It was also the ideal opportunity to observe his lordship off duty and among his own. Was there some dark side to the Earl of Langdale that had caused a man like Ben Elliot to risk everything to kill him? Murdo's assessment was that Elliot kept things to himself. There was still a niggling doubt, however, and she wanted to be sure. Perhaps there was a score to settle beyond the rewilding fund? Who knew what someone might let slip when they thought no one else was listening?

Chapter 26

Heavy rain had arrived from the west and was battering the window of the CID office as Shona worked through the overtime sheets, headphones on, listening to a playlist that Becca had created for her. It was a curious blend of Fleetwood Mac, Paulo Nutini and Stormzy. Perfect for summer in Scotland, many would say. The rain wouldn't reach the high moss until later but whatever Becca was up to at the dig, Shona hoped it was under shelter. As August neared its end, it felt like autumn had wiped its feet on the mat and begun to tramp up the hall, making itself well and truly at home.

Her High Pines planner, shared with Rob, was open on the screen and she could see he'd made some additions. Luckily, there were plenty of local festivals to extend the B&B season through to Kippford Arts in October, followed by Halloween, St Andrew's night, the harbour Christmas lights, Hogmanay and then on to Burns Night in January, which would start the year all over again. They already had plenty of bookings and, with luck, would recoup what they'd lost by the enforced closure for Rob's trial in London. But during his absence, she'd felt something shift. Perhaps she was just tired, but the prospect of returning home from a gruelling day dealing with the worst of society only to hear about a guest who had complained that their towels were too thick had lost its comic quality. But she'd chosen Rob and this life. What else could she do? And what about Becca? These were questions she couldn't answer.

She signed off on the CID budget sheets, sat back in her chair and stretched her arms, releasing the tension in her shoulders. The days were already an hour shorter than they'd been two weeks ago, when she'd dropped Becca at the campsite. The window for Dr Armstrong's recovery of Olivia Thomson's remains this year was closing. Shona picked up her phone, finger hovering over the redial button on a recent call.

Ravi tapped on the glass partition. She signalled back that she'd be two minutes. She'd done all she could under the radar. Time to come clean. Well, nearly clean. Super-intendent Davies needn't know everything. She picked up her phone and dialled his number.

'The position hasn't changed,' he said sternly, when he'd listened to her proposal. She'd held back from revealing she'd seen the Girls in the Glen file already, or from criticising the original investigation, but instead emphasised that the original case had been focused on securing a conviction. Bringing home Lilly Scott's and Olivia Thomson's remains had slipped down the priority list once it became clear how many resources it would consume. Hundreds of officers, many on overtime, had searched the moor until the coffers had run dry and beat officers were needed elsewhere.

'This wouldn't be an active investigation, sir,' she said. 'Not even a case review. It's just to get us up to speed ahead of media interest, which'll continue to be intense and may even go on for years with this crowdfunding in place. It'll damage the force's reputation if some journalist discovers that key information's been sitting in our files all along, and someone will have to carry the can for it.'

She heard Davies pause and weigh up whether that person could be him. It was obvious Division considered the case closed. With the killer dead, and no DNA record, it would be difficult, and potentially expensive, to prove or disprove a forensic connection to any new evidence uncovered. Historic issues had a nasty, unpredictable way of biting the bums of current officers.

'It's proactive policing,' Shona persisted. She thought of revealing Cam's personal connection to John Maxwell, but knew that Davies would see the archaeologist's journey of genetic penance as something best pursued through private therapy rather than supported by Police Scotland's budget. 'It would emphasise we never forget the victim's families. Could be a huge PR win for us if handled properly.'

She'd dangled some soundbites. Was it enough to reel him in?

'There are no grounds for allocating resources,' Davies said.

Damn, Shona thought, a wasted fishing trip. She'd been wrong to approach him. Now he'd be scrutinising her every move to make sure she toed the line.

'However,' Davies continued. 'A short briefing for Division could access funds from the press and public relations budget. Do you feel you're qualified to produce a *short* briefing?'

'Yes, sir,' Shona said, and punched the air.

'Just remember, DI Oliver, if this turns into a PR disaster, and the force is brought into disrepute, I doubt the subsequent disciplinary outcome will be in your favour.'

Ravi had returned to the glass panel of her office, his look quizzical. She gave him a thumbs-up. He quietly got up and opened her door.

'Davies has greenlit a briefing document on the Girls in the Glen,' she said when she'd ended the call.

'Ya dancer, boss,' he grinned. 'How'd you manage that?'

'Let's just say I took a leaf out of the Border reivers' book and made him an offer he couldn't refuse.' Shona gave him a cryptic smile, but the truth was she wasn't at all confident this would end well for either herself or the families of the murdered girls.

'Well, as long as we don't have to ride aboot the hills wi' swords. Ponies are pure chaffing.'

Shona rolled her eyes, but couldn't prevent herself from smiling. 'Just get everyone in the conference room.'

—

After her initial euphoria, the sombre reality of the task presented by the Girls in the Glen case settled on Shona and her team. When Shona sketched out what they had already discovered, Kate gave Ravi a brief, resentful look from the other side of the table: *I knew you were up to something*. Ravi stared back at her impassively, his minor victory of upstaging his rival DC with a big case complete.

The civilian staff sat under the window that ran along one side of the room. Shona turned to address them.

'Chloe, Vinny, I'm not expecting any digital stuff to come your way, but I want you up to speed, just in case.'

Both specialist investigation officers nodded to show they understood.

'Also, can you work with Hannah on the scanned records when they arrive? I want a clear chronology, particularly regarding witness statements. Who knew what, and when. I'm also looking for anything that might shed light on John Maxwell's motives or that might give us an insight into his choice of deposition sites.'

Hannah Crawford, a highly efficient fifty-something civilian data input operator, who had something of a crush on Murdo, said, 'You've not seen the file yourself then?'

'I've seen elements,' Shona replied without elaboration.

'We could build you a GIS map of the terrain,' Vinny Visuals said. 'Add in the known deposition sites, along with locations associated with Maxwell, his home and work places. Since Lilly Scott was found at the midden site, we should cross-reference it with Canmore – that's the online archaeological record developed by the Royal Commission on the Ancient and Historic Monuments of Scotland – and exclude anywhere that's been excavated in the last thirty years.'

For a moment, everyone stared at Vinny. It was the longest and – to Shona's ears at least – most profoundly useful statement he'd ever made of his own free will. She'd read something recently about the proposed introduction of Geographic Information Systems mapping software to identify locations and reasons communities felt less safe, but it sounded like Vinny was ahead of the game.

'We've made a wee start,' Chloe smiled coyly.

'We're the police. I don't think it's right that a uni archaeologist might find Olivia Thomson before us,' Vinny said bluntly. He folded his arms and scowled, blissfully unaware that his approval rating with the room had just rocketed.

Vinny had come to the team via the distinctly unacademic route of a community service order. A few years ago, Murdo had got wind of a kid who, by day, was stacking supermarket shelves, and by night hacking exam boards and selling papers to financially grateful students. He'd shepherded Vincent towards the light via a consultancy firm that the police used for gathering digital evidence. Shona had eventually brought him in-house. She was never sure if Vinny had fully hung up his black hat, but reasoned that if the FBI came calling, she'd at least know where to find him.

'That would be great. Well done, guys,' Shona said.

Vinny stared at his tablet but acknowledged, with a tilt of his head, that he'd heard her. Shona gave Chloe a complicit wink. That pairing was working out a treat.

'As far as the recovered remains are concerned,' Shona said, 'one of the Edinburgh CID guys emailed me this morning. He's got some background on the second victim, Cindy Jardine, the forty-five-year-old sex worker who disappeared off the street.'

She opened the message on her tablet. 'There's no family left who knew her at the time, and none of her friends are still about, but the officer spoke to a retired detective who knew her. Kate, Edinburgh is your neck of the woods. Fancy a trip home?'

'You want me to go and talk to this guy?' Kate looked doubtful.

'Your mum and dad will be pleased to see you,' Shona smiled. 'I'm forwarding the details.'

Kate wore a new and expensive-looking gold bracelet, and, Shona observed, had brushed off Ravi's one-upmanship with uncharacteristic ease. Perhaps career progression was no longer her primary concern. In that case, the earl would drive her to Edinburgh. He could meet the folks. That way, the travel costs wouldn't come out of her budget, Shona thought with cynical satisfaction. She didn't care if Alexander Douglas made a fuss with Division about the resurrected reputational damage to the area and its impact on his estate plans. Her investigation was sanctioned, and Davies could deal with the earl.

Kate shrugged, opened the forwarded email on her own tablet and added a note. She resumed combing her fingers through her long blonde hair, which was usually in a high ponytail but was now low and over one shoulder.

'Ravi,' Shona said. 'Where are you up to? Did you talk to Dan Ridley?'

Kate's fingers stopped halfway down and she frowned at Shona. 'What do the Girls in the Glen have to do with Cumbria Police?'

'The first victim came from Keswick, that's in Cumbria,' Shona snapped. 'You're the one with the geography degree.'

A faint blush crept up Kate's cheeks, and she folded her hands in her lap and looked down.

'So, Dan found a sister for Harriet Jackson,' Ravi said. 'Cathy Fraser, as she is now, was twenty at the time and can remember Harry – as she calls her – leaving after a row with their parents. When she disappeared, they were all sure it was the lorry-driver boyfriend, Jimmy Fraser. He was found hanging in woodland near Langholm three months later and the family thought it was a guilty conscience, but his alibi was solid. He was loading at a forestry clearance, collected his wages at the site office and went for a drink. Multiple witnesses.'

Both Shona and Ravi caught Kate's expression of puzzlement. Shona would have been disappointed in her detective constable if she hadn't picked up on Ravi's unheralded direction of travel. Shona gave a faint nod, indicating he should proceed.

'As to potential unlinked cases,' Ravi went on, 'Dan's come up with two women who disappeared in similar circumstance during in the first half of the 1980s, with connections south of the border, to match the three I've identified north of it. None have been traced.'

'What about after Maxwell's conviction?' Shona said.

Ravi blew out a long breath. 'A few possibles. I need to do more digging.'

A wave of exchanged glances ran around the table, followed by murmurs of unease.

'At this point...' Shona said loudly, and waited for the voices to subside before continuing. 'We're not expanding the scope of the original enquiry. But I don't have to tell you there are precedents for this.' She wouldn't say the names of the men who'd been the subject of previous, large-scale operations. Men who'd gone to jail for ending numerous women's lives, only to boast the figure was much higher, and for it to be proved that was substantially true.

'But Ravi's talking about later cases, too,' Kate said. 'D'you think John Maxwell's conviction was unsound?'

Eager eyes had turned to her. Even Vinny looked up from his tablet.

'I'm approaching this with an open mind,' Shona said, carefully. 'Early enquiries have thrown up some other lines of enquiry.'

'John Maxwell confessed,' Kate said. 'And there was forensic evidence.'

Ben Elliot confessed, Shona thought, and I still have doubts about that.

'I'm aware,' Shona said briskly. 'Our job is to produce a briefing document for Division. It may touch on some of what's been mentioned this morning, or it may not, but one thing it will be is thorough.' She looked into each of the faces around the table to make sure her words had sunk in. 'I'll not have us caught out on our own patch. Remember, for most officers, cases like this come along once in a career, and you don't want it to define that career for all the wrong reasons. Do the best I know you're capable of, that's all I'm asking. Any questions?'

'When will Murdo be back?' Hannah said.

'Soon,' Shona replied. 'Until then, come to me or Ravi. Anything else?'

No one had any queries, and notebooks and tablets closed.

'I don't have to tell you that this doesn't leave the office. The media will go after anything related to the Girls in the Glen. If they get as much as a sniff of this, someone will get their jotters.' She looked around the circle again, coming to rest lastly, and deliberately, on DC Kate Irving.

Kate caught the look and her chin dipped as she packed up her things. Shona wasn't being any tougher on her than she would on other, male, officers in the same situation. Kate had made her choice. It was up to her to convince Shona she could still be trusted.

Chapter 27

Murdo took an iced bun from the bag and leaned on his elbows on the metal parapet of Thomas Telford's bridge. Beneath ran the dark waters of the River Esk, fleeing from the forests and moors to meet the sea at the Solway.

Lads and lassies in their black uniforms, out for lunch from Langham's high school, clutched cans of Irn–Bru and chocolate bars advertised 'for sharing'. Not the way to stay healthy for an afternoon of learning. Murdo glanced at the bun. He wasnae one to talk.

A night at the Elliot farm had left him craving a sweet treat. He'd hardly slept. As the ancient farmhouse had settled in the dark, every creak and sigh of its timbers against the stone walls sounded an alarm that woke him. Grace had accepted his presence on her father's orders, but when, in the small hours, Murdo left his blanket on the sofa to investigate a noise, he found her in the hallway in front of the empty gun cabinet. She gave him a look of disdain that said the police seizure of the farm's rifles and shotgun was not ameliorated in any way by his presence.

Despite Wee Shona's insistence that his wife should accompany him, Murdo had come alone. Joan's work at the hospice was as important to her as his was to him. She'd accepted he was going alone to the Elliot farm, and loaded him with food from the freezer in her stead. He'd

played down the potential threat, citing his old friendship with Ben Elliot as the primary motive for his act of
charity. One thing he was clear on: if there was trouble,
he wouldn't put his Joan anywhere near the firing line.

The Elliot girls – even Flora, bandaged and bruised
– were now at the dig, safe under Dr Armstrong's and
the shoot staff's supervision. He had to admit, Shona had
been right. Grace, Flora and Ashley had sunk his attempts
to impose any kind of schedule on them. They'd kept
to the rhythms of the farm. He'd at least been allowed
to help with the heavier jobs that morning and check
the buildings for security, but they continued to split up
and re-form, feeding stock and checking their moorland
sheep, like a small flock of birds oblivious to any circling
hawks.

When the weather turned, they'd school books to
work through, and had commandeered one corner of the
lambing shed as a temporary art studio, with cans of spray
paint and papier mâché animal heads.

With her father gone, Grace had brought the two
sheepdogs – Bess and Fly – from their barn pen into the
kitchen at night. Even they seemed to resent Murdo's
presence. He soon learned not to get too close to their
spot by the Rayburn, or mother and daughter circled
behind him and nipped his heels.

Murdo straightened up from the bridge parapet, dusted
off his fingers and walked the short distance to his mother's
house. The day was overcast. There was a pressure behind
his eyes that heralded another early autumn storm. Bright
colours already licked at the trees like tongues of flame.
It was the English August bank holiday at the weekend,
summer's last hurrah, with a reputation for extremes of
weather: either a heatwave or a washout.

He was in his mother's house only long enough to fill the kettle, when there was a knock on the door. One of the neighbours must have seen him arrive. He steeled himself for the sympathetic words about his loss that still flowed over him each time he returned. Enquiries about possible rental had crept into the mix now. Perhaps it was time. Maybe he and Joan would retire here, eventually, returning to the streets where they'd played as children. Murdo went to answer the knock.

Alan Kerr, his brother's killer, stood on the front step.

The two men locked eyes. The air seemed to stretch and buckle under the pressure of Murdo's glare. Finally, he stepped back and made to slam the door.

Kerr's hand shot out, coming to rest on the green painted wood, just below the brass knocker.

'Please,' he said.

Time had shrivelled Kerr. While some men made use of the prison gym, he obviously had not. His once thick fair hair had become close-cropped, marching backwards behind jutting cheekbones and faded blue eyes. He was a scarecrow, his overlarge white T-shirt tucked into baggy jeans gathered at the waist by a worn leather belt where an extra hole had been punched.

Murdo could probably lift him with one hand.

'There's nothin' fur ye here,' Murdo said quietly, and increased the pressure of the door on Kerr, but the man didn't budge.

Across the street, an old neighbour woman in a print dress and cardigan had come out to watch, arms folded, on her doorstep. She said something to an elderly couple who were passing, bulging bags-for-life shared between them, and they stopped and looked across at Murdo's mother's house. At this rate, the entire street would join the audience.

Kerr was calm, his eyes pleading.

Murdo released the door. Kerr staggered but regained his balance.

'In,' Murdo said.

He marched Kerr through to the kitchen at the back of the house and pulled out a chair.

'Sit.'

Murdo switched on the kettle and, more from habit than hospitality, dropped two teabags into mugs.

He turned to face Kerr, who was tracing the pattern of roses on the wax-cotton table cover with his right index finger.

'Say yer piece.'

Kerr looked up at him, a picture of contrition. 'I'm sorry.'

Murdo turned and filled the mugs from the boiled kettle. His mouth was clamped in a tight line, causing him to breathe heavily through his nose. He fished out the teabags, then turned and placed a mug before Kerr, resisting the urge to slam it down on the tabletop. He picked up his own tea and stood, resting his back against the worktop, arms folded across his body.

'I ne'er stopped thinking aboot yer brother,' Kerr said, eyes on the roses.

'He wis cried Drew,' Murdo said, through gritted teeth.

Kerr nodded. 'Aye, Drew. I kent that.'

Murdo waited. Kerr lifted his cup, the scalding tea wet his lips.

'It made it worse tha' he wis so blameless,' Kerr continued. 'Why couldnae I have kilt someone who deserved it? Ah met plenty inside. Rapists, paedophiles.

Guys who mugged old biddies fur their pensions cos they needed a fix. People who preyed on their fellow human beings.'

Murdo wondered why he was here and how much of what Kerr said had been prepared in order to elicit some fellow feeling. He was pretty sure the terms of his parole didn't require Alan Kerr to apologise in person to his victim's family.

'I'm no' asking you to forgive me fur what I did,' Kerr said.

There was a long pause while Kerr studied the table-cloth and Murdo looked beyond the seated figure to the garden and his father's shed, painted the same colour as the front door for economy's sake, and his mother's washing line, still looped in an orderly manner around the far clothes pole.

'That all?' Murdo said, eventually.

Kerr nodded without looking up.

'Best be on yer way,' Murdo pushed off from the counter-top and poured what was left of his tea down the sink. He took Kerr's cup and did the same, signalling the end of the visit. He followed Alan Kerr to the front door, reaching past him to open it. The neighbours were still on the far pavement. Kerr went out without a word and moved left, back towards the town centre. Murdo lingered on the step, raising a hand to the neighbours, who shuffled around, suddenly caught out in their surveillance. Murdo looked straight ahead, but out of the corner of his eye, he watched Kerr walk to the end of the street, until he turned and disappeared.

Murdo gave the neighbours a last nod, then went inside and closed the door.

Back in the kitchen, he lifted Kerr's mug from the sink and dropped it in the bin. He stood, looking out through the kitchen window at the gunmetal clouds and the first spots of rain, then reached into the bin, retrieved the cup and placed it back in the sink. Waste was a sin, his mother used to say.

Murdo was the last of his family. His legacy was to remember. Or, more importantly, not to forget. *Forgive each other, as the Lord has forgiven you*, the Bible said. But was it possible to draw a line and from there walk on unaccompanied by the burden of the past? Murdo didn't think so.

Aileen Armstrong O'Halloran would never have forgiven the man who killed her son, but Murdo's father might have seen things differently. His grandfather had come from Northern Ireland, and Murdo's father had spent time working there and visiting family. He'd lived to see the Good Friday Agreement, and Murdo could still remember the tears in his father's eyes as he'd watched the announcement on television. 'At last,' his father had said, 'there's hope for a different future.'

Murdo thought about Olivia Thomson, still lost on the moor, and all the other Girls in the Glen. Lilly had lain in the peat, starved of oxygen, yet preserved by her anaerobic state. She, like the others, didn't get the chance to forgive; to decide what should be remembered and what should be left behind.

Murdo, however, had that chance. But it didn't mean he had to take it.

Chapter 28

On the edge of the River Esk, the Langdale Mountain Rescue team, snug in their yellow dry suits, picked
between the boulders. Helmet lamps danced like fireflies
in the gloom, and reflections sparkled on the dark surface
of the fast-flowing water, swelled by the earlier rain. Up
on the moor, the sunset had been spectacular, and Shona
and Tommy McCall had been loath to leave The Douglas
Arms, but for different reasons. She had enjoyed the view
and good food; he, the reunion with Freya.

Now, strands of birch and fir stretched like cathedral
pillars along both sides of the river, and Alexander
Douglas, Earl of Langdale, master of this land, was in
his element. The arc of his smile was perpetual, white
teeth caught by the torch beams. Like the Cheshire Cat,
Shona reasoned, it would be the last thing to fade when
the twilight eventually dimmed to full dark.

He'd arrived with men from the estate, including the
head gamekeeper, Charles Bell. Some difficulty ensued
finding the earl a dry suit that was tall and broad enough at
the shoulders. Shona sympathised, though her difficulties
were at the other end of the scale.

Earlier, she had looked in on Murdo at the Elliot farm
and all seemed quiet. The girls obviously resented the
invasion into their territory, but had been mollified by
Joan's lasagne. To Shona's annoyance, Joan herself was

nowhere in sight, and Becca was now installed in the twin bed in Grace's room. Shona was intent on reading Murdo the riot act, but he looked so dejected she deemed it pointless. With four lassies in the house, he'd learned the hard way. *Hell slap it intae ye*, as her gran used to say. Shona gave it twenty-four hours before he called his wife for reinforcements.

On the riverbank, under Tommy's direction, the men began entering the fast-flowing river. They practised defensive rescue swimming, how to get yourself out of the current and safely back to shore. When Shona's turn came, she jumped in. The cold squeezed the air from her lungs. She turned onto her back until she could control her breathing. Her feet faced downstream and were close to the surface to fend off rocks or the entanglement of fallen branches. The trees of the gorge swept above her like sentinels in the dark, the fir-tops jagged against a small patch of velvet sky. As the riverbank curved, she hit an eddy in the current and saw one of the mountain team signalling with a torch. She rolled onto her front and swam strongly towards the bank. The smooth rocks became mud and gravel as she clambered out.

The earl was right behind her. He shook the water from his eyes and hair, and grinned.

When everyone had had their turn, Tommy got them all together.

'Well done, team. We'll move on to the throw-bag exercise. That's recovering a casualty fae mid-flow. We train for this in the dark 'cause you need vigilance to pick someone oot, and the lack of visual reference points makes it harder to judge speed.'

In the pool of light from their helmet torches, he held out an orange, circular RNLI bag, the size of two toilet rolls stacked on top of each other. It had a loose drawstring opening and was filled with coiled neon-yellow rope.

'Water current flowing at even walking speed will exert a pressure of sixty kilograms on the body,' Tommy continued. 'So you'll be pullin' against that additional force. Now, I could throw wee Shona in, but that would make it far too easy.' There was a round of laughter. Tommy went on, 'So, which one of you bonnie lads would like to be the first casualty?'

The earl immediately held up his hand, and stepped forward to appreciative whistles and cheers.

'I graduated from a mountain adventure school in the Rockies,' he confided to Shona as he moved past her. Smugness radiated in his tone. 'Used to do this all the time when we white-water rafted through the Grand Canyon,' he announced to the group.

'Good,' said Tommy and reached up to pat the earl's solid shoulders. 'I like a challenge. Let's hope you didn't have a big dinner afore ye came.'

There were more laughs.

'We'll keep this as the recovery point,' Tommy continued, and turned to Alexander Douglas. 'You'll go back up the path tae the first entry position wi' Jim here.' Tommy indicated a young member of Langdale Mountain Rescue, his face ruddy and shining above the tight black seal of his immersion suit. A walkie-talkie was clutched in his hand. 'And float down as you did before. We'll throw. You catch. Simple.'

'What happens if I miss?' the earl said.

'You can say hello to the Muckle Toon when you get there, an' call a taxi,' Tommy said, to appreciative chuckles from the team.

Tommy raised his hands to simmer down the hubbub.

'His lordship makes a good point,' he said, seriously. 'We'll hae everyone in a line on the bank, ready to throw. If you miss them all,' Tommy shook his head in theatrical disbelief that the earl could be so incompetent, 'there's a reason we practise self-rescue as the first exercise. Get yersel to the bank and wait there for one of the team to bring you back up.'

Alexander Douglas gave a good-natured nod, apparently happy to be the butt of jokes. He stepped aside, sweeping his arm out to indicate that a rather overawed Jim should precede him up the path.

Charles Bell, the head keeper, smiled at Shona. 'His lordship is desperate to be accepted for the local volunteer fire service flood rescue team. It protects Langholm and surrounding villages in case of emergency.'

'You can't fault him for effort, can you?' Shona smiled. It was hard to reconcile the man she saw wading through mud and cold water in the dark with the image Elliot had painted of Alexander Douglas as a vengeful individual at war with nature, his neighbours and the moor.

Bell shivered. 'Aye, well, I'm hoping he develops his interest in malt whisky soon. I'd happily follow him there.'

Shona went round the group, handing out throw-bags. 'Hold the end of the rope in your dominant hand and throw with the other. The most dangerous part of the procedure is when the casualty catches hold of the line. Be sure you're anchored and ready, and not pulled in after them.' Most of the men were experienced, but they listened patiently. The angled light from the head torches on sombre faces, marked by sun and weather, gave them the look of natural forms carved out of the darkness.

The younger team member, Jim, who had been dispatched by Tommy to position the earl, asked the best way to detangle. Shona emptied out the rope, turned her back on the pile and then fed the line rapidly over her shoulder from behind into the throw-bag.

When she looked back at him to confirm he'd understood, a thought struck her. 'Why aren't you with his lordship?'

'He sent me back. Said he'd done it before, and it'd be more realistic if you dinnae know when he was coming.' He must have seen Shona's expression, even in the dark, because he suddenly touched his radio, unsure if he'd done the right thing.

'Did you confirm this was okay with Tommy McCall?' She thought it was unlikely Tommy had agreed, as pairing up in low visibility situations was standard procedure.

'His lordship sent me back,' Jim repeated, as if the earl's authority couldn't be trumped.

As she turned to look for Tommy on the shore, a shout went up.

The glow from the earl's helmet flicked between the trees on the bank as he came around the river bend. But the light was all wrong. It was muted, like the moon behind scurrying clouds. A second later, she knew why.

'Tommy,' she roared, and started forward.

The earl was floating face down in the water.

Shona plunged past Tommy and the others, and into the Esk's churning blackness. The force of it pushed against her knees and thighs. Stones knocked at her ankles. She fell forward and the river gripped her. Rocks rose up, flashing in the tumbling beam of her head torch like the rounded backs of kelpies, beasts intent on claiming lives. Shona kicked out into the fastest current. The floating mass of the earl swung towards her.

She tried to read the surface: piled-up river ridges or V-shapes of white water, signs of obstruction below. It was too dark. She was moving too fast.

She spat out a mouthful of water, surprised it wasn't salty. Instead, it had the bitterness of peat. The sea was vast and overwhelming, but here the water was concentrated fury; a creature powerful enough to consume the rocks it flowed over.

Above the spray, pinpricks of light streamed in a constellation along the bank. Some had followed her into the water. She kicked out and accelerated as she hit the main current. The river closed the gap between her and the earl faster than she'd thought possible.

She grabbed him and they spun together. Only the relentless press of water told Shona which way was downstream. Reaching under Alexander Douglas, she fumbled at his chest until her fingers closed on the shoulder strap of his buoyancy aid. She tugged hard and he rolled over. A splutter of water, rank with the smell of vomit, hit her in the face. Their red helmets smashed together like pool balls and the webbing of his life jacket bit through her gloves, but she clung on. Rafted together, Shona kicked towards the bank, but the earl's greater momentum kept them out in the fastest flow. His limbs hung in the water, with only faint animation, a trick of the river that didn't tell Shona if he was alive or dead.

She craned her neck for a throwline, simultaneously aware she was unlikely to catch it while one hand gripped the earl.

They were barrelling downstream in the darkness. Suddenly, thick beams of torches caught and tracked her. She picked out Tommy's voice above the shouts and the roar of the river. Ahead loomed the arches of a high granite bridge. Even if they survived the Esk dashing them against one of the uprights with all its might, the undertow caused by the piers would suck them into a never-ending circle below the surface from which there would be no escape.

Shona's anger at the earl's bravado and stupidity exploded inside her. Her hands were becoming numb and stiff with cold, and the force of the water had breached the seal at the neck of her immersion suit, sending icy trickles down her back. She thought of Becca and Rob, but not for a second did she let go of the earl. She turned her face away from the bridge, thrust her chin upwards, gulped at the air. The river grew heavier as she kicked with all her strength and gathered great armfuls of water with her free hand.

But then a pair of stars converged on her like arrows of hope. Below the helmet lights, she saw gritted teeth and unfamiliar eyes half-closed against the spray. The two men from Langdale Mountain Rescue, tethered on ropes held by their colleagues, grabbed her and the earl, and she felt the Esk's bite lessen.

'Let go,' they shouted. One reached over and uncurled Shona's fingers from the earl's life jacket. She was dragged at right angles to the flow. Mud and rocks caught her heels, and a moment later she was on the bank.

She rolled onto her hands and knees, and panted. A thread of watery saliva stretched from her nose and mouth, and her eyes streamed. The earl was on the ground, surrounded by brightly uniformed figures. She made to get up, but hands pushed her into a sitting position.

'Is he alive?' she spluttered to the first-aider.

He ignored her question, running through his checklist. Head, neck, limbs. How much water had she swallowed?

'More than I'd like,' she said impatiently. Then: 'Sorry, pal. I'm fine.' She squeezed the kneeling man's arm, then used it to haul herself up.

The mountain rescue team's pickup, lights ablaze, engine running, stood at the top of the steep wooded incline that led to the road by the bridge. The buzz of radio chatter competed with the rush of the river, as Tommy issued instructions. Alexander Douglas lay strapped to a spinal board.

Shona felt her heart soar. Clamped to his face was an oxygen mask. She pushed her way through the group. His helmet had been removed and he wore a cervical collar.

'Xander, can you hear me?' she said, and gently brushed back the blonde hair, plastered dark to his forehead.

His eyelids fluttered, lips forming a shape beneath the mask.

She leaned close and tilted the side of the mask upwards, away from his cheek.

'He hit me,' he wheezed. 'Pushed.'

Shona stepped back. The split to the bridge of the earl's nose seemed to confirm he'd been struck in the face. Thank God he'd been wearing his helmet. If he'd gone in without it, the Esk would have bashed his brains out. But even if that had happened, the river would not be culpable of his homicide. Whoever had pushed him in would.

Chapter 29

The next morning, forensics searched the riverbank. Shona tasked Murdo to liaise with Sergeant Graham and the Langholm cops over statements from the mountain rescue team. She'd gone in the ambulance with the earl to Dumfries Royal Infirmary, where he was diagnosed with concussion. His breathing was still ragged, so he'd been kept on oxygen overnight to avoid secondary drowning, where even a small amount of water in the lungs later proves fatal. There was little else he could tell her other than that he'd been aware of a dark shape, been hit in the face and pushed into the river. The doctor confirmed blows to the back of his skull, injuries to his face and hands, and general bruising, but couldn't say which had been sustained before he entered the river.

Shona pulled into The Douglas Arms and parked next to Tommy McCall's van. She'd been driven home to High Pines in the early hours by Kate, who'd driven back from Edinburgh, then insisted on returning to the hospital, the line between her duties – official and personal – never thinner. Kate would need to fight Lady Lucy for the prime bedside spot in the private room where the hospital had placed the earl. Uniform had two officers standing guard, but at least Shona could be sure her DC would relay any clue to the earl's attacker straight away.

Shona found Tommy McCall sitting alone at the bar, an empty coffee cup in front of him. Having given his statement, he was free to go. He eyed the bruise on Shona's cheek.

'Got yersel a shiner there,' he said.

'Could have been a lot worse,' Shona said with a grin. 'Thanks for hauling us out.'

'Shouldnae have happened in the first place.' He shook his head.

'It wasn't your fault someone decided to banjo the earl,' Shona said sternly, then lowered her voice. 'If the Sundance Kid hadn't gone off on his own, none of this would have happened.'

'I shouldae considered the river levels were up and strung a grab line across, well before yon bridge.' Tommy pushed the teaspoon around the saucer.

'It wouldn't have helped the earl.'

'Aye, but it would've helped you.' Tommy looked her full in the face and only then did she realise how shaken he was. 'Maybe it's time for me to step down as helm if I cannae rely on my own decisions in an exercise I've run dozens of times before.'

Shona put a hand on his arm. 'I didnae doubt for a second you'd haul us out.' Then she stepped closer and hugged him just as Freya came through from the kitchen. Shona felt a moment of awkwardness, but the woman gave her an understanding smile.

Tommy patted Shona's back and let her go. 'His lordship got any idea who pushed him?'

'None,' Shona replied. 'D'you think it was one of the mountain rescue lads?' The interviews so far indicated everyone's movements were accounted for, but in the dark, it was hard to be certain.

'Doubt it,' Tommy said. 'You could switch off your ain head torch, try creeping up on the earl, but the minute you got close to him, thon hi-vis dry suits light up like Christmas trees.'

Shona agreed. 'I'm off to see forensics now, but I'm not hopeful.'

'He seems a braw lad,' Tommy said. 'Just the sort you'd want for the area.' The earl had won over Tommy, but perhaps Freya, whose job relied on the earl's expansion plans, was at the heart of his thinking. 'Who's he upset? Some husband, mibbae?'

Shona shrugged and looked from Tommy to Freya, sensing she had an opinion on the matter. The Douglas Arms was near opening fully, and had already drawn a fair amount of locals into its orbit. Freya, though Orcadian by birth and outwith the historic system of loyalties and enmities, was well-placed to hear local whispers.

'Well, there's plenty of lassies around here who've had a dalliance with the earl, a few of them already with husbands, but that's folk for you, and nobody else's business,' Freya said.

Did Kate know what she was getting into with the earl? Shona thought it unlikely, since it seemed so at odds with his morally upright, clean-cut image, but if his romantic track record after eight months in the area was already common knowledge, it might not be long before Kate had a rude awakening.

'I don't like to speak ill of my employer,' Freya continued, 'but if Xander Douglas has put a foot wrong, it's over the community land buyout.'

'The habitat restoration proposals?' Shona said.

'Folk are no' saying the police were wrong to arrest Ben Elliot,' she reassured Shona, 'but it doesnae change the fact they'd rather see the moss as a place they can be proud of and bring in visitors from all over the world, not just a few rich ones to shoot the birds. The earl, with all his good intentions to save the moss, isn't listening. Local people's connection to this land is as deep as his.'

The idea the earl was suffering from a Messiah complex chimed with what Shona knew of him. The only place he led from was the front, as his insistence on forging ahead alone on last night's exercise had shown.

I wanted him gone from this glen, and for that, you must arrest me. Ben Elliot's words came back to Shona. She'd thought the shooting was a personal escalation of their poaching dispute, but did others in the community group feel just as strongly?

Shona nodded. 'I'm on my way down to the scene now. Thanks, Freya. That's very useful.'

She patted Tommy on the shoulder as she passed him, heading out the door.

'You should go home and get some rest. I'll see you later.'

He'd been up half the night and his low mood was likely brought on by tiredness. Rest would give him some perspective on events and there was a confidential counselling service at the RNLI he could use, if needed.

Murdo was at the riverside when she arrived, talking to Suzanne, a forensic assistant. Shona had worked with her before and found that her apparent youth belied her skills and experience. Her previously dark cropped hair was now icy blonde and – paired with the white forensic suit and set against the greens of the riverbank trees – she had the look of a seriously displaced snow figure.

Shona joined them.

'The scene is just too trampled and muddy,' Suzanne said. 'We've multiple footprints from people, horses and dogs. No sign of any weapon or clothing fibres on the surrounding vegetation. Any transferred DNA on the victim from the attacker would have been lost in the river.'

Given the remoteness of the location, there was no question of CCTV or nearby traffic cameras. The irony that the crime had occurred when the riverbank was having its busiest night of the year, with more than twenty potential witnesses, wasn't lost on Shona. A lack of physical evidence was what she'd expected, but disappointing all the same.

'Thanks, Suzanne,' Shona said, and the forensic assistant began picking her way between the trees, crablike and weighed down on one side by her equipment case, back to her van parked on the road by the bridge.

'I know Ben Elliot's confessed to the attack on Nicola Baird, but you don't think one of her little friends has switched targets?' Shona said.

'You mean Darren Porter?' Murdo nodded.

'He's capable, and the earl stands for many of the same things as Nicola Baird. Porter knows we're after him. Perhaps he saw it as a challenge?'

'None of the witness statements mention any strange faces or unaccounted-for individuals,' Murdo said.

'With his background, he could have had the earl under surveillance from a distance and escaped cross-country,' Shona mused. 'Get Vinny to check if Porter's surfaced anywhere electronically since we last looked. Phone, bank account. He might have driven, but check CCTV for buses.'

'Will do,' Murdo said.

'We need to talk to the rewilding group,' Shona said.

'Think they're in the frame for this?' Murdo said.

'Freya at The Douglas Arms said there's more ill feeling about the buyout than the earl realises.'

Murdo pursed his lips and nodded. Then he indicated the bruise on Shona's cheekbone. 'That happen when the earl got his dooking?'

'It did.'

'No chance you were the target?'

Shona shook her head. 'None. Unless the attacker confused me for a six-foot-three American, which is unlikely. Even in the dark.'

'Willie Graham's still checking for CCTV of Archie Nixon's car, but it's not looking hopeful.' Murdo's frustration at their inability to nail him for Flora's hit-and-run was evident in his expression. 'The slippery bastar' had his car cleaned that morning, so forensics will likely draw a blank. Best if you don't go up to the moss on your own.'

'If I *was* the target,' Shona replied.

'Don't kid yersel. You were the target, all right,' Murdo replied. 'Only Becca and Flora knew you weren't inside that coat, and neither of them was driving. But dinnae worry, we'll get him.'

'I know you will,' Shona replied. Surely someone would come forward with information. Flora could have been killed. It had gone past intimidation into serious crime. 'Everything okay at the farm?'

Murdo looked shattered, and his manner was uncharacteristically brusque.

'Aye,' Murdo said. 'Well, no. There's a letter from the estate. Grace refuses to open it, but I've had word fae one of the land agents in the toon that the estate approached him about marketing the Elliot farm.'

'Eviction?' Even though she'd known it might come, the swiftness with which the estate had moved against the Elliot girls had taken her aback.

'It'll be a notice to quit,' Murdo said. 'On the grounds the leaseholder can't carry out his obligations.'

Shona sighed. 'I'm surprised. You'd think they'd at least wait till after the trial. Maybe Kate can have a word with the earl?'

'You think?' Murdo said, looking a little less downhearted.

'Mind you, it'll be Lady Lucy behind it, but Kate could big up how bad it'll look for the estate. No point appealing to her humanity. I'm fairly sure it doesn't exist. Might buy the girls some time.'

Murdo nodded. 'Worth a try. Let's get up to George Robson's farm. He's the guy you met the other day at the Elliots'.'

'With the white beard?' Shona said.

'Aye, be our best bet. He's an elder at the church. I think if he knows anything, he'll tell us.'

Robson's place ran up through a wooded glen off the A7 and was a more favourable spot that the Elliot's hill farm. Thick hedges of hawthorn lined the road, and bounded the sheep and cattle pastures beyond. By the river, the light wind brushed through level fields of barley like ripples across the surface of a golden sea.

George Robson climbed down from a tractor parked in the yard and shook their hands.

'It's all over the town about his lordship. I can't believe it,' Robson said. 'How can I help?'

He was clearly surprised, but not angered by Shona's questions. Was someone from the rewilding group behind the attack?

'I can't see what it would achieve,' Robson said, seriously, shaking his head.

'I've spoken to the earl myself about the habitat restoration plan,' Shona said. 'He's convinced his grouse shoot is the better way to provide jobs rather than turning the land over to rewilding.'

'It's not an either-or situation. The restoration of wild places and the regeneration of the rural economy go hand in hand. We've been looking at this for over a decade, and leading charities like the RSPB, the Woodland Trust and Rewilding Scotland support the buyout project.'

'The old earl wasn't in any state to make decisions for years before he went,' Murdo said.

'Aye, that's true,' Robson said. 'But things have moved on now. We need regeneration to start happening round here, with the environment at the heart of it. We're planning small-scale businesses to develop technology that can help landowners understand the potential for carbon storage on their land and inform land-use decisions. The raw data exists – often from satellites – but we need it processed by land managers. Make sure, for example, the right native trees are going in the right places.'

Robson had honed his pitch before investors and the press, but the neat prosperity of his farming enterprise, complete with solar panels on the barn roof and a wind turbine behind the steading, gave weight to what he was saying. He clearly practised what he preached.

'It's not just about the moss,' he continued. 'These are globally important peatlands. Scotland's been praised internationally for its ambitious climate change targets. The eyes of the world are on us. We've raised over 2 million pounds from supporters in dozens of countries who'll be able to follow the restoration journey through digital media.'

The Border reivers had made their own ways in the Debatable Land for centuries, Shona thought. They'd known how to work the political and economic systems beyond their borders, playing the parliaments in England and Scotland off against each other. Now, it seemed, their descendants were using that skill for the greater good, as well as personal gain. They were making the world an offer it couldn't refuse because, if it did refuse, it wouldn't be a raid of fire and sword that would follow, but environmental Armageddon. It was a powerful argument, but it also emphasised how high the stakes had climbed.

'So you're telling me the removal of Alexander Douglas wouldn't be a welcome development for the rewilding group?' It was the only motive Shona could see that linked Ben Elliot's actions with the attempt last night on the earl's life.

'We were all shocked at what Ben did, Inspector,' Robson said. 'We pray he finds a path to redemption, and we will do what we can to support his girls, but we condemn utterly his action. It's not in our interest to see the earl removed.'

'Why?'

'Because I think he'll come round to our view,' Robson said. 'He's an educated man, a Yale business school graduate. Bield Moss will win his heart and his head, I'm sure of it. If he went, who knows what the next earl might be like? We could end up with someone like Jack Douglas.'

'He isn't in the line of succession,' Shona said, puzzled.

'Aye, I know. But he was a great favourite of the old earl, before they fell out and he went off with the hippies to France. He'd have had us all living in communes and eating mushrooms as a business plan.'

Shona suppressed a smile. Jack's reiver tourism and foraging courses obviously didn't come up to scratch with the rewilding group.

'And if his lordship died,' Robson continued, 'there'd be a risk the moss would go on the open market, and we'd be priced out. A lot of corporate investment firms are banking land in Scotland.'

Shona recalled Rob and Becca debating the 'green lairds' trend: banks and large companies buying moorland to offset their own carbon emissions, but bringing little benefit to the local economy.

Shona's phone buzzed in her pocket. She checked the screen. Dr Armstrong. She declined the call. He'd sent her a couple of chatty texts the previous day, asking how she was, as though they were somehow friends again. Shona hadn't answered. She had to wonder if he was blind to what he'd done, or if he was angling for forgiveness.

'What about these pranks played on the earl?' Shona said. 'Your members behind those?'

Robson shook his head. 'Not that I know of, but I hear the earl took it all in good part. Anyway, there's a difference between spray painting some sheep and nearly drowning him.'

'I agree,' Shona said. She looked at Murdo, who gave a slight shake of his head, indicating he had no more questions. 'Thank you for your time, Mr Robson,' Shona said and held out her hand.

He shook it, then indicated to Murdo he'd just be a minute. He disappeared inside a steading building and returned with a box. Shona saw eggs, shrink-wrapped packs of sausages and a bag of potatoes inside.

'For the Elliot girls,' Robson said. Murdo took the box and Robson waved away his thanks. 'God bless you, Murdo, for all that you're doing.'

When they were back in Shona's car, she said to Murdo, 'What d'you make of that?'

'Robson's got a point. Better the devil you know when it comes to landlords.'

'You didn't see the earl's face when I raised the community buyout with him,' Shona said as she stared the engine. '*Over my dead body* was his response.'

'Well, let's hope it doesnae come to that,' Murdo replied.

Shona could only agree.

Her phone buzzed again. There was an email from the pathologist Professor Sue Kitchen that she'd overlooked earlier, and a string of missed calls from Cam Armstrong.

'Hang on, Murdo,' Shona said. 'I better see what he wants.' Two of the shoot staff were still at the dig, but if there was any trouble, she'd send Sergeant Graham and his constables to deal with it.

At first the voicemail message hissed and cut out, but then Cam's words came through loud and clear.

'Shona, you better come. We've found a child's body.'

Chapter 30

A Land Rover from the Earl of Langdale's shoot was waiting for them at the car park. Shona and Murdo got in and they made the ten-minute climb up the track. The driver reported that early this morning a student working in one of a number of test pits on the far side of the site, sunk to check if there was a boundary ditch, had uncovered what looked like a child preserved in the peat. The students had been sent down to the camp at the Elliot farm until more was known. Shona tried to catch the forensic assistant Suzanne, but she'd already been diverted to a job in Glasgow; she needed to submit a fresh request.

But when she reached the dig, Shona saw the lone figure of Professor Sue Kitchen waiting by the dig gazebo, a cup of tea in her hand. The forensic pathologist rarely graced the recovery of remains and was most often found in the post-mortem suite at Glasgow's Queen Elizabeth Hospital. The professor saw Shona's look of surprise. She poured Shona a cup of tea from a flask and handed it to her.

'It's not an official visit. Cam called me,' Sue said. 'I was in Galashiels for a junior fencing tournament. It's easier to get here from the east, with all the trees down. Just a hop over the hills.'

Shona suppressed a smile as she pictured her tall, broad-shouldered friend as a giant striding over the Southern Uplands.

'Given the circumstances,' Sue continued, 'I thought I better have a look. I've been meaning to see the site for myself anyway. And see you, too,' she added, her face serious. 'How are you holding up? What's happening with Rob in London?'

'I'm fine. Rob's barrister is happy, but it'll run into next week,' Shona sighed. 'I'll go down, soon as I can.' She was aware of Sue studying her carefully and making her own diagnosis on the toll the fraud case was taking.

Sue gave her a sympathetic nod, the manifestation of a bedside manner the pathologist no longer required for patients and now usually reserved for the bereaved. There was that word again, *bereaved*. Olivia Thomson's mother, frail and desperate on the evening news, flashed up in her mind's eye and Shona tilted her head towards the covered pit, partly hidden by the heather, on the far side of the excavation.

'You had a look?' she said. 'What d'you think?'

Murdo, notebook out, stood alone by the tarpaulin, the two Langdale men having gone back down to the student camp. There were no birds, and the wind dropped to an uneasy calm. Under the grey sky, the moss seemed to hold its breath and the familiar air of disquiet settled again on Shona.

'I've been waiting for you and Cam. Here he is,' Sue replied, and drained her cup. The archaeologist's Land Rover was visible halfway up the track.

Shona swallowed the last of her tea and concentrated on the vehicle, impatient for Cam to arrive. It would make sense if the remains were Olivia's. The girls were taken together, so surely it was likely they'd been buried close to each other?

'Did you read my email?' Sue said.

'I haven't got to it yet,' Shona replied, still watching the Land Rover's approach, one finger tapping on the rim of her cup. What was so important that he had to leave the site instead of just getting on with it?

'Your friend DCI Frank Paterson from the Historic Cases Unit called,' Sue said, breaking into her thoughts. 'We had a discussion about new forensic techniques which might be applied, *in theory*, to the Girls in the Glen, should it ever *officially* be reviewed.' She gave Shona a complicit smile. 'I thought it might be a good exercise for my students.'

'Did you find something?' Shona turned, momentarily distracted from Cam's arrival by the seriousness in Sue's voice.

'The acidic environment of the peat bogs affects DNA, and we're not quite there yet with a reliable method of analysing it, but Paterson arranged access to the stored evidence. There's not much, but there was an envelope of tapings, taken from the recovered victims, to look for clothing fibres transferred from the killer. What they couldn't do then, but we can now, is extract DNA from those sticky-tape strips.'

'And?'

'We've male DNA on two of the victims, Karen Anderson and Cindy Jardine. It could be John Maxwell's.'

Shona felt a jolt of surprise and hope, but Sue held up a moderating hand.

'We don't have Maxwell's DNA on the UK database. He refused to give a sample and, as you know, it's only been possible to do that without consent in Scotland since 1995. I suppose with the case closed, and since he wasn't rearrested for other offences, no one pursued it. The prison disposed of his belongings after his death, and there's no known blood relative we can ask.'

Shona's eyes slid to Cam Armstrong's vehicle and quickly back. She hadn't discussed her doubts over his father's case with him and would need to be very careful how she phrased it if she asked him for a DNA sample.

As Murdo had already discovered, Cam's birth certificate was in a sealed file in the National Records office. A court order would open that, but it still wasn't absolute confirmation that Cam was Maxwell's *biological* son – just that he was registered as such. It might just prove, once and for all, that the original investigation had got it right, and lead to closing other historic cases. She could see Detective Superintendent Davies's satisfied smile and the resulting media coverage. Even without modern forensic techniques, Willie Graham's local knowledge and good old-fashioned policing had got the right result. But if the DNA samples didn't match, either Cam wasn't Maxwell's biological son as he'd thought, or another individual was linked to the Girls in the Glen killings. Either result would have huge implications for both Armstrong and Police Scotland.

Sue was watching her and had partly guessed Shona's line of thought. 'You're wondering if confirming Maxwell's DNA will implicate him in other murders?'

'It's a consideration,' Shona admitted. 'Are you part of Dr Armstrong's plan to set up a forensic archaeology team at the University of Glasgow?'

'I'm interested,' Sue replied. 'An interdisciplinary model for forensic science and medical training is an attractive one. Dundee University already has its Centre for Anatomy and Human Identification, and we've a lot to offer in terms of expertise.'

Dr Armstrong, it seemed, had recruited a powerful ally in Professor Kitchen.

As the Land Rover neared, Shona saw there was a slight, dark-haired figure in the passenger seat, who she assumed was the student who'd made the find. But, as the vehicle came to a halt, all the optimism and hope Sue's news had brought plummeted as swiftly as if Shona had stepped into one of the moss's sinkholes. Shona composed her features into a professional smile and pulled open the passenger's door.

'Mrs Thomson,' Shona said. 'I really don't think this is the place for you today.'

Olivia Thomson's mother was even more bird-like in the flesh than she'd appeared on television. She ignored Shona and edged forward in her seat, determined to get out of the vehicle.

'You'd be more comfortable at The Douglas Arms,' Shona said and glared at Cam, who'd come around from his side of the Land Rover to take Mrs Thomson's arm. He avoided Shona's look. In what universe did he think offering the woman a ringside seat at her murdered daughter's disinterment was a good idea? She'd have to close the site and declare it a crime scene.

'The police have had their chance. It's Dr Armstrong's turn. I'm going to sit in thon tent,' Vicky said, certainty in every syllable. 'Tell me when you're sure. All I ask is a few minutes near her.' She stopped her faltering steps and turned to Shona. 'Olivia's lain oot here for near thirty year. I'm her mother. I brought her into the world. You can give me a wee while here, at the place she left the world, to make peace wi' the fact I couldnae stop that.'

Vicky took a series of shallow breaths and Shona could see the physical price she was paying. She'd travelled from Glasgow and must be exhausted, driven on by a single-minded determination to be there for Olivia.

Professor Kitchen had come over and had been listening to the exchange.

'Mrs Thomson… *Vicky*,' she said. 'I'm Sue Kitchen and I'll be looking after Olivia when she leaves the moss. If it's all right with Shona, I'll sit with you, and you can ask me any questions you have.'

Shona had the sense she'd been ganged up on, but perhaps they were right. The crime that had led them all here had been solved long ago, and the perpetrator had died in jail. No evidence chain would be compromised by Vicky's presence. This was about giving a final justice to the remaining family, resurrecting Olivia not as a victim but as a departed daughter whose mother would be joining on the other side shortly. It was a setting to rights, and who had the greatest right to decide how that might be accomplished? The law might say it was Shona's decision, but in that bleak and overwhelming landscape, it felt to her that an older and more natural justice should prevail. The justice of mother and child reunited. Becca had been right. If Shona were in Vicky's shoes, she'd want to be there, however painful the moment.

'All right,' Shona said. 'But if I think you're distressed or unwell, Professor Kitchen and I will take you back to The Douglas Arms and get you checked over.'

They made Vicky Thomson comfortable in the gazebo. Cam brought a tartan rug from the back of the Land Rover, and Sue poured a mug of tea. When she was settled, Cam and Shona made their way to where Murdo stood, hands clasped before him in respectful vigil at the graveside.

'When I called Vicky this morning, she got straight in a taxi,' Cam said. 'I couldn't stop her.'

'You should have talked to me first,' Shona replied. She'd dealt with enough grieving families to know Vicky Thomson's action was entirely foreseeable. Once Olivia was in Professor Kitchen's care, Shona would ask for a Glasgow officer to act as family liaison to deal with the resultant media attention and funeral arrangements.

They had cut back the dry heather tops around the test pit, revealing the delicate cushioned stars of sphagnum moss, lime green and blood red, that sheltered beneath.

Cam pulled back the tarpaulin sheet. He kneeled close to the edge and reached into the metre-square hole to pull back a second cover. A long plait of reddish hair coiled across the surface of the exposed peat.

'Tannic acid of the peat stains everything this colour,' Cam said. 'The original hair could be dark or light, but it appears to be the remains of a young female.'

Olivia's photo in the press had shown her with black hair held back by an Alice band, but it was certainly long enough to be styled this way.

Shona kneeled beside Cam as he carefully trowelled back the peat, which had already begun to dry out. The head and one shoulder of a small figure slowly emerged. She appeared curled on her side, her hands to her face, almost as if hiding.

'We'll need to extend the test pit in order to preserve her forensically,' Cam said.

'Is it her?'

As soon as Cam was sure, Shona would call the fiscal. Forensics could take over and remove the surrounding turf, in order to lift her and any associated evidence.

With painstaking care, Cam teased back the peat. The skin around the child's forehead was ochre and the texture of rubber.

Above them, the disc of the sun shone through thinning clouds, pale as the moon. In the trench, Cam gripped its tiny twin between his fingers, allowing crumbs of damp peat to fall from its face. A silver coin. He sat up and peered at it closely, examining the raised pattern on its surface.

Shona stared into the pit where Cam had been working. 'Where was that?'

'Sitting on her cheek, next to her hand,' Cam said.

Holding the coin between his finger and thumb, Cam rotated it from one side to another.

'It's a quarter merk,' he said, as he handed it to Shona. 'Scottish. Probably seventeenth century.'

Shona gently turned the coin in her hand. One side showed a worn design of a thistle, and the other, a shield with a lion rearing up on its hind legs. She passed it on to Murdo, who stared at it fascinated, holding it gingerly in his palm.

Cam's attention had returned to the metre-wide hole. A moment later, he was upright again, shaking the damp soil from his trowel.

'The surrounding contexts look undisturbed. The body appears to be *in situ*.' He sat back on his heels, his shoulders slumped. 'It's not her. It's not Olivia.'

Without another word, he got to his feet, and left Shona and Murdo by the pit.

They watched as Cam crossed the heather and kneeled by Vicky Thomson. He took her hand as he delivered the news. She bowed her head in acknowledgement that her hopes had again been dashed and her slight frame shook as tears fell.

'Who does he think it is?' Murdo said.

'A reiver's child,' Shona said. 'It's what he was looking for in the first place. Evidence of settlement, a place of sanctuary. It proves his research was right.'

But at this moment, what had proved him right had also proved him wrong. Olivia Thomson was still out there. It was as if Bield Moss was toying with them. It had folded the girl into its dark layers and saw no reason to give her back. Shona was overcome by the immensity of the place which stretched out to every horizon. She thought of all the times she'd been at sea with the lifeboat, searching for a person in the water, their head no bigger than a football, visible for a fraction of a second between the waves' peaks, but only if you were looking in the right direction in the first place. The lifeboat wasn't always successful, but when they were, it was worth all the effort. A life saved.

Shona couldn't save Olivia, but perhaps she could save her mother from dying without her child, and that was why she had to keep on looking.

–

'I'm sorry,' Shona said, when she returned to the tent and crouched down by Vicky.

'Don't be,' Vicky said, her iron composure regained. 'Out here, I feel near her, and what I've seen today gives me hope. If anyone can find her, it'll be Dr Armstrong.'

Once Mrs Thomson had gone with Cam and Professor Kitchen in the Land Rover, Shona stood with Murdo on the edge of the moor. His normally steadfast expression had taken on a low and settled scowl.

'That poor woman,' he said. 'It's no' right she's still going through this. Maxwell destroyed all those lives, and he's still doin' it fae beyond the grave.'

Shona told him about Professor Kitchen's finding and the possibility of matching Maxwell's DNA to other outstanding cases.

'Suppose that's something,' he said, grudgingly. 'But plenty of folk knew what Maxwell was. If somebody had stopped him earlier, we'd awe hae been better off.'

'Different times, Murdo,' Shona replied. Victims of violence, such as Cameron's mother, were treated with less understanding and compassion than today. Perhaps his mother had carried the guilt all her life that if Maxwell had been locked up for his attacks on her, he wouldn't have had the opportunity to kill other women and girls. But that hadn't been her responsibility.

'They're no' different enough for my liking. Just look at Flora, and Archie Nixon coming after you,' Murdo said, then turned towards the corner of the moor and the test pit where Dr Armstrong had made his grim discovery. 'I mean, that's no' a Christian burial. There's a wee reiver's lassie who came to harm and was left oot on the moss. Lilly's the same. When you think of it like that, it's hard to argue we've come as far as we should in the last 300 years.' He wiped the back of his hand across his eyes. 'This wind.'

'I agree,' Shona said, her face serious, not fooled for a second that the wind was responsible for his damp eyes. 'There's always more to do.'

She heard the roar of the shoot Land Rover coming to collect them and took a last look around the moss. The sun had retreated and the dark clouds, banked up on the Solway, were again heading their way.

'I need to check if they've released Alexander Douglas from hospital,' Shona said. 'I've got Kate with him. She promised she'd have a word about the Elliot girls and the farm. You okay? You know if there's anything you want to talk about, my door's always open, Murdo.'

'Aye, I'm fine,' Murdo said, his jaw set. 'I'll head back tae the farm, if you don't need me, and mibbae have a wee chat with those shoot fellas over a cup of tea. They might let slip something about the earl, or what's being said about Archie Nixon coming after you.'

'Thanks, Murdo. We'll catch up later.' Shona knew some of Murdo's old friends from the town were among the shoot staff, and thought that perhaps that cup of tea would serve another purpose. Whatever burden Murdo was carrying could be set down in their company, at least for a while.

Chapter 31

Once Murdo had left, Shona stood for a moment by the Audi. The Debatable Land, it seemed, was not ready to give up all of its dead. Bield Moss stretched in an endless sea of heather to the horizon. For three centuries it had been owned by neither Scotland nor England, but though battles had raged, it had also been home to families who'd sought sanctuary in its wild havens. Soon, new forces would try to change it once more. Whether that was the earl, or the community rewilding group, remained to be seen. Alexander Douglas and Flora had narrowly escaped death. It was Shona's task to make sure there were no more casualties along the way.

Her thoughts returned to the small corpse that had been uncovered on the moss. Murdo was right. That was no Christian burial. It was likely she'd also met her end through violence. A child in the wrong place at the wrong time, just as Lilly and Olivia had been. Shona couldn't shake the sense she'd let both Olivia and her mother down. If Vicky Thomson had had the strength, perhaps she'd have raged against this failure but, if anything, her simple acceptance that the police were no longer interested in finding her daughter stung Shona more than any angry outburst would.

She thought again about Professor Kitchen's discovery of the DNA, and forwarded the email to Ravi, asking him to run checks on partner databases, such as Interpol. Maxwell had worked abroad in France and Germany in the late 1970s and early 1980s. Vicious serial offenders often began their criminal careers early. DNA evidence from a reviewed, but unsolved, rape or murder abroad might give them a break.

The car park was empty, but she heard the sound of a vehicle approaching up the single-track road. Sergeant Graham's fourbie swung into the car park. Dour resentment clouded his heavy features as he got out. Someone, perhaps one of the shoot staff, had alerted him to Shona and Murdo's arrival at the dig and now Willie Graham's nose was out of joint at not being informed about possible developments on his patch.

'It's not Olivia Thomson,' Shona said bluntly, as he approached.

Graham stopped a few feet from Shona, his weight on his rear foot. He hooked his thumbs into the armholes of his stab vest and stared out across the moor, the muscle of his clenched jaw working. After a moment, he gave a curt nod.

'How's it coming with Archie Nixon?' Shona could keep this professional and civil, as long as Sergeant Graham remembered his place.

'We've found nothing to link him to Flora's accident.'

'We're calling it an accident now, are we? What about the CCTV from the town?'

'Nothing,' Graham said.

Shona balled her fists in the pockets of her coat and wondered again if Graham was doing his job properly. Then she remembered Murdo's involvement, and knew he'd have expressed his disapproval and cracked the whip if he thought anyone was slacking or potential avenues were being left unexplored.

'Can you think of anyone else you might have upset?' Graham said.

'Apart from you?' Shona challenged.

'Aye, well, I've an alibi,' Graham replied.

Shona glared at him, then took a step closer and jabbed a finger in his chest. 'You're perilously close to a suspension for misconduct, Sergeant.'

'You've no' exactly handled things with kid gloves, have you?' he said.

'I don't need kid gloves. I'm the polis,' Shona said. 'It's my job to get the bad guys, not win polls for popularity.'

'You'd no' last five minutes in a toon like this,' Sergeant Graham spat. 'It was local knowledge – people coming to us cos they can trust us – that locked up John Maxwell in the first place.'

'It was your brother, wasn't it? Your brother was the gamekeeper that Maxwell confessed to.'

'Aye, it was, and before you make any accusations about a fit-up, he wasnae the only one who heard him. Jack Douglas knew aboot it, too, and backed my brother up.'

'What was Jack Douglas doing hanging out with gamekeepers?'

'He spent summers here as a lad and then worked for the old earl. Old Douglas was fond o' him and there was talk at one point aboot Jack taking o'er the estate, but he's a distant cousin so that wasn't gonna happen.' He stopped at the look of surprise on Shona's face. 'What? No one tell you? Common knowledge, but maybe nobody felt like sharing it wi' outsiders.'

There was no statement from Jack Douglas in the file, but perhaps that wasn't surprising given the poor record-keeping and intervening passage of time. Jack would have been in his early twenties, like Ben Elliot. At that age, he might have resembled his cousin Alexander in his desire to be accepted, especially if it looked like he might have a hand in running the estate. Perhaps he thought he was performing a community service and agreed to whatever seemed expedient at the time to lock up a man who was obviously a vicious and violent menace.

'Who else was in the frame for the murders at the time?' Shona demanded. Now Graham had broached the subject, she could challenge him on the points that were bothering her.

'No one,' he said, clearly taken aback that she would even ask that with the killer dead and no further victims found. 'Maxwell was a bad bastar'. Knocked his wife and kid about. Raped and beat a few lassies in the toon, though we couldnae get him for it. There's nothin' more to be said where he's concerned.'

His tone suddenly turned accusatory and tinged with pain. 'Ye ken, you should have called me if you thought that was Olivia. I retire next year. The only thing left to do is find the last Girl in the Glen. An' that's down to thon Armstrong lad, no' you. I'd a right to be there.'

He turned without another word and stalked back to his vehicle. Shona stared after him as he got into his patrol car and drove away. The Girls in the Glen case was eating at Willie Graham in a way Shona hadn't realised. Was it, as he said, a sense of a job left unfinished as he neared the end of his career? Or was there something else?

Her remark about Willie Graham being behind the wheel of the car that targeted her had been a knee-jerk response to the absence of proper respect for a senior officer. His assertion of an alibi had been a little too quick for her liking. But if he'd truly wanted to dispose of her, she'd just handed him the perfect opportunity. An empty car park and 10,000 acres of moorland. And, if he'd come because he thought Olivia had been found, where were his constables? The ones he'd need to seal off the crime scene and keep the press at bay?

But Sergeant Graham had been on shift the night Flora was knocked down, his patrol car arriving within ten minutes of the 999 call. Shona had only worn her parka that day, although for the past week it had been visible in the back of the car, with her overnight bag, for anyone who'd cared to look. No, it was unlikely that he'd hit Flora, mistaking her for Shona, however much she'd like to pin it on him.

But now she wondered if his resentment of her very presence was about more than her being an outsider on his patch. Had he cut corners, strayed outside the letter of the law, to get the result he wanted? Sergeant Graham had built his career on the Girls in the Glen case. Shona was sure of one thing. He really didn't want her poking about in the past.

Chapter 32

Later that evening, Murdo sat in his car, parked in a pool of darkness between the sparse streetlights, waiting. A quick call to the local police office was all it took for him to find Alan Kerr's registered address, in a dead-end street barely a quarter of a mile from his mother's house. Tonight Kerr's flat, in the two-storey Victorian terrace by the river, was quiet.

The Elliot girls had settled in front of a David Attenborough DVD that Shona had previously brought up at Becca's request. They had strict instructions to call Murdo at the first sign of trouble. The sheepdogs would raise the alarm if anyone came even close to the farm.

Murdo was patient. He'd probably be here till after the pubs closed. His message to Alan Kerr would be short. Get out of Langholm. You have no right to be here.

If Kerr didn't take the hint, Murdo would have a word with Willie Graham. The slightest violation of his parole and Kerr would go back inside to serve the remaining four years of his sentence. It would be a public service.

Murdo tapped the steering wheel and leaned his body back into the seat, easing the muscles he'd pressed into service hauling bales of hay around earlier in the barn for the goats' amusement. It was a relief to swap his jeans and sweatshirt for his customary suit.

Kerr's house had been empty when Murdo rang the bell. The curtains were open, but the lights were off. Murdo had cupped his face to the window. Behind the grubby nets, the front room was minimally furnished. Sofa, coffee table with two mugs on it and the red light of a TV set. The building, like many in the area, had been split into cramped flats sometime back in the 1980s. The former dining room was now a bedroom, with a tiny kitchen and bathroom out back. Landlords of these properties weren't fussy who they let to.

A car turned into the street, its headlights making a staccato sweep of the railings that lined the river. Murdo slid down behind the steering wheel in case he was spotted. The car stopped outside Kerr's house. Murdo caught the silhouettes of two men. The driver opened the door and the courtesy light clicked on.

And there he was: Alan Kerr, out on parole and banned from driving, bold as brass behind the wheel.

Murdo felt an unassailable swell of rage and vindication as he flung the car door open. No licence. No insurance. Kerr had gone away for the maximum term for the crime of causing death by dangerous driving, yet the minute he was back out, here he was, at it again. This little jaunt would add to his stay inside.

Murdo crossed the road and grabbed hold of Kerr before the man knew what was happening. His companion in the passenger seat stared, eyes wide with alarm. The rank smell of booze hit Murdo. Kerr had been drunk when he killed Drew.

Murdo was incensed. He hauled Kerr out of the car by the scruff of his neck and shook him hard. He felt featherlight, a husk of a creature, and Murdo could almost hear his bones and teeth rattle inside his worthless carcass. Kerr's hands shot up to protect his face.

For one brief moment Murdo was tempted to run the man headfirst into the house wall. He'd never felt such a white-hot rage, not even in his rugby-playing youth, when he'd sometimes been on the receiving end of the dirtiest, potentially career-destroying tactics from local rivals.

By ending this bastard's life, he could revenge Drew and stop this vermin wrecking any more families, or living to the ripe old age of the kind denied Murdo's brother. Kerr was pleading, but the words rushed over Murdo in a torrent of meaningless sound.

The man in the passenger seat made a move and Murdo, on his guard, caught the action. As Murdo swung to face the threat, still grasping Kerr, the shocked faces of two young children, their eyes wide with fear, came into view. A boy and a girl, strapped in car seats in the back. That Kerr could drive drunk with bairns was beyond Murdo's comprehension. The boy began to howl and struggle against his harness. The front passenger opened the door and vomited onto the road.

'It's okay, Dylan. It's okay,' Kerr soothed, twisting in Murdo's grip. 'Wait, please, Murdo. You dinnae understand.'

Blood rushed in Murdo's ears. He looked from the drunken, white-faced passenger who swayed, held upright only by his seat belt, to the children in the back. The girl, older by a year or so, but still no more than four or five, tried to comfort the boy.

Murdo pulled Kerr's arms behind his back and slipped the cuffs.

'Please, wait,' Kerr pleaded, squirming, his voice muffled as Murdo pressed him against the side of the vehicle. 'Ma sister, Sophie, has got the breast cancer. Her man struggles wi' his mental health and drinks. Been unemployed for a long time.'

It was the sort of sob story Murdo had heard many a time on the beat. He pulled out his phone and thumbed through his contacts for the local police office. The man in the passenger seat mumbled to himself.

'That's ma brother-in-law,' Kerr said. 'He called from thon car park at the other end of the toon, by the river, wi' the kids asleep in the back. I just ran, didnae think. I couldnae leave him in case he drove intae the river. I couldnae call him a cab. They'd report it to the polis or Social Services.'

Murdo's hand paused. 'It's all right, son,' he said to the child, who sobbed and sucked the corner of a blue blanket.

He manoeuvred Kerr against the front of his house and turned him round.

'Sit,' he ordered.

Kerr slid down the brickwork. 'I'll no' run, Murdo, but please, just listen.' His face was urgent and pleading. 'These kids are a reason to stay out of jail, ma chance to make amends. I'm no' just paying a debt to society. It's selfish,' he shrugged. 'I want a chance tae redeem myself in ma own eyes. I know what I'm like. If I'm no' careful, I'll just go back tae the drink and the drugs. I need a purpose for living, and living well. Dinnae deny me that, Murdo.'

To Murdo, it sounded like the well-rehearsed plea of a guilty man, caught out and clutching at straws.

No doors had opened, and no lights were on in the neighbouring houses. This was the kind of place a tussle in the street didn't raise even an eyebrow. But a slight woman, in a patterned skirt and denim jacket, approached along the pavement from the far end of the street.

'If you wouldn't mind, ma'am,' Murdo said, indicating she should step into the empty road to pass. But she halted uncertainly a short distance from the car.

'What's going on?' she said. She had fair hair cropped close. A gold cross around her neck caught the orange of the streetlights as she looked from Kerr to Murdo. Her eyes fell on the open car door and her hand shot to her mouth.

'Oh Alan, you didn't?'

'Who are you, ma'am?' Murdo said and planted himself on the pavement in front of his prisoner.

'I'm Karen Johnson, Alan's partner,' she said. 'I'm a prison visitor with the New Dawn.'

Murdo recognised the name as a church-based organisation working in offender rehabilitation.

'You should have waited for me,' she said to Kerr. It was obvious from her look of sorrow and rebuke that she recognised the seriousness of Kerr's transgression.

She produced a key from her pocket and turned to Murdo. 'Is it okay if I take Gordon and the kids inside?'

Murdo nodded and opened the rear door of the car. Karen leaned in. The kids obviously knew her. The little boy dropped his blanket and reached up, wet-eyed, to be lifted. Karen spoke softly to the girl and unclipped her seat belt, then took the boy. The little girl picked her way across the footwell. Murdo held out his hand, and she took it gingerly and jumped onto the pavement.

'Where's the mother?' Murdo said softly to Karen.

'Dumfries Royal Infirmary,' Karen replied. 'We're hoping to get her home soon.'

Murdo looked at Kerr, who sat up a little, smiled at the kids and gave them a nod of reassurance.

'Here,' Murdo held out his hand to Karen for the house key.

Karen looked back uncertainly at Gordon, who'd fallen asleep with his head against the door frame.

'Just leave him tae me,' Murdo said. 'You sort out the bairns.'

When she'd gone inside, Murdo closed the door. He pinched up the knees of his suit trousers and squatted down in front of Kerr. There was no smell of drink from the man and a breathalyser might well prove negative. But there was still the matter of his void driving licence and no insurance. It would be enough to put him back inside.

'If ma sister dies,' Alan whispered, 'the kids will likely go intae care. I know what I did tonight was wrong. Karen wants to be a force for good, and so do I. Dinnae deny me that, Murdo.'

Through the lit window, Murdo could see the kids on the sofa, the TV tuned to cartoons as Karen cast anxious glances at the street outside.

'I know what I did tonight was wrong,' Kerr said again. 'All I'm askin' is you think aboot this afore ye call the local polis.'

Murdo looked at the pathetic figure before him. The anger had drained, leaving a bitter sense of defeat. He saw Drew again, with his brilliant smile, snuffed out like a candle. Murdo had what he needed to put Kerr back behind bars. It was unlikely Karen Johnson was lying, but even if she was, there would be phone evidence and CCTV from the shops in town that must have caught Alan Kerr's return journey at the wheel of his brother-in-law's car.

It would be enough.

'Get up.' Murdo pulled Kerr to his feet. He swung him again to face the wall, then unlocked the handcuffs. He pointed to Gordon, still passed out in the passenger seat. 'Help me get him inside.'

Kerr rubbed his wrists and peered at Murdo. He followed Murdo around to the passenger door and together they half-dragged, half-carried Kerr's brother-in-law into the house. The children were sitting on the sofa, eyes fixed on the TV. They deposited him in the bedroom.

'This means you're letting me go?' Kerr said.

Murdo shook his head and stepped back out into the road. He couldn't look at Kerr without seeing Drew's face. But now he also saw the boy sucking on a blanket and the frightened little girl. Kerr wasn't the right person to watch over them.

'I can't do that,' Murdo said.

'I won't run,' Kerr repeated, almost defiant.

A call to Langholm police office was all Murdo needed to do now. The white-hot need for revenge would be sated. He wanted Kerr off the streets and now he had the power to do that. He turned and walked away.

Chapter 33

Shona spent Friday morning dealing with a serious assault in Gretna Green motorway services. After a fight at a wedding, round two had broken out at the KFC, and a man was now in Dumfries Royal Infirmary. Members of both families were due to join the happy couple on their honeymoon in Magaluf. Shona wondered if she should put in a call to the Majorcan police and warn them to get the cells ready, but concluded that there was only a fifty–fifty chance the party would even make it to the airport.

At lunchtime, she walked to a nearby cafe, as much to clear her head as to buy a sandwich. Shona was halfway back up the stairs at Cornwall Mount when her jacket pocket buzzed. She let the strap of her handbag slide to the crook of her left elbow and held her takeaway coffee high, out of harm's way, as she fished out her phone and answered Kate's call.

'The earl's fine,' Kate said, before Shona could ask the question. 'I mentioned the Elliot girls' notice to quit the farm. He didn't know. He's going to look into it.'

Perhaps the rumour that the estate was taking back the Elliot land to farm themselves, with the farmhouse part of The Douglas Arms expansion plans, had all been cooked up by Cousin Jack and Lady Lucy behind the earl's back. His intervention would give the girls a stay of execution, but Shona had little doubt what the ultimate outcome would be.

Shona pushed through the swing doors with her shoulder. The main office was busy. Ravi got up from his desk and came towards her.

'Thanks, Kate,' Shona said. 'Anything else?'

There was a brief pause, then Kate said, 'I'm just on my way back from Langdale…'

'Need to have a chat, boss,' Ravi mouthed, getting Shona's attention.

'Hang on, Kate,' Shona said and put her hand over the mouthpiece of her phone. 'Is this something we all need to hear, Rav?'

'Aye.' There was an air of suppressed animation about Ravi's features, as if he was bursting to tell her right now.

Shona went into her office, put her coffee on the desk and jabbed her thumb over her shoulder to indicate Ravi should get everyone into the conference room.

'Sorry, on you go, Kate,' Shona said, and let her bag slide to the floor.

'I went to check over the earl's statement, to see if he'd remembered anything else.'

'And?' Shona prompted.

'He thinks he may have been mistaken about an attacker.'

Shona stopped, her coffee halfway to her lips. 'How d'you mean?'

When Shona had tilted the earl's oxygen mask as he lay on the riverbank, she'd clearly heard him say someone had struck him. *He hit me. Pushed.*

'He now says he may have walked into a branch in the dark, and fallen into the river,' Kate said.

So much for graduating from mountain school. To knock yourself unconscious against a branch, while wearing a helmet equipped with a torch, would take some going, but Shona had known the lifeboat called out for people who'd done sillier things and ended up in just as much danger as Alexander Douglas.

'I think he's a bit embarrassed,' Kate continued. 'He wants to join the volunteer flood rescue team. He's worried they won't have him.'

'You're kidding me,' Shona said, exasperated. 'He's Alexander Douglas, Earl of Langdale. They'll let him play.'

The gamekeeper Charles Bell had mentioned this. So, the earl's pride was dented and, because of that, Shona had spent most of yesterday, and a chunk of her budget, running after a ghost. But then she remembered the earl's shocked words. *He hit me. Pushed.* Not the embarrassment of someone who'd stumbled in the darkness, but the reaction of a man who believed himself a target and had a fair idea who his attacker might be. If it was the same individual who'd previously pranked him, then the incident had gone beyond a practical joke. Why Alexander Douglas wasn't willing to share any of this was a different question and one Shona, for the moment, couldn't answer.

'So, can I tell him we're closing the case?' Kate said.

'Well, unless we get all the riverbank trees in for an ID parade and he picks out the one that whacked him, I guess we'll have to,' Shona sighed. Kate obviously didn't share her doubts. 'How far away are you?'

'Half an hour?' Kate said. 'There's a bit of traffic.'

'Okay, we're just going into conference. We need to press on with the Girls in the Glen briefing document, so see you shortly. You can update us on what the Edinburgh detective said about Cindy Jardine.'

Shona ended the call, then quickly checked her emails. She tried Murdo, but his phone went straight to voicemail. She left him a brief message about the earl's change of mind, then took her coffee into the conference room where Ravi and the civilian staff were already seated.

'Ravi, we'll go to you first, but before we do, there's an update on the Earl of Langdale.' Shona told them of Alexander Douglas's recent recollection that he'd been alone when he went into the water. 'So we can stand down the hunt for Darren Porter, among other things.'

'Porter's excluded himself,' Ravi said, unfolding a printed sheet from his notebook. 'There's a system flag for a DNA on remains spotted in Lochaber by a couple of climbers. They've been positively identified as Darren Porter's.'

'When were they recovered?' Shona said, taking the sheet and searching for a date.

'Couple of weeks ago,' Ravi said. 'But it looks like his body's been lying out there for months. Found at the base of a cliff. Open verdict on cause of death but it's likely an accident or, given his mental health history, suicide.'

A small smile of triumph appeared on Vinny's face. 'I said there was a reason I couldn't find him.'

'Well, he didn't die just to prove you right,' Shona said.

Vinny looked affronted, as if Shona blamed him for Porter's remains not turning up sooner.

'Does this mean we've tied off all the lines of enquiry related to Nicola Baird's shooting?' Shona said. 'No outstanding persons of interest?' If the file was ready to go to the fiscal, that would be something.

'There's just the three unidentified individuals from the drone footage,' Chloe said.

'Let me see.' Shona put her glasses on. There were a couple of people in green waterproofs, hoods up, making it difficult to tell their age or gender. The day had been dry, but the wind was strong, so perhaps the head coverings were protection from the chill.

'The local cops had no luck with this pair?' Shona said, and Chloe shook her head. Both figures carried large rucksacks, so perhaps Kate's theory about long-distance walkers leaving this remote area without realising what had happened was valid.

The second photograph was from directly above, not much more than a shape against the heather. A blurred bullseye of pale hair was visible on top of their head.

'This is from before the shooting, right? You have any wider shots of this individual?' Shona said.

When she saw the figure within the expanse of moor, she had no doubt. Off to the left, a short distance away, were two other blurred objects that at first glance could have been deer.

Shona tapped the photograph. 'They're ponies. It's the earl's cousin, Jack Douglas. He spends half his life up there. Did no one think to cross-check his statement?' She threw the snaps on the table. 'Right, well, I'm happy we've identified everyone we can who was on the moor that morning, so the file can go to the fiscal. Anyone else got any queries over this?'

There were head shakes around the table. With the case complete, the Procurator Fiscal could set a hearing date, and the next stage of Ben Elliot's journey through Scotland's justice system would be underway.

'Okay.' Shona leaned forward and on the table. 'The Girls in the Glen briefing file. The child's body recently located at the university dig on Bield Moss was a historic deposition, but that just emphasises that we need to be prepared. There'll be far more interest from the media as the crowdfunded project, led by Dr Armstrong, enters its next phase.'

Shona paused. 'Our other objective is to identify, evaluate and progress any information that might help to recover Olivia Thomson's body.' She got up from her seat and pushed her chair to the side, clearing the space in front of the whiteboard. 'Ravi, will you do the honours?' She handed him a marker pen.

'Now, as I said at the last briefing, I want a clear chronology, particularly on the witness statements and anything that throws any light on Maxwell's motives. So let's go through what you've found, victim by victim, starting with number one: Harriet Jackson, from Keswick.'

Ravi wrote the name on the board, along with the date she disappeared and where she was found.

'Only thing to add,' Hannah Crawford began, 'is that Harriet's boyfriend, Jimmy Fraser, was accused of stealing diesel from the Langdale estate and selling it on. He was sacked soon after she disappeared. Three months later he was found hanging in woodland nearby and it was thought the loss of his job was a contributory factor in his suicide.'

'Okay, thank you, Hannah,' Shona said.

No one had anything to add, and the team had uncovered no new connection between Harriet and John Maxwell.

'Okay. We'll leave our second victim – Cindy Jardine, from Edinburgh – until Kate gets back.' Shona glanced at the time on her phone. She shouldn't be long.

'Victim number three, Karen Anderson. We now know her husband Craig worked for the Langdale estate on a land conveyance, but he'd only brought her with him because there'd been trouble at home with vandals and he was worried about leaving her alone overnight. Thoughts?'

Ed, a young intelligence processor and part-time special officer, cleared his throat. 'I looked at this. In common with Harriet Jackson's abduction, the investigation concluded that Maxwell's targeting of her was opportunistic.'

'I've traced the land deals,' Vinny said, 'and added them to the GIS map.'

Shona took a deep breath. 'So now we come to Lilly and Olivia. The motive put forward by the prosecution was that Maxwell took revenge on his neighbours, the Thomson family, because of the father's interference in Maxwell's domestic violence.'

She got up and took the pen from Ravi. 'But Ben Elliot told Murdo and I that, at the time, Lilly's father, Findlay Scott, had dealt out rough justice to a couple of poachers and it was thought by many people that they'd taken the girls to teach him a lesson, but something had gone wrong.'

She wrote *poachers* with a question mark, beneath Olivia's and Lilly's names.

'Elliot couldn't remember the names, describing them only as *a couple of the Nixon callants*, which means *lads*, according to Murdo. The Scott family home was set alight, and livestock targeted. Any sign in the files that this was pursued as a line of enquiry?' Shona said.

Hannah tucked a strand of her short, grey bob behind her ear and flicked through the pages in from of her. When she came to a list of names, she ran her finger down them, marked two with her highlighter pen and nodded.

'Malcolm Nixon and his brother Archibald were interviewed once about the fire, but they denied any involvement in it, or in the girls' disappearance, and were released.'

'Archibald Nixon?' Shona said. 'Is that the Archie Nixon who's in the frame for knocking Flora down? Murdo says he's got form for vehicle-related incidents.'

Hannah checked the details and nodded. 'It's the same guy.'

'Just supposing,' Ravi began, 'that what Ben Elliot said was right, and the girls were taken in a tit-for-tat that got out of hand. In which case Nixon might have targeted you, not because of the incident in the pub car park and the bad publicity, but because he thinks you're getting closer to the truth.'

Shona considered this for a moment. It made sense. Both Sergeant Graham and, more importantly, Murdo had interviewed Archie Nixon. But, from what Shona could tell, Nixon was a classic bully. She was itching to have a go at him herself, just to see what his reaction was now the tables were turned and he wasn't in a car park, backed up by his mates, or anonymous in the dark behind the wheel of a car.

'Good point, Ravi. Let's go and have a chat with him this afternoon.'

She didn't care if she stepped on Sergeant Graham's toes. Telling her to leave the original Girls in the Glen case alone was the biggest mistake he could have made.

'I keep coming back to Maxwell's motive,' Shona said. 'Maxwell didn't know these women, but he knew Lilly and Olivia. We assumed the motive was sexual, but the forensics doesn't fully back that up. What other possible motive links all these cases?'

The discussion circled the room. Robbery, drugs, jealousy. None seemed to fit.

'All we've got is the confession from John Maxwell,' Ravi said. 'It's rambling, but paints the initial three murders as opportunistic. He saw the women and felt like killing them. Taking the girls was an act of revenge on his neighbour.'

'See, that rings alarm bells for me,' Shona said. 'Suddenly, he starts planning things.'

'The forensic evidence is centred on the murder weapon: a knife, and rope used to bind the victims, both found in Maxwell's vehicle,' Ravi added.

'Yes, but in a rural community back then, did people even lock their cars? Anyone could have planted them. Oh, Hannah, any statement from Jack Douglas about him backing up the confession?'

Hannah looked puzzled. 'Should there be?'

'According to Willie Graham, the earl's cousin confirmed Graham's own brother's account of a confession, but I haven't seen a record of this anywhere.'

'My audit shows it's likely a single archive box, representing about 10 per cent of the original documentation, is missing,' Hannah said, with her customary precision. 'I can pull the court transcript for you, see if he was called?'

'Thanks, Hannah, but it's probably quicker if I just ask him,' Shona said. She hoped the intervening years and his hippy lifestyle hadn't dimmed his memory. Then again, hearing a confession like that wasn't something you forgot easily.

A message from Kate flashed up on Shona's phone: *15 mins away. Trees!*

'Let's take a quick break till Kate gets here.' Shona's eyes fell on Chloe and Vinny Visuals. 'I want to see your GIS map and talk about any deposition sites. Kate's the expert on Langdale.'

'In every sense,' Ravi smirked.

The news of Kate's liaison with the Earl of Langdale had obviously leaked. Keeping anything quiet in an office full of cops was like juggling jelly – impossible, and often with messy results.

Everyone trooped out of the room. Shona heard the clatter of cups above the noise of the boiling kettle while other, more discerning, coffee addicts chose to make a quick dash to the Italian cafe up the road.

'Ravi,' Shona said as her DC returned, hopefully to take her order of a double espresso. He had his notebook in his hand, but his sombre face told her it wasn't refreshments he had in mind.

'Just got an email from Interpol,' he said. 'There's a hit on the DNA that Slasher Sue recovered.'

Shona sat up. 'And?' she prompted.

Ravi looked at his notebook. 'A Jacques Darceleaux. They're sending the file over.'

Shona took a moment to process what this meant. They'd know more when they saw the documentation, but the case had taken on a European dimension.

'Maxwell worked abroad,' she said. 'He could have used an alias?'

Ravi nodded his agreement.

'You're not asking Dr Armstrong for a sample?' he asked.

'From our chat last week in the interview room, I doubt he'd give one, and I want this kept between you and me until we've seen the file.' It was highly unlikely Cam Armstrong would reveal his connection to the Girls in the Glen killer to the press. But, as Detective Superintendent Davies had previously pointed out, the slightest sniff of a Maxwell DNA link to other cases would be catnip to journalists, and the last thing she wanted to do was add fuel to that fire before she knew exactly what she was dealing with.

Chapter 34

Shona used the breaktime to call Jack Douglas at the pub, but it was Freya who answered and informed her he was out with the ponies on the moss. Mobile? No, it was behind the bar. No signal, no point taking it. Shona had more luck with Murdo who, it turned out, had a bone to pick with her. The David Attenborough DVD box she'd brought up at Becca's request in fact contained the disc of the horror film *A Nightmare on Elm Street*. All four girls had been up all night as a result. Shona was mortified at her daughter's behaviour, but Murdo had been warned.

'I'm sorry, Murdo, but you were telt. Get Joan up there, pronto.'

Murdo had come into Langholm police office for a cup of tea and a sit-down. He'd found the local cops had greeted with irritation and amusement in equal measure the earl's reframing of events surrounding his fall into the River Esk. Murdo relayed to Shona how someone had mocked up a 'Dunkin Douglas' poster, with the earl as a doughnut. Shona hoped Xander's stamina as the butt of jokes was in good order. He was going to need it.

When Shona told Murdo she wanted to talk to Archie Nixon herself, he went quiet for a moment, and then agreed to arrange a meeting for later that day. She was just about to get herself a refill of coffee when Cam's name came up on her phone. She dearly hoped he hadn't changed his mind about the reiver's child.

'I've just heard from Sue Kitchen about the potential Maxwell DNA,' he said without preamble. 'Why didn't you say something?'

Because it's not your business, Shona wanted to reply, although as Maxwell's only surviving relative, perhaps it was his business more than anyone else's.

Instead, she said, 'Sue shouldn't have told you.'

'Sue doesn't know about my...' Cam hesitated. 'About my connection to the cases, beyond that I was helping Vicky Thomson.'

'Do you want to volunteer a DNA sample?' Shona asked.

There was a long pause, then Cam said, 'I'm not comfortable with the idea.'

It was the reaction Shona had expected. Despite the fact that Cam knew who, and what, his father was, to be reminded in black and white that you shared half your genetic make-up with a serial killer – no matter what your wife had convinced you about nature and nurture – would never be easy. 'Cam, I'd advise you to put it out of your mind. When we know more, I promise I'll tell you.'

Cam gave a derisive snort. 'So, how many? How many others did he kill?'

'That's beyond the scope of our current enquiry,' Shona said, falling back on a neutral response in the hope of calming the exchange.

'You're not looking at other cases? If it's beyond the scope... you saying you think it *wasn't* him? Is that why you asked me what I could remember about other people at the house?'

'Cam, listen...' Shona began, but the line went dead. Whether he'd ended the call or the signal had dropped, she wasn't sure. Redial went straight to his voicemail. All she could do was leave a message. 'Cam, I appreciate your concern and promise I will update you as soon as I can.' She wasn't about to share the Interpol hit with anyone, least of all with Cam Armstrong, until she knew what it meant.

As she finished the message, Kate arrived in the office, loudly bemoaning the tree cutters who'd managed to clear the roads, but had now introduced mobile contraflows as they began logging the timber from the verges. The start of the English bank holiday weekend increased traffic across the border, and long tailbacks had formed in Langdale.

'Just let me grab a coffee,' Kate said, as Shona came out of her office.

Vinny Visuals plugged his laptop into the screen on the opposite wall from the whiteboard and everyone shifted their chairs around. Soon they were swooping with a hawk's-eye view across the Langdale estate, with its moors and farms. The 10,000 acres of Bield Moss appeared. Stripped of its cloak of heather, the contour lines clumped together and spaced apart with no obvious logic, but betrayed sinkholes and fissures in the bedrock far beneath the peat.

'The red markers are the deposition sites,' Chloe said. 'The yellow show the work, home and social matrix of Maxwell's known movements.'

Shona noted the overlaps. Cindy Jardine and Karen Anderson had both been found close to where Maxwell, as an assistant gamekeeper, had been monitoring red grouse numbers. But Ben Elliot had discovered Karen's body while drystone walling on the edge of the moor in a team with several other local men, so knowledge of the area shouldn't have been the primary factor in pinpointing Maxwell for arrest. There were pink blocks for archaeological sites and a few brown squares over the baseline green colour.

Shona wasn't sure what she'd expected from the map. A small part of her had hoped that when she viewed it, the deposition sites would mark out an identifiable shape: a pentangle, or some ancient reiver's rune on the landscape, with the location of Olivia's body revealed at the missing point.

'Thanks, Vinny, Chloe,' Shona said, and turned to Kate, who'd opened her tablet and set it before her on the table, ready to give her report.

Shona noted how tired her DC looked. The trip to Edinburgh, followed by the rush back to the earl's bedside, had taken their toll. Kate's smoothed, low ponytail of the last few weeks was now a hasty updo, with a pen sticking out from the messy bun at the back of her head.

'Cindy Jardine disappeared—' Kate began.

'Hang on a minute,' Ravi said, as he got up and resumed his position at the whiteboard, forcing everyone to wrestle their chairs around again like particularly unco-operative four-legged beasts.

'Okay.' He ignored Kate's irritated scowl and picked up the marker pen. 'Fire away.'

'Cindy disappeared in early November 1985 and was found in January 1986,' Kate began again. 'The retired detective I spoke to, Andy Russell, was working on an allegation that she was part of a sex-sting to blackmail a High Court judge.'

'Who was the judge?' Shona said.

'A Lord Broadford. He died in 2012. Andy Russell suspected Cindy had been paid to disappear. When her body turned up, and she was linked to the Girls in the Glen, he assumed she'd taken the money and run, only to land in a whole different kind of trouble. There was nothing missing from her flat, not even a suitcase.'

'What happened with the blackmail case?' Ravi said, turning from the board.

'Quietly closed,' Kate replied. 'His lordship stepped down on health grounds. Ended up as a non-executive board member with a couple of big agriculture companies. One thing that always struck Russell as odd was where she was found.'

'The field drain on the estate?' Shona said and nodded to Vinny who, by tapping a key, caused a red block to light up and a drop-down box, complete with Cindy's photograph, to appear.

'It was more the connection to her alleged victim that he thought odd,' Kate replied. 'Lord Broadford, or James Macleod to give him his ordinary name, was married to Margaret Douglas, so that made him the 13th Earl of Langdale's brother-in-law.'

Shona raised her eyebrows. That the current earl's grandfather had a connection to one of the victims was quite a coincidence.

'Was that pursued at all?' She opened the question to the rest of the staff sitting around the table, but no one had anything to offer.

'I got the sense that Andy Russell had a bit of a soft spot for Cindy Jardine,' Kate said. 'She was a vulnerable individual, and he thinks her death was a bit too convenient for some people and tidied up too quickly. He also thought Lord Broadford, who wasn't wealthy himself, was using his wife's money to pay off the blackmailers.'

'Bet that made him popular at home,' Shona said. 'Has Russell any evidence to back his allegations?' Shona said.

Kate shook her head. Retired, and with time on his hands, Andy Russell had clearly fallen victim to the curse of *what might have been*, and the cases that got away.

'Okay, thanks everyone,' Shona said. 'In the absence of Murdo, can you each give me a one-page briefing before you go tonight? Highlight gaps, and we'll look again on Monday. Hannah, give me your timeline of the case and put in a request for the missing box.'

'Already done,' Hannah said, swiping her tablet.

'Right, crack on,' Shona said. 'Kate, wait a minute.' When the others had gone, she continued, 'Thanks for having a word about the Elliot girls.'

Kate sighed. 'It's not looking good for them, is it?'

'It makes you think the families come off worst sometimes,' Shona agreed. 'Can you chase something up for me?' She explained about the missing statement from Jack Douglas, confirming John Maxwell's confession. 'Call The Douglas Arms again. His mobile is behind the bar, but can you check if he's at Langdale Hall? Don't tell him the documentation is lost. Make something up about not being able to read his signature, or the like.'

'Okay, no problem,' Kate said. She looked at her watch. 'Mind if I pop out for an hour? My washing machine's packed up. There's a guy coming to fix it. I'd have taken it as my lunch break, but the traffic…'

'Sure,' Shona said. 'Off you go.' It was on the tip of her tongue to make some crack about Kate not having to worry about such things once she was Countess of

Langdale, but it seemed out of kilter with the seriousness of what they'd just been discussing.

Once alone in the conference room, Shona studied the whiteboard again. Perhaps Cameron Armstrong was right. John Maxwell was an evil and opportunistic killer, and to look for his motive would be as fruitless as searching for his conscience. She thought of Vicky Thomson, living next door for years to the man who went to jail for killing her child, and wondered how much she'd tortured herself for not seeing that threat. Cam was right. It was a huge part of what drove Shona: recognise evil and you can be a shield for others.

She turned to look at the GIS map that Vinny had left open on the screen. Kate, who knew how to interpret landscape and read its mysteries, had seen no additional clues or pattern in the deposition sites. They were indeed, as Cam had noted, all on or close to places associated with the Border reivers, but was that just a coincidence? She went back through her briefing notes, then stared at the screen until the blocks began to swim before her eyes.

Ravi came in with a cup of coffee and a disgruntled expression. 'There's a problem, boss.'

He took his tablet from where it was tucked under his arm and swiped the screen.

'Jacques Darceleaux,' he began, 'was jailed in 1994 for the murder that year of his girlfriend Rema Chaput's five-year-old daughter, Luna. That's why he's on the Interpol DNA database. He served twenty-two years in a French prison. Released three years ago, whereabouts unknown. And get this: he was a lorry driver.'

As Shona looked at the file before her, she felt the whole case against John Maxwell sink as surely as if it had fallen onto the bottomless mire of Bield Moss. By 1994,

Maxwell was in prison, serving multiple life sentences for the Girls in the Glen killings, and couldn't have committed this murder in France. Jacques Darceleaux was not the alias of John Maxwell. They were two different people. The fact that the French lorry driver's DNA had turned up on two separate Scottish victims – Karen Anderson and Cindy Jardine – murdered and buried on the moor months apart put him, not Maxwell, squarely in the frame for the killings.

'Shit!' Shona said. Darceleaux was a lorry driver, which fitted with the initial line of enquiry back in the 1980s that it had been a 'Yorkshire Ripper' scenario. A man who passed regularly through the area and had become familiar with the deposition sites via his job. 'Doesn't say if he ever drove in the UK. D'you think he could have picked up Harriet Jackson when she was hitch-hiking?'

Ravi nodded, considering the idea. 'Possibly. The clothes fibre tapings are from Karen Anderson and Cindy Jardine but similar items from Harriet's case might not have survived in the evidence stores.'

'Okay, put his details on the board. We don't know where he fits in yet, but we need to share this with the team in case they've come across something in the case file. Well done, Ravi. See if you can trace his movements with the French authorities prior to his conviction, or post-release – and a photo of him would be great.'

After Ravi left, Shona made a conscious effort to clear her mind and look at the rest of the evidence with a fresh eye. As a lorry driver, Darceleaux's visits might have been fleeting. She noted down the murder dates. The three women were killed from October to December, although Karen Anderson wasn't found until April 1986. Then, there was a gap in the killings until February 1986, when the girls were taken. The DNA only connected the Anderson and Jardine deaths, but the method of strangling and sharp force trauma was common to all the recovered victims. The time gaps fitted with someone not resident in the area, but passing through. She perched on the edge of the desk and chewed her pen.

When should she tell Cameron Armstrong about this new development? Darceleaux may have known Cam's father, but he'd already told her he was unable to remember anyone who came to the house.

Shona studied the deposition sites again. Why would a French lorry driver carry Lilly Scott's body to the top of Bield Moss and bury it in an ancient midden? It was possible he'd worked on the estate, perhaps as a seasonal labourer driving a tractor, as Maxwell himself might have done when he'd worked abroad. But the winter dates of the killings made that less likely. She was still musing over the possibilities when Kate came back.

'Spoke to Jack,' she said. 'He confirmed his statement backing up Eddie Graham's account of the confession. He was suspicious, but I think I got away with it.'

'Okay, thanks,' Shona said. 'Kate, what are the brown boxes on the map?'

Kate moved the cursor and clicked on a box, expanding it out to show a colour key. 'Brown is the plots of land sold when Craig Anderson was acting for the estate.'

'But one had a red box on it?' Shona said.

'Yes, a deposition site.' She clicked on the red box, and Karen Anderson's round face and pixie-cut dark hair appeared on screen. 'The others overlap with yellow for archaeological sites.'

'So Karen Anderson was buried on a plot of land that her solicitor husband Craig was selling on the estate's behalf? Is that odd?'

'Ben Elliott found her. Blackriggs farm.' Kate read the details on screen, then looked around at her boss's reaction. But Shona was deep in thought. Kate gazed past her to the whiteboard. 'What's that?' She pointed to Ravi's recently added note.

'Slasher Sue's students recovered DNA from fibre tapings taken from two of the victims. Ravi got a hit from Interpol. A lorry driver. We need to explore further and determine if there's a connection.'

'Darceleaux?' Kate stared at Shona, white-faced. 'You know what Darceleaux means? "Black water". And Douglas is from the Gaelic *Dubh gleas*. Black water. Jacques Darceleaux is French for Jack Douglas.'

Shona blinked at her. 'Jack Douglas told me he lived in a hippy commune in the Pyrenees.' Was it possible his stay in France was under a different name and in an entirely different kind of establishment?

'Xander said,' Kate began, 'that his father and uncles fell out with the 13th Earl over Cousin Jack's influence on the old man and what they called Jack's "obsession" with the estate. But that's the reason Lady Lucy wanted Jack back, because he knows all about the place, and loves it.'

Shona stared at the details of the killings again, and this time, they shifted and began to re-form before her eyes.

'What if...' Shona jumped up from her chair. 'Karen Anderson's husband's law firm was severing their connections with the estate over the 13th Earl's violent behaviour. Cindy Jardine had blackmailed the earl's brother-in-law. Ben Elliot told me it was well known that Lilly Scott's father, Findlay, was in dispute with the estate over grazing

317

rights and his livestock had been harmed, but everyone assumed it was poachers.'

She took the marker pen and began adding to the whiteboard. 'Harriet Jackson's boyfriend was sacked for stealing diesel from the estate.' She turned back to Kate. 'It's not the women and girls that are linked, it's the men.' Shona stabbed her pen on the whiteboard. 'Every one of the victims had a father, boyfriend or husband who was in a dispute of some kind with the Langdale estate.'

'Except Cindy Jardine.' Kate still looked doubtful.

'Yes, but if your detective is right, Lady Douglas's cash was going to the blackmailers, and that made it estate business.'

'So why not kill the men?'

'We don't know he didn't.' Shona picked up her tablet and began flicking through the files. 'Craig Anderson's partner, Edwin Bell, who did most of the estate work, died in a car crash around the same time. Findlay Scott had an apparent heart attack soon after the trial. They found Jimmy Fraser hanging in the woods above Langholm, and his death was attributed to suicide.'

'Cindy Jardine had no family,' Kate said. 'What about Olivia's father, Alex Thomson? He didn't die until a few years ago.'

Shona tapped the pen on the board. 'It was assumed Maxwell's motive was a dispute with Alex Thomson and Lilly was taken because she was there. What if it was the other way around? Lilly was the abduction target, and Olivia was taken because she witnessed it.'

'But why would Jack Douglas do this?'

'He was obsessed with protecting the estate,' Shona said. 'Perhaps the 13th Earl told him he'd make him his heir. Cam said the old Border families were like the Mafia. Every Mafia family needs an enforcer.'

Shona wondered if Kate's loyalty to Xander, and the potential social position and riches offered as a member of the Douglas family, was blinding her to their potential sins.

'Look at the body depositions,' Shona continued. 'Jack Douglas knows everything about the reiver sites, including the unrecorded ones. Cam was even picking his brains about them. Look at the dates, all in the winter, all at night. He's taking a twisted reiver's revenge on not just the men, but the families, too. I bet Jack concocted John Maxwell's confession, and Willie Graham's brother, Eddie, who depended on the estate for his livelihood, just went along with it. The whole town wanted Maxwell locked up.'

'But how do we prove any of this?' Kate said.

'Ravi's tracing Darceleaux's movements with the French authorities. We might have a picture soon, and...' Shona went to the door and shouted for her other DC. When he came in, she said. 'Where was this Darceleaux living when he killed his girlfriend's daughter?'

Ravi thought for a moment. 'A commune-type place in the French Pyrenees.'

The look on Kate's face said she'd heard Jack's story of taking the cheese to market on horseback, too. 'Oh my God. It is him.'

Shona snatched up her phone. It was as if the last piece of the jigsaw had fallen into place and suddenly the whole picture was clear before her. 'The car that hit Flora. The witnesses said a dark blue or black hatchback. There's a dark green hatchback at the pub, and Jack Douglas saw me go up to the dig with Cam, wearing the parka.'

319

She punched in a number, her face grim. 'Murdo, forget Archie Nixon. We're going to The Douglas Arms.'

Chapter 35

On Bield Moss a storm was brewing. The windows of The Douglas Arms were dark, its door firmly shut. As heavy clouds rolled in, the granite walls seemed to reach their roots down into the peat, the ancient inn clinging ever more firmly to the hillside.

Kate had reported that Jack Douglas was suspicious of her questions over the confession, but if the earl's cousin hit Flora believing she was Shona, he must already believe she'd strayed too close to his secret.

Shona had called Freya earlier. Jack hadn't come back yet, and his mobile was still behind the bar. 'Get out now,' Shona told her. 'Coat, handbag, don't stop for anything else.' Murdo was waiting fifty yards up the hill, out of sight of the pub.

Kate rang Langdale Hall. Only Lady Lucy's pony was in the stable. Jack had left a couple of hours before, saying he was returning to The Douglas Arms. The light was falling. He was out there, somewhere, on Bield Moss.

'Firearms are on their way,' Kate said, unfolding a map on the bonnet of the Audi.

Murdo and a local unit were parked in a passing place up the hill from The Douglas Arms, watching for anyone who approached the pub. Cam wasn't answering his phone. Much to Shona's relief, Murdo had discovered that the students weren't on the moor, but at the small museum in Langholm for a community archaeology event, showing their initial finds to local people. He'd rung the curator to keep them there.

Shona had brought four uniform units with her to add to three patrol cars belonging to Langholm police office. She'd let Murdo handle Sergeant Graham. All Willie Graham knew was that Jack Douglas was wanted for questioning about his time in France, and that it concerned a serious crime and he should be approached with caution. The helicopter wouldn't be here for at least an hour, and with 10,000 acres of moorland she needed to narrow down her options on where to search first.

'There are marked bridleways,' Kate said as she traced the route from Langdale Hall. 'But Lady Lucy said they rarely followed them, as Jack and the ponies knew their way about.'

'The local boys are blocking off the access roads,' Shona said. 'But send one of our own units to check Langdale Hall.' The place was a literal fortress. *Four fires meant a great many horsemen… but none of them ever got inside this tower*, Alexander Douglas had said. Kate might believe the earl would hand over his cousin Jack, but she wasn't so sure.

'We'll search the pub,' Shona said. 'Murdo can watch our backs.'

Freya had left the door unlocked. Shona knew the layout and they moved quickly through the public rooms downstairs, the kitchen and back office, and the upstairs guest rooms. In an annex at the back, Jack Douglas's bedroom had the kind of large, carved oak bed that would feature in a medieval fantasy. The rest of the room was sparse, like a prison cell, except for the walls, which were covered in drawings of the same reiver scenes that featured in the bar. A shelf contained a few historic volumes on the same topic, but no passport or personal papers. Jack Douglas was a man who travelled light.

Back outside in the car park, the sun had dropped further. Shona went to the garage at the back and shone her phone between the crack in the doors. The dark green hatchback was still there.

Shona called Murdo on the radio for an update. 'Any sign?'

'Nothing, boss.'

She walked beyond the parked police vehicles to the edge of the car park. The view down the glen had folded into shadows; the lorries on the main road were a stream of lights. If Jack Douglas knew she was waiting for him at the pub, he could easily lose his pony, flag down a vehicle and hitch a lift. She couldn't contain him on the moor; she'd have to get a public appeal out.

Shona glanced up the road, and saw Murdo and the patrol car. Beyond them, the sky held a faint smudge, and the glow of sunset. But her internal compass, refined by time on the expanse of the Solway Firth, told her something was wrong. She leaned out over the wall that bounded the car park and saw Cam Armstrong's Land Rover speeding up the track to the Elliot's where a pinpoint of red blossomed against the grey.

'Murdo! Behind you!' Shona called into the radio as she ran to the Audi. 'The Elliot farm. Fire!'

Kate, in the passenger seat, alerted fire and rescue, as Shona floored the accelerator behind the speeding patrol car, blues and twos blazing. They hit the main road and five minutes later took the turning up to the Elliot farm. Shona cursed as the Audi's underbody ground on the rough track with an ominous scraping noise, but she pushed on.

The barn was alight, and the house not far behind, as smoke oozed like sweat from beneath the roof tiles.

Flora Elliot was in the yard, training a garden hose over the front of the farmhouse in an ineffectual bid to stop the flames spreading. Cam stumbled from the building's open door, carrying a box of papers and valuables. Shona saw Grace and Becca herding the farm's terrified goats and chickens across the field, the sheepdogs at their heels.

'What happened?' Shona grabbed hold of Cam to stop him running back into the farmhouse.

'Murdo said to keep the students at the museum, but the girls had already gone. The house phone was down. I came up, saw the flames.'

Murdo had taken the hose from Flora. A Special backed the farm tractor away from the buildings and others broke out the emergency extinguishers from their vehicles.

'Is everyone safe?' Shona shouted above the bleats of the sheep and goats, and the barking dogs. Murdo was with her. Flora, Grace and Becca in the field. 'Where's Ashley?'

There was a loud bang from behind the barn. Shona and Cam flinched. It sounded like a gas canister had gone up. Murdo shouted for everyone to get back and Shona grabbed Cam's arm again to haul him away.

Then, among the sparks carried high on the wind, she saw a horseman on the hill, the pony pale against the darker moorland. Shona's grip tightened and she felt the corresponding tension in Cam's arm. Smoke swept the yard, but she wasn't hallucinating.

'That Jack Douglas?' Cam asked Shona, but she didn't answer.

'Ashley!' Shona cried, turning and sprinting into the field. 'Ashley!'

Cam was close behind her.

The animals huddled in the far corner, penned in by the dogs and their own terror, while the girls tried to soothe them. At the sound of Shona's and Cam's cries, Grace, Becca and Flora began wading among the stock, taking up the call for the youngest girl. When they turned to Shona, their faces told her all she needed to know.

Cam grabbed Shona by the arms. 'He's taken her, hasn't he? That bastard Jack Douglas?'

He let Shona go, but she stumbled after him and grabbed at his jacket as he raced to his Land Rover.

'Wait,' she said. 'The chopper's coming. We'll find her.' But even as she said it, she knew it would be too late.

Cam shook off Shona and pulled open the driver's door of the Land Rover. She scrambled into the passenger seat, and he swung the vehicle in a neat arc and headed back down the track. He took the fork up towards the dig site. She radioed that they were in pursuit of a suspect and a possible hostage.

Shona pictured the GIS map. The dig track would take them to the top of the moss. With darkness falling, they'd never find him, but they might be able to relay approximate co-ordinates to the helicopter for the search.

'Why are the police here?' Cam shouted. 'Tell me!'

'The DNA Professor Kitchen found on two of the Girls in the Glen victims. We got a match. I think Jack Douglas went to prison in France under another name.' Then, because she saw no reason to hide his crime, she said, 'He killed a child.'

'He was just playing me!' Cam Armstrong slammed his hand onto the steering wheel. 'He knew things about the

Girls in the Glen cases, things to do with reiver sites. I was convinced what he knew would lead me to Olivia. Now you're saying he was in league with Maxwell all along.'

The idea that Maxwell's conviction could be unsound hadn't yet occurred to Cam, but it was only a matter of time and Shona thought it would cause irreparable harm to their relationship if she kept it from him.

'Jack backing up Maxwell's confession was the basis of the case,' Shona said. 'It should have had further investigation.'

He shot her a look.

'Watch the road,' Shona said, firmly. 'We can talk about this when we've found Ashley.'

They slid to a stop at the top of the track and got out. There was nothing but the wind. The pewter sky beyond the dig was filled with an eerie light, a false dawn. They reached the crest, and saw why. It wasn't just the Elliot farm on fire. The whole of Bield Moss was burning, too.

'Look,' Cam said.

A line of ghostly figures headed towards them. A moment later, Shona recognised the head gamekeeper, Charles Bell. The men were beating at the flames with their jackets and flails on long poles.

Shona and Cam waved their arms and called out.

'The last fire like this burned for three days,' Charles Bell panted, his face sweaty and muck-stained. 'They had to get a helicopter up from Yorkshire to douse it.'

Shona didn't have three days.

'Jack Douglas… He's taken Ashley Elliot. Did you see him?'

Bell looked horrified, then shook his head. 'Willie Graham called me an' said you were after him. I didnae realise... We came along the bridleway. He's no' passed us.'

Panicked birds, their feathers on fire, careered over them. A mountain hare running in circles doubled back into the blaze and Shona heard its screams.

'He'll be headed south,' Cam said. 'Towards Foulsyke. Come on.'

Bell sent half the men with them, while the others, many of whom were reserve firemen, tackled the blaze around the dig site. The men led Shona and Cam through the moss, beating at flames that sprang up like waiting warriors from the tinder-dry heather tops.

'If you see Douglas, leave him to me,' Shona warned.

She stumbled over tussock, Cam forging ahead. She shouted at him to slow down, so no one would be separated in the fire and darkness, but he ignored her warning. She looked down to concentrate on her footing but when she raised her head again, men were shouting, and a wall of fire was all around them. Cam had disappeared but she heard him call her name. Suddenly, an enormous, pale spectre loomed and Shona threw herself out of its path. Jack Douglas's terrified pony careered like a spirit through the smoke, turning in frenzied circles until one of the shoot staff grabbed its bridle.

'Watch oot for Foulsyke edge!' someone shouted.

For a second, the flames in front of Shona buckled, as if a great hand had swatted them aside. She saw two figures in the clear ground beyond. She pulled her jacket over her head and thrust herself through the opening. The flames scorched her face while her feet plunged into the bog beneath. She dropped to the ground and rolled in a yielding patch of sphagnum moss, assaulted from every direction by the heat of the flames and the sucking chill of the bog water.

Cam was ahead of her, wrestling with Jack Douglas; Ashley lay motionless on the ground nearby.

Shona crawled forward and felt for the faint fluttering of a pulse beneath the girl's neck. Her eyes opened, and she screamed hoarsely and struck out. Shona shushed her, ordering her to stay still as she wrapped her with her own soaking coat to protect her from the flying sparks. All around them, the shouts of the beaters mingled with the crackle of the fire as the moss took light.

Shona scrambled to her feet. 'Ashley, don't move.'

The flames danced on the knife in Jack's hand. Cam staggered back and for a moment she thought he'd been stabbed. Jack Douglas was taller and broader than Cam, but the archaeologist was an ex-soldier with a grievance. He circled, waiting for his chance. Behind them, the moor dropped into blackness, lit only by the fast-flowing ribbons of flame.

'Drop your weapon,' Shona ordered, putting herself between Jack and Ashley. 'Cam, stay back.'

'You've no powers out here,' Jack shouted. 'Your laws mean nothing.'

For Jack Douglas, this was still the Debatable Land.

But for Shona there was no debate. She was taking him from this moor. He would stand trial for his crimes and the Girls in the Glen would get the justice they deserved. With the true killer revealed, finding Olivia Thomson's body was a step closer.

'Give me the knife, Jack,' Shona said. 'There's nowhere to go. The shoot staff are all around you.'

It was a bluff, as she wouldn't risk civilian lives; she'd order them back if Jack came closer. The heat from the heather broke in waves against her cheek. She heard Ashley whimper.

'You think my cousin's men will stop me?' Jack grinned. 'Sure you're not the one surrounded?'

Shona stole a glance behind her. Further off, the shoot staff were still beating at the ground, but, where the flames had died, Douglas men were turning, suddenly aware of the drama unfolding on the cliff edge of Foulsyke. Shona tensed. The nearest beater stepped closer, and she recognised him as the lad who'd found the cartridge among the heather and been rewarded from the earl's own whisky supply.

Jack's grin widened, but in that moment, Cameron Armstrong sprang at him. Jack Douglas raised the knife, lashing out. They rolled together to the edge of the heather and disappeared.

'No,' Shona shouted, and leaped forward, but the earl's men rushed past her. They hauled up a single figure, patting out the smouldering embers that clung to Cameron Armstrong's slight frame.

Above she heard a long rumbling roar as the storm broke. The first drops fell like heavy tears. She edged forward and peered over into the pit of fire below the cliff. A minute later, the ghylls and sykes seemed to swell like pulsing veins. They ran pitch-dark with the ashes of the moss, and Jack Blackwater lay dead among them.

Chapter 36

Bield Moss rose, steep and watchful, behind St Cuthbert's kirkyard. Shona and Murdo arrived on Monday morning, dressed in sombre black suits. Grass grew tall between the gravestones and the seed heads of spent wildflowers caught the early sun. A crowd was scattered along the roadside and through the graveyard, punctuated by journalists and cameras.

Despite Shona's efforts to trace relatives, Lilly Scott had no living family left to bury her. The Procurator Fiscal and the local council agreed she should be laid to rest among her own people. Both parents had been cremated, her father in Glasgow and her mother in Australia, so the thirteenth century St Cuthbert's, outside of Langholm, was chosen. The ancient church had lost its roof to a fire in the eighteenth century, set perhaps by the last of the hell-bound reivers, but its ivy-clad walls still stood and a few burials, for those with links to the area, continued each year. The minister from the new kirk in the Muckle Toon agreed to officiate.

At Dr Armstrong's suggestion, the reiver's child would be buried alongside Lilly. In Scots law, all human remains have 'a right to sepulchre'. Beyond a small tissue sample taken for DNA records, the university had no wish to keep her body for research purposes. The Girls in the Glen, past and present, would be laid to rest together. It seemed fitting that the reiver's child should lie near the old church where she might even have been baptised, the small circle of her life closed at last.

As Shona and Murdo made their way through the crowd to the graveside, she saw Nicola Baird, her arm still in a sling, milking the press attention, until faces turned from her with the arrival of the earl. There was no Lady Lucy. Shona had heard, via the jubilant housekeeper at Langdale Hall, that her ladyship had been driven back to London not by rain or midges, but by her perceived close association with the man locals were already calling 'Black Jack'. House staff had ignored her orders. A woman in Langholm had spat at her. Public opinion was kinder to Xander, who most considered an innocent party. A divorcee ex-model was expendable. A young earl, intent on bringing jobs and prosperity back to the area, less so.

DC Kate Irving had also opted not to attend the funeral, her romance with Alexander Douglas having ended. Shona hadn't got the full story. Perhaps it was the gossip over his affairs, or having a serial killer in the family, that had put her off. Shona wondered if, for Kate, the attraction had been, at least partly, about her rekindling her first love: the moor and its geography.

Olivia's mother, Vicky Thomson, was too ill to travel. While she could not witness or be comforted by the grief still shared, after all these years, by her community, she was at least spared the sense of what might have been. Her own daughter still lay somewhere on the moor.

A soft breeze brought birdsong as the archaeology students, led by the minister in his black gown, carried the small coffins in procession. Professor Armstrong, incongruous in a dark suit, his face still scorched and his hands bandaged, walked behind.

The ceremony was simple and short. When it was over, Murdo came towards her, Grace Elliot at his side.

'You can talk to Shona,' he'd told Grace, and left them to it.

Grace wore a dark jacket over a fitted black dress, her pale hair loose. Shona was struck once more by the maturity the girl exuded, far more than her eighteen years, but there was a nervousness in the way she chewed her lip.

'How's Ashley?'

'She's okay.' Grace fixed Shona with her serious grey eyes. 'Thank you for saving her.'

Shona smiled. 'You don't need to thank me.'

Grace cleared her throat. 'And Ashley's sorry for what she did.'

'There's nothing for her to be sorry about,' Shona said, puzzled. It was true the lassie was a handful, and had been warned not to go out of sight, but she had hardly gone off with Jack Douglas willingly.

'It was just a joke,' Grace continued. 'We were having a competition, ma sisters and me. We wanted to see who could knock thon feathered bonnet off the earl. We're sorry for the MSP. We didnae mean to hit her. Murdo said I should tell you but you'll no' make me say in court it was Ashley who shot the woman.' The words tumbled out, and suddenly Grace looked both defiant and afraid. 'We wanted the earl and his cronies to get off our moss.'

For a moment, Shona couldn't take in what she was hearing. Then, she remembered the earl's hat, with its ridiculous pheasant tail feathers, which he'd been wearing when she'd first arrived at the shooting lodge. This whole case had been a prank gone wrong, but somehow, as she looked at Grace's anxious face and thought about what this revelation meant for the Elliot family, Shona felt her initial stab of anger tempered by the idea that several possible futures stretched out before the three sisters and their father. The decision she took now would decide which path they might take.

'You were behind the tartan sheep, and the grouse in his car,' Shona said.

Grace nodded, defiance edging out the fear.

'Did you push him in the river?'

'No!' Grace said, indignant. 'That mighta kilt him.'

'And aiming a rifle at his head wouldn't?' Shona, whose firearms training emphasised gun safety as a paramount operating procedure, failed to see the logic.

'We're all good shots wi' the wee deer gun,' Grace said. 'It was an accident. We're really sorry.'

Shona let out a long breath. What a mess. But among the tangled strands of blame and recklessness, she saw a chance to put something right. That Ben Elliot was willing to spend the rest of his life in jail was a testament to how far people were prepared to go to protect their family. Jack Douglas had been the evil flipside of that compulsion. Perhaps both impulses had their roots in their reiver blood, but Shona was clear: she didn't want these particular girls in the glen to face a future marred by violence and retribution. They deserved credit for owning up to their mistake.

'Ashley's only eleven, isn't she?' Shona said.

The age of criminal responsibility in Scotland had recently been raised from eight to twelve years old and no one younger than that could be arrested or charged.

'I think ma dad guessed what we'd done, but thought if he didnae confess you'd keep investigating, and Flora and Ashley would end up in care.'

It was a reasonable fear, in the circumstances. Ben Elliot's previous conviction for assaulting a neighbour, coupled with poor firearms security and the impression he was struggling as a single parent, might lead Social Services to take action.

'D'you want to see an innocent man go tae jail for something he didnae do?' Grace pleaded. 'If ma dad withdraws his confession, the fiscal will drop the case, won't he?'

She was right. There was little chance of a successful prosecution on the forensics alone. The bullet recovered from Nicola's shoulder would link the rifle, but not who fired it. The stumbling block was Nicola Baird. She'd never let it go.

'I understand you're sorry, Grace,' Shona said. She leaned in and squeezed the girl's hand. 'You did the right thing telling me. Thank you. Go home and look after your sisters. Let me see what I can do.'

When Grace had gone, Shona walked up to where Nicola Baird was chatting with mourners, and asked for a minute of her time. A direct approach was best; neither woman had time or patience for small talk. Shona outlined what Grace had told her, in broad terms: that the shooting had been a prank gone wrong.

'Thing is, Mrs Baird, it may not be in anyone's best interest to pursue this.'

'What do you mean?' the MSP's eyes were hard and suspicious. 'The little witch shot me. She deserves to be punished.'

'We're talking about an eleven-year-old girl who narrowly survived the attentions of a serial killer. Is it really in your political interest to pursue a child over this?' Shona paused to let the potential headlines of such an action sink in. 'Say nothing and I can wind the investigation down with a conclusion that exonerates your friend the earl of any blame, and you'll go on being a woman whose toughness in public office has been proved beyond doubt.'

Shona could see Nicola's mind working and had no doubt she could spin this in a way beneficial to herself. But she knew better than to appeal purely to Nicola's better nature, which she was fairly sure didn't exist.

'We could, of course, continue to investigate.' Shona spread her hands wide. 'Perhaps I'm wrong. Maybe there is a political, personal or financial motive and we just haven't found it yet?'

Nicola's eyes narrowed. 'What do you mean by that?'

'We can keep on digging and digging,' Shona said. 'Who knows which of your many associates could have harboured harmful intent?'

The threat was subtle and implied. Accept the official conclusion that this was an accident, probably a stray rifle shot from deer poachers disturbed by the shoot, or have the police pick over every aspect of your life – from your tax returns to who you might have been sleeping with – in the hope of finding a motive, and face the consequences in the press.

Nicola Baird shot her a look of pure venom, then composed her features into an official display of piety. 'I'm in favour of the efficient use of police time and resources.'

'Thank you,' Shona said and watched as the MSP walked quickly away and began to work the crowd.

'Well done, Murdo,' Shona said, quietly, when she joined him at the graveside. Persuading Grace to trust him, and the sensitive way he'd handled what she'd revealed, meant Ashley would have a second chance. The consequences of her foolish act of violence would end here and the family would have the opportunity to heal.

'You've squared it wi' Nicola Baird?' Murdo said.

'Yes, there'll be no comeback,' Shona replied and hoped it was true. 'You okay?'

Cam and the students had already left, Becca with them. Most observers had begun to drift away, but her sergeant was still staring at the mound of flowers. He'd barely said a word all morning.

'Fine, boss.' He paused, raising his eyes to the moss. 'I had a brother,' he began. 'He died.'

'I'm sorry, Murdo. I didn't know that.' Shona touched his arm briefly in an act of condolence.

'It was ten years back. No reason why you would.' Murdo shrugged. 'His name was Drew, and he was a bit older than me.'

Shona sensed there was more, and that he would tell it in his own time.

'I've a wee errand to run,' Murdo said. 'Might pop off now, if you don't need me back in the office.'

'Sure, Murdo. I'll call you later.' There was one more matter with which Shona needed to deal.

The earl had begun to edge through the crowd towards the gate. Shona intercepted him. He shook her outstretched hand.

'I hear you're selling Bield Moss to the community habitat restoration project,' Shona said. 'Quite the change of heart. You're a local hero.' Her face was neutral, and she fought to keep the sarcasm from her tone.

The chair of the rewilding group, George Robson, had called her earlier with the news. Now, Alexander Douglas stood before her and accepted the idea that he was indeed a local hero, as if it was his birthright.

'It's gonna take thirty years to rewild the moss, maybe more, and subsidies on land set aside for carbon capture won't be on-stream for a while. The estate doesn't have thirty years.'

It wasn't an act of generosity. He was offloading a loss-making enterprise at a profit.

'I'm afraid the pub will have to go,' he said, seriously. 'Can't have the brand associated with what happened. The business is changing focus. Push on with the eco-lodges. Might turn the inn into a backpackers' hostel. Walking is good business.'

'What about the staff?' Shona asked. 'Will they want to stay?' She was thinking of Tommy's girlfriend, Freya.

'They're welcome to stay. I'm aware how unpopular shutting a local business can be.'

That word again. Business. Would the killings – the grief and anger that stretched back more than thirty years – just be filed as an unfortunate matter of business by the Douglas family? But of course it wasn't just thirty years, it was centuries of tradition and vested interest.

'Mrs Baird will help secure investment and job creation grants,' the earl said, glancing towards the MSP, who was working the crowd of mourners like it was a political rally. As he took his leave, he touched Shona's shoulder lightly like a politician, implying implicit trust and confidence.

The earl and the MSP had a lot in common. If the project was a success, Nicola Baird would claim part of the credit. An alliance of convenience.

'What really happened on the riverbank?' Shona asked, putting out a hand to stop Alexander Douglas moving away to the safety of his Range Rover. 'It was Jack, wasn't it? He was very close to your grandfather. Did he think you weren't measuring up to the old man?'

It was evidence of his self-possession that he didn't even bother to deny it or cover his lie with a show of indignation. His face was a pleasant neutral. Anyone watching would think they were exchanging small talk, the proper conclusion to the day's events.

'Probably my own fault. An accident.' He shrugged. 'You know how it is, Detective Inspector. They've asked me to join the flood rescue team. All water under the bridge seems appropriate.'

Shona took a step nearer and lowered her voice. 'I risked my life to save you and all I get for my trouble is a glib remark.'

'You mustn't think me ungrateful, Shona,' the earl said, his face composed, blue eyes like glass. 'Of course, your husband should call me, and we'll set up a deal for your B&B.'

Oliver, tenants and vassals of the Douglas, the map in Langdale Hall said. Not likely.

Chapter 37

Traffic streamed through Langholm's narrow high street. Most shops and cafes were open to take advantage of the English visitors crossing the Anglo-Scottish border eight miles south for their bank holiday Monday.

Murdo pulled into the car park behind the small museum, with its elegant clock tower, a gift from a wealthy mill owner. It had once housed the town council offices and been the police station, standing on the site of an earlier gaol that had held many a reiver in its day: Nixons, Armstrongs, Douglases and Elliots among them.

Murdo took the cardboard box from the boot and went inside. A cheerful young woman with long red hair and a sleeve of tattoos that stretched up one arm introduced herself as Georgia Fitzwilliam, the museum curator.

'It's a grand title,' she said. 'But I do everything from looking after the archives to making the tea. Would you like some?'

'That'd be nice,' Murdo said.

She led him to a side room where the walls were lined with newspaper volumes, bound in red and green leather. *The Eskdale and Liddesdale Advertiser* and *The Langdale Gazette* were among the titles stamped in gold on their spines, with dates stretching back to the 1840s. Georgia indicated he could put the box down on the polished mahogany table that took up most of the room, but Murdo found his hands would not obey him and he held it close. She gave him a small smile of understanding, put her tablet and keys down, and left to make the tea.

He sat down with the box in his lap. After a moment, he folded back the cardboard top and took out Drew's space encyclopaedia, complete with Neil Armstrong's signature. Next to it, he placed a tiny piece of a lunar meteorite encased in a clear plastic block that had been a birthday gift. There were rolled-up posters, metal badges, mugs and pens. A model of the Apollo 11 Eagle lander. Colourful sew-on mission patches and commemorative coins. A scarf of lunar tartan made by a local textile mill.

Forgiveness wasn't about forgetting.

He didn't forgive Alan Kerr for killing Drew. But since that night when Kerr had gone to aid his desperate brother-in-law and his bairns, he'd found he was no longer as angry as he had been. There were no great wheels of fate turning. Kerr was a bad driver who'd made bad decisions because he was drunk.

It had taken Murdo all weekend to decide, but he wouldn't report him for the incident on Friday. He felt no great lifting of the burden of grief at this realisation and he didn't want to see Kerr again, but he'd make sure the partner, Karen, knew his decision. In a quiet way, through the church. Let Alan salvage what was left of his life and perhaps the next generation of that family wouldn't be so destructive to themselves or others.

Georgia returned with two mugs of tea. The curator was from Manchester originally. If she knew the story of Drew's killing, she gave no indication. Murdo found himself chatting about the town where he'd grown up, filling in gaps for the curator and promising to put her in touch with some locals for an oral history project she was planning.

'You do realise this memorabilia has huge value now?' Georgia said. 'Not that I want to talk you out of bringing it to us.'

'Och, I could never sell it,' Murdo said. That morning he'd phoned the builders to get the renovation work started on his mother's house. It was only then he'd made the decision to bring Drew's collection to the museum, but he knew he wouldn't change his mind.

'Well, I'm thrilled,' she said, her face alive with enthusiasm. 'If you're happy, we'll call it a permanent loan. That way it'll stay in the museum after you and I are gone, and won't be sold on without permission. It's not often we get material of international importance that tells such a wonderful story about our own Muckle Toon. You and your family will come back when it goes on display, won't you?'

Murdo nodded.

'I can't wait to get this on our website. It'll interest people all over the world and be a huge draw for us. Thank you, Murdo. Oh, I almost forgot.' She picked up a tablet and tilted the screen towards him. 'I'm digitising the archive. There's so much to get through, but I wanted to show you this.'

A black-and-white film of Langholm sprang to life. There was the high street outside the building they now sat in, thronged with people. Neil Armstrong and his wife, Janet, surrounded by dignitaries, walked among the crowd. Hands were thrust out to shake, men and women, old and young alike, awed and proud of their town's famous son.

A boy of about ten, in a duffle coat and bobble hat, with his back to the camera, held out a book. The moon man smiled as he signed it, then briefly rested his hand on the boy's shoulder in recognition of the bond they shared, their joint fascination with space flight and the heavens.

Murdo touched the screen, and the image froze. Here was Drew as he himself would choose to be remembered. Murdo picked up the space encyclopaedia and held it close to his chest.

Georgia looked from the tablet to Murdo, then her eyebrows went up and her mouth formed a delighted 'O'.

From now on, each time Murdo came home, he'd see his brother's name in the museum, not just in the graveyard, and so would others. If there is life beyond, then perhaps this was it – to live in the minds of others and be known for the things you yourself loved.

Chapter 38

Shona stood at the tall windows in High Pines and watched the lifeboat turn circles on the glassy surface of the estuary. Tommy was running through a helming and general handling exercise with two recent recruits. The curves of the far bank were a gold-tinged border of green between two sweeps of blue, sea and sky. Enjoy the view while you still can, she told herself, as it might not be yours much longer. She could hear her daughter's music floating up from the floor below. Shona would need to talk about their future here, soon.

Ben Elliot had been released. Murdo had let her know. Ben was giving up the farm to take on a smaller place. It was further up the glen, off Douglas land. Grace would be joint tenant and take it over, when the time came. The family were putting down new roots but would still be involved with the habitat restoration of their beloved Bield Moss. The strength of their ties to the land, and to each other, would see them through.

Her phone buzzed. Cameron Armstrong's name bloomed – an incoming call. Her finger hovered over *decline*. Was that what she was going to do now? Turn people away while she dealt only with her own pain? She pressed *accept*.

'Cam, how are you?' Shona said.

'I'm okay,' he said. 'I'm not sure if you've heard the news. Vicky Thomson died this morning.'

'Oh, Cam, I'm sorry.' While their friendship would never be what it had been, she and Cam shared a deep and genuine grief that neither of them had been able to grant Olivia's mother her last wish.

'I told her,' he said. 'I told her who I was. She remembered me. Said I used to come to her house and play with a big red bus.' She heard him sob. 'Vicky said she'd often thought of me and was so pleased to see what I'd become, that...' he stopped and took a gulp of air, 'it seemed right she was leaving the search for Olivia in my hands.'

'I'm pleased you were both able to have that conversation,' Shona said. 'What will you do now?'

'Keep going until I find the last Girl in the Glen,' he said simply. 'What about you?'

If she walked away from Rob now, she would be closing the door on any prospect of a resolution. Suddenly, she knew she couldn't do that. A potential guilty verdict for Rob had to be faced. She had to support him. After all, they were still a family, and in that family, she would find the strength to face whatever was coming.

'I'll keep going, too,' Shona said, and meant it.

Acknowledgements

I have many people to thank. First my wonderful editors Katy Loftus and Louise Cullen at Canelo, who along with Alicia Pountney have worked so hard to produce this book. Particular thanks also go to my agent Anne William at KHLA for bringing DI Shona Oliver out of the shadows in the first place. The meticulous and all-knowing development editor Russel D McLean, copy editor Daniela Nava and proof-reader Miranda Ward have my admiration and warmest thanks.

Once again, I owe a huge thank you to the lifeboat crews, particularly Steve Austin at RNLI Cleethorpes and Gareth, Ross, Laura, John, Lilli and James of RNLI Kippford for their patience answering of my incessant questions. I am truly in your debt.

The Girls in the Glen grew out of my fascination of both cold case investigations and archaeology. I'm sure the archaeology aspect has its roots in the castle holidays of my childhood and also witnessing Roman treasures unearthed at the Antonine Wall excavations close to where I grew up. After a marvellous year working as a photographer at The Hunterian Museum, University of Glasgow, life took me in a different direction. Later, I was able to circle back via Lincoln Archaeology Group, where I'm currently a committee member. It is to LAG's intrepid volunteers, and archaeologists Dr Craig Spence, Zoe Tomlinson, Dr

Duncan Wright and Dr Martin Huggon, that I owe much of the inspiration for this story. A special mention must go to Charles Simpson for detailed guidance on the excavation of human remains and insights into the archaeology and heritage of space.

For perpetual encouragement there are no better cheerleaders than my fellow alumni of the University of East Anglia MA Crime Writing course and I'm truly thankful for their continued support. My thanks also go to my home team of husband Mickey and to Leo, Chloe, Sam and Thomas for allowing me to rattle on about latest fascinating discoveries.

The Girls in the Glen contains many real places and entirely fictitious events although the Border reivers and their escapades in the Debatable Lands are a matter of historic record. I'm indebted to George MacDonald Fraser's *The Steel Bonnets* and Graham Robb's *The Debatable Land*, both of which are entertaining and informative reads and added greatly to my research. My thanks also to Tarras Valley Nature Reserve and the Langholm Initiative for information on habitat restoration and community land purchase. Gilnockie Tower, home to the Clan Armstrong Museum, is a great source of reiver knowledge and one of the few surviving pele towers open to the public. The story of Murdo's brother, Drew, was inspired by Neil Armstrong's visit to Langholm and some old newsreel film is available online. If you look closely, you may just see a familiar face or two in the crowd.

CANELO CRIME

Do you love crime fiction and are always on the lookout for brilliant authors?

Canelo Crime is home to some of the most exciting novels around. Thousands of readers are already enjoying our compulsive stories. Are you ready to find your new favourite writer?

Find out more and sign up to our newsletter at canelocrime.com